# FOLLOW ME

# ALSO BY TIFFANY SNOW

*In His Shadow*, The Tangled Ivy Series

*Shadow of a Doubt*, The Tangled Ivy Series

*Out of the Shadows*, The Tangled Ivy Series

*Power Play*, The Risky Business Series

*Playing Dirty*, The Risky Business Series

*Play to Win*, The Risky Business Series

*Out of Turn*, The Kathleen Turner Series

*No Turning Back*, The Kathleen Turner Series

*Turn to Me*, The Kathleen Turner Series

*Turning Point*, The Kathleen Turner Series

*Point of No Return*, The Kathleen Turner Series

*Blane's Turn*, The Kathleen Turner Series

*Kade's Turn*, The Kathleen Turner Series

*Blank Slate*

# FOLLOW ME

## A CORRUPTED HEARTS NOVEL

## TIFFANY
## SNOW

Text copyright © 2016 Tiffany Snow
All rights reserved.

Published by Montlake Romance, Seattle

www.apub.com

Amazon, the Amazon logo, and Montlake Romance are trademarks of Amazon.com, Inc., or its affiliates.

ISBN-13: 9781503938397
ISBN-10: 1503938395

Cover design by Eileen Carey

Printed in the United States of America

*For my sister, Tonya. Your praise and encouragement
have meant more to me than you'll ever know.*

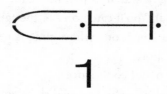

1

"The Doctor is dead."

"Again?"

"Yeah." I adjusted the Bluetooth in my ear so I could still hear my grandma, then grabbed the netted scoop next to my fish tank.

"Did you remember to feed him? I told you that you work too much at that job and then you come home exhausted. You forget to feed yourself, much less—"

"No." I cut her off before she really got rolling on my lifestyle choices. "I fed him all the time." The little goldfish floated on top of the water and I sighed as I removed him. Another one bites the dust.

"Then that's your problem. You're *over*feeding him."

"I thought fish were supposed to be easy to take care of," I complained, flushing the corpse down the toilet. An ignominious end, but what was I supposed to do with a dead fish? Bury it in a tiny cardboard box? I'd have half a dozen minigraves in the backyard if I did that.

"They are," Grandma assured me. "You'll just have to try again."

"You know, the whole reason I got a fish was that watching them and listening to the water bubbling in the tank was supposed to be relaxing. Instead, I'm stressing out even more about killing them."

"They *are* relaxing to watch," Grandma said. "You just haven't got the hang of it, that's all. You'll catch on . . . though maybe you should ask for an old fish this time, one whose time is near. That way you're not cutting a life too short."

"Thanks for the vote of confidence."

"I'm just being realistic. Do they sell fish by age? I wonder how you tell how old a fish is?"

"No clue. Size maybe?"

"Then get a big one this time."

I kept my grandma's advice in mind as I perused the goldfish tank at my local pet store. They'd seen me come in a few times now and the employee loitering by the fish tanks was giving me the side eye.

"Having some trouble keeping the little suckers alive," I said with a forced laugh. The guy didn't smile, so I dropped my grin, too. Maybe he took fish lives way serious. I tried to look harmless, which wasn't hard since I barely topped five two.

Pushing my glasses up my nose—a nervous habit I couldn't break—I asked, "So can I get an old fish?"

"They're all about the same," he said, scooping up a random gold-fish and depositing it inside a water-filled plastic bag. He tied off the bag and handed it to me. "Good luck."

I paid and hurried outside, hugging my flannel shirt tighter over my T-shirt and wishing I'd thought to grab a coat when I left home. It was early October and the sun was shining—a gorgeous Sunday morning—but I was too skinny and perpetually cold.

My Ford Mustang shone in the sun, giving me the warm fuzzies and dissolving the twinge of guilt I had when I looked at the blissfully oblivious fish I carried. The car was my one indulgent purchase when I'd graduated from MIT and gotten a job paying well into six figures. It was fully loaded, complete with a performance package.

I'd been stopped for speeding numerous times, but had yet to get an actual ticket. The cops usually took one look at me—short, bespectacled, unruly mass of hair yanked back in a ponytail—and snorted with laughter. The last time I was pulled over, the officer even asked if I had to use a phone book to see over the steering wheel. Smart-ass.

I appreciated the Men in Blue, but not always their sense of humor.

Sunday was Admin Day—the day of the week I reserved for administrative tasks like groceries, errands, laundry, bill paying, and talking to my grandma.

The cherry red of my Mustang gleaming in the far corner of the lot—furthest away from any other car—beckoned me. The purr of the engine was like an old friend greeting me, only this friend spoke in mechanics and gasoline, via tachometer and speedometer. Those signals were blessedly easy to read, as opposed to actual people with all their body language, obfuscations, doublespeak, and insinuations.

As was my routine, I stopped at Retread, the pop-vintage store that was on my way home. I'd been searching for a mint version of Van Halen's *5150* album and so far, nothing had come in. But there was always a chance one had shown up, or something else was just waiting to be discovered in the stacks the owner hadn't yet sorted. I could use eBay or search online, but finding it myself in a store was its own unique reward. Typing in Google's search box and clicking the Buy It Now button didn't offer the same kind of gratification.

"Hey, Buddy," I called out as I pushed open the door to the shop. A little bell clanged tunelessly as it bumped against the glass, announcing my arrival even if I hadn't spoken. But I always spoke anyway, just so he knew it was me.

A head poked out from behind a dilapidated bookcase toward the back of the shop. The shelves were bowed with the weight of books and records piled up, and I had serious doubts as to how much longer they would hold out.

"Hey, China. How's it going?"

That's me. China Mack. Well, not really. My name was China, which was weird enough, but my last name was fifteen letters long and unpronounceable by anyone who'd had the misfortune of having to attempt it. So I went by a shortened version of my middle name—Mackenzie. Thus, China Mack.

"The usual," I said, wandering over to the "Just Arrived" section, though that was a misnomer. Buddy was so behind, there was stuff that had "Just Arrived" for more than six months now. It wasn't really his fault. An acute case of ADHD meant Buddy was easily distracted. Kind of like when you start watching a YouTube video on how to repair your iPhone screen and end up two hours later bleary-eyed and watching a compilation video of cats falling off furniture set to the tune of "Flight of the Bumblebee."

"No *5150* this week," he said, disappearing again behind the bookcase. "But I got an absolutely pristine version of the Beatles' *White Album*."

I grimaced. "I'm an Elvis fan, not Beatles," I reminded him, crouching down.

"I keep hoping to convert you."

"Not gonna happen." Hmm. I saw the corner of something that looked interesting, buried under about twenty other albums. Glad I didn't care if my jeans got dirty.

"The Beatles were groundbreaking musical geniuses," Buddy said, his voice slightly muffled from behind the bookcase.

"They were bubblegum pop who had lucky timing," I shot back.

"I should bar you from my store for that."

"Then you'd lose half your customers." I grinned. The Elvis vs. Beatles argument was ongoing between us, with each of us making insults as to the other's idol of choice.

Buddy grumbled as he worked, but I knew he got a kick out of our friendly rivalry as much as I did. And I wasn't joking about the customers. How he kept the shop running, I had no idea. I didn't even know if Buddy was his real name. He'd introduced himself as Buddy and the few people I'd seen come in the store called him that. I assumed it wasn't his actual name. Who'd do that to a kid? Of course, I wasn't one to talk. I'd taken a lot of crap over the years because of my name.

I pulled out the album that had caught my eye, grinning. A near-mint condition of Madonna's *Like a Virgin* album. Sweet.

"Hey Buddy," I called. "I'll give you twenty bucks for *Like a Virgin*."

"Fifty."

"Twenty-five."

"Done."

Thrilled by my new acquisition, I set the album aside and moved farther into the store. I dug around the store every week and still hadn't been through all the nooks, crannies, and crevices that were filled to the brim with old records, books, and various vintage paraphernalia.

I passed three boxes that held familiar clay figures. "Buddy, I told you to quit accepting Chia Pets. No one buys them." I shook my head. Buddy could dicker over prices all day, but he couldn't turn down free merchandise.

"They discontinued Chia Teddy Bear," he said. "It's rare."

"No, it's not," I absently told his disembodied voice. "They began reissuing it as Chia Bear in 2006." I was distracted by a milk crate full of paperbacks, and crouched down. *Vintage Harlequins . . . cool!* My grandma had read them by the bucketful when I was little. She still did. She was going to be ecstatic at getting a box of these.

"How do you know this shit?"

I let out a girly scream and fell back onto my butt at the voice right next to me. Buddy had come out from behind the bookcase without me even noticing.

"You scared the crap out of me, Buddy!"

"Sorry," he said, looking abashed. "Still, I don't know how you know all the crap you do." He shook his head and walked away as the bell on the door tinkled again.

I went back to pawing through the collection of romance novels. Yes, I had a really good memory for completely useless crap and anything to do with my work, but ask me to tell you last year's Oscar nominees for Best Actress and I'd give you a blank look.

Whoever had dropped off the books had dug them out of a dust pile because they were coated in dirt and cobwebs. I brushed them off as I stacked them—Silhouettes to one side, the Harlequins on the other—grimacing at the layer of grime starting to coat my hands and clothes. My nose itched and I sneezed, then sneezed again.

"Bless you."

Eyes watering, I glanced over to see a very nice pair of Italian leather shoes, which were at the end of long legs encased in black slacks. I looked up, then up farther to a leather belt and a button-down black-as-coal shirt of thick cotton. I swallowed, reluctantly lifting my eyes until my gaze fell on a familiar and wholly unwelcome face.

"Find something worth buying, China?" my boss asked.

*Oh shit oh shit oh shit.*

Jackson Cooper owned the company where I worked and, for anyone else, seeing their boss outside of work wouldn't be a big deal. For me, it was a disaster of gargantuan proportions. Tall with eyes a deep, warm brown and chestnut hair, he had the intellectual stamina of a genius and prodigy rolled into one. Combined with the business acumen of a savant and the smoldering sexuality of Christian Grey, he was the epitome of every woman's fantasy man. Well, maybe not *every* woman, but definitely me.

Which meant, of course, that my limited social skills fled in his presence. At work, I could at least pretend to be occupied with my computer and keep my earbuds in when he walked by. Now, he was looking at me and talking to me and obviously expecting some sort of halfway-cogent response.

"Um, yeah" was the best I could come up with. I felt my face get hot and nervously shoved my glasses up my nose.

Jackson waited, apparently in the vain hope that I'd say more, but I just pressed my lips together and stared. It wasn't hard to stare at him. I did it all the time from the limited privacy of my cube.

"Okay then," he said, offering me a polite half smile. "Enjoy your books."

He walked past as I sat there on the floor, surrounded by paperback romances, their covers adorned with women and men in clinches and bodies half-naked as an invisible wind tore at their clothing.

*Oh God.* I wanted to die right then. He probably thought I was actually going to buy all these romance novels, which, who was I kidding, I probably would, but that wasn't the point. They were for my grandma, not me.

A moment later, I heard the door open again and Buddy call out a stammering "Bye. C-come again," which meant Jackson had left. Buddy always *tried* to be friendly, but it usually just came across as awkward and vaguely creepy to people who didn't know him.

"Did you see that?" Buddy asked when I set a stack of two dozen paperbacks on the counter.

"Yep," I said.

"*The* Jackson Cooper was in my store." Buddy's voice was a mixture of awe and fear.

Everyone knew who Jackson was. And why wouldn't they? He was a genius bazillionaire who looked like Brad Pitt circa 2000. Women practically killed each other in their rush to land him, and he'd made the *Forbes* Ten Most Eligible Billionaire Bachelors list. Twice.

He'd hacked into the NSA at fourteen and started working for secret government agencies by the time he was sixteen. By twenty-one, he was disillusioned (or so the rumors said) and left the government to start his own business in the private sector. And he'd done phenomenally well, creating a social media platform that hit huge. Which he then sold for top dollar.

With his new hundreds of millions, he'd founded Cysnet. Companies who couldn't find anyone else to solve their tech problems came to Jackson. They were charged exorbitant rates, but got what they paid for—Jackson made sure of it. From the development of sci-fi tools such as flexible, paper-thin computers, to biotechnology and bridging the gap between computers and humans, Cysnet was on the cutting edge. Everyone knew Apple, of course—developers of the beloved iPhone and iPad devices. Apple was to Cysnet what Wile E. Coyote was to the Road Runner.

To work at Cysnet was an industry coup—it meant you were the best of the best. But it also demanded long hours and dedication to the job. I'd been approached by Cysnet as I was finishing up my degree at MIT. Even if they hadn't dangled a jaw-dropping salary at me and the chance to move to Raleigh, North Carolina, which was one of the top-ten tech cities in the country, I would've jumped at the chance to work for them. Bragging rights alone were worth the fifty- to sixty-hour weeks I put in.

"I still can't believe you work for them," Buddy said, shaking his head as he rang me up. "It's so freaking cool. I bet you guys work on like supersecret stuff."

"Could tell ya, but then, well, you know the drill." I smiled and winked like it was a big secret, and it was (we weren't ever supposed to discuss what we worked on), but when it came down to it, I just worked long hours in a cube in front of a computer screen. Not exactly the stuff movies are made of.

Buddy rolled his eyes as I handed him my money. "Yeah, you're about as threatening as a miniature dachshund. I remember the time you screamed bloody murder because a spider was in one of the stacks."

"It wasn't just 'in the stack,'" I argued. "It *attacked* me, like *jumped out*"—I used my hands curved as claws to demonstrate—"and *landed* on me." I pawed the air like I was a cat. Buddy just looked at me. I dropped my arms in defeat. "It was a big spider."

He nodded the way one does when there's no point in arguing and handed me my change, then a paper bag overflowing with used Harlequins, plus the Madonna album. "See you next Sunday," he said.

"Bye, Buddy."

Back at home—my three-bedroom duplex in a complex that boasted nearly a hundred of them—I lugged everything inside. I carefully deposited The Doctor in his new home and watched him swim around as he inspected the sunken SpongeBob pineapple house and plastic scuba diver.

"Welcome home," I said to him. "I hope I don't kill you." Not exactly comforting words, but it wasn't like he could understand me.

I was behind on my schedule but had caught up by 7:00 p.m. Seven to ten was laundry time and I ironed in front of the television, watching classic reruns of *The Bionic Man*. Lee Majors had been quite the hottie in his day.

Since the autumn equinox had passed, it was officially a new season, requiring a different set of pajamas. I'd packed away my summer *Star Wars* pajamas (Tatooine and Boba Fett graphics) in favor of my fall *Star Wars* (Endor with Ewoks) pajamas. Hoth with tauntauns was reserved for the winter. (The only spring set I'd ever found had Naboo on them, with Queen Amidala and Anakin in a love clinch. Since I pretended the prequels didn't exist, I couldn't buy those.) I set a glass of water on my nightstand (on its coaster), checked my alarm clock, and climbed into bed at precisely ten thirty with a sigh of satisfaction.

I loved being on schedule and having everything exactly right and in its place. It gave me a warm, comforting feeling of being in control. I lived alone by choice because people were just too upsetting and taxing. They took a lot of effort. I got a little lonely sometimes, but it was okay.

Overall, my life was pretty close to perfect.

At exactly seven in the morning, I walked into Cysnet. Security required my ID badge and handprint scan before I was allowed through. Four armed guards manned the two entrances to the building and they weren't the friendly, chatty kind of guys. I always tried though.

"So . . . busy morning, right?" I asked, giving the one scrutinizing me a nervous smile. He didn't smile back.

"Backpack, please," he demanded, polite but no-nonsense. I hurriedly handed it over and waited as he pawed through, wincing slightly as he touched my carefully arranged things. Now I'd have to reorganize and straighten it.

He handed it back and I fixed what he'd mussed before heading straight through the lobby to the set of glass stairs leading to the second floor where my cube was located. For about the thousandth time, I wished I could move to a different area. I sat right outside Jackson Cooper's office, which was nice sometimes when I was feeling—a certain way. I could watch him covertly and admire how very handsome he was, how broad his shoulders were, and how very nicely he filled out a pair of slacks.

But most of the time, he made me nervous, so I tried to block him out the best I could with my earphones and never-ending classic-rock playlists. Once I got into my coding, it was easy to forget where I was.

Stowing my backpack in the bottom drawer, I sat down and logged in. I checked out the project I'd been working on, grabbed my notebook, a Red Bull from the minifridge underneath my desk, and began.

I knew when it was ten o'clock because that's when my cubemate, Randall, rolled in. He was a night owl and liked to code long after everyone had gone home for the day, but the latest management would let him come in was ten in the morning. I pulled out one earbud and caught the package he tossed my way.

"Bacon-egg McMuffin with cheese," he said.

"Thanks." My stomach was growling since I hadn't yet eaten. Who could eat at the crack of dawn anyway? Maybe the same people who killed themselves at the gym before the sun rose, running miles on a treadmill or climbing endless stairs. Not my thing. "I'll get lunch."

Randall nodded, already sitting down and unwrapping one of his four sausage burritos. This was our normal routine. He'd grab breakfast—I'd spot him lunch. It worked out pretty well because by the time we were ready for lunch, I needed to stretch my legs.

It was another hour and I was in midchorus of "Highway to Hell" when I felt a tap on my shoulder. I jumped, startled, spinning around in my chair to see who the hell hadn't gone through protocol—i.e., step in front of my cube so I could see them.

It was Jackson Cooper.

My irritated reprimand died on my tongue and I yanked out my earbuds, hoping I didn't have any McMuffin on my white *I* ♥♥ *NNY* T-shirt.

"Yes, sir?" I asked.

He opened his mouth to speak, then stopped and frowned, glancing down at me. I waited until my nerves couldn't handle the suspense and I looked down. Nope. No crumbs.

"How can you sit like that?"

Oh. *That's* what he was looking at. Okay, I did sit kind of weird, but I was short. I crossed my legs and sat on my feet, so my legs were in the chair, knees pointing to the side. Then I'd settle my Bluetooth keyboard on my lap and work.

"It's, um, it's fine for me," I said, then hurriedly added, "but I could stop, if it's like . . . against the rules, or something—" Were there rules for sitting? I'd read the employee handbook cover to cover and could recite most of it. I scanned my memory for anything that mentioned employee posture and came up empty.

"No, it's fine," he interrupted. "It was just a question. Listen, China, can you come into my office for a few minutes? I have something I'd like to discuss with you."

My mouth was hanging open and I shut it with a snap. "Sure. Yeah." I scrambled up from my chair—not the most graceful of moves—and grabbed my notebook. Looking around my desk, I didn't see my pen. I shuffled some papers . . . nothing. Opened my drawer and peered inside . . . nothing. Stepped back and looked at the floor . . . nope.

"What's wrong?" Jackson asked.

"I can't find my pen," I said. Yes, I had other pens but I *liked* a certain one. Where the hell was it?

"You mean this one?"

I looked up in time to see him standing right next to me, reaching for my hair. I froze in place and felt the slide of metal as he pulled the pen from where it had been tucked behind my ear.

"Voila." He smiled a crooked half grin which, combined with him being so close I could tell just exactly where the very top of my head met his shoulder, made my knees want to melt like Field's metal stuck into a mug of boiling water.

I was mesmerized by his eyes. I didn't think I'd ever stood this close to him before. He had cologne on—I could smell it. And he'd touched me . . . My eyes fluttered shut and I rocked forward slightly, inhaling the sweet aroma—and bumped my nose right into him.

"You okay?" he asked, grabbing my shoulder. My eyes flew open. "You're not going to faint, are you? Did you stand up too fast?"

My face turned so red I could feel the heat radiating from my neck upward. "I'm fine. Sorry." I snatched the pen from his hand. "Yeah, just stood up too fast." I forced my lips to curve in a smile and shoved my glasses up my nose. He was going to think I was so bizarre.

Jackson looked quizzical for a moment, then turned and headed for his office. "Follow me," he tossed over his shoulder, and I rushed to obey.

I felt eyes on me as I walked. Jackson usually only met with the managers, not the staff directly. I reported to a guy named Brad who happened to be on vacation this week. I supposed that was why I was heading into Jackson's office instead of Brad. Whatever it was, it obviously couldn't wait.

"Have a seat," he said, gesturing to the seating arrangement in his office. His desk stood to one side, diagonal to the windows that lined the wall. A sofa and two chairs were arranged facing each other on the opposite side, which was where he'd pointed.

Okay then.

*Sofa or chair . . . sofa or chair . . .*

I stood in indecision, frantically going through the pros and cons of each seat inside my head. *The chair would be good but it faces the windows and there's a glare. I'll be squinting. Sofa is better but what if he sits beside me, then I'll be craning my neck to see him and my feet won't touch the floor. The other chair is in a better location but it's higher than the sofa and if he sits on the sofa then I'll be above him and that may be insulting since technically I'm not "above" him—*

"China," he interrupted my train of thought, brushing past me and taking the chair I'd been leaning toward choosing. "Have a seat."

That was a command. I could recognize the tone. So I plunked myself down in the nearest spot, which put me on the sofa. Except I'd misjudged the softness of the cushions and I sank, putting me even lower than I thought I'd be, as I faced him. I forced a smile.

"Cushy couch."

Okay, that was something a teenager might say. Not a grown woman with degrees piled behind my name and several years of experience under my belt. My smile turned into a grimace. I started fiddling with my pen and shoved my glasses farther up my nose.

"Brad would usually be the one to hold this discussion," he began, "but since he's out of the office right now, I thought I'd handle it."

My palms began to sweat and I went cold. This sounded like the beginning of a conversation I wasn't going to like. I searched my brain, trying to think of what I could've done to bring about a disciplinary meeting with the CEO.

"If this is about that argument between me and Toby last week, then I want you to know it's resolved. He dinged my Mustang and refused to admit it, but when I had the paint samples compared, they totally matched."

Jackson gave me an odd look. Okay, that wasn't it then.

"And I'm not the one who keeps stealing Janine's Diet Coke from the fridge," I blurted. "It's Megan in accounting. I caught her but she swore me to secrecy because she saw me borrow one of Blake's Kit Kat bars that he keeps in the freezer." I took a breath. "*Borrow*'s not really the right word, I guess, since I ate it. But I did replace it the next day." I grimaced. "And ate it again. But I really am going to bring him more. I swear."

Still nothing. His eyes were a bit wider though. Surely that couldn't be a good sign?

"And I'm not the one that keeps adding *h-o-g* to Liam's nameplate." The guy's last name was *Hedge*. Really, he was just asking for that one.

"Or—"

"Stop!"

I clamped my lips shut.

Jackson cleared his throat. "While I appreciate your willingness to, um, clear your conscience . . ." he paused, "none of those things are why I brought you in here."

"Then why did you?"

"I was getting to that, before your impromptu confessional."

Oh. I shut up again.

"I had a project come in and need a programmer with certain skills," he said. "You seem to be the only person on staff familiar with LISP."

I was still processing the "need a programmer" part so my brain took longer than usual to catch up.

"LISP?" I asked. "Um, yeah. I went through a phase where I was studying the first programming languages. I learned FORTRAN and LISP. Not a lot of stuff being written in those nowadays, but it's helpful to learn for maintenance purposes." I shrugged. "Besides, I was bored."

"You were bored," Jackson echoed. I nodded. "And how old were you?"

"Thirteen." Not every thirteen-year-old girl wanted to host sleepovers and paint their friends' nails . . . Okay I *had* really wanted to have a sleepover, but the smell of fingernail polish gave me a headache. And since there was no one to have a sleepover *with*, I learned coding languages.

"I see." He sat back in his chair and crossed his legs, one ankle resting on the opposite knee. My eyes were drawn to his shoes.

I had a thing for a really good pair of men's shoes. Not to wear or anything—I wasn't *that* weird—but I could appreciate the expense and quality of well-made leather footwear. And Jackson Cooper always wore nice shoes, polished to a gleaming shine. His clothing was almost always the same palette of gray or black pants paired with a button-down shirt, also in a gray or black. He never wore a tie, and his shoes were never the same two days in a row.

I could feel his gaze on me and I kept mine on his hand, which was draped on his ankle. His hands were large and looked strong, but weren't roughened by manual labor. The fingers were long and tapered, almost like a pianist's. Looking at them made my thoughts wander in an unprofessional direction and I hastily averted my eyes.

It was nerve-racking, being in here alone with him. I'd worshipped him from afar ever since he'd first made his name in tech. Yes, empirically speaking, he was closer to the Ten on a scale of One to Ten and I wasn't blind. But his main draw, at least in my opinion, was how smart he was. Compared to him, most of the population were just jabbering monkeys, myself included.

Whereas my hands had been cold, now they were clammy with sweat and I had to consciously stop myself from wiping my palms on my jeans. That would look really gross. I pushed my glasses up my nose instead and focused on Jackson's eyes rather than his body.

Oh geez. It felt wrong to even be *thinking* that word in reference to my boss. *Body* . . .

". . . currently working on—the version upgrade for MTS—let's take you off that for now," he was saying. I nodded like I'd been listening all along. "I'll e-mail you a brief of what I need and the project outline. You can look that over and we'll meet tomorrow to work out anything that needs clarification."

Which was a really nice way of saying *anything I didn't understand*, because I had no doubt that I'd have to wade my way through what Jackson would view as a light bedtime story.

Jackson looked like he was waiting for an answer or some sign that I was comprehending the words coming out of his mouth.

"You betcha!" I blurted, then inwardly cringed at how ridiculous I sounded. I forced a smile that widened until my lips were sticking to my dry teeth. This time he didn't even bother with a polite perfunctory smile back. I couldn't blame him.

"Okay, thank you," he said, rising to his feet and heading for his desk.

I was up and off the couch like a shot, or I would've been if the couch hadn't fought me. There was a gravitational pull of black-hole proportions and it wanted my ass to stay right there. After fumbling for a moment in the depths of the cushions, I struggled my way to my feet. I could feel Jackson's eyes on me and my face burned, but I didn't dare look at him as I hightailed it back to my cube.

Only after I'd curled up in my usual semisquat in my chair did it hit me: I was going to be working side-by-side on a project with none other than Jackson Cooper.

*Holy shitballs.*

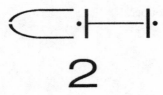

## 2

Monday night was when I worked late, which wasn't hard on this particular Monday, and ordered pizza on my way home. It had taken me the entire day and the better part of the evening to read through what Jackson had e-mailed me. As I'd figured, it wasn't exactly entry-level stuff. I took notes and highlighted, wrote down questions, and dug out my old tech books. I forgot to eat lunch and lost track of time. It was a challenge and I loved it.

So long as I didn't think about having to work with Jackson, I was fine.

"Hi Reggie . . . yeah, it's China," I said into my Bluetooth. "I know I'm late . . . seven minutes . . . yeah, the usual, please—no, wait. Let's go crazy. Add extra cheese."

I heard a laugh in my ear. Reggie got a kick out of my detailed routine and it had taken him about two months to figure out I called at precisely the same time every Monday night and ordered exactly the same thing. The only two variations were last February when I'd ordered dessert (in honor of Valentine's Day), and tonight. Being asked to help the boss on a project was cause for some celebration, I thought. Therefore, extra cheese.

Ordering from the car ensured just enough time for me to get home, change clothes, and pop open a Red Bull before the doorbell rang.

I liked to keep my apartment warm, so wearing a thin pair of sweats and a tank was perfect. *It felt good to be out of jeans and a bra.* I wiggled my toes. *And shoes.*

Grabbing some money from the envelope I kept in a kitchen drawer (put there for this purpose), I jogged for the door and yanked it open.

"Perfect tim—" I stopped. Because it wasn't the pizza guy at my door, it was Jackson.

I was so shocked, I stood there gaping at him for a moment, then blurted, "What are you doing here?"

He ignored my question. "Can I come in?"

I couldn't compute. "This isn't right. You're supposed to be at work. Not at my house."

"I'm not at work twenty-four seven, China," he said mildly.

"No no, I mean, yeah, I know that, but you're at my house . . ." My words faded away as common sense took over. I was making my boss stand on my stoop in the dark, moths dancing around his head in the light I'd left on for the pizza guy. "Crap. Yeah, sure, come in."

I stepped back inside and he followed me. Everything was all awry. I wasn't dressed properly. He shouldn't be here—how did he even know where I lived anyway? The pizza guy would be here any minute and was there enough for two people? Of course there was, but then I wouldn't have leftovers tomorrow and would have to do something different for lunch. I hated different. And he'd undone another button on his shirt, not that I'd noticed.

"I'm sorry to arrive unannounced like this," Jackson said as I closed the door behind him. I reached up and tightened my ponytail, then shoved my glasses up my nose. A twofer in my nervous jitter repertoire.

"It's fine." Which was such a lie. This wasn't fine. Not at all. What was I supposed to do with him? The only men I had in my apartment were my *RuneQuest* squad and I didn't really count them as men of potential romantic interest since two of them still lived at home with their parents and the other two lived together in the Biblical sense. Jackson Cooper was most definitely a *man* in all the ways that mattered most to a female.

Something to drink. Yes. That would break the ice. And would give me something to do.

"Do you want something to drink?" I asked.

"Sure. That'd be great."

Okay. He said yes. I spun on my heel and hurried to the kitchen, then realized I hadn't asked him *what* he wanted to drink. Shit.

"Um, so, yeah, I have water . . ." Duh. Everyone with a sink had water. I opened the fridge. "Milk . . . Red Bull . . . cranberry juice . . ." I think I had one dusty bottle of merlot someone had given me. I could offer him that. "Wine—"

"Red or white?"

I jumped at his sudden proximity and shut the door too hard. He'd come into the kitchen without me realizing, since my head had been buried inside the refrigerator.

"Um, red, I think." I pushed my glasses up again and moved past him to get the bottle from my cupboard. I'd just realized I didn't own a wine-bottle opener corkscrew thing when I saw it was a screw-top cap. Thank God. Disaster averted.

I poured him a glass then thought I should pour myself one, too. I handed his to him. "Here you go."

He said "Cheers" and held up his glass to toast just as I took a big gulp. I choked.

"Easy there," Jackson said, slapping my back, which just made things worse.

Coughing and spluttering, I grabbed a dish towel and coughed into it. My eyes were watering but even so, I could detect the pity in his eyes. Could this get any worse? And I still didn't know why he was here.

The doorbell rang just as I was getting myself under control and Jackson went to get it before I could stop him.

"Who're you?" was the first thing out of Reggie's mouth.

"I'm Jackson." He took in Reggie's uniform and the flat box he held. "How much do we owe you?" He reached for his wallet.

"We? Where's China? I ain't never seen you before, mister."

"You deliver pizza here often?"

"Every Monday night. Like clockwork."

"Here, Reggie," I said, squeezing between Jackson and the open doorway and holding out money. "Thanks."

Reggie gave me a look I couldn't figure out—people were so hard—and handed me the box before turning around and leaving. Okay, one problem solved. The other problem was standing so close, our bodies were touching.

"Want some pizza?" I asked, taking the warm, aromatic box into the living room. I set it on my coffee table. It was almost time for *Supernatural.* I liked to watch it live so I could tweet about it. How long was Jackson going to stay? "Did you want a slice?" I asked.

"I don't want to eat your dinner," he said, which wasn't really a *Yes* or a *No.* I was afraid it was one of those phrases that had some kind of societal propriety behind it, which meant I had no clue whether he really wanted a piece or not.

I was too tired for this. I'd already worked all day and there was a reason my primary partner was a computer. If he wanted a piece, I hoped he'd just say so.

"Okay," I said with a shrug. Grabbing a slice and my wine, I sat cross-legged on my couch and took a bite, my gaze on Jackson who was likewise watching me. He looked good, really good, and my gaze was drawn to the patch of skin revealed by the undone buttons. The pizza was suddenly hard to swallow and I had to wash it down with a chug of my wine.

Jackson took a drink as well and sat down next to me on the couch.

Seven minutes until *Supernatural*.

"As I was saying, I apologize for arriving unannounced like this," he said. "There were a couple of things I needed to discuss with you before we move forward on this project."

"And it couldn't have waited until tomorrow?" I took another nervous bite of pizza. *Jackson Cooper was in my apartment. Jackson Cooper was sitting on my couch. Jackson Cooper was drinking my wine. Jackson Cooper was close enough for me to smell his cologne . . .* I shut those thoughts down right there and shoved in more pizza.

"It's not something I wanted to talk about there." His gaze dropped.

Oh my god, was he checking me out? No. No way. But what if he was? Should I do something? Let him know I was interested? *Was* I interested? I was a twenty-three-year-old virgin whose only kiss had been a very awkward and wet experiment with my lab partner at MIT who hadn't known how to kiss at all.

I bet Jackson Cooper knew how to kiss—*really* knew.

He turned away and set his glass on the table. I momentarily panicked. Would he ask before he kissed me? Or would he just do it? Should I do something alluring? Like toss my hair? Girls did that, right?

Without thinking it through, I did this weird little thing with my head that was supposed to make my ponytail drape over my shoulder. Instead, a sharp pain went right through my neck.

"Ow ow ow ow owowowow!" I dropped my pizza on the table with a splat, my hand going for the crick in my neck.

"Are you all right?"

"Um, yeah, I'm fine," I managed to get through my gritted teeth. This is what I got for trying to act like a girl. "Just got a crick in my neck."

"Here, let me."

I had no time to reply before he'd moved my hand out of the way and was massaging my neck. His hands were much larger than mine and felt way better. Like *waaay* better. Wow . . .

"Still hurt?" Jackson asked after a minute or two, and I desperately wanted to say yes, but I was a terrible liar.

"No, it's much better, thank you."

"And you have some sauce . . ." He gestured and I looked down. I had a streak of bright red pizza sauce on my chest, right above the top edge of my tank.

And my mortification was complete.

I grabbed a napkin and wiped off the sauce. No, he hadn't been checking me out. He'd been staring at what an absolute pig I was, wearing my dinner. Talk about misinterpreting signals. Epic fail. Who was I kidding anyway? The idea of Jackson Cooper checking *me* out, much less kissing me, was so ludicrous as to be laughable. Except I didn't feel like laughing.

"So what did you need to tell me?" I asked, jerking my thoughts back into work. Work was the reason he was here, not some only-just-now realization of how he'd been struck with an overwhelming attraction for me. I really needed to quit reading my grandma's Harlequins.

My slice of pizza looked forlorn, sitting half-eaten on the coffee table, but no way was I going to try to eat again in front of him.

"This project we're working on is highly classified," Jackson said.

I shrugged. "So is ninety-nine percent of everything we do."

"It's not just that," he continued. "The people who hired us aren't exactly trusting."

"What do you mean?"

"I mean that coding, writing the software that runs the world, can sometimes be dangerous. I want to make sure you are fully aware that it's highly probable you'll be monitored and/or followed."

"There's a clause in all Cysnet employees' contracts that absolves the company of any indemnity 'should the employee be hurt or deceased due to or as a direct result of any customer involvement.'" It had been an eye-opening and gulp-worthy clause, but I'd signed it, choosing not to think too deeply about the reasons why that was in there.

"Yes, but words on paper and actually seeing the paranoia and lengths some clients go to in order to protect their investment and intellectual property are two different things. I wanted to remind you of that as well as the confidentiality and non-compete in your contract."

"I'm not looking for another job," I said.

"Good."

"And I know my contract, but thanks for the warning." I wondered just who was the customer for this particular project. It hadn't been listed anywhere in the materials Jackson had e-mailed me.

"All electronic communication between us will remain encrypted," he said. "And if you write anything down, shred it before you leave the office."

"Understood." So weird, that he was telling me all this, which prompted my next question. "So . . . who's the client?"

Jackson took his time replying, opting for another swallow of wine first. "Wyndemere," he finally answered.

Oh. Oh wow. No wonder he'd shown up tonight. "The defense contractor?" I asked, hoping I'd misheard.

"The one and the same."

Wyndemere was the premiere software contractor for the government. You had to have a security clearance to know 90 percent of what they did, and top-secret clearance to know the remaining 10 percent.

"So the project we're working on is really . . . for the government," I said, feeling slightly lightheaded.

Jackson glanced at me, his mouth set in a grim line. "Most likely."

No wonder his warning earlier. I'd been involved with that kind of work once before at MIT's government laboratory. We'd worked on technology that could identify someone in total darkness based upon their infrared thermal signature.

The whole time we'd been working on the project, I'd been monitored. They hadn't known I'd found their wiretaps or saw the car that kept tabs on my comings and goings, but none of it escaped my notice. It had been unnerving and I'd been glad to finish that particular project.

The military implications of what we'd done and how the technology could be used by people with less than altruistic purposes still kept me awake some nights, but that was the thing with advancement in technology. It wasn't as though you could put the genie back in the bottle. Once something was achieved, there would always be people who could turn even the most innocuous thing into a way to kill people.

He drank the rest of his wine in one long swallow and I tried not to watch the movement of his throat. Then he was on his feet and I was scrambling to keep up.

"Did you have a chance to go over everything?" he asked as he headed for the door.

"Yeah. I should be ready to start tomorrow."

"Good. Let's meet first thing in my office to go over the schematic and database structure."

"Okay."

He opened the door, then paused. "You've been with Cysnet for four years, China, and from your performance reviews, I can see you've been doing an excellent job. I'm looking forward to working with you on this."

My face grew warm again, but for once it was from pleasure rather than embarrassment.

"Me, too, sir."

"Call me Jackson."

"Yes, sir. I mean, Jackson." First-name basis with the boss? Um, yes, please.

"Have a good night, China." He glanced at his watch. "I think *Supernatural* should be on in about sixty seconds."

I looked over my shoulder at the clock. Hot damn, he was right. That warm fuzzy feeling of being back on my schedule curled inside my tummy. When I looked back, Jackson was already sliding into his silver Mercedes. I would've stuck around to watch him pull out of my driveway, but my fictional boyfriends Jensen and Jared wouldn't wait.

It was only after the first commercial break that I wondered how he'd known what I watched on Monday nights.

The phone was buzzing. The phone shouldn't be ringing. It was . . . I glanced at the clock by my bed . . . nearly midnight. I'd gone to bed at ten-thirty, like always. And now my cell phone was buzzing.

Only my Favorites could make my phone buzz when it was in Do Not Disturb mode, so I grabbed it. The caller ID said "Big Bro Oslo."

"Yeah?" There was never a good reason for a call at this hour and my thoughts immediately went to my dad, who lived alone on our farm.

"Hey, Chi, sorry to wake you," Oslo said, "but we have a problem."

I sat up. "What's wrong? Is Dad okay?"

"Yeah, Dad's fine. It's Mia."

Mia was Oslo's oldest daughter. He'd had her with his first wife, who'd up and left him so he'd filed for divorce. He'd remarried several years later and had two more kids, a girl and a boy, but Mia was sixteen whereas the next oldest was only seven.

"What's wrong with Mia?"

"She's decided she's running away from home. We had a big argument about her grades and not applying herself to her studies. Next thing I know, she's packed and gone."

I rubbed the sleep from my eyes, grimacing. "Did she leave a note or anything?"

"Yes, thank God, which is why I'm calling you. Apparently, she bought a plane ticket to Raleigh. She said she was going to go live with you."

My eyes shot open. "Me?" I squeaked. Mia and I had always gotten along all right—after all, there were only a few years between us. But she wanted to come *live* with me? "Why me?"

"I don't know, but she talks about you all the time. How you're the only who understands her and there's no other women in the family for her to talk to—"

"What about Heather?" Heather was Mia's stepmom.

He sighed. "They haven't been getting along lately either. I know it's probably just a teenager stage, but I need you to go get her from the airport. Her flight lands in thirty minutes."

"She flew here? Tonight?" I scrambled out of bed. The Raleigh-Durham airport wasn't big, but I didn't want Mia to be wandering around it alone at this hour.

"I know. Teenage spontaneity, i.e., stupidity." Oslo sighed.

"All right. I'll text you when I have her. What airline?"

He told me and I ended the call, shucking my pajamas in favor of jeans and my *Hooray Sports! Do the Thing, Win the Points* T-shirt. I grabbed my jacket, keys, and cell, and was out the door.

I lived halfway between the airport and downtown so it didn't take long before I was pulling into short-term parking. Ten minutes later I was standing by baggage claim when Mia came around the corner.

"Aunt Chi!" she exclaimed, her face breaking into a wide smile as she hurried forward and flung her arms around me.

Mia was as different from me in looks as night and day. Whereas I had dark hair and pale skin that made a snowbank my best camouflage in the event of the zombie apocalypse, she was taller than me by two inches with pure golden-blonde hair that hung to her waist. Perfect white teeth and baby-blue eyes meant that she turned heads even at the young age of sixteen, though she was blissfully unaware of her own stunning beauty.

I hugged her back, her light cloud of perfume enveloping me. Mia was as girly as they came. From her carefully manicured nails to the collection of fashion magazines she adored. Smart as a whip, she aced her classes with ease then grew bored at the lack of anything to challenge her. Whereas I was into computers, her area of obsession was math.

"I'm so excited to come visit you," she said, stepping back and flipping her hair easily over her shoulder using the move that had nearly sent me to the chiropractor earlier tonight.

"A little more warning would've been nice," I said dryly. Mia also had a habit of ignoring unpleasant things. Perpetually cheerful, she simply refused to acknowledge anything that upset her. Even to the point of "running away," apparently.

She frowned. "Dad called you."

"How else would I have known you were coming?"

"I just need a little vacation," she said. "Please don't send me back. They just don't get me." Her eyes begged me, and I sighed. I'd always had a weak spot for Mia. Kids and I didn't generally get along, but she and I had clicked from the first moment I'd laid eyes on her little swaddled newborn body. To my seven-year-old eyes, she'd seemed like the most amazing and perfect thing I'd ever seen.

"All right," I said. "But you're calling your parents in the morning and we'll discuss it."

Her face lit up and she squeezed me again. "Thank you! I knew you'd understand."

I texted Oslo as we waited for her suitcases—a duo of pink-and-white *Hello Kitty*–themed pieces—then led her to my car.

"No way! This is your car?"

That's right. Mia hadn't seen my Mustang, though I'd posted pics of it on Facebook.

"Your parents still won't let you have a Facebook account?" I asked, unlocking the trunk for her suitcases.

"No. They said that 'teenagers don't appreciate the permanence of what's posted on the Internet.'" I could tell by the way she said it that she was quoting, and it did sound like Oslo. Mia rolled her eyes. "I mean, like, whatever. I understand social media better than Dad or Heather."

I silently agreed with her. Oslo had always been a reluctant tech user, and Heather still thought MySpace was cutting-edge.

Mia talked nonstop all the way to my place.

". . . and this stupid football player asked to copy my homework. As if! Like some hulking hot guy who smiles at me is worth getting a zero for cheating. Then he got all pissy with me. Not surprised . . ."

She chattered as we parked, unloaded her luggage, and went inside. Only one thing interrupted her.

"What's that?" she asked, pointing to the floor in front of my fish tank.

I glanced down, then gasped. "Oh no! The Doctor!"

The little goldfish was lying on the hardwood, not moving. I scooped him up and dumped him back in the tank, hoping we hadn't been too late. He did nothing for a moment, just began to sink, then twitched and flipped over. He wasn't moving fast, but he was moving. I let out a sigh of relief.

"That was weird," Mia said. "How'd he get out of the tank?"

"I have no idea. Maybe word has spread and he was trying to commit suicide before I kill him."

She looked at me oddly. "You kill your goldfish?"

"Not intentionally. It just . . . happens." I gave a helpless sort of shrug.

"Okay then." She looked around. "So where do I sleep?"

"Umm." I hadn't thought that far ahead. "I mean, I guess there's the couch?"

Mia snorted. "I am *not* sleeping on a couch when I know you have three bedrooms." She brushed past me and headed for the stairs. I hurried to catch up.

"But one of those is my bedroom, one is my office, and one is for storage." Though *storage* probably wasn't the right term . . .

"Then I'll just make room in your office," she said. "Don't you have a futon in there or something?"

"It's really not set up for sleeping," I protested, nearly tripping on the top step. Mia could move fast when she wanted to.

"You're being all OCD again, Aunt Chi." She opened the door to my office. "See? I could set up an air mattress in here, no problem. Though that would probably give me nightmares." Mia headed for the life-size Iron Man Mark 42 suit that stood in the corner. "Is it real?" She reached out—

"Don't touch it!" I slid between her outstretched hand and the suit. "It cost me eight grand," I said. "*And* it's a limited edition."

Mia rolled her eyes. "If that's in here, then I'm afraid to ask what you have in storage."

"No, wait—" But I was too late to stop her. She was out the door and had thrown open the storage room by the time I skidded to a halt behind her.

"Wow."

I winced. Yes, I kept the Mark 42 in my office, but the masks for the Mark 17 and Mark 41 were in here . . . along with my life-size Boba Fett and my TARDIS. And that didn't encompass the bookshelves lining the walls filled with other memorabilia.

"This is . . . amazing," Mia breathed. "How long have you been collecting?"

"Since forever." Which was true. I still had the metal *Star Wars: A New Hope* lunch box I'd bought when I was seven. I hadn't used it, of course, because then it would no longer be New In Box. I'd taken my lunch to school in brown paper bags.

She headed for one particular corner as if drawn there by a magnet. I should've known she'd go there first.

"I have never seen a Harry Potter collection this good." She stood on her toes to get a closer look at the Sorting Hat replica. "So what House are you?"

I hesitated, unable to ascertain if she was serious or if she was being sarcastic and making fun of me. That particular nuance was tough to distinguish. Oh well. If she was making fun of me, it wasn't as though I wasn't used to it.

"Ravenclaw, of course," I said.

"Me, too!"

"Really?"

"*Or yet in wise old Ravenclaw, If you've a ready mind, Where those of wit and learning, Will always find their kind,*" she recited.

I grinned. She hadn't been making fun of me.

"People always want to be Gryffindors," she continued, "but I think that's just because of Harry. Not everyone is a true Gryffindor, who are brave, yes, but reckless. I totally think Hermione should've been a Ravenclaw."

"I know, right?"

"Every House gets a bad rap except Gryffindor. I'm always arguing on Reddit that each House is of value, *not* just Gryffindor."

That launched more discussion as to the Houses chosen for more characters as Mia perused my extensive collection.

It was nice, really nice, to have someone who appreciated a fandom obsession. I had a theory—and thus far it was proven correct in about seven out of ten cases—that tech and science geeks were actually the most creative of all personalities. Not the Hollywood screenwriters or the actors on Broadway. Those who enthusiastically embraced the most outlandish and exotic ideas about life and fantasy were more often in a position to turn those imaginings into reality.

"Okay, so I'll sleep with you tonight and we'll get an air mattress tomorrow," Mia said. "And so long as Tony doesn't attack me in my sleep, I'll let him stay."

Good, because that suit weighed a ton and it had taken two burly deliverymen to get it upstairs for me. I'd tipped them well, but they'd still been muttering under their breath and giving me dirty looks when they left.

Mia and I hauled her luggage upstairs and she set up camp in my bathroom for over thirty minutes. I was just about to head to my guest bathroom to brush my teeth—again—when she finally emerged.

"It's about time," I grumbled, moving past her. I stopped short.

It looked like the makeup counter at Macy's had blown up in my bathroom. Every available surface was covered with bottles and jars and tubes. I felt the kind of dismay every single guy must feel when his girlfriend decides to move in with him.

She'd left me a tiny little corner on the counter that held my electric toothbrush.

"Thanks heaps," I muttered.

But it was way past my bedtime so I didn't bother trying to move anything. It was deeply unsettling, as was climbing into bed with her beside me. She had pink earplugs in her ears and a black eye mask with *Fuck Off* embroidered on it.

Okay then.

I lay down on my back and tried to pull up the covers. She was lying on them. Grimacing, I tugged, but she was a dead weight as a soft snore emitted from her half-open mouth.

Staring at the ceiling, I plotted exactly how much my brother was going to pay for this, until I finally drifted off.

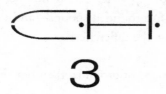

## 3

My Tuesday morning was immediately thrown off when I woke to find Mia already in the shower. I banged on the door.

"Hurry up! I have to get to work!"

"I'll be right out!"

I stood there fuming and counting the seconds ticking by. After three hundred and fifty-two of them, I heard the water turn off. Another one hundred and ninety-six seconds later, and the door opened.

"You're going to make me late," I snapped. "I need to shower and get ready for work."

Mia stared at me. "But . . . you don't have to be at work for an hour."

"Yes, but I still need to make my coffee, eat breakfast, and read the paper."

"Did you make the coffee yet?"

"No. I make the coffee *after* I shower. Not before."

More staring.

"Are you done in there or not?" I said impatiently.

"Yeah, sure, I'm done." We exchanged places. "I'll just go make the coffee."

I yanked the almost-closed door back open. "Fill the coffeepot with the distilled water, not tap water, to the number ten line. The coffee is in the freezer. Use five rounded spoons—and I mean rounded, not heaping. Do you know the difference?"

She nodded.

"Five *rounded* spoons of grounds, then put the coffee back in the freezer."

"Okay. Got it."

Slightly mollified, I closed the door and rushed through my shower, trying to make up time. I pulled on my jeans, a navy-blue *Bad Wolf* T-shirt, and layered a white-and-navy plaid shirt over it. It was one of my favorites because it was so soft, a brushed-cotton flannel.

The smell of coffee, and that I was only three minutes off schedule, went the rest of the way to easing my mood. Until I walked into the kitchen.

"You opened the paper?"

Mia was sitting at the kitchen table, wrapped in the fluffiest pink robe I'd ever seen, her hair still up in a towel. And she had the paper spread open in front of her.

"You said you read the paper, so I grabbed it off the stoop," she said, taking a sip of her coffee. "I just took the entertainment section. Do you want it?"

"I don't read the entertainment section."

"Oh good. Then see? It all worked out." She smiled.

No, it really wasn't *all worked out*. I gritted my teeth and forced a smile.

"Is this your OCD thing again?" Mia asked, her smile fading into a look of sympathy that would have been appropriate for hearing news that I was afflicted with a fatal illness.

"Of course not." I faked a laugh. *Yes, Aunt Chi was weird.* Passing her by, I poured myself a cup of coffee. This whole wrench in my routine was upsetting, but Mia wasn't just anyone—she was family. Surely I could suck it up for a few days . . . even if she *had* opened the paper first and removed a section.

We drank our coffee in mutually agreed silence, each perusing the paper. Thankfully, she hadn't taken any of the other sections and twenty-six minutes later, it was time for me to go.

"Call your dad today," I reminded her as I gathered my stuff. "Try to talk things out. You can't stay here indefinitely."

"All right, all right," she grumbled.

"How much school are you missing anyway?"

"It doesn't matter. It's not like I can't catch up. Besides, I brought my books with me so I won't fall behind."

She was unconcerned, and with good cause. Mia would probably be ahead of the class by the time she returned home.

"I'll call you later," I said as I headed for the door. "And don't eat all my Fig Newtons." They were my guilty pleasure and I had two of them every night before bed along with a cup of chamomile tea.

She mumbled something about "gross" and "disgusting," but I was already outside. It took exactly thirteen minutes to drive between work and home. Unfortunately, traffic interfered 93.6 percent of the time on my drive to work, but only 17.8 eight percent of the time on my way home since I rarely left before 6:00 p.m.

Today was one of the 93.6 percent days and it took twenty-seven minutes to reach the offices of Cysnet, which still put me there two minutes before eight o'clock.

I was in my warm, fuzzy place as I settled into my chair with my Red Bull and logged in. I was just about to put in my earbuds and crank the tunes when Jackson suddenly loomed over my cube wall.

I choked and Red Bull came out my nose, which burned like hell.

"Didn't mean to startle you," Jackson said, handing me a white handkerchief from inside his sport coat. "Why don't you come on into my office when you're . . . ah . . . done here?"

He disappeared, striding toward his office, while I mopped up my face and keyboard. Damn, was I cursed to always look like a complete klutz in front of him?

I locked my computer and grabbed my notebook and my favorite pen. Unfolding myself from my chair, I hesitated, then picked up my Red Bull. I still needed the caffeine.

The handkerchief—a real honest-to-God handkerchief—was stained now and had my slobber on it. It even had his initials embroidered on the corner—JMK. I wondered what the M stood for. It needed to be washed before I could return it, otherwise that was just *ew*.

So when Jackson said "first thing in the morning," apparently he really meant first thing in the morning. He was seated behind his desk when I tapped on his open door. Glancing up from his computer, he gestured me inside.

"Go ahead and close the door, please."

I pulled the frosted glass door closed and the edges fit snugly into the rubber casing, providing a solid seal. This helped prevent anyone from overhearing anything said in Jackson's office. I also knew that his office, just like those of other senior management, was set up with a high-tech audio masking system. Laser listening devices could be used through glass windows from a good distance away, but I had no doubt that Jackson was aware of that fact and was protected.

"Have a seat." This time he pointed to one of the two chairs in front of his desk, so there was no internal debate on where to sit.

"Give me just a minute to finish this," he said.

"Sure. Take your time."

His fingers sped over the keyboard, drawing my eye. People viewed IT and computers as technical, and they were. But coming up with ways to solve problems and accomplish tasks using technology required a unique kind of mind—one that was both intensely creative but also methodically logical.

Jackson was a genius in both areas. Perhaps he was more akin to an artist than anything else in the work he did.

I surreptitiously admired him as he worked. He'd discarded his sport coat and was wearing black slacks and a black shirt with thin gold and burgundy pinstripes. It looked really good on him and I could tell it was made from quality material. The creases on his sleeves told me his dry cleaner was as fastidious about his clothes as Jackson was.

His eyes were intent on the screen, the set of his jaw hard, and I was glad I wasn't on the receiving end of whatever e-mail he was typing. Speaking of jaw, it was smooth, probably from his morning shave. I wondered if he was one of those exercise nuts who worked out in the morning . . .

That led to vivid Harlequin-inspired images of Jackson inside my head. He was pumping iron, shirtless, with sweat glistening on his chest—all it needed was a wind machine and sound track . . . what would suit him working out? AC/DC? Def Leppard? Bon Jovi? *Mmmm . . . You give love a bad name . . . yeah . . .*

I was abruptly yanked from my fantasy by Jackson saying, "All right, that's done." His gaze swung to meet mine.

I felt a rush of heat to my cheeks. Dammit. Thank God telepathy didn't exist.

"Yeah, great!" I said brightly, smiling for all I was worth.

He gave me that odd look again, the one I couldn't decipher. I figured it either meant: *She's just so weird* or *I'm a bit gassy today.*

"Here's the database schematic I sketched out last night," he said, handing me a trifolded piece of paper. I opened it to its full length, pushing my glasses up my nose as I inspected the tiny print. There were roughly a hundred tables or more on the sheet. "It's pretty rough," Jackson continued, "but I thought that would give us a starting point in addressing some of the issues they're having."

Picking up a small remote, he dimmed the lights slightly, then a projector above us came on. The database he'd just given me was displayed on the opposite wall. Another button and the walls on either side of a large whiteboard folded up like an accordion, making the whiteboard huge.

"We can set up the rest here," he said.

Okay then. Time to get to work. I could almost feel my brain shutting down the social/personal interaction section—which was underdeveloped anyway—and the technical part of my brain taking over, immersing itself in the labyrinth of connections.

For the next three hours, we discussed primary keys, inner joins, outer joins, and reference tables. By the time my stomach growled so loudly even Jackson could hear it, the database had grown to three times the original draft he'd created.

"Did you get breakfast?" he asked, glancing at his watch.

I thought of Randall and the bacon, egg, and cheese McMuffin probably cold and congealed on my desk.

"Not today," I said.

"Then let's grab an early lunch." He hit the same buttons and the wall closed over the whiteboard, the lights came on, and the projector turned off. The fan still whirred, cooling the machine.

"Back in an hour?" I gathered up my things, my Red Bull can long since empty.

"We should be. There's a Mexican joint right around the corner. I go there a lot. You'll like it, if you like Mexican. You do, don't you?"

I stared at him, my mouth agape. We were going to lunch? Together?

He was still looking at me, waiting for an answer.

"Um, yeah. Of course! I mean, who doesn't?" I laughed awkwardly. "I mean, I practically live at Taco Bell."

There was that look again. That had been an appropriate response, right? Taco Bell was Mexican. Sort of.

"Well, hopefully it'll be better than Taco Bell." Jackson slipped on his sport coat and held the door for me. I put my notebook back down and walked out of the office. I heard the snick of the lock as he secured the door behind us.

My nerves hit full force as we headed to the parking garage. I fell into step behind him as he walked toward his car. Now his car . . . his car I could appreciate without getting his weird look. It had been hard for me to get a good look at it last night in the dark, and he parked on a special level reserved for management. As we got closer, I could see why.

"Oh my God. Is that the 2017 Cabriolet?" I asked, my voice filled with awe.

Jackson glanced at me, his lips twisted in a little smile and a question in his eyes. "You know it?"

"Mercedes stopped making the Cabriolet in 1971," I said. "Is this the AMG S63?"

"Yep." He reached for the handle and the door automatically unlocked.

I stood on the passenger side, staring at the most beautiful car I'd ever seen. "Wow," I breathed. I heard a slight chuckle as Jackson got in.

Sliding inside the car was as close to a religious experience as I'd ever had. The interior was brick red with leather seats and black trim. Jackson flipped a switch and the soft top folded back on the convertible. The purr of the engine made my eyes drift close.

"This car can do zero to sixty in three point nine seconds," I said. "It has five hundred seventy-seven horsepower and a peak torque of six hundred sixty-four pounds per foot."

The car didn't move and Jackson didn't say anything, so after a moment, I opened my eyes to find him looking at me.

*Oh no. Had I said something wrong?* I went over my last few sentences in my head, but could find nothing offensive about them. And he was still staring. I pushed my glasses up my nose and cleared my throat.

"Really amazing that you got your hands on one early," I said, pulling my lips back in my best smile imitation. I wished I was one of those people who could pull off a genuine smile on demand, but experience had shown I just sucked at it. But societal convention meant I had to try. A lot.

Jackson visibly winced. "Why do you do that?" he asked.

My fake smile disappeared. "Do what?"

He backed out of the spot, talking as he drove. "Use that awful fake smile."

"People expect smiles. It makes them feel more comfortable." My mother had drilled that into me before her death.

"Screw what people expect. Their expectations aren't your responsibility to fulfill."

I blinked at him. That had always been what I thought, but had never dared to speak aloud.

"And you certainly don't have to fake it with me," he continued. "I value honesty more than worrying about expectations."

He slipped on a pair of designer sunglasses that, combined with being behind the wheel of such an amazing car, made him look incredibly sexy. Mia would probably say he was *smoking hot*. As if Jackson needed help in that department. Unfortunately, I felt like the frumpy little sister in the passenger seat next to him.

I overlapped the edges of my flannel shirt, hugging it to me. Rarely did I contemplate my looks. I'd come to terms a long time ago that while I was cute, I didn't have the patience or ambition to spend a lot of time on things like hair, clothes, and makeup. I had good hair, thick and long, but never knew how to style it so always settled on a ponytail.

My dad had tried to get me contacts when I was in high school, but I couldn't get the damn things in. Not even the optometrist could pry my eye open long enough to push the little lens inside. I didn't really care. The idea of sticking my finger in my eye twice a day grossed me out anyway. Yuck. I'd stick with my glasses, thank you very much.

Seeing Jackson's nice clothes reminded me of my own, and I glanced down at my faded jeans. I couldn't remember the last time I'd gone shopping. I ordered all my stuff online and if it was too big—which the jeans usually were—I just used a belt and rolled them up. My wardrobe consisted of about five dozen T-shirts, numerous jeans in various states of wear, and a rainbow of long-sleeved shirts I used for warmth (I was perpetually cold)—and to conceal my less-than-curvy figure.

The only things I wore that were expensive were my bra and underwear.

I was on an ongoing quest to find a bra that would actually make my (barely) B-cup chest look like I had actual cleavage, and I stalked Victoria's Secret on a regular basis. And I couldn't buy the pretty bras without buying the matching panties and I certainly couldn't *wear* a mismatched set, which meant every day I wore ridiculously expensive lingerie underneath my T-shirts and jeans.

Though I'd yet to find that perfect bra, I didn't mind searching.

Jackson seemed content to let the wind rushing by fill any need for conversation, which suited me just fine. I was nervous enough as it was, just thinking about having to carry on casual conversation during lunch without also stressing about what to say while he drove.

The awesome thing about this convertible was that the car was designed in such a way that you didn't get blown to pieces just because the top was down. It also had a climate system that sensed the temperature and kept you warm from the neck down—in my case, the eyebrows down—so even if it was a bit chilly like today, I was still toasty warm. It was an absolute dream car and I didn't want to know how much he'd paid or what part of his soul he'd sold to get it before it had been released to the market.

Unfortunately, the restaurant really was right around the corner, as in less than a mile away, so I didn't get to ride in it for very long.

The staff knew Jackson on sight and the host smiled, rattling off something in Spanish to which Jackson readily replied. Apparently, he knew Spanish.

A gorgeous, filthy rich, multilingual genius. Was there anything this man couldn't do? Maybe animals hated him. Or he was stumped by a Rubik's Cube. I bet he had ugly feet. Oh, who was I kidding? His feet were no doubt as perfect as the rest of him.

We were led to a booth and I slid in on the far side. The host set a menu in front of me and another in front of Jackson. I immediately began studying it as though preparing to take a pop quiz.

"The enchiladas are particularly good here," Jackson said.

I took that as a decent suggestion and when the waiter showed up, ordered the enchilada trio. Jackson ordered the same thing, plus a margarita with Patrón. Now it was my turn to stare.

"Did you want a margarita as well?" he asked politely.

"I don't really drink much," I said. "But thank you." Which was an understatement. I drank once in a blue moon, mostly because I couldn't hold my liquor. Zero tolerance plus a body weight barely into triple digits meant I could handle approximately one and a half drinks before I was drunk. Being drunk wasn't a particularly good look for me, so I avoided alcohol.

Once the waiter had brought my water and his margarita, Jackson smiled and said, "So tell me a little more about yourself, China."

My mind went blank, like a deer caught in headlights.

"Um . . . well, uh . . . I, um, guess there's not a lot to tell," I said at last.

"Sure there is. I read your employee file. You're quite extraordinary, actually. And you come from the Midwest, right?"

I was blushing from the "extraordinary" comment, but managed to nod. "Omaha."

"You have siblings?"

"Two older brothers."

"I see. So you're the baby of the family, then."

"I'm the youngest, if that's what you mean," I said. I'd always disliked being referred to as the "baby." Maybe it was because of my size. My brothers both topped me by a foot or more and nearly a hundred pounds each.

"Are your brothers similarly gifted?"

"That's a trick question," I said.

Jackson's lips lifted ever so faintly. "How so?"

"Well, *A*, I don't think of myself as 'gifted' and *B*, my brothers are extraordinary in their own ways. I'm not 'better' than them just because my IQ is higher."

"So then tell me what these *extraordinary* older brothers do for a living," Jackson said, and I had the feeling he was being sarcastic, but I couldn't be sure.

"Oslo is a risk analyst for an insurance company," I said. "He's the oldest. Jack is the middle child. He runs my dad's farm now. Oslo is twelve years older than me, Jack is eight."

"So you came along late?"

I nodded. "My mother really wanted to have a girl, but they had trouble getting pregnant again. I think they'd given up and then wham! I showed up."

Jackson smiled slightly. "Are you close to your parents?"

That struck the part of me that always hurt when I thought about my mom. "I was close to my mom," I said, ignoring the twinge of sadness. "But she died in a car wreck when I was eight."

"Oh. I'm sorry to hear that." He seemed sincere, which was a nice change since up to now he'd had a slight edge to his questions, as though he was humoring me or finding me amusing or something like that. It was hard to say, which only fueled my frustration and irritated me.

I couldn't fake a smile now even if I cared to make the effort, which I didn't. "Yeah. It was . . . hard." An understatement. I'd spent years longing for my mother, wishing she'd been able to give me advice. She alone had understood me and how difficult it was for me to interact with people. She'd guided me and "translated" when I just couldn't understand. Were they laughing *at* me or did I say something funny? Is that person sad or angry? Was that a sarcastic statement or were they serious? I missed her every day.

Mom had been the one who'd fought to keep me with other kids my age, saying they could get me tutors to advance my schooling, but that my social development was important, too. Once she'd died, Dad had quit fighting the schools that recruited me, dangling scholarships in front of us and saying it would be a crime to not allow me to explore my full potential.

"And your dad?" Jackson asked, pulling me from my thoughts.

"He coped okay. He's never remarried and he's stayed on the farm. Jack worked for ConAgra for a while, then started working with my dad when he needed help. He's gradually taken over more and more as my dad has gotten older." I didn't want to keep talking about myself, so I turned the conversation toward him, as my mom had taught me. "What about you?"

The waiter interrupted, setting two identical plates down in front of us. The food smelled heavenly and my stomach let out another growl in anticipation.

"Not much to tell," he said. "Only child. Parents still alive, but divorced."

I burned my tongue on the enchilada, of course, and had to gulp down some water, so it was a moment before I could respond. "Do they live around here?"

Jackson shook his head as he chewed his own enchilada, which obviously didn't burn his tongue. "They both live in Florida now."

"Did they know you were . . ." I faltered. *Special* didn't sound quite right, and I wasn't sure I could say *genius* without sounding like I was sucking up.

"Did they know I was gifted?" he supplied. I nodded. "They found out pretty quickly. I was speaking in full, complex sentences by the time I was two. Reading by the time I was four. Math development was similar. Things took a pretty advanced path after that."

I nodded, then drew a blank on what to ask next or how to keep the conversation going. I settled for taking another careful bite of my food.

"How do you know about cars?" he asked.

Shit. That's what I got for not having another question prepared. Now I had to talk about myself again and he'd see just how boring I actually was, if he didn't realize already.

"Nothing special," I said. "Self-taught."

"But why? You just like them?"

"It was something I could talk about with my dad and brothers." If I was being bluntly honest, and really, that's the only way I knew how to be. The art of subtle obfuscation escaped me.

Jackson paused in his chewing, his brown eyes intent on me. I was rethinking that blunt honesty thing when he spoke.

"Why would you think you needed to find something that interested them? Couldn't they have been the ones to find a commonality between you?"

And again, I couldn't think what to say. But he was waiting for an answer, so again that honesty thing came out.

"I've never thought that way," I said with a shrug. "They're normal. I'm not."

"Bullshit. You're better than normal."

He said it so matter-of-factly, taking another bite of his food afterward. My throat thickened and with horror I realized my eyes stung.

Oh my God . . . was I going to *cry*??? I never cried. Ever. It would have to be while I was having my first, and probably only, lunch with my boss that my girly emotions decided to let me know they really did exist.

The waiter walked by and I reached out and grabbed his arm. "Margarita on the rocks, no salt."

"*Sí,*" he said with a smile and nod before hurrying off.

I cleared my throat and applied myself to eating my food, avoiding looking at Jackson. If I'd been unsure what to talk about before, now I was at a total loss.

The food was good and I was starving. I pushed the unsettling conversation to the back of my mind and ate every bite on my plate. The margarita arrived and I sucked that down, too, ignoring the little voice of warning in my head that said it might not be the best idea.

The waiter took away our plates and I expected him to bring the check, but instead he brought fried ice cream and set it in front of Jackson.

"I always get fried ice cream," he said, pushing it into the center between us. "Have some."

My last date had been five years ago. It had been with my lab partner at MIT, Rolf. He'd taken me to Cracker Barrel for dinner, then had spent an inordinately long amount of time in the bathroom. There hadn't been a second date. But we'd both gotten an A in the class. However, we *hadn't* shared dessert.

Jackson dug into the ice cream like it wasn't a big deal to be sharing with me, though it felt very different from my side of the table.

Tentatively, I picked up my spoon and scooped a bit of ice cream. It was good. Jackson ate more than I did.

It felt so odd to see him like this, casual and relaxed. In the office, he was unapproachable—the lord presiding over the peons. At least, that's how I felt. Others spoke of him with admiration and awe. My interactions with him, until now, had been minimal and perfunctory at best. A "good morning" or "good evening" exchanged, but nothing more. And now I was sharing dessert with him.

Surreal.

I was feeling that margarita now, belatedly regretting my sucking down tequila in the middle of the day. It loosened my tongue, and, given my already dysfunctional social thermometer, that was a Bad Thing.

"What's it like being you?" I blurted.

Jackson's eyebrows climbed as he scooped up the last bit of fried ice cream. "What's it like being me?" he echoed.

I nodded. "You're like . . . perfect." My voice got dreamy as I elaborated. "Supersmart, handsome, rich, famous. You have it all, right? What's that like?" I couldn't imagine. I was smart and yes, made a good salary, but that was where our similarities ended.

He grimaced. "It's not as great as you make it sound. I live in a bubble, every move is scrutinized in the gossip rags, the finance pages, and the tech blogs."

"Oh." I was kind of let down. Jackson was likely the closest I'd ever be to an honest-to-goodness superstar.

Maybe Jackson sensed my disappointment, because he added, "But it does get me the Cabriolet." And he winked. I smiled. "And apparently you think I'm handsome."

My smile disappeared. "I-I'm sorry," I stammered, cursing Jose Cuervo. "I didn't mean——"

"You're not going to take it back, are you?" he asked, and he was still smiling, so I catalogued that as him teasing me. I relaxed.

"Nope." I downed the final big swallow of margarita, ignoring the creeping embarrassment that would surely harangue me later when I was fully sober.

He paid, which I gave token protest to, but he overrode me with ease.

"Thanks," I said, preceding him.

"You're welcome."

I felt a touch on the small of my back as we went out the door, and it felt as though I'd been given an electric shock. He'd touched me.

Jackson. And I'd had just enough alcohol to appreciate it way more than I should have.

We were in the car when his cell rang. He answered and I tuned out the conversation, too busy studying the amazing stitchwork on the leather seats, until Jackson said, "I'll be right there."

"Is everything okay?" I asked as he ended the call.

"A friend of mine," he said.

"Yeah?" I prompted when he didn't continue.

"He's dead."

That sobered me right up.

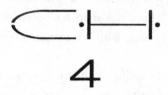

# 4

I didn't say anything as Jackson passed the turn to Cysnet and accelerated onto the highway. It appeared I'd be going with him . . . wherever we were going.

We headed north of downtown and twenty minutes later pulled into a nice, heavily treed subdivision. My eyes widened at the homes—beautiful, expansive brick structures with no two looking alike. It was a gorgeous neighborhood, especially with the leaves starting to turn, which is why it was so jarring to round a corner and see a line of emergency vehicles outside the last home in the cul-de-sac.

"C'mon," Jackson said, parking on the other side of the street. He was up and out of the car before I'd even processed that he meant I should come, too.

I hurried to follow him, his long strides eating up the pavement and making me have to jog to catch up. He intercepted a fireman heading back to his truck.

"What happened?" he asked.

"I'm afraid I can't say," the man replied. "Privacy issues."

"Fine. Where's Madeline?"

"Who?"

"The resident." Jackson sounded impatient.

"Oh. Yes, she's inside. I believe the paramedics were seeing to her."

Jackson was off before the man had even finished his sentence, heading for the front door, which was ajar. He went through and I followed.

The inside was as beautiful as the outside and tastefully decorated. The hardwood floor gleamed and the chandelier sparkled overhead in the sunlight, conveying a cheerful effect in stark contrast to the woman seated on an ottoman in the living room. She glanced up as Jackson reached her, and the expression of devastation on her face was painful to witness.

"Jackson, thank God," she said, lifting her arms as her eyes welled with tears.

He crouched down and hugged her. I stopped a few feet away, feeling like an intruder.

The woman was older, perhaps in her fifties, and Asian. Her hair was beautiful: black, shot through with silver, and wavy down past her shoulders. Slim and long-limbed, she wore a long-sleeved wrap dress in a turquoise-and-white pattern.

"Tell me what happened," Jackson said gently, pulling back and taking both her hands in his. His position put them at eye level as he crouched in front of her.

"I was out of town," she said softly, and I had the sense she was trying to keep her composure. My heart went out to her. Obviously, the man—Jackson's friend—had been her . . . husband? That seemed about right. "And I called last night. Tom was distracted, worried, but didn't want to discuss whatever was bothering him. I don't think he wanted me to worry.

"He said he had some work to do," she continued, "so we didn't speak for long. This morning, I tried to call him before I flew back, but he didn't answer. When I got home, I couldn't find him, and the house smelled funny." Tears rolled down her cheeks now, but her voice remained steady. "I went into the garage, and that's when I found him. The car was still running."

Oh. Oh wow. She'd found her husband after he'd committed suicide. That was just . . . just horrible. It was hard for me to even begin to comprehend how Madeline must be feeling.

"Did he leave a note?" Jackson asked.

Madeline shook her head. "No. I just can't believe he would've done this. I know he trusted you—that's why I called. I thought you might know if he was in trouble somehow."

"You're thinking foul play."

"It has to be, Jackson. You knew Tom. He wouldn't have done this."

I felt like an intruder, listening to them, so I backed off to give them some privacy. The police were wrapping things up and I saw the ambulance drive away. The fire truck was likewise gone.

A couple of cops were in the kitchen talking quietly when I walked in. They both glanced at me.

"Sorry. Didn't mean to intrude. I was just giving the widow some privacy."

"Sure, no problem," one of them said. The other gave me a nod as he walked by and headed outside. "You're a friend of the family?"

Easiest way to answer that was "Yes."

"I'm sorry for your loss."

"Thank you." I hesitated, then said, "Madeline thinks foul play might be involved. Could that be true?"

The officer grimaced. "They all want to think that," he said. "I don't blame them. It's easier to think their loved one was killed than that they'd take their own life."

"But you don't think it was."

"No. There's nothing to suggest that. It's pretty clear-cut."

I nodded, thinking about what he said versus what Madeline had said.

"If you'll excuse me, we're going to clear out of here."

"Yeah, sure."

He moved past me. "You might not want to leave her alone tonight," he suggested. "She'll need some time to process this and we wouldn't want her doing anything rash once the shock has worn off."

I understood what he was saying. "Yes, good idea. We won't."

I waited a little longer in the kitchen, then drifted down a corridor to a set of French doors that were slightly ajar. I could see into the room beyond and it looked like an office. Maybe it had been Tom's. Curiosity had me pushing open the door the rest of the way.

It was like any other office with a computer on the desk and three monitors attached. Papers were scattered and I moved closer, glancing over them.

Notes, it seemed, and a list of program errors in the software he must've been working on. Half of them had been checked off.

"There you are."

I jumped at Jackson's voice and spun around. "You startled me." My heart was racing.

"I didn't know where you'd gone." He looked at me with that strange expression again. "Might be a little impetuous for you to wander the house, but you probably didn't think of that."

Oh shit. I'd done something rude and hadn't even realized. I pushed my glasses up my nose. "I'm sorry. I didn't mean—"

"It's fine," he interrupted. "Like I said, it probably didn't even occur to you. It's not as though you were being deliberate about it."

I couldn't tell if he was angry or not, and since he hadn't outright *said* he was mad, I went with not.

"The cops said it was a clear-cut suicide," I offered.

Jackson winced. "He was a friend of mine," he said.

I understood what he meant and immediately wanted to crawl into a hole. Could I have been more insensitive? This was why interacting with people exhausted me and left me feeling inadequate. Sometimes I just said the wrong thing. Oh, who was I kidding—not *sometimes*, *ALL* the time.

"I-I'm sorry," I stammered. "I'm not good at this. Can I do anything? Do you need something?" Being given a task would be so much easier than finding the right words to say. "Would you like some hot tea? I drink chamomile every night and it's very soothing."

"No. I was actually coming in here to have a look around," he said. "And you don't have to apologize. You're probably the one thinking the clearest at the moment, without emotions affecting your logic."

I wasn't sure about that. Embarrassment was doing a pretty good job of impeding my thinking, but I didn't say anything.

"Did anything catch your eye?" he asked.

"I hadn't looked around very much."

"Madeline seems to think foul play was involved."

"I know. I heard," I said. "But if the police can't find any evidence, then I don't know what else you can do."

"Well, if he was murdered and they made it look like a suicide, they wouldn't leave evidence now, would they?"

I didn't argue, just resumed my trip around the office, stopping in various spots to peruse the dead man's effects. "Where did he work?"

Jackson looked at me. "Wyndemere."

Oh. "I really hope that's just coincidence," I said. "Because otherwise it's a little . . . disconcerting." I was proud that I'd found a better word than the one that had immediately come to mind, which was *terrifying*.

"Me, too."

Although we went through the office, neither of us found anything. No work files that looked incriminating or worth killing over, and no suicide note. I even dug through the trash, but came up empty.

"Let's go ahead and leave," Jackson said at last. "Madeline's sister is on her way to stay with her and I don't want to intrude further."

We said good-bye to Madeline, and Jackson promised to be in touch. He didn't say anything on the way back to the office, appearing deep in thought, so I stayed quiet, too. Until my phone began shrieking at me.

"*It's me! Your favorite niece. Pick up the phone! I know you're there. Answer me—*"

I scrambled for my cell, digging in my pocket and pulling it out. It was even louder now. Mia must have changed my ringtone. When the hell had she done that?

"Yeah?"

"Hey, Aunt Chi!"

"What did you do to my phone?" I hissed as Jackson glanced sideways at me.

"Oh yeah, you like it? Way better than that boring ringtone you had, and now you know it's me without looking!"

"I like *my* ringtone."

"Seriously? It was some weird western song."

Jackson was listening, I could tell, so I turned away slightly so he wouldn't hear me. "It's the theme to *Firefly*."

"To what?"

"*Firefly*," I said louder.

"What's that?"

I sighed and closed my eyes. It wasn't worth it. "What did you want?"

"Oh yeah, why I'm calling. I want to make brownies but I can't find your flour."

"You want to do what?"

"Make brownies."

I didn't even know if I owned a pan to make brownies in, much less have flour. "I don't do a lot of baking, Mia. If you want brownies, you'll have to buy them."

"Okay, but homemade is better. I'll walk across the street to the drugstore then. They'll have brownies."

Was that okay for her to do? Was she old enough? Would a good parent tell her no, she shouldn't do that? I had no idea. I guessed if she thought it was okay, then it probably was? I had no clue.

"Ah, okay, I guess. Hey, did you call your dad?" The sooner I could send her back home to her parents, the better we'd all be.

"We had a long talk, yes, and guess what?" She sounded terribly excited, which I instinctively knew meant I *wouldn't* be. "He said I could stay with you for a semester! And I researched it and everything and the high school here is only four miles away. I called and got an appointment to go in and meet with them and register."

My mouth was gaping, but it took me several long moments to realize it.

"Aunt Chi? Are you there?"

"Um, yeah, I'm here. Listen, let me call you back in a little bit. I'm not in the office right now."

"'kay. I'm so excited! Bye!"

My next call was to Oslo, and I didn't bother going through conventional social niceties when he answered.

"You told Mia she could stay with me? For a *semester*?" That came out kind of squeaky. I cleared my throat, glancing at Jackson, who seemed not to be paying attention.

"Please, China," Oslo said. "She and Heather are going through a rough time right now. They're bickering constantly. If Heather says the sky is blue, Mia says it's . . . orange." He paused. "It's because of her mom leaving, China, I know it is. I tried to get her to talk to a therapist, but she won't. It's been years, but that kind of thing . . . it doesn't ever go away. Your own mother abandoning you. I mean, hell, it was excruciating for me and I was just married to the woman. She wasn't *my* mother. Please. Can she stay?"

Damn it. No way would I say no now, and Oslo knew it. "I don't know how to deal with a teenage girl," I said, in one last futile attempt. "She's going to hate staying with me."

There was an awkward silence, and it clicked.

"Oh," I said. "That's what you want. If she hates it here, she'll realize how good she has it there, and will change her tune. Nice, Oslo."

He must've heard the hurt and anger I couldn't disguise. "It's not like that, China," he said. "But . . . yeah. I'm hoping a few months there will . . . change her perspective."

"You're lucky I like her," I said, then ended the call. And I did like Mia. I could understand how she'd feel about her biological mom leaving her. Although I knew that my mom hadn't wanted to leave me when I was eight, the stages of grief included an anger phase where you do blame the person who died for leaving. Very common.

I stared out the windshield, my mind racing. I wasn't equipped to deal with a teenager. I'd have to be like a pseudo-parental figure or something. I couldn't even keep a goldfish alive, so my qualifications for caring for another actual living person were pretty slim.

"Everything okay?"

Jarred from my thoughts, I turned to Jackson. "Yeah, I guess. I mean, no, not really."

"No? Or yes?"

"No, well, I don't know."

He was looking at me like I was an alien and I thought I should explain.

"It's just that my niece, Mia, decided to run away from home last night and flew here. Now I guess she's convinced her dad—my brother—to let her stay here with me for a semester."

"Is she a problem kid? On drugs or something like that?"

"Of course not. She's a good kid, not into alcohol or drugs. Too smart for her own good and a downright prodigy at math."

"Then what's the problem?"

Now it was my turn to look at him like he was an alien. "I'm not a mother! I don't know the first thing about how to deal with a teenager, even if she is related to me."

"Well, they're just like normal people, right? Just younger."

He'd obviously not dealt with many teens.

"I think there's a little more to it than that," I said. As to what the "more" part of it was, though, I had no clue.

"I'm sure you'll figure it out."

I appreciated the vote of confidence.

". . . so all we have to do is designate you my temporary guardian and then I can enroll," Mia finished.

I continued dishing up the beef and broccoli (Tuesday was Chinese night) onto two plates, along with fried rice and eggrolls.

"Did you get sweet-and-sour chicken?" Mia asked.

I paused. "You didn't say you wanted sweet-and-sour chicken."

"Everyone loves sweet-and-sour chicken."

"That's not really Chinese food. It's Chinese food for Americans who don't like Chinese food."

"Then what do you call beef and broccoli? That's about as un-Chinese as you can get."

I decided to ignore this rather than argue the merits of beef and broccoli versus sweet-and-sour chicken. Grabbing my plate and fork, I headed into the living room. Mia followed me, plate in hand as well.

"So?" she asked. "Will you do it?"

I curled up cross-legged on the sofa and clicked on the television, digging into my apparently pseudo-Chinese food.

"Aunt Chi?"

What choice did I have? I'd researched the public school Mia wanted to go to and it was a really good school, better than her one back home, with an accelerated math and science track. Oslo had e-mailed me PDF copies of Mia's medical records, birth certificate, and insurance information—in short, everything I needed to take care of her for the next however-many months.

I swallowed my mouthful. Although I'd told Oslo I'd take care of Mia, I still wanted her to work for it. "Yeah, I'll do it."

"Yes!" She pumped her fist.

"But—" I interrupted her celebration. "But you have to promise to obey my rules and dedicate yourself to your homework. This isn't some kind of vacation. You'll need to work, especially at this school you want to attend."

"I swear, I'll work hard and I won't be any trouble."

I wasn't sure about that last part, but if Mia needed to have a few months away from home for whatever teenage reasons were bothering her and coming between her and Heather, then I could give that to her. She was family.

Navigating the DVR menu, I pulled up the episode of *Castle* that I recorded. Tuesday night I watched the shows I'd recorded—*Castle, Doctor Who, Downton Abbey,* and *Rizzoli & Isles.*

"Ooh, I love *Rizzoli & Isles,*" Mia said, grabbing a blanket off the back of the couch and tucking it around her legs. "Let's watch that first."

"But I watch it last," I said. "Not first."

"Does it matter?"

I hesitated. "It's just . . . how I do it."

"Okay, that's fine," she said, backing down. "It's your thing so we'll watch however you want."

She was making me feel crazy OCD again, but obviously didn't want to rock the boat since she was now a semipermanent houseguest.

There was a loud thump outside, interrupting our conversation.

"What was that?" I asked, setting down my plate.

"Probably your new neighbor," Mia said.

"I have a new neighbor?" I headed for the door as another thump sounded.

"Yeah. They moved in this afternoon. A couple of moving guys, but I didn't see who it was."

Pulling aside the curtains in the front window, I peered outside. The duplex next door had been empty for a couple of months. A new neighbor would be nice, so long as they didn't play music too loud or smoke.

I couldn't see who it was, but could see a man bent over behind a sofa, apparently trying to move it himself. Hurriedly, I opened the door.

"Here, let me help you," I said. He was going to hurt himself. I rushed forward to grab the other side of the sofa, then realized I'd vastly underestimated how heavy it was.

A low chuckle made me look up from where I was straining to lift the furniture, and I forgot how to breathe.

The man on the other end of the sofa was probably the most beautiful man I'd ever seen. No. Scratch that. He was *definitely* the most beautiful man I'd ever seen. Wavy black hair and crystal-blue eyes like the best incarnation of Superman ever. Dimples creased his cheeks as he gave me a thousand-watt, whiter-than-white, perfectly-straight-teeth smile.

His wide shoulders and muscled arms were giving the cotton of his black T-shirt a run for its money as it stretched to accommodate his body. I couldn't see the rest of him because of the couch, but I had no doubt he was as perfect below the waist as he was above it.

That sent my thoughts spiraling in a direction straight out of the racier Harlequins that I kept meaning to send to Grandma. And I would send them . . . eventually. Just as soon as I finished *Love's Pure Delight*.

"I'm Clark," Superman said, reaching a hand across the sofa toward me.

"No way," I murmured. His eyes were *so* blue—

"What was that?"

I made myself blink, breaking the spell of his amazing eyes. "Nothing," I said, thrusting out my hand. "I'm China."

"China?" His hand engulfed mine.

"Yeah." I shrugged. "My parents met there. It's better than being named *Beijing*."

Clark laughed and I was mesmerized—a throaty chuckle that made me want to record it just so I could hear it over and over.

"Good to meet you, China."

He looked down and I realized I was still holding his hand. I snatched it away, my face burning.

"So, yeah, I came out to help you," I said, trying to act natural, or at least what passed as natural for me. "Because you, ah, looked like you, ah, needed help."

"No offense, China, but I'm guessing this couch weighs nearly three times what you do. I appreciate the offer, but I can get it. It's just a little awkward." He smiled again.

"I'm Mia."

She popped over my shoulder, wearing a brilliant smile, her long blonde hair blowing softly in the breeze. Some aunt I was—I'd completely forgotten her presence once I'd seen Superman.

"Hi, Mia." Clark glanced between the two of us. "Are you sisters?"

"I'm her niece," Mia said. "I'm here visiting for a few months. So you're moving in next door?"

I wanted to shush her for being so nosy, but I was dying to know, too, so I didn't say anything.

"Yeah, I closed on the lease a few days ago," he said. "My work relocated me here from Huntsville."

"Alabama?" I asked.

"The very one."

"So what do you do?" Mia asked. "Don't tell me . . . you're a model."

I was mortified, but Clark just laughed.

"Thanks for the compliment," he said. "But I'm actually in human resources."

"That's great," I said, grabbing Mia's arm and squeezing. "We'll just leave you alone then."

"We should help him," Mia said. "Between the two of us, we can help."

Before I could say anything, she'd taken a position next to me. "Okay, on the count of three."

Clark grinned and bent to grab the couch. "One, two . . . three."

We all heaved. Mia and I scrabbled backward through the door.

"Ouch!" I'd banged my side against the handle as we maneuvered.

"You okay?" Clark asked, not even huffing slightly, whereas I was trying not to grunt with the effort I was exerting. She-Ra, I was not.

"Yep . . . fine," I gritted out.

We managed to get the couch inside, where Mia and I unceremoniously dropped it, both of us out of breath.

"Thanks a lot," Clark said. "That went faster than I thought it would." He pushed the couch a few times and I admired the muscles bulging in his arms and back. Then the couch must have been arranged to his satisfaction because he stood back to take a look.

"Glad we could help," Mia piped up. "Hey, we just ordered Chinese food. Have you had dinner?"

My jaw was somewhere in the vicinity of the floor. I never in my wildest dreams would just invite a man over for dinner—*especially* a man who looked like Superman.

"Actually, I haven't," Clark said, glancing at me. "I'd love some Chinese, if it wouldn't be too much of an imposition."

When I didn't say anything, Mia dug her elbow into my side and I winced. "No, it's fine. We'd love the company," I said on cue.

"Great! Thanks! Give me a few minutes to clean up and I'll be right over." Another full-wattage smile.

"Awesome! See you soon," Mia said, taking my elbow and dragging me out the door.

It wasn't until we were back inside my place that I regained full cognizance.

"What did you do?" I asked, turning on Mia. "You invited a total stranger here? For *dinner*? Are you insane?"

"Correction," she said, going to the kitchen to get another plate and fork. "I invited the *completely awesome hot guy* to dinner. That's way different and totally acceptable."

"We don't even know him," I protested. "He could be an ax murderer."

She paused on her way back to the living room, her expression dreamy. "There are worse ways to go."

There was no reasoning with a hormonal teenage girl.

Luckily, I'd doubled our order tonight because I hadn't known how much Mia would eat, so there was plenty of food. But that didn't do a thing for my nerves as we waited for Clark's imminent arrival. I redid my ponytail twice and pushed my glasses so far up my nose, my eyelashes were brushing the lenses.

I was feeding The Doctor when a knock sounded on the door. Mia bounded over to answer before I'd even put away the fish food.

"Hi again!" Mia said as Clark walked in.

He grinned and looked around the room, his gaze stopping when it rested on me. "Hi," he said.

I was so nervous, I didn't know what to say, even though I felt a smile curve my lips. It was impossible *not* to smile when a man who looked like Superman said hello to you. His sexy grin should have been outlawed, as should the jeans that clung to his hips and thighs and . . . oh God. I really needed to stop reading those damn romance novels.

"We have tons of beef and broccoli," Mia said cheerfully. "Hope that's good with you."

"Beef and broccoli sounds great," Clark said, heading toward me. "Is this your fish?"

"No. It's just this huge tank of water I use for decoration. I can't keep the fish out of it." The smart-ass reply popped out before I could stop it. To my relief, Clark didn't take offense. Instead, he laughed, the warm, rich sound filling the room and lighting up his already-sparkling blue eyes.

He'd laughed at my joke. Maybe he thought I was funny. *Funny* as in Ha-Ha, not *funny* as in Weird.

"Do you like fish?" I asked.

"Yes, but usually filleted and sautéed in a nice butter sauce," he said with a grin.

I looked at him. "Goldfish are technically edible—they're a freshwater fish—but I wouldn't think they'd taste very good."

"Not literal, Aunt Chi," Mia hissed to me as she walked by. "Here you go," Mia said more loudly to Clark, handing him a plate heaped with food.

Oh.

"Thanks," he said.

Unsure what to do, I headed back to the sofa and my lukewarm beef and broccoli. The television was paused at the beginning of *Castle*.

"I love that show," Clark said, sitting in the middle of the sofa between Mia and me. "But I'm a big Nathan Fillion fan."

"You are?" I asked.

"Yep. He even tweeted me once."

"No way, really?" I'd had a crush on Nathan Fillion for years.

"Yep," he said, taking a bite of his food. I waited while he chewed, then he said, "It was Valentine's Day and he was throwing his annual virtual party—"

"I've been trying to get into his parties forever," I interrupted.

"I know, right?" Clark grinned. "So I tweeted him and said 'I know lots of useless trivia, like the last line spoken in *Return of the Jedi.*'"

"'He's my brother,'" I quoted.

He grinned. "Very good. Anyway, I didn't think anything about it but when I checked Twitter about eight hours later, he'd tweeted me back and said I was in."

"Oh my God! That's so cool!" My nervousness was nearly forgotten, the mutual excitement over Nathan Fillion obscuring my natural shyness.

"He was amazing in *Firefly*," Clark said, taking another bite.

Now he was talking my love language. We spent the next thirty minutes talking *Firefly*, *Buffy*, and all things Joss Whedon.

"Did Mia go to bed?"

I glanced around at his question, just then realizing that Mia was nowhere to be found and my bedroom door was shut. The little shit.

Nerves hit hard as I realized we were alone together and, to mask them, I grabbed our plates and carried them to the kitchen. To my dismay, Clark followed.

"So what do you do?" he asked, leaning against the counter.

I began rinsing the dishes. "I'm a programmer," I said. "I write software, things like that."

"Really? That's pretty impressive."

"Thanks." I couldn't help the kernel of pleasure his words gave me.

"How long have you been doing that? You don't look old enough to be out of college."

"I'm twenty-three," I said. "I've been out of college for four years."

Clark blew a low whistle. "Wow. So you're like one of those genius kids."

*Genius kids.* Hmm. Not really how I wanted the hot neighbor guy thinking of me. I briefly wished I'd lied, said I was a secretary or beautician or something. Then he wouldn't be looking at me as though I was from a different planet.

When I didn't answer, he seemed to hesitate. "Hey, I'm sorry. That wasn't meant as an insult. It was a compliment."

I smiled to let him know I hadn't taken offense, but didn't really know what to say. "It's fine," was what I settled on. "Can I get you anything else? Do you want an eggroll? Or a fortune cookie?"

"I'd love a fortune cookie."

Reaching into the bag, I pulled out a handful of cookies and set them on the counter. "You're supposed to choose your own fortune," I said.

He picked up a cookie at random and so did I. We opened them together.

"Huh," Clark said, looking at the slip of paper in his hand. "Mine says, *The end of the world is near . . . and it is all your fault.*" He looked up at me. "That's kind of a downer. What does yours say?"

I glanced down. "*Today is probably a huge improvement over yesterday.*" True so far.

Clark smiled. "I don't think I've ever gotten such odd fortunes before."

"They're all like this at that place," I said. "Some are pretty bizarre, others are hilarious."

"I think I should pay you back for dinner. It's the least I could do."

"Oh no, that's okay. Consider it a welcome to the neighborhood."

"No, I insist. Are you free for dinner tomorrow night?"

It took a moment for me to process that, and my heart leapt into double time once I had. Superman was asking me out to dinner? Like . . . a date? The fortune was right. Today was most certainly way better than yesterday.

No, wait, he said he was paying me back. So *not* a date. A return favor.

"That's really nice," I said, swallowing my disappointment, "but I have plans—"

"No she doesn't!" Mia called out from behind the closed bedroom door. "She can go!"

I spun around. "I'm going to put you on the next plane home!"

Silence. I let out a frustrated breath, turning back to see Clark grinning broadly. He raised one eyebrow. "Are you sure you're not sisters?"

"She's . . . impetuous," I said. "And I love her . . . when I don't want to strangle her."

"So how 'bout it?" he asked. "I've never had to work so hard to convince a woman to have dinner with me before." That smile again, full wattage and double dimples.

*Aw hell . . .*

"Yeah, that would be great," I said, not quite believing I was saying yes. But really, how could I possibly say no at this point? And Mia would probably kill me if I did.

"Fantastic. I'll be by about seven." He headed for the door and I followed. "Thanks again for helping with the sofa. And the Chinese."

"Anytime."

I watched him go back into his place before I closed and locked the door.

"Is it safe to come out now?" Mia called.

I pushed open the bedroom door. "Yes."

She was sitting on the bed, a book in her hands. "And the plane home?"

"You can stay," I said. "But no more interfering. That could've gone really bad." For me.

"But it didn't." She stood, closing the book with a snap. "And you're having dinner with the total hot-guy neighbor, two nights in a row." She brushed by me with a flip of her hair and whiff of light perfume. "You're welcome."

Smart-ass.

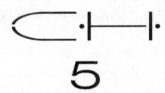

5

Jackson called me into his office the next morning. Thankfully, it was *after* I'd scarfed down my bacon, egg, and cheese McMuffin.

As I took a seat opposite his desk, I said what I'd rehearsed inside my head. "I'm sorry for your loss. I don't remember if I said that yesterday or not. How is Madeline doing?"

"She's doing all right," he replied, leaning back in his chair. "The best that can be expected, I suppose."

He looked good today, as always. He wore black on black, which made his eyes appear even darker. But there was a soberness to him that made me think the usual wardrobe had another meaning today as he mourned his friend.

"I called you in here because I was contacted by Wyndemere last night."

I stiffened. That couldn't be good.

"In light of Tom's death, they've given the entire project to us and need someone to manage it," he continued. "Someone who doesn't need to be trained and who can get up to speed quickly. I'd like you to take that position."

"Me?"

"Yes. You're the most qualified and we're already working on part of it. You'll need to coordinate all the different pieces Tom had going on and manage them. Your interoperability with non-techies is the best in the company."

That was high praise indeed, especially coming from the boss. I felt like I was glowing inside. The people pleaser in me was twirling in glee. Though in reality, it wasn't hard to be the go-between for techies and users—I'd been doing it all my life in my family.

But he also wanted me to work for Wyndemere. All the whispers and rumors I'd heard about the secret government projects they worked on gave me pause. The private sector was always preferable to the government. I racked my brain for an excuse.

"I don't have a security clearance," I said. "There's no way—"

"Already taken care of," he interrupted, shooting down the only objection I could think of. "They cleared you a few minutes ago. As far as they and I are concerned, the sooner you start, the better. The deadline on this project is in two weeks."

Two weeks? I was supposed to walk in cold, wrap my arms around a project I knew nothing about, and deliver it in two weeks?

"That's . . . a really tight timeframe," I said.

"I know, which is why I'll be helping, too."

Okay, that made me feel better. I'd been an on-site consultant before, though a lot of Cysnet's projects were done in-house. It was still like starting a new job, which was incredibly stressful.

"So when do we start?"

"Let's plan on heading over there this afternoon," Jackson said. "You can ride along with me, if you like."

Ride in his awesome Cabriolet convertible again? Twist my arm.

"Sounds like a plan," I said cheerily.

"Okay. Come by about one and we'll go."

I nodded and took that as my dismissal. A few minutes later, I was back at my desk and Randall wanted to quiz me.

"So what's going on?" he asked, popping his head over the cube wall. "You've been in Jackson's office a lot. You in trouble or something?"

IT people were as nosey and as big gossips as anyone else, perhaps more so because interaction with actual people wasn't very common. Anything out of the ordinary stirred their interest, especially if it didn't involve themselves.

"He and I are working on a project together," I explained.

"You're working with Jackson? That is so awesome!" Randall's enthusiasm made me smile. "I've never gotten to. Jeremy has though, and he never stops bragging about it."

"Weren't there like ten people on that project?"

"I know, right?" he scoffed. "Like it even counts. How many people are on your project?"

"Just him and me."

He emitted a low whistle. "No way. Wow."

"Gotta get back to work, Randall. Thanks for breakfast. I'll spot lunch. Taco Bell?"

"Yep. The usual."

I nodded and he disappeared back down into his cube as I settled into my chair.

Wyndemere was in Research Triangle Park—RTI—as opposed to downtown where Cysnet was located. They owned a sprawling two-story building that took up acres of land, most of it hidden behind a thick growth of trees that surrounded the property.

It took the better part of two hours to get our temporary IDs, set up our fingerprint, voice, and retinal scans for security, and go through and sign paperwork that detailed the fine print of their nondisclosure agreement. Finally, we were taken to a small conference room where a woman was waiting for us.

"Hello, I'm Freyda," she said, rising to greet us. "Freyda Jain. I interface between Wyndemere and the customer, be it government, foreign, or domestic contracts."

"Jackson Cooper, and this is China Mack." Not even the great Jackson Cooper attempted to pronounce my last name.

We shook hands all around.

"Thank you for coming on such short notice," she said. "Please have a seat."

Jackson and I took adjacent seats next to Freyda and she set identical file folders in front of us, about an inch thick.

"This should help bring you up to speed. You can look over it here, but all materials must remain on-site at all times."

"Understood."

"Your team." Another folder, thinner this time, one to each of us. "You'll meet with them tomorrow morning. I thought you could use some time to acclimate first."

I glanced at my watch. An hour before quitting time. Thanks heaps.

"The project cost estimate is just that—an estimate," Jackson said. "Real hours will be billed, not to exceed twenty percent of the original estimated cost without written approval."

"Agreed," she said. "Any other questions?"

"Yes," he said. "Is this a government project?"

"I'm sorry. I'm not at liberty to say."

That didn't make me feel any better, but it wasn't as though there was anything I could do about it.

"Let me show you to your office." Freyda rose and we followed her from the room.

The office was severe in design, proving more functional than luxurious. It did have two desks, which was nice, though it was obvious the second one had been moved in last-minute as it didn't really fit with the layout. Windows were on one wall, providing a view of the parking lot and trees outside.

"Security went over procedure with you?" Freyda asked.

"Yes, thank you," I replied while Jackson inspected our computers. Each was hooked up to three monitors, which was nice.

"The lock on the office door has been keyed to your fingerprints," she said, handing me a business card. "Just dial my extension if you need anything."

"I'll do that."

Freyda left and I sat down in one of the two chairs at the small conference table in the corner. Flipping open the thinner of the two file folders, I began to read. Jackson sat down opposite me and did the same.

I was halfway through the thick file when my phone rang.

*"It's me! Your favorite niece. Pick up the phone! I know you're—"*

"Yes, Mia?" I answered.

"Where are you?"

"Work," I said, glancing at my watch. I wasn't that late. "Why? Did you need something?" I'd left her money to go grocery shopping in case she needed anything I didn't have, like brownie mix.

"You have a date tonight," she said. "Remember?"

Shit. I'd completely forgotten. "Oh no." It was already six thirty and Superman—I mean Clark—had said he'd be by at seven.

"You bet, *oh no*," she said. "Please tell me you're on your way home because I will personally cry on your behalf for breaking a date with a guy that looks like Zac Efron on steroids."

Okay, I was drawing a blank on who Zac Efron was, but I got from the context that he was akin to Clark.

"Yeah," I began throwing all the papers together and back in the folder. "I'm leaving in two minutes." I hung up. Traffic wouldn't be too bad, I hoped, but it still looked like I'd be going to dinner dressed in what I was wearing. Jeans, a T-shirt—*Tea. Earl Grey. Hot.*—and the white button-up I'd thrown on over it was fine for tech work, but probably not a date.

And it was Wednesday. I always had dinner with Bonnie on Wednesday. We'd met when she had a flat tire on the side of the road, in the rain no less, and I'd stopped to help her, though the statistics argued against such a thing. She'd looked like a miserable, drowned rat, her attempts at removing lug nuts proving futile. I'd helped her change her tire, she'd cooked me dinner as a thank-you, and we'd been best friends ever since, despite the barely edible dinner. Bonnie was in culinary school and loved trying her new recipes on me, bless her heart.

*Bless her heart* came naturally when thinking of Bonnie and cooking. Try as she might, she just couldn't get the hang of it and would get her recipes 97 percent right, which was good, but the 3 percent that was wrong was *really* wrong. Her family was wealthy, though, so her father had paid for her continued training.

I'd completely forgotten about the date, much less having to cancel with Bonnie. She was going to kill me. She hated when I cancelled and thus removed her default guinea pig.

"I've got to go," I said, opening one of the file drawers and locking the folders inside. "Sorry. But I'll come in early tomorrow." I headed for the door. I could call Bonnie on the way and see if we could get together tomorrow night. Thursday night was breakfast-for-dinner night, but maybe Bonnie could be convinced to make pancakes. She couldn't mess those up that badly. Could she? Hmm . . .

"Aren't you forgetting something?" Jackson asked.

I stopped, racking my brain. I hadn't taken anything with me. Was I supposed to do something else?

"I drove us here," he said.

Oh. "Um, yeah, I guess I forgot. But that's okay if you're not ready to go. I can Uber back to the office." Which would take even longer so there was no way I'd be home by seven.

"No need for that," he said, gathering up his files as well. "I can take you home if you're in a hurry."

"Really? That would be a huge help." It wasn't like I had a date every day. Or even every month. Okay, fine, every *year* if you wanted to get particular about it.

"Of course."

We locked up and exited the building, me trying not to look like I was in a huge hurry. Half my brain was focusing on each minute that passed, the other half on what I should wear when I got home. I didn't have anything that was date-like. Maybe my *Mulder, It's Me* T-shirt? Dana Scully and Fox Mulder were pretty hot together so that was romantic, right?

"I live in Brier Creek," I said. "That's—"

"I know," Jackson cut me off.

Oh yeah. Duh. He'd been to my house.

"So you have plans tonight?" he asked.

"Um, yeah." Should I say I had a date?

"Mia?"

"No," I hesitated. "I . . . have dinner plans. A new neighbor moved in."

"Oh? What's her name?"

Why would he assume it was a girl? "*His* name is Clark." There may have been a note of affront in my tone.

"So you have a date?"

If I said it, that made it official, right? "Um, I guess so, yeah."

"And he just moved in?"

"Yesterday."

"Wow. That's quick. You don't find that at all . . . strange?"

I turned to look at Jackson, replaying his words in my head. Any way I looked at it, technically that was an insult.

"It's strange that a man would ask me out on a date?" It hurt somewhere inside my chest when I said that.

"Of course not," Jackson said. "But . . . he just moved in and already asked you out?"

"Technically, I guess I asked him out first. He had dinner with us last night."

"Are you always so forward with strangers?"

*Forward?* What was this, the fifties? "He literally lives right next door. We were being neighborly."

"Just keep in mind, you work in a very important position in a highly secretive field, and getting close to you would be a coup."

I went from zero to hurt and angry in two seconds flat. "Are you accusing me of discussing my work with outsiders?" Because that would not only be questioning my discretion, but would also be impugning my *honor*, and I wouldn't stand for that.

"No, I—"

"Because I would *never* do that," I interrupted. "And I greatly resent your implication."

"I'm not implying anything," he said, pulling into my subdivision.

"Yes, you are." I was incredibly hurt, but it was easier to handle and voice anger than hurt. Hurt implied vulnerability. Anger was going on the offense. "If you have a problem with my personal life, then take it up with HR. I'm sure you have plenty of lawyers at your disposal."

I was up and out of the car like a shot, too upset to care that I might be overreacting and he'd think I was nuts. I'd worry about that tomorrow.

Mia was waiting for me. "It's about time," she said. "C'mon. I've got your clothes ready. I only have a few minutes to do your hair and makeup."

Wait a minute . . . hair and makeup?

She dragged me into the bedroom before I had a chance to complain and whipped off my T-shirt.

"Here," she said, thrusting some fabric into my hands. "Put this on."

It was some kind of black shirt, but it looped in wraps and I couldn't figure out how to get it on. I fumbled for a couple of minutes before she grabbed it back from me.

"For goodness' sake," she muttered, holding it open for me.

I pushed my head and arms in. "It's not my fault it's a weird shirt," I said, my voice muffled by the fabric over my head.

"It's reversible, and it has side wraps that help push your boobs up and pull your waist in."

My head was out and she began fidgeting with the fabric, pulling it this way and that. I noticed a problem right away.

"I can't wear this, it's cut way too low." The deep V-neckline plunged between my breasts, nearly exposing my Very Sexy Flirt Demi bra in purple rapture.

"Which is *exactly* why you're wearing it," Mia said, stepping back to take a look. "Perfect."

"It's too small," I complained, pulling at the fabric. She brushed my hands away.

"It's not too small. It actually *fits* you, for a change. And it's supposed to be tight."

I wasn't sure about that, but Mia was the expert on fashion, not me. My ponytail had come loose so I reached up to redo it.

"Nope. No ponytail tonight," Mia said, knocking my arms aside and pulling out the elastic band. "Wow, you have awesome hair." She started running her fingers through it, fluffing it. "Not even a ponytail dent. Sheesh."

"It's a pain when it's down," I said. "It gets in the way."

"Of what? Being pretty? Please. And look at all the waves in it. Damn, Aunt Chi. You look totally hot right now, and I haven't even done your makeup."

I pushed my glasses up my nose, wondering if bad vision ran in the family and Mia needed to have her eyes checked. I'd have to make her an appointment with my optometrist.

"Do you have contacts?" she asked.

"I can't wear contacts. My eyes are too sensitive and dry. Trust me, I've tried."

"Okay, well, it doesn't matter. They're such a pretty blue, you just need some mascara and eyeliner to make them pop."

Making my eyes *pop* didn't sound pleasant, but before I could respond, the doorbell rang.

"Stay here," Mia commanded me. "I'll be right back."

I did as she said, chewing my nail as I heard her answer the door, then the deeper voice of Clark. My stomach lost touch with gravity as nerves assailed me. Was I really going on a date with someone I hardly knew?

Which is exactly what I said to Mia when she came back in, closing the bedroom door behind her. She gave me a strange look.

"That's kind of the whole point of a date," she said.

Oh.

"C'mon," she tugged on my hand and pulled me into the bathroom. "I have a great sparkly topaz cream shadow that will look awesome on your eyes."

She sat me on the toilet lid, took off my glasses, and proceeded to open several fabric makeup cases, revealing an alarming amount of brushes and gizmos and palettes. I couldn't tell which was for cheek, lip, or eye. They all looked the same. Mia obviously knew what she was doing, though, because she said, "Close your eyes," and that was that.

Ten minutes later, she said, "Open," and handed me my glasses. I'd tried valiantly not to twitch during her eye makeup application, but the tone of her mutters was decidedly irritated. I slid my glasses back on.

Mia scrutinized me, then smiled broadly. "I am so freaking awesome."

"What did you do?" I stood up and looked in the mirror.

Wow. She *was* good. The woman staring back at me had artfully tousled hair with thick bangs over her forehead, smoky blue eyes that looked almost mysterious, glistening pale-pink lips and a flawless ivory complexion. The shirt she'd given me made my waist look tiny, and I even had a bit of cleavage.

"How did you do that?" I asked.

"It's not like you're a troll," Mia said with a snort. "You just need to accentuate the positive and wah-la."

"It's *voila*," I automatically corrected.

"Whatever, and you're welcome."

I smiled, impulsively giving her a hug. "Thank you."

Mia's cheeks pinkened and she looked pleased. "Not a big deal. Now go, he's waiting. Have fun and don't worry about me if you don't come home until morning." She waggled her eyebrows.

"Mia!"

But she just laughed at me.

I couldn't even imagine . . . Clark and me . . . until morning—

Nope. Not going to go there. This was dinner. That's all.

Mia remained in the bedroom, giving me a firm shove out the door and closing it behind me. I stood for a minute, my stomach doing somersaults, then took a breath and walked into the living room.

Clark was sitting on the couch, one ankle resting on the opposite knee, watching whatever Mia had playing on the television. He wore jeans and a button-down shirt the precise blue of his eyes. His shoes and belt were both the same honey-brown leather, and his jaw looked freshly shaven.

Wow.

As if he'd heard my unspoken thought, he glanced over and our eyes caught. His mouth fell open slightly and he didn't move for a moment, his eyes tracking me from head to foot and back. It felt like one of those movie moments, where the librarian lets her hair down and suddenly she's this bombshell—only it wasn't a librarian but just me, a nerdy IT girl—and I certainly wasn't a bombshell just because I had on eye shadow and for once wasn't wearing my hair in a ponytail.

But it felt nice, all the same.

"Sorry I'm late," I said, heading toward him. "Work took longer than I expected."

He smiled broadly as he got to his feet. "It was definitely worth the wait."

A charmer, too. Not surprised, though, with his looks, I wondered how often he had to use charm to get a date.

I cleared my throat, unsure what to say to the unexpected compliment, nervously tucking my hair behind one ear. This was why I always wore it up. There was just so *much*, it was constantly getting in my way. "You look really nice."

"Thanks," he said, standing. "I hope you like Italian."

"Italian" was basically flour with sauce and was my least favorite ethnic food. But I smiled and said, "Sounds great." I could eat salad. Every Italian place had salad.

Clark led me to his car—a ten-year-old Honda in sky blue. Not what I would have pictured him driving, that was for sure. A glance at the odometer when he opened the door for me said the car was nearing one hundred and fifty thousand miles. Wow.

"Sorry it's nothing fancy," he said as he slid behind the wheel. "I used to drive something nicer, but had to downsize recently."

"Oh?"

"I had my own real estate business, but when the market crashed, it did, too," he explained. "It's taken a year or so to get back on my feet, but I finally sold the house and got this job, so I moved here."

"Where did you live before?"

"Wakefield Estates."

I knew that was a really nice area in Wake Forest that catered to the superrich. Jackson lived there. Clark must have lost quite a bit when his business went under, which explained him moving into a duplex, and the car.

"And you're in HR now?" I asked. He nodded.

"Not exactly what I was doing before, but it suits me."

I was awful at small talk and we fell silent after that. My nerves were still on edge and I fidgeted with the neckline of my shirt, trying and failing to expose less skin.

"So how was your day at work?" Clark asked.

It flashed through my mind what Jackson had said, but I dismissed it. Asking about someone's day was perfectly normal chitchat. Or at least, that's what Mom had always drilled into me.

"It was all right. I've started a new on-site consult."

"Oh, you're a consultant? I thought you were a programmer."

"I am, and sometimes our contracts don't require an on-site presence. This one does."

"So which company do you work for?"

"Cysnet."

Clark frowned slightly. "That sounds familiar. Why does that sound familiar?"

"You've probably heard about the owner, Jackson Cooper," I said. "He's one of those self-made billionaire-genius types."

"Ah. Yes. That's why. So you work for him? What's that like?" He sounded impressed, which made the butterflies in my stomach land temporarily.

"It's interesting. And a challenge."

"I bet you've got to be really smart to work at a place like that," he said.

I felt my face get warm at the unexpected compliment and I didn't know what to say. *Yeah, I am,* just sounded wrong.

"So you have to be on-site somewhere else now?" he asked. "Where?"

"I'm doing a project for Wyndemere."

He issued a low whistle. "Wow. I definitely know who they are. And you're consulting for them? That's pretty cool."

It wasn't often that anyone knew or cared what I did for a living, much less thought it was "cool." The butterflies in my stomach went away completely and I felt myself relax.

"Do you know anything about computers?" I asked "Or coding?"

Clark shook his head with a small laugh. "What I know about computers could fit in a teacup. Maybe you could put it in layman's terms, what you do."

"We basically write custom software," I said. "Businesses have problems or need a better fit for their niche and we come up with the best solution for them, then write it from scratch."

"So that's what you're doing for Wyndemere?"

"Something like that." No sense getting technical. "I'm not really supposed to discuss our customers."

"Oh yeah, sure, sorry. Wasn't trying to pry." He smiled at me again as he pulled into a parking lot.

"Not a problem." I got out of the car, looking around at the restaurant he'd brought me to. It was a chain, but a nice one. A typical middle-class working-family establishment.

The hostess couldn't have been older than twenty and could barely take her eyes off Clark as she led us to a table.

"Can we have a booth instead?" Clark asked.

The beaming smile on the hostess's face faded a bit, but she reluctantly led us to a booth. I slid in one side, Clark the other. She handed us menus and drifted away with one last longing look in Clark's direction. To his credit, he didn't seem to notice.

"What do you like?" he asked me. "Is wine your thing? Or do you want to start with a cocktail?"

"A cocktail sounds nice." So long as I sipped it.

"What's your poison?"

"Um . . ." Since I rarely drank, I had no idea what to order. But I *had* read an article on classic American cocktails one time. "A sidecar," I decided, scanning the article in my memory and choosing the one with the prettiest picture. "Please." That sounded sophisticated, right?

Clark's brows went up. "A sidecar. Really?" I nodded. "Okay, sounds good." The waitress came by and he ordered me a sidecar and himself a gin and tonic.

I glanced at the menu, scanning the columns for something without noodles. They had chicken and beef, too, and I went with the chicken marsala.

"To new neighbors . . . and new friendships," Clark said, raising his glass.

I clinked mine against his, then took a sip of my cocktail. It had a sugared rim, so how bad could it be? It was ice-cold and tart and I liked it right away. I took another sip as I turned over his toast in my head, knowing I shouldn't read anything into it. But the way he was looking at me with those eyes, intent and unblinking, made my heart skip into overtime.

"If you don't mind my saying so, you seem awfully young for that kind of job," Clark said.

Ah, the age question. I got it a lot. It's what happened when you graduated MIT at nineteen, which is what I told him. Clark was chewing some of the bread they'd left on the table and he paused.

"Seriously?"

"Yeah. I've always been a little bit . . . precocious," I said. Which was a nice way of saying *smarter than anyone in a thousand mile radius.*

Clark frowned. "It must've been really hard for you when you were young."

That was putting it mildly. Bullies had nothing on how mean "nice" girls could be.

I didn't know what it was—maybe the way Clark was looking at me with sympathy rather than pity. Or maybe it was the atmosphere in the half-empty restaurant with the dim lighting and candles on the tables. Probably it was the brandy in my glass already flooding my nervous system. Either way, I found myself talking.

"One time, I was invited to a sleepover," I said. "I was thirteen. I'd never been to a sleepover before. They said it was a dress-up party— come in costume. I was so excited, I could hardly wait." I remembered it as though it had just been yesterday. I'd been so proud to tell my dad that I'd been invited to a real high school party.

"I dressed up in my favorite costume—a Star Fleet science officer. Even took along the tricorder I'd fashioned. It beeped and whirred the real noises when I pressed the buttons, I made sure of it. My dad dropped me off, told me to have fun, and that he'd be back in the morning to pick me up.

"I walked up the sidewalk and I could hear the music inside and people talking and laughing. For once, I was going to be one of the cool kids. Maybe I'd find someone who liked the things I liked. Someone I could talk to and laugh with. So I rang the doorbell." I paused. The pain from that night still ached even after all these years.

"What happened?" Clark asked.

"They opened the door and I saw it not only wasn't just a handful of girls at a sleepover, but most of the high school was there. The next thing I noticed was that it wasn't a costume party."

Clark winced.

Follow Me

"They laughed, took my tricorder, and locked me in a trunk. You know, one of those old-fashioned, traveling-type trunks?" He nodded. "Anyway, they were drinking and forgot about me. I spent the entire night locked in there. It wasn't until the next morning that the parents got home and let me out."

I'd been shaking with fear and had wet myself because I hadn't been able to hold my bladder any longer. They'd tried to apologize and wanted to call an ambulance, but I'd run out the door. I'd walked the three miles to my house and snuck in the back. I'd cleaned myself up before my dad saw me. One look at my face and he hadn't asked how it went.

"Oh my God," Clark murmured, looking stunned.

I'd almost forgotten that I was telling the story, rather than reliving it. And here I was, sharing one of the most shameful things that had ever happened to me, with the most gorgeous man I'd ever seen, on what could possibly be argued was our first date.

*Nice way to break the ice, Chi.*

"I know, right?" I said, forcing a laugh. "Kids are mean. But to answer your question, yes, it was a bit difficult when I was young."

It appeared I'd struck Clark speechless, because he seemed utterly at a loss as to what to say next. Ah, knowing when was the right time to say things and when it would be a really bad time—I needed to work on that. I tried to think of some way to get back on chitchat footing.

"I mean, it's okay," I said quickly. "I got the last laugh, right? I have three degrees from MIT—two undergrad degrees in computer science and biological engineering plus a master's in engineering—and make more money at twenty-three than most of them will probably see by the time they're fifty." I forced another laugh that kind of petered out when Clark didn't laugh with me. I took another nervous sip of my sidecar.

83

"What they did to you was awful," he said at last, breaking the uncomfortable silence. "I can't imagine."

"Bad stuff happens sometimes," I said. The sidecar was really good and I turned the glass so I could get more sugar off the rim. "You get over it, right?"

"That's very . . . pragmatic of you."

"A necessity sometimes."

"And how often was 'sometimes'?" he asked.

I sensed he was getting close to pity. Our food arrived before I could figure out how to head that off, thank goodness. Now I could make pleasant noises about the food. I took a good look at my plate.

"Wait, there's mushrooms in this," I blurted.

"Yes, the marsala is a mushroom-based sauce with Marsala wine," the server said.

"I don't eat mushrooms." I'd thought for sure I'd asked for them to leave the mushrooms out, but maybe I'd been too preoccupied with staring at Clark and hadn't.

The server grabbed my plate. "Absolutely. We'll get you a new dish right away."

"I'm so sorry," I apologized. "I didn't realize—"

"It's fine. I'll be back soon." She hurried off.

"You don't eat mushrooms?" Clark asked, finishing off his cocktail. I noticed he wasn't eating yet, which was weird. His food was going to get cold.

"It's fungi. I don't eat fungi."

Clark nodded sagely. "I see. And why is that?"

I looked at him like he was nuts. "It's *mold*. Do you eat anything that's molded?"

"Not if I can help it."

"Exactly."

"I like mushrooms though. Especially portabellas. They're delicious."

"If you say so." I looked at his plate again. "Your food is getting cold."

His lips twitched. "It's impolite for me to eat before you've gotten your meal."

How strange. "So you'd let yours get cold and inedible because of societal niceties?"

Clark chuckled. "I suppose that's one way of looking at it."

Huh. "Please don't wait," I said. "It's not a logical thing to do. And really, I don't mind watching you eat." Which sounded weird when I heard it said aloud. "I mean, please, go ahead."

Clark just smiled, considering me in silence until the server brought back my plate. This time sans mushrooms, thank goodness. I dug in. I was starving. Only then did he begin eating his lasagna.

"Better?" Clark asked.

"Much. Thanks." I'd finished my sidecar and took a sip of the merlot Clark had ordered for us. The sidecar must've been pretty powerful, especially on my empty stomach, because I was feeling really relaxed. The butterflies were a distant memory.

We ate in companionable silence and I finished my glass of wine. Alcohol was the best thing ever, I decided. Why hadn't I drunk more before? I didn't even care that we weren't talking, whereas usually I'd be stressing and desperately trying to think of something to say.

"So tell me about yourself," Clark said. "Have you always been a prodigy?"

"You want the Brief History of Me?" I asked, taking another bite. He smiled.

"I guess you could call it that."

"There's not much to tell. I graduated high school at fourteen. Got a college education from MIT at nineteen. I've been working for Cysnet ever since."

"Are you from here?"

"No. Omaha, actually."

"A farm girl?"

"My dad's a farmer, yeah." I finished off the mashed potatoes, scooping up the last of the mushroom-free sauce.

"Siblings?"

"Two older brothers. One married, one not."

"And your niece lives with you?" he asked as the server took our empty plates.

"For a short while," I replied, sipping my second—third?—glass of wine. Clark was looking better and better, not that it was a hard thing. Those blue eyes and smile . . . I heaved a long sigh. *In my dreams.* "What about you?" I asked, sick of talking about my boring life. "Family? Siblings? Hometown?"

"Parents married forty years, now retired. Only child. Allentown."

"That's quite . . . succinct," I said with a laugh. Clark smiled, too. He leaned forward and to my shock, placed a hand over mine so that we were almost holding hands, but not quite.

"I haven't led a terribly exciting life," he said, which I hardly heard. I was too focused on the feel of his skin against mine, warm and dry, and how it was suddenly hard to breathe.

"Uh . . . really?" was the best I could come up with because now he was stroking his thumb across the top of my hand. It was the most erotic thing I'd ever felt and, all the while, his eyes were gazing into mine as though he was looking into my soul.

"No, though there was this time I traveled to Singapore . . ." He continued, telling me a story about getting lost in the back streets of Singapore and hit on by a prostitute, though I couldn't focus. His hand was on mine and he'd begun idly playing with my fingers as he talked until all I could think about was that I wanted him to touch me more.

The bill came and he paid, then led me out of the restaurant. My senses were heightened from the alcohol and his hand on my lower back felt like a brand through the thin fabric of my shirt.

"Can I talk you into dessert at my place?" he asked as we drove back.

I glanced at my watch. It was getting late. Bedtime was in twenty minutes. I had to be at work in the morning.

"Thanks, but I can't," I said. "But dinner was really nice. Thank you."

"Did you have a good time?"

"Absolutely!" Okay, maybe a little *too* enthusiastic there. "I mean, yeah, of course." That was better. *Play it cool, Chi.*

He smiled that thousand-watt smile again. "Me, too. Maybe we can do it again? Soon?"

Was he asking me out on another date? Like . . . *two* dates? With the same guy? And not just any guy . . . but Superman?

Clark parked in his driveway and turned off the car before looking at me. His smile faded. "I'm taking your silence as a no?"

"No! I mean, yes, I would, sorry. I was just—" I cut my words off just before I embarrassed myself. The alcohol was slowly wearing off and my better sense was oozing back into my brain.

"Just what?"

But I shook my head, not wanting to finish the thought, because *surprised you'd want to see me again* sounded so incredibly pathetic.

"I . . . think I know what you mean," Clark said. He leaned toward me and the dim light from the lamppost shining through the windows made his eyes gleam. I could smell him now and I took a deep breath, memorizing the slightly spicy scent.

His body was bigger than mine, his shoulders wide enough to block my view out the windshield. I was frozen in place as he lifted a hand to cup my jaw. It felt surreal, like I was in a dream as he leaned closer. Carefully, he removed my glasses, setting them on the dash as I watched, transfixed.

The touch of his lips on mine was nearly shocking, it had been so long since I'd been kissed, and never by a man like this. My eyes were still open as his mouth caressed mine, the gentle coaxing sending waves of heat and energy through me.

My eyes drifted closed, my body felt like warm caramel flowed in my veins, and the touch of his tongue against the seam of my lips was velvet. Instinctively, I parted my lips and his tongue surged inside, caressing mine. He tasted of the wine we'd drunk and his own flavor, which I knew immediately I would never forget.

His hand moved to cup my neck and for once I felt as though my small frame *wasn't* a detriment. Clark was strong and male, a perfect complement to me, which was an incredible turn-on.

He deepened the kiss further and our breaths mingled, an intimacy that struck me. I could kiss him like this forever. Tentatively, I lifted my hand to the back of his head, my fingers itching to touch his dark, wavy locks. They were as soft as I'd imagined. I luxuriated in the feel of it, which he seemed to like because he moved even closer, his kiss becoming more urgent.

It was lovely to be wanted like this and I reveled in it. Like one of Grandma's novels come to life . . . *my* life. Which was, frankly, insane.

I felt the light touch of his fingers drift down my neck to the deep V of my shirt. It was unexpected and I was too unused to such a thing for me to control my reaction, which was to jump and pull back.

"I-I'm sorry," I immediately apologized as Clark lifted his head to gaze down at me. "I-it's just that—"

"It's okay," he said, his lips curving slightly. He tucked a thick lock of my hair behind my ear. "It's my fault, moving too fast. You're just . . . very beautiful and so smart. I . . . lost my head for a moment."

Dumbfounded, I simply stared at him, blinking. Up close, I could see him, but everything else was a blur.

He brushed a kiss to the tip of my nose, then handed me back my glasses. "I'll walk you to the door."

I was still at a loss as to what to say when we got to my door and I turned to face him. I went for manners.

"Thank you for dinner," I said.

"I'm looking forward to seeing you again," he said, standing much closer than the usual eighteen inches preferred by Americans. I found that, for once, I didn't mind the invasion of my personal space.

"Me, too." Okay, now I definitely sounded like one of those breathless heroines in Granny's romance novels. I stared into his eyes, breathing in his scent as he leaned close and pressed his lips gently against mine. This time, my eyes closed right away and I savored the touch.

"Good night, China," Clark said, his voice a low throb of sound. Then he was gone, moving into the darkness to his place next door.

Wow.

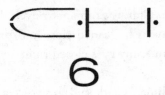

# 6

Mia wanted to hear all about my date, so I gave her a brief rundown, leaving out the kissing part because I was still trying to process that.

"Did he kiss you goodnight?" she asked, despite my censoring.

"Um . . ." I hesitated and heat flooded my face.

"He did!" she crowed. "It was the eyes. Sparkles *never* disappoint, am I right?"

Her enthusiasm had me grinning like an idiot, the really great evening finally sinking in. I was walking on air, excitement bubbling inside me like a bottle of champagne.

I washed my face and braided my hair before going to bed, moving quickly. But although I was in bed on time, it took a while to go to sleep. My mind kept reliving the evening, looking at it from every angle. It was surreal. I stared at the dark ceiling, remembering the feel of Clark's mouth on mine, the smell of his cologne, the softness of his hair in my fingers.

I smiled into the darkness, the bubble of joy threatening to burst inside my chest. Tonight had been one of—no, correction—*the* best night of my life. And he wanted to do it again.

It was a long time before I went to sleep.

I had to get up extra early the next morning to get a cab to pick up my car from Cysnet and still arrive at Wyndemere on time. Even so, I didn't beat Jackson there as he was already in our shared office space.

Nerves assailed me as I headed inside. I'd been pretty angry last night and had no idea how to handle things with Jackson this morning. He'd been an ass, which was unexpected. I'd idolized him for so long, been so excited to work with him, then he'd insulted me in a very personal way.

The phrase "the bloom is off the rose" seemed apt.

"Good morning," I said stiffly to him as I folded myself into my temporary chair at my temporary desk. I'd snagged a Red Bull from home and popped the top while my computer logged on.

"How was your date?" Jackson asked.

I was glad I'd already swallowed or I would have choked again on that opening inquiry, especially considering how we'd left things last night.

"It was fine," I said, avoiding his gaze by getting out the papers I needed from the locked cabinet.

"Just fine?"

I sensed another insult, but couldn't pinpoint it. But the question didn't make me feel any more compelled to like him. "I had fun, though it's really none of your business."

"And you spoke nothing about your work."

I gritted my teeth as anger surged again, and I looked over at him.

Jackson wore black, as usual, and his dark gaze was leveled on me. He had an edge to him that was so unusual for someone in our profession—a white-collar computer job, as generic as they came. He was anything but "generic." Maybe it was that edge that had compelled him to work as hard as he had and build his company from the ground up. Or maybe he did karate in his spare time and that's where he got it from. Either way, I didn't care.

"I told you I wouldn't," I said. "He asked where I worked and I gave the most basic reply. *Where* I work is not a secret. What I *do* is, which is why I take my employment agreement very seriously."

"Good."

Our gazes held for another moment before he looked away.

"That meeting with the rest of the team is this morning," he said. "I want you to run it. I'll attend as well, but I'd rather not be the point person for the team."

A knot of nerves coalesced in my stomach. Having to talk tech wasn't an unknown thing for me, though I'd never managed a team before. But it wasn't exactly like I could tell my boss, *You know, I'm not really comfortable with that.* At least, not if I didn't want to get fired. "Understood."

"Let's run down the list and make sure we have a meeting agenda ready to go."

I agreed—a concrete plan of what I was going to say sounded good—and that's what we began putting together. At this point, I was ready to work as many hours as necessary to finish this project, just so I wouldn't have to be around Jackson anymore. He'd been Not Nice to me in a big way and while I always pretended I had a thick skin, the truth was far from it.

Two hours later, we headed down the hall to a conference room. Three other people were already there. Jackson held the door for me and I preceded him, choosing a chair at random from the remaining five situated around the oval table. He sat on my right. The glass windows were tinted against the morning sunshine, which was nice.

A quick glance around the room and I smiled a generic greeting. I'd found that people always responded better to smiles—even my crappy fake one—regardless of whether you spoke. It set them at ease. Two of the three people were men and there was one woman. I knew we were missing one more man, though it was time for the meeting to begin.

"Who are we waiting for?" I asked the assembled people.

"John," replied the woman. "He's usually running a few minutes behind."

"You must be Lana," I said. Easy guess, since she was the only female aside from myself on the team. My memory served up her employee file like flipping through a Rolodex. Lana Miller, graduated from Berkeley with a BS in computer science, got a master's at Caltech, been working for Wyndemere for over a decade. Had climbed steadily in the company and been promoted until she was head of her division. Not married. No kids. *Enjoys basket weaving and long walks on the beach in her spare time*, my inner smart-ass added.

"I am," she said with a friendly smile. She appeared in her early forties with short brown hair and was dressed nicer than I was, in slacks and a pale-blue blouse with heavy silver jewelry.

The door opened and a man I assumed was John came rushing in, looking harried. "Sorry I'm late," he said, sliding into a chair.

"It's not a problem." Which was a total lie. I hated tardiness. But getting irritated certainly wouldn't get things off to a good start.

"John," he said, confirming my assumption. My mental Rolodex flipped pages. John was a mechanical engineer who'd begun programming when he'd been laid off from his previous job. Divorced, he'd bounced around a few other jobs before landing at Wyndemere. I was surprised he'd been promoted as quickly as he had, given his background. But perhaps he had influence or some other reason for how well he'd done at Wyndemere.

*And that other reason certainly wasn't punctuality.*

"I'm China Mack, and this is Jackson Cooper." I nodded toward Jackson. "We've been brought in—" And I paused because, at that point, no one was paying a bit of attention to me. Their eyes were all glued to Jackson with varying expressions of stunned amazement and awe on their faces.

I resisted the urge to roll my eyes, but just barely. I'd been just like them less than twenty-four hours ago.

Clearing my throat did nothing, so I did it louder and more obnoxiously until all eyes swung back to me.

"As I was saying, we've been brought in to finish this project. My condolences to you all on Tom's death." An uncomfortable silence then, though I saw Lana's eyes tear up. "Unfortunately, the due date is still firm and needs to be met. Can we get a status report from each of you to start?"

No one spoke. In fact, they looked at one another in confusion. One of the men spoke up.

"That's against protocol," he said. "I'm Terry, by the way." He was grizzled in the way I was used to seeing from coders. Khakis and a button-down shirt that should've been ironed and a scraggly beard that needed trimming.

"Nice to meet you, Terry," I said by rote. *Two master's degrees from MIT. Been at Wyndemere his entire career, which was over fifteen years.* "What do you mean *against protocol?*"

"We discuss our parts of the project individually and in private," he clarified. "Tom didn't like doing it that way, but the specs for the project made it clear."

"Deviation from specs is cause for immediate termination of employment and a breach of confidentiality suit," the last man said. He was the oldest of the group, perhaps in his sixties.

"George?" I said, though it wasn't really a question. The process of elimination meant it had to be him. *Graduated from UMass in the seventies. Been in tech since apple was still just a fruit.*

He nodded. "I've been working here for over twenty years and I've never seen anything like it. But rules are rules." He shrugged and took a sip from the Styrofoam cup of coffee in front of him.

I'd read through the file and I was certain there'd been nothing like that in the contract, which meant Tom must have made that up.

It looked as though Jackson had come to the same conclusion because when I instinctively glanced at him, his mouth was set in a grim line and he didn't speak.

Okay then.

"Of course," I said. "We'll continue operating according to . . . protocol . . . and meet separately. We'll begin this afternoon and I'll e-mail you the time."

"Are we meeting with you or him?" John asked, motioning toward Jackson.

"You'll be meeting with China," Jackson answered. "She's project leader, not me. Defer to her for direction and if you have any questions or problems."

"But . . . you're Jackson Cooper," John said. "Surely you'd be best suited—"

"Actually China is the most qualified to step in here," Jackson interrupted. "We're working together on this account, but she knows more about the language than I do."

That silenced them . . . and me. I knew I shouldn't look so surprised at his recommendation—I just couldn't help it. It took me a moment to recover.

"So I'll e-mail you all and we'll meet this afternoon. Individually. Please bring whatever materials you think I'll need."

Various nods of assent from around the table. I stood to leave. "Thanks, everyone. Good to meet all of you." I let out a sigh of relief. It was over and I hadn't collapsed from nerves.

They filed out, leaving Jackson and me alone.

"I appreciate your support," I said to him. Women in IT were rare, so I was used to my abilities being questioned, especially factoring in my age. I'd gotten over being offended about it years ago.

"I wasn't being nice. I was being truthful."

Well. He'd effectively planted himself on my Good Side again. Dammit. And I didn't know what to say except, "Um . . . okay then." Picking up my things, I walked back to the office, not checking to see if he followed. As it turned out, he did.

"I'm heading back," he said as I set my stuff on my desk. "Let's meet tonight and discuss your meetings this afternoon."

"Tonight?" It was Thursday. I'd texted Bonnie last night and she'd gotten irritated that I'd waited to cancel until the last minute, but the moment I'd said "date," she'd gone all squealy on me. I'd sworn to her I'd fill her in tonight.

"Yes. Why?" Jackson's expression had gone all hard again. "Another date? I do hope your job isn't interfering with your active social life."

Was I imagining the snide snark in his tone? It was so damn hard to tell. Was he being a jerk or just blunt? I went with the latter but I suspected the former, though why he cared if I had another date was beyond me.

"Yes, actually. With my friend Bonnie. But she's a chef so I doubt she'll be interested in my work." I sounded just this side of bitchy, but I didn't care. Why had I never noticed what an ass Jackson could be? Oh yeah, I'd been too blinded by hero worship.

"I see."

When he didn't say anything else, I said, "So do I need to cancel, or can we talk tomorrow?"

"First thing tomorrow. My office."

"Yes, sir."

I watched him leave, feeling my whole body relax when he was out of sight. I absolutely could not figure Jackson out. Yesterday, he'd seemed so nice. Then it was as though he flipped a switch. Maybe it was me? Maybe I'd been too familiar with him or something and he was reminding me of my place? Either way, he was as intimidating as hell.

But I had a job to do, so I shoved thoughts of Jackson aside and got to my e-mail, which was really Tom's e-mail but now mine.

There were four distinct parts of the project and Terry was responsible for Software Integration. I met with him first.

". . . and all current web browsers are ready to go. My team is still working on social media software. Gaming consoles are proving the toughest to crack."

I could believe that. Gamers—some of the most suspicious people on the planet—had their own encrypted communication via their device of choice.

"And of course each has their own proprietary method," he continued. "But we're making progress."

"Does your team need additional resources?"

"Not at this time."

Terry was matter-of-fact and professional, both qualities I appreciated. We talked through more specifics and he gave me an inch-thick packet of papers. It was the better part of an hour before we were through, then it was on to George, who was in charge of Tracking, Lana who was Testing Coordinator, and finally John with Deployment.

By the time I was finished, it was after five and my head was throbbing. I was sick of talking. And I had a stack of papers on my desk nearly a foot tall.

There was so much to process, I decided to deal with it later. I needed a break, and I had a best friend cooking a bad dinner just for me.

I called Mia on my way home.

"Hey, Aunt Chi! I got bored today, so I rearranged your closet. I hope you don't mind."

The car swerved and I nearly dropped my phone trying to right it.

"You did *what*?"

"I cannot believe how many T-shirts you own," she went on. "Seriously, where do you get them all?"

"You rearranged my T-shirts?" Oh God, it was hard to breathe. "They were by fandom!"

"Well now they're by color."

"By color? Why? That's a ridiculous way to arrange a closet!"

"No it's not. It makes perfect sense. Just wait until you see it. You're going to love it, I promise."

I didn't love it, but she was so pleased at having "helped" me, that I didn't have the heart to put them back the way they had been. I invited her with me to Bonnie's, but she said she'd met another girl her age who was coming over to watch *Pitch Perfect* with her and order pizza. That was fine with me. I'd rather pluck the hairs on my arm one by one than watch a chick flick.

"It's about time you got here," Bonnie said as she opened her door. "The kale's almost ready."

Kale. Yippee. So much for my hinting that waffles and bacon sounded really good.

Bonnie lived in a nice upper-class neighborhood in a house that was about two thousand square feet too large for one person. She had a gourmet kitchen with all the bells and whistles—gas stove with hood, double oven, copper pots and pans hanging above a granite island in the middle, and a professional knife set that had cost a small fortune.

I sat at one of the leather stools at the expansive breakfast bar, smelling the aromas that were a combination of good . . . and a hint of bad. Something was burning. I hoped it was the kale.

"So tell me about this date," she said, stirring a steaming dish on the stove. Bonnie was tall, her skin a warm honey that perfectly matched her hair. She was also the only woman I knew aside from Giada on the Food Network who looked good in an apron. "Who's the guy?"

"He's my new neighbor," I said, reaching for one of the little bites from the tray on the counter. I couldn't tell what they were, maybe dumplings. I took a small bite and gingerly chewed . . . not bad. I stuffed the rest in my mouth and talked around it. "Name's Clark. Looks like Superman."

Bonnie stopped stirring to glance at me. "No shit?"

"No shit."

"Wow." She stirred some more. "That's pretty cool. You haven't had a date in forever. It's about time there was a guy with a big enough set of balls to ask you out."

I ate another dumpling. "Yeah, because *that's* the reason why I don't get asked out." Bonnie was funny and smart and pretty. She had dates on a regular basis.

"You don't get asked out because all you do is work," she retorted. "If you'd come out with me sometime, you could meet people."

"I don't drink, you know that." Which wasn't exactly true anymore. "Though I did drink last night."

"You drank on your date?" She removed the pan from the stove and poured the contents over chicken breasts spread out on two plates. "What happened?"

"Nothing . . . just that it probably explains why I let him kiss me in the car." I'd hoped for a good reaction, and I got one.

"Oh my God!" she squealed, giving me a blinding smile. "That's awesome! Good for you."

I grinned at her like a lovesick loon.

"So?" she asked.

"So . . . what?"

She rolled her eyes. "So how was it? Was kissing Superman everything you'd thought it'd be?"

Her teasing had me blushing, but I still nodded. "Yeah. Better, actually."

Bonnie laughed. "This calls for a celebration." Opening a miniature wine refrigerator, she took out a bottle. "Start at the beginning and don't leave anything out."

So I did, adding in the news of my new houseguest as well. Combined with her questions—"Mia did *what* to your closet? Is she crazy?" because of course that was one of the first things I told her—catching her up on my life took the entire dinner. But that wasn't a bad thing. It helped distract her from the fact that I wasn't eating very much. The sauce was really good, but the chicken was overcooked and dry, and the kale tasted like a soggy mass of seaweed in my mouth. I'd managed to spit it into my napkin when she wasn't looking.

"So what do you think?" she asked, motioning to my plate. "Is it a repeat?"

"The sauce was amazing," I said. "Definitely a repeat."

"And the kale?"

I hesitated, then just made a face. She looked crestfallen. "I'm sorry!" I blurted. "You know I'm not a greens kind of person!" Bonnie had been trying to get me to eat cooked greens forever, from spinach to collard and now to kale.

"I know, I know," she sighed. "Weeds with good PR." Which was my line for said greens.

"So what do you think about Clark?"

"He sounds like a hottie, and that he's got baggage if he's had money problems. But if you're looking to get in the dating scene, he sounds like a better prospect than most."

"What about the kissing stuff?" I'd been honest with her about the episode in the car. Bonnie and I didn't keep secrets from each other. "Was it . . . normal . . . for him to try for second base?"

She laughed and refilled our empty glasses of wine. "Men will try to get away with whatever you'll let them get away with, no matter the timetable. Don't get me wrong. You're beautiful, and a genius, and have an awesome job, and you're fun—"

"Stop it," I interrupted. "You're embarrassing me. Get to the point." Bonnie was my biggest fan who loved me as much as I loved her, but

I thought that probably biased her opinion of my fabled beauty and charm.

"I'm saying, I want you to have fun, but you should be careful. This is new to you."

Okay. She was probably right. I should be careful. It just seemed so strange to me, given my sadly lacking love life, that this incredibly gorgeous guy I'd just met would be so smitten with me. Romance novels weren't real life. Things like that just didn't happen, which was of course why women read so many of them, including me.

I really needed to ship Grandma the latest stack I'd bought, even though I was right in the middle of *Forbidden Enchantment*.

We chatted some more and Bonnie told me about her latest cooking mishaps in class while I made sympathetic noises.

". . . but I may have an in on a job at a new restaurant downtown," she said.

"What's the in?"

She grinned. "Another guy in the class, who's totally cute. His sister is the one with the restaurant and she's looking to get good help cheap. It would be good for the experience in a real restaurant kitchen, you know?"

"That's great, yes, it would," I agreed. Bonnie definitely needed more experience if she was going to make her dream of being a chef come true.

We discussed the pros and cons for a little while as we finished the wine, then it was time to go.

"Gotta get home by bedtime, right?" Bonnie asked with a laugh. "You're so predictable, China."

"Yes, I know." I gave her a hug. "It's part of my charm. Thanks for dinner, as always."

"Let me know about Superman."

"Will do."

I waved as I headed down the sidewalk to the driveway. It was a pretty dark neighborhood and I heard a dog bark somewhere nearby. My breath made puffs in the cold night air and I wrapped my arms around myself. Unlocking my car door with my remote, I slid behind the wheel, wincing as the chill from the leather seeped through my jeans.

A click by my ear startled me and I jerked, instinctively turning my head.

"Don't."

Hard metal pressed against my temple and I froze. *Someone was in my backseat.* The thought hit, then the fear and adrenaline. It felt like ice water had been shot into my veins, an immediate rush that I'd never felt before. Part of my mind was analyzing this physical reaction while a second part was assessing the situation and yet a third was busy having a panic attack. I went for door number two.

It was a man. He had a weapon, obviously a gun. It was pointed at my head and chances were high that it was loaded. He didn't want me to see him. That fact plus that he hadn't killed me yet gave me a better than even chance that he wasn't planning on killing me. Which left the question of what did he want? Was this a carjacking?

"I'm here to deliver a message," he said. His voice was a low rasp and sent a chill through me. "You're involved in a project that's very important to us."

Wyndemere immediately came to mind. Dammit. I knew nothing good would come out of working for them.

I swallowed. "I work on a lot of important projects."

"This is a special one, and we want it finished."

"Who's 'we'?"

"Not your concern. But you should know that Tom was a casualty. It'd be too bad if you were, too."

Tom. Apparently not a suicide after all. My heart sank. "Why would you kill Tom?"

"Tom was having second thoughts about turning over the software to us," he said. "We want to make sure you don't follow the same path."

"Why wouldn't I give the customer the software?" I asked. "And who is 'we'? Who do you work for?"

"You can say I work for your . . . customer. Indirectly."

Sneaky, damn government agencies. All that crap you saw in movies about just how deadly the government could be . . . was absolutely true. So a government mercenary. Even better. "And if I don't?"

"Do I really need to answer that question?" He paused. "Think of this gun I'm holding to your head." He pressed it harder against my temple and I winced. "Then think of identical ones pointed at everyone you care about. Have I made myself clear?"

Tears stung my eyes, which pissed me off. Being bullied at a young age combined with my overall lack of height and strength had made me feel vulnerable for much of my life. I hated feeling that way and the tears were more from frustration than fear.

"Yes." My reply was simple enough, but laced with *fuck you*.

"Good. Just so we're clear. Tell no one about this. I'll be in touch."

He was out the door before I could retort. I whipped around to see him, but the shadows had already swallowed him up.

I gripped the steering wheel, trying to control my shaking hands. I'd never in my life had a gun pointed at me, much less had one held to my head. My immediate reaction was that I wanted to run back inside Bonnie's house, but that wouldn't be doing her any favors.

After taking a few more deep breaths to slow my racing heart, I started up the car and headed home, my brain already puzzling together the pieces of what I'd learned today. I was missing something big about the program, obviously. Something someone would kill for.

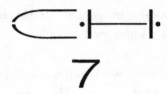

# 7

I had another surprise when I got home.

"Clark came by," Mia said as she poured powdered cocoa mix into a steaming mug of milk. "He said he'd be up for a while if you wanted to come over." She waggled her eyebrows at me.

I didn't know if I was up for that, not after my unexpected non-carjacking.

"You're going, aren't you?" Mia asked when I didn't reply.

"Um, I don't know. I'm pretty tired." And still recovering from my close encounter.

"Don't start the hard-to-get thing so soon," she said. "Especially when he came by. You don't have to stay long. You should go."

"I don't look like I did the other night," I said with a sigh. Plain-China was back, my hair in a ponytail, and wearing my *Driver Picks the Music & Shotgun Shuts His Cakehole* T-shirt.

She reached over and, in one quick grab, pulled out my ponytail. "That's better," she said, fluffing my hair with her fingers until she was satisfied. "You look great."

I rolled my eyes as she took a careful sip of her cocoa, but I obediently headed for the door, unable to be anything less than pleased that Clark had come by, regardless of Bonnie's warning inside my head.

Maybe romance in my life wasn't so farfetched of an idea.

Clark answered the door right away and I stopped breathing.

He was bare chested, just wearing jeans, and had a towel slung around his neck. His dark hair was wet, the water making it black, and tiny rivulets were tracing leisurely down his neck to kiss his chest.

"Hey! It's you! Come in." He stepped back, which is when I realized my jaw was hanging open and I was staring.

"You look . . ." *incredibly sexy and mouthwatering* ". . . like you're busy," I hedged, not moving from my spot on the stoop.

"Not at all. Come in and have a seat."

He turned away and I ogled his back, the muscles rippling as he dried his hair some more and grabbed a white T-shirt.

Wow. Even with his hair all mussed, Clark looked like a model. And his arms were much bigger and more defined than his shirt had let on. Like, only-seen-on-TV kind of defined—the trapezius muscles above his shoulders were curved and there was an actual indentation between his deltoids and biceps.

Then he turned around as he dragged the shirt over his head and I was treated to a six-pack carved abdomen, clear definition of his obliques, and a dark trail of hair that went from his navel down to disappear under the waistband of his jeans.

I was staring. Still.

Forcing my gaze away from Clark's Man of Steel body that the thin fabric couldn't adequately conceal, I stepped inside and shut the door behind me. Then I was immediately faced with another seating quandary.

"I was just having a glass of wine. Can I get you one, too?" he asked.

Absolutely. "Yes, please." This had to be a record for alcoholic beverages I'd consumed in a week.

"How was work?" he asked, pouring another glass half-full of garnet-colored wine. I watched him with too much interest.

"Same stuff, different day," I said vaguely. "You?"

"Not bad. It's always difficult, starting a new position. I expect I'll feel more comfortable in a few weeks." He handed me my wine.

*Keep your eyes above his neck. Keep your eyes above his neck.* I repeated the mantra inside my head.

And that exhausted my ability to chitchat. "Mia said you stopped by?"

"I did." He sat on his couch, stretching one arm along the back. "Come sit down. You look like you've had a long day."

Gee, thanks. That was right up there with *You look tired* and *Are you sick?*

I gingerly sat on the couch as well, careful to leave eighteen inches of space between us.

"Is everything okay?" he asked, frowning. His blue eyes studied me. "You look really pale."

Pale was my normal color, but I could well imagine that the panic I'd endured still showed in my eyes.

"Um, I was almost carjacked," I said, deciding to go with a half truth. "He had a gun and . . . it was terrifying."

"Oh my God, China." He set down his wine and leaned forward, taking my hands in his. "Your hands are like ice. Did you go to the cops? What happened?"

"It was outside my friend's house," I explained. "He got in the backseat. But someone was out walking their dog and scared him off, I guess. It didn't last long, thank God." A lot of fibs there but at least I could tell someone I'd been traumatized tonight, and it wasn't like I wanted to tell Mia and make her worry.

"Are you okay?"

I nodded. "Yeah. Totally. I mean, I'm fine. He didn't hurt me." Not that he'd promised he wouldn't . . . eventually. I blinked rapidly, trying to clear my suddenly blurred vision. Taking off my glasses, I rubbed my eyes.

Clark cursed softly under his breath, then drew me toward him, scooting me closer like I weighed nothing before wrapping his arms around me.

"Shh, it's okay. I'm so sorry that happened to you." His voice, low and soothing in my ear, made me lose my battle with the tears and they spilled out, trailing down my cheeks to drip onto Clark's chest.

His arms felt amazing around me. I'd never felt anything like it. Strong and warm, holding me close. I could smell soap from his skin and feel the rasp of his whiskers against my hair as he tucked my head under his chin.

I didn't say anything, *couldn't* say anything. I wasn't dumb enough to think moments like this came along every day, and I catalogued everything my senses could take in. As for my emotions . . . well, logic was taking a backseat right now to my being a girl.

"Is there anything I can do?" Clark asked. I shook my head, which had the added benefit of rubbing my cheek against his chest. I wanted to purr like a cat, but he'd probably look at me funny.

We stayed like that for a few minutes—I was loath to move, though internally I was tracking the time, wondering when it went from the Acceptable/Comforting phase to the Awkward-She-Won't-Get-Off-Me phase. Was it three minutes? Five? Longer?

Five minutes came and went with neither of us moving apart. His hand was rubbing soothingly up and down my back, then it slowed, going from soothing to . . . something else. My breath sped up and the guy with the gun was a distant memory.

Clark moved his hand to my hair, pushing his fingers into the thick strands, up to my scalp, then down, combing through the mass as it lay in loose waves down my back. He repeated the motion over and over, slow and unhurried.

I didn't know what to do. Should I touch him back? Was this sexual? Or just a friendly hug? I was willing to bet it wasn't the latter, but didn't want to just assume. What if I was wrong? What if I touched him and that was the wrong thing to do? I'd be mortified.

The question was solved for me when he tugged on my hair, pulling my head back. Our eyes met and I was transfixed. He was looking at me the way I'd only read about in books, and it took my breath away.

I wanted him to kiss me again and, as if he'd read my thoughts, he lowered his head until our lips met.

This kiss was no less thrilling than the first one had been, though my surprise was substantially less. I kissed him back with perhaps too much enthusiasm, but he didn't seem to mind.

He suddenly pulled back. "I'm sorry. You've had a rough night and I'm sure this is the last thing you want right now."

"Actually, I find it quite . . ." Arousing. Exciting. ". . . soothing," which sounded less enthusiastic than I'd intended, but his lips twitched and he started kissing me again so who cares if I found the exact right word or not?

My fingers were itching to touch him and I twisted around so I could put my palms flat against his chest. His skin was warm, the muscles beneath were hard, and every thought flew out of my head.

His tongue stroked mine as I learned the curves and lines of his chest and shoulders, then I felt him tugging the button-up I wore down my arms. Next thing I knew, he was pulling the hem of my T-shirt up and over my head, leaving me in just my bra and jeans. There was a moment of *so glad I wore my gray and pink lace push up*, then a hit of cold reality.

Clark was kissing my neck, his hands tugging at my hips until I was on my knees, straddling him. It didn't look like he was going to stop anytime soon so . . . was I ready to do this?

Being my age and a virgin was a real pain in the ass. I felt ridiculous, for one. And two, if it didn't happen now, then when? Not everyone got married, so no sense holding out for that fairy tale. It might never happen. And frankly, there were a lot worse guys I could be having my first time with—at least Clark was nice and really attractive, plus he seemed to like me a lot, with an added bonus of me really liking him.

I didn't have to worry about birth control. In a fit of optimism, I'd gotten an IUD a couple of years ago and it was good for five years. Most women my age were probably on the pill, but I didn't like taking pills. Then there was the whole "safe sex" thing to consider, but I was sure Clark probably had condoms lying around somewhere.

So . . . decision made. Full steam ahead. Which was easier said than done because as soon as I'd flipped the switch from Possibility to Certainty inside my head, nerves struck.

Clark's hand moved up my back to my bra strap and quicker than I could do it myself, it was unsnapped. I had just processed the slide of elastic down my arms before his hands were cupping my breasts, his thumbs brushing the tips and sending a shiver through me.

My heart was beating so fast, it felt like it would burst from my chest any moment. His hands were touching me, his lips were kissing their way down my neck, and I could feel the hard length of him pressing between my thighs.

My bra was gone and he pulled me closer, until my breasts touched his chest. His skin against mine was the most amazing thing I'd ever felt. He was warm and hard against my softness, his arms around me made me feel protected—like our bodies were made to fit into each other in just this way.

Then his hands moved to the button on my jeans and I went stiff and rigid in his arms.

I couldn't help it. I was excited but scared, too. This was all new to me and moving so fast . . . maybe this wasn't the right decision? Should

I decide something like this in the heat of the moment? But maybe this was the only "moment" I'd get and what if I let it pass me by?

"What's wrong?" Clark whispered against my shoulder. His warm breath fanned across my skin. "Do you not want to do this? We can stop."

"No," I blurted. "I mean, no. Don't stop. I'm just a little nervous, that's all."

"What are you nervous about, sweetheart?" The low murmur of his voice in my ear made my eyes slide shut. Butterflies still danced in my stomach, but it felt like they were migrating south.

"Mmmm . . ." My thoughts were jumbled the more he touched me. He'd stopped trying to undo the button on my jeans and he'd moved his hand between my legs, rubbing me through the denim. I struggled to form a coherent sentence. "I've just never—" His hand moved over a certain spot and I gasped.

"Never what?" he asked, his lips trailing from my collarbone down the slope of my breast. "Never had sex on the second date?" He chuckled lightly. His mouth fastened over my nipple and I pried my eyes open, looking down at the sight of his head, so dark against my pale skin. I slid my fingers into his hair, holding him to me.

It was indescribable, how he was making me feel. I felt wanton, sexy, desirable. Gone was the awkward China with two left feet and a knack for saying the wrong thing at the wrong time. In her place was a woman somehow sexy enough for a man like Clark to want. It was like being given the best Christmas present ever.

Clark pulled back slightly, his tongue caressing me in such a way that made my hands close into fists in his hair and my eyes slam shut. Wow. He was really good at this. I'd definitely made the right decision.

"Never what?" he repeated.

It took me a second to remember what I'd said. "Never had sex before," I murmured. I pressed a little on his head, hoping he'd get the hint and do that thing with his tongue again. That wasn't rude, was it? He'd seemed to like it, too, so surely that was okay.

And apparently I could still say the wrong thing at the wrong time because you would've thought I'd told him I was really a man in disguise. He sat upright, his eyes widening for a split second in surprise.

"You're joking," he said.

Ouch. I forced a laugh, feeling acutely exposed in more than one way. Instinct made me cross my arms over my breasts.

"Um, nope, not joking," I said with a tentative smile. "I . . . didn't think it would make that big of a difference. Does it?" In all my romance novels, the hero *liked* it when the heroine was a virgin. But Clark didn't look as though he liked it. Not even a little bit. I swallowed, bitter disappointment and embarrassment curdling in my gut.

"Um, yeah, China," he said, rubbing a hand over his face. "I don't think—"

I scrambled off his lap before he could finish, my face burning, and snatched up my T-shirt. I yanked it over my head and shoved my arms through the holes.

"China, wait a second—"

"I've gotta go," I said, cutting him off. Shirt, bra, glasses—check, check, and . . . check. I avoided looking at him. I was mortified and close to tears, which I really didn't want him to see. I'd had plenty of embarrassing moments in my life, but this took the cake. This was why I chose computers as my primary companion. People didn't work out so well.

"China—"

"Catch you later." And I was out the door. Five seconds later, I was walking into my house, praying Mia was asleep already.

The house was dark and the television was on mute. I saw Mia's huddled form underneath blankets on the couch and the telltale sound of light snoring. I breathed out a sigh of relief.

Tiptoeing past her, I made it to my bedroom and shut the door. Now that I had the privacy to cry, I found I couldn't. The shock of Clark's reaction had worn off, leaving only cynicism in its place. As usual, I hadn't been able to predict someone's reaction accurately. And it had hurt me, in a very private and personal way.

*Chalk it up to live and learn*, I thought bitterly. My gaze caught my reflection in the mirror and I paused, looking more closely.

My T-shirt was on backward.

Of course it was.

I left for work earlier than usual the next morning, detouring by Cysnet first. No one was in yet except the one person I thought would be and who I'd come to see.

"Come in," Jackson called out when I knocked on his door. He glanced up when I entered. "On your way to Wyndemere?" he asked as I took a chair in front of his desk.

I nodded. "Yeah, but I needed to come by and tell you something first." Even though I'd been told not to.

He frowned and relaxed back in his chair. "What is it?"

Taking a deep breath, I answered. "A man was in my car last night. He had a gun. He threatened me."

Jackson's eyes narrowed and he leaned forward, one fisted hand resting on the desk. "Did he hurt you?"

"No. He just told me I had to make sure to deliver the software. That Tom had been having second thoughts about delivering it and that . . ." I hesitated. "That was why he was dead." I winced, hoping what I'd said hadn't been completely insensitive.

His fist tightened and the look in his eyes made me shrink a little in my chair, though I knew he wasn't angry with *me*.

"Should we go to the police?" I asked.

Jackson shook his head. "If they got to Tom, we'd be dead by morning. The police would take your statement and that's all they could do. No crime was committed. Did you even see his face?"

I shook my head. "Then what do I do?" I swallowed the lump that had jumped into my throat. "I don't want to be the next one who 'commits suicide.'" I used air quotes for that. "The police even examined the scene and they're positive it wasn't foul play, which means whoever killed him is really good."

"Just finish the software then," he said. "Go, do your job, and be careful."

I looked at him. "I feel less than reassured as to my safety."

Jackson rested his arms on the desk and leaned forward. "I understand. I'll tell my security people what happened. They can look into it and be more aware. You'll be okay."

Stiffening, I said, "I know that. It's just . . ." then faltered. I had to look away from his penetrating gaze, glancing toward the window. Only then did I realize my fingers were gripping the arms of the chair.

"It's just what?"

I couldn't look at him and my words were barely audible. "It's just that . . . I'm scared."

He took something from his drawer and stood. Rounding the desk, he crouched down in front of me so we were eye to eye. Prying my fingers from the armrest, he opened my hand and placed a gun in my palm.

"Take this. Keep it on you at all times."

I stared, wide-eyed. "I . . . I can't take that."

"Of course you can," he said, standing. "I just gave it to you."

"But that's against the law."

"Giving you a weapon?"

"And I have no training or license to carry . . ." I babbled on, still staring at the foreign object I was holding. "Here. Take it back." I thrust it toward him.

"Christ, China," he said, pushing my hand so the muzzle wasn't pointed in his direction. "I take it you don't know how to use this."

I gave a vigorous shake of my head. "They scare me."

He sighed, which I interpreted as either frustration or impatience. Neither reaction was positive for me.

"All right then. Let's go." He grabbed his keys from the corner of his desk, then took the gun from me. He headed for the door. I jumped up and scrambled to follow.

"Where are we going?"

"To teach you how to use this."

I just had to ask.

The gun shop he took me to reminded me of the one and only shop I'd been inside back in Omaha. My dad had taken me with him one time on an errand for bullets. The noise from the range in back was as loud as that other store had been, the smell of gunpowder hanging heavy in the air.

It didn't take long for Jackson to get two targets, a box of bullets, and two sets of goggles and earmuffs. We were assigned a booth number and he led me into the back.

No one was on either side of our assigned booth and I watched as Jackson clipped the targets and sent them down the line. Glancing up, he beckoned me.

"Ready for your first lesson?"

No. "Yes."

"Parts of a handgun. Muzzle. Grip. Safety. Trigger. Barrel. Slide. Sight. Magazine. Magazine release. Hammer." He pointed to the various parts and I memorized them.

"First, make sure the safety is on, then eject the magazine. Like this." He showed me. It popped out of the bottom, then he pushed it back in. "You try."

It took four tries and hurt my fingers, but I finally got the magazine out. Jackson just watched, making me feel inadequate.

"Time to load the bullets." He showed me that, too.

"Kind of like a Pez dispenser," I observed. He paused, looking at me. "What?"

His lips twitched but he said nothing. We were standing so close, I could smell that damn cologne again, even over the gunpowder.

The magazine was loaded, then he pushed it inside the grip again. He put on his goggles and I followed suit, then the earmuffs, keeping one ear slightly uncovered so we could hear each other.

"This is a semiautomatic, which means it'll load the next bullet for you each time you pull the trigger. But you do need to load the first bullet. To do that, you rack the slide. Like this." He did that move I'd seen action heroes do a thousand times in the movies, the sound much more frightening in real life.

"Hold it like this, hand firmly around the grip, resting in the cup of your left hand. Never point it at something unless you want to shoot it. Switch off the safety, aim, squeeze the trigger."

He did all these things, pointing the gun down the range toward the target. His body was absolutely still as he aimed, then I jumped about a foot when he fired.

"It's really loud," I blurted.

Jackson glanced around at me, a smirk curving his lips. "Yes, China. It's loud. Now come here."

Nerves twitched up and down my spine, but I obediently moved closer until we stood side-by-side, nearly touching inside the little space.

"Right now, there's a live round ready to go," he explained. "If you're done firing, switch on the safety. Move the slide to eject the bullet." He did that, the bit of brass falling onto the counter. "Safety off. Point downrange. Pull the trigger." A click of an empty chamber. "Safety on. Set it down, muzzle always pointed downrange."

I glanced at the target he'd shot at and swallowed. A small hole was nearly dead center in the head. Apparently, this wasn't his first rodeo.

"Your turn."

My hands were sweaty and I wiped them on my jeans. "Um, okay. Step one, rack the slide." I tried . . . and didn't move it a millimeter. "It's too big," I said. "My hand won't fit around it." I tried again, but was stopped by a muffled snort. I glanced up at Jackson, who appeared to be holding back a laugh. "What are you laughing at? It's hard."

His eyes twinkled. "I'm not laughing at that."

"Then what?" I replayed my words in my head, turning them over for a double meaning . . . and realized. "Oh." My neck and face burned and I went back to trying the slide again, avoiding Jackson's eyes.

"Here, try this grip instead." Taking my hand, he turned it so I was pushing the slide toward me rather than trying to pull it. I lost track of what I was doing for a second, too focused on the fact that he'd touched my hand. He had to prompt me. "Now try."

To my surprise, I could rack the slide this way, though it was still hard. I hoped if the time ever came when I actually had to use this thing, I'd be able to do it.

"Safety off, point downrange—"

"Spread your legs a little farther," he said.

Okay, that didn't help the blush I could still feel, but I moved my feet farther apart.

"Sight the target . . ." I lined up the bull's-eye in the center of the chest. "Squeeze the trigger."

Even though I knew it was loud, I was still surprised at the hard jerk of the gun in my hand. A thrill of fear went through me and I realized I was shaking.

"Good job, China," Jackson said, stepping up behind me. "You hit the target. Now you need to adjust your sight based on how the gun shot for you. Like this."

He put his arms on either side of mine, pointing the gun toward the target. I promptly forgot everything I was supposed to be doing as he tried to tell me how to change my sight. His face was right next to mine, pressing lightly on my cheek as he looked down the sight as well. My eyes drifted close and I took a deep whiff of his scent, luxuriating in the feel of his body pressed against my back. And his cheek was so smooth against mine . . .

"Try that."

I was startled from my lapse into fantasy territory and pulled the trigger without even realizing. A sudden burning sensation inside my bra had me yelping and I dropped the gun. I danced around, yanking at my T-shirt.

"Owowowowow! It burns!"

"Hold still." Jackson grabbed my arm and hauled me close, then to my shock, he reached inside the V-neck of my T-shirt. His fingers delved into my bra, brushing briefly over my breasts and nipples before pulling out a bullet casing. He showed it to me. "They can burn you if they touch your skin. Are you all right?"

My jaw was somewhere around the vicinity of the floor. "Did you just . . . ?" *feel me up* was what I wanted to say, but the words wouldn't come.

"Save you from being burned?" he asked. "You're welcome."

"You copped a feel!" I blurted, his arrogant self-assurance pricking my anger. And my pride. He'd totally touched my . . . well, *me* . . . and hadn't seemed to even notice.

He had the audacity to look affronted. "I was saving you!"

My words of outrage caught in my throat as I studied his eyes. Earlier, they'd been twinkling with humor. Now, there was something else there, and he still had a hand on my arm. Though it wasn't a tight grip, he kept me close. Was he . . . flirting? And if so, what was I supposed to do?

"M-my apologies," I stammered, thinking fast. "Though maybe y-you should be thanking me rather than the other way around." I lifted one eyebrow and took a step back. I had no clue where *that* had come from, but I thought I'd pulled it off. At least it hadn't come with a crick in my neck.

We shot some more—without any more cleavage incidents—until Jackson was satisfied that I could operate the gun properly and at least hit the target somewhere in the black.

"Carry it in your purse," he said as we climbed into his car.

"I have a backpack," I said.

He glanced at me, his mirrored shades concealing his eyes. "No purse?"

Yeah, let's finish putting that nail in the you're-so-not-a-girl coffin. Oh well. I shrugged. "It's practical."

He mumbled something under his breath and I didn't ask for clarification.

When we got to the office, he parked by my car and I got out. I was unlocking my door when he rounded the car and stopped in front of me.

"Do you feel better now?" he asked.

Actually, I did. "Yes. Thank you."

"Good." Reaching behind me, he opened my door, placing us in close proximity again. I was suddenly reminded of his fingers inside my bra, touching me. "Be careful."

"I will."

I could see him in the rearview mirror, watching me as I drove away.

Work was piled up when I got to Wyndemere, and I had to leave the gun in my glove box, knowing I'd never get it through security. So I worked, burying myself in a coding error that George had e-mailed about. There was a memory leak somewhere in his team's segment and they were having trouble finding it.

While part of my mind was scanning through lines of code, the other part was turning over the big picture inside my head. There was a reason why Tom had wanted only one set of eyes to know all the pieces to the puzzle: it was missing a key part. I hadn't realized until I'd started going through the modules that built the software, but it was glaringly obvious the deeper I dug. I hoped I was wrong because if I wasn't, Jackson wasn't going to be happy about it.

A knock at my door caused me to glance up. It was John. I motioned him in.

"You didn't follow through on sending me the synopsis and status report I requested," I said as he sat down opposite my desk. Might as well cut right to the chase. Pleasantries were so overrated.

"I haven't had time to catch you up," he said, an edge of disdain in his voice. "I'll ask my secretary to get something over to you later today. Is that all you wanted?" He stood back up.

His insolence set my teeth on edge and I stood up, too. "No, that's not all." My voice was sharp and he paused on his way to the door to glance back around. "And I didn't ask for you to have your secretary do it. I want *you* to do it. Concisely and immediately. Is that understood?"

We had a staring contest for a moment, then he smiled in an unfunny kind of way.

"Overcompensating because you're a girl, right? You may work for Jackson Cooper but it doesn't take a rocket scientist to see why." He gave a scathing glance down and back up my body. "I'll see what I can do. But stay out of my way. I've got a job to do and don't have time to hold your hand and explain my work." Then he was gone.

Shit.

I plopped back down in my chair. My blood pressure was raging, I was so mad, and I took a deep calming breath. Okay, I took *several* deep calming breaths.

*Jerk.*

This put me between a rock and a hard place. If I couldn't manage the team, then Jackson would have to replace me, which would be a bad scenario all the way around. It would make me look incompetent and make Cysnet look unprofessional. Ditto if I asked anyone for backup on handling John. Plus, Jackson would be disappointed and, all in all, disappointing my boss was something I usually tried to avoid.

I'd have to figure out a way to outmaneuver John, that was all. Sure. Easy peasy.

Right.

Another knock at my door and I glanced up. It was Lana.

"Hey," she said with a smile as she stepped inside. "I thought you might want to grab a late lunch?"

A glance at my phone told me I'd worked through lunchtime and hadn't even noticed, though now my stomach was growling. Lunch with a near-stranger, though, where I'd have to make small talk and not only discuss work. I shied from that, but thought I should go anyway. She'd worked with John for several years—maybe she'd know why he was being such an ass.

"Sure, that sounds good. I haven't eaten yet."

I locked my computer and secured my office, grabbing my backpack before following Lana outside.

"I can drive," she said, leading me toward her car. It was a recent model Lexus with lots of bells and whistles.

"Nice car," I complimented her once we were inside. "So where are we going?"

"There's a little lunch place nearby," she said. "Soup, sandwiches, salads. Is that okay?"

"Sounds perfect."

"How long have you been with Cysnet?" she asked.

"This is my fourth year."

She glanced from the road to me, her eyes wide. "You must be really smart to have started there so young."

Rhetorical statement, so I just gave a bland smile. "What about you?" I asked. "You've been at Wyndemere a long time."

"Yes. I like it here, though it's taken a while to get to the position I have."

She pulled into a parking lot then, so conversation ceased as we went inside, found a table, and looked through the menu. Once the server had taken our order, I picked up where she'd left off.

"I did notice that," I said. "John certainly rose through the ranks quickly, given his background."

She rolled her eyes. "Don't get me started on sexism in the IT industry. I'm sure you get it all the time."

We shared a look of mutual understanding. "It's nice at conferences, though," I said. "There's never a line at the restroom." Which was absolutely true. I'd enjoyed seeing the men's room line piled up fifty deep.

Lana laughed. "Obviously I need to go to more conferences."

"Two words: DEF CON. It's insane and I love it, but still—ninety percent men."

"I'll have to check that one out then."

We fell silent as the server delivered our lunches and I pondered if I should ask more about John as I picked the frisée out of my salad— I hated that stuff. Just like eating a weed. Maybe Lana would have some insight into how to handle him. But I didn't have to say anything because she brought him up first.

"You might want to go easy around John," she said. "He's sometimes a bit . . . grumpy."

"I have noticed he's already taken a dislike to me," I replied. "I'm not sure why."

"John is really good at his job, but playing well with others isn't his specialty. It's caused problems with his management style and he's had some complaints. Honestly, I don't know why he hasn't been fired. His sexism is quite obvious as well."

"Have you had trouble with him?" I asked around a mouthful of romaine.

She nodded, swallowing before answering. "I was here before him, but he can still be an ass. Occasionally, I have to remind him of that. He doubts everyone's abilities until you prove yourself."

"I'm not going to be here long enough to 'prove myself,'" I said dryly. "He's going to have to just deal with thinking I'm incompetent because I have a vagina instead of a penis."

Lana snorted iced tea, choking and laughing at the same time as she dabbed her face with a napkin.

My cell buzzed and I dug it from my pocket. Mia.

"Are you coming to take me to register?" she asked. "The guardianship papers came today, so we're all set."

Oslo'd had the guardianship papers drawn up and FedExed to me. I still couldn't wrap my head around the fact that I was now legally liable for another human's welfare.

"Yeah, yeah, of course. I just lost track of time," I said. I still had time to get home, pick up Mia, and get to school before office hours ended. "I'm on my way."

"I'm so sorry," I explained to Lana. "My niece, Mia, is living with me and I need to register her for school today."

"No problem. I'll take you back to your car. I was finished anyway." The server had dropped our check and I reached for it, but Lana beat me to it. "My treat."

"You don't have to do that," I protested. "I should be buying *you* lunch."

She just winked. "I'll expense it and you can get the next one."

I grinned back. "Sounds good. Thank you."

She dropped me off by my car and I tossed my backpack in the backseat. I knew I'd need to come back tonight. Too much work still needed to be done. Hopefully, it wouldn't be that late.

Unfortunately, it took longer than I thought it would to register Mia—the bureaucracy of the public school moved at a glacial pace. She loaded up on science and math courses, reluctantly adding a history and English course.

"You have room for a study hall," the counselor suggested, eyeing her with misgiving.

"Can I take Advanced Calculus instead?" Mia asked.

The counselor hesitated, glancing at me. "Well, your grades are very good, but I'm hesitant to load your schedule up with such intensive classes."

"I'm good for it," Mia said, flipping through the course description book.

The counselor looked at me again, which I took to mean I should say something.

"She's very advanced for her age," I said. The counselor seemed unconvinced. "I'll keep an eye on her, too, and if she's overwhelmed, we'll let you know." Like that was going to happen. Mia may look like Teenage Barbie, but her IQ was well into triple digits.

We picked up tacos on the way home—because Friday night was also Mexican night—and I dropped Mia off with strict instructions to ignore Clark if he came to the door. Not that I was expecting that. After last night, I doubted I'd see him again. But just in case.

"Why can't I talk to him? What happened last night?" she asked, avid curiosity in her eyes.

"Nothing. Don't worry about it. Just do what I say, okay?"

"Was he a jerk?"

I didn't answer, which apparently was answer enough. Mia snorted.

"Figures. The pretty ones always are. Asshat. Don't worry, Aunt Chi. If he comes by, I'll tell him to go screw himself."

"First, that's anatomically impossible," I said. "Second, I'd rather you just not answer. He'll get the hint. Please."

She reluctantly nodded and I sighed in relief. I just wanted to forget all about Clark and the disaster of last night. I should've known things wouldn't end up like a romance novel. After all, who really got the man of their dreams and a happily ever after? Not me, that was for sure.

I was so distracted trying *not* to think of last night, that I was halfway back to Wyndemere before I realized I was being followed.

The black sedan stayed two cars behind me, no matter how many lanes I changed or how I sped up or slowed down. After the threat last night, I wasn't about to ignore this as a coincidence.

The area I was in was unfamiliar to me and my first thought was to get to Wyndemere as fast as I could, but then I realized a vast, empty parking lot surrounded by woods probably wasn't the best place to be. My second thought was to go to the police station. Unfortunately, I didn't know where it was. After discarding both those ideas, a final idea struck me.

I sped up, the purr of the engine turning into a growl as the car leapt forward. I weaved in and out of traffic, leaving irate honks in my wake. At that point, the sedan gave up the pretense and sped up as well. Literally, I was now in a car chase. Surreal. Good thing I didn't just own my Mustang for looks, but actually knew how to drive the thing.

The wheels ate up the pavement as my speedometer edged toward ninety, the sedan not far behind. I'd give anything to have a cop pull me over right now, but, of course, there was never a cop when you needed one. Go twelve miles an hour in a ten-limit parking garage and they came out of the shadows to give you a ticket. But ninety on the highway? Nothing.

Rubber squealed as I made a sharp left into a subdivision, my headlights bouncing crazily as they cut through the darkness. I'd never driven to this particular location before, but I knew the address and exactly how to get there, thanks to Google Street View and my penchant for occasional cyberstalking.

I was far enough ahead of the sedan that I couldn't see if it had followed me or not, and I didn't want to slow down to check. Taking another turn that made my tires squeal, I gunned it up the hill, then a hard right and down a long driveway. I didn't slam on the brakes until the front door of the house was just yards away.

Grabbing my keys, I leapt out of the car and ran for the front door just as headlights turned up the street, going too fast in this neighborhood to be anyone other than my tail.

I banged on the door, which had to be twelve feet tall, and glanced around for a doorbell. My palms were sweaty as I clutched my keys in my hand. I didn't know what would happen if they caught up to me, and I didn't want to find out. But I was in plain sight here on the front porch . . .

I hit the door again with the side of my fist, desperate to get inside. Just when I was about to give up and make a dive for the bushes to hide, the door was yanked open.

"What the hell?" Jackson asked.

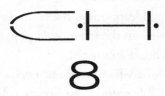

## 8

"Please let me in," I blurted. "Someone's following me."

His gaze swung up behind me and I glanced over my shoulder, then gasped as Jackson's hand closed on my arm and hauled me inside. He pushed the door shut and hit the light switch, dousing the foyer in darkness.

Letting me go, Jackson went to the window and moved aside the curtains a bare inch.

"Who's following you?" he asked. "And where's the gun I gave you?"

Shit. "I have no idea . . . and I kinda forgot about the gun. But they know where I live because I noticed them tailing me on my way to Wyndemere from home." I chewed my lip, now worried about Mia.

Jackson pulled out his cell phone and hit a button. "There's an unfamiliar car in the neighborhood, driving around," he said. "Possible threat. Let's get the plate and follow. Don't detain though." He listened for a moment. "Good. Keep me posted." He ended the call and slipped the phone back into his pocket.

"Security?" I asked. He nodded. Of course he had security. He was worth millions. It was a miracle I'd gotten to his door without being tackled to the ground.

I watched him while he watched out the window, both of us silent. The lights from outside cast his face in uneven shadows, making him appear menacing in his vigil. His dark eyes glinted slightly and his jaw was set in a sharp line. He was still dressed for work, in slacks and a button-down shirt, but he'd undone another button at the neck. I could see the curve of his Adam's apple in the line of his throat.

It hit me then, now that my panic had passed, that I'd felt safe the moment I'd seen Jackson. An odd thing that was. Maybe because he was my boss? Or perhaps because he always seemed so capable and in control. Nothing fazed him and he was the smartest person I'd ever known. And not just book smart. He'd built his company from the ground up. He was street savvy as well—his success was proof of that. Watching how well he'd handled that gun this morning didn't hurt either.

"I think they're gone," he said, dropping the curtain and turning toward me. "Are you okay?"

My fists were clenched and my heart was still pounding, but I didn't particularly want to share either fact with Jackson. I wanted to appear as in control as he was, even if I had to fake it.

"I'm fine."

Jackson studied me for a moment. "You look like you could use a drink," he said. "Follow me. And you can explain to me how you 'forgot' about a semiautomatic in your possession."

It didn't sound as though I should argue with him, so I didn't. He led me out of the foyer and down the hall, our footsteps echoing on the hardwood floor.

His house was massive and beautiful, but it had an empty feel to it, as though it wasn't lived in very much. It was a lot of space for just one person.

He opened a set of double doors and stepped aside to let me precede him. I took two steps inside and stopped in my tracks.

"Wow."

It was a massive library. Like *Beauty and the Beast* kind of massive library. A circular room, there was even a winding staircase that went to a second level that lined the walls, leaving the center ceiling stretched high above us into a turret. Dark wood was everywhere, and leather, and the smell was deep and rich without being musty.

"Do you like it?" Jackson asked, startling me. He'd come up right behind me while I'd been staring in awe.

"It's fantastic," I said, which was still inadequate.

"It's the reason I bought the house," he said, heading to a table in the corner. There were several glasses and a crystal decanter half-filled with amber liquid sitting on the table. "It's too much space for just me, but I couldn't resist the library."

"Don't you have any staff? Like a housekeeper or something?"

"I have a man—Lance—who takes care of the house. He cooks and handles the day-to-day upkeep." Jackson poured an inch of the whisky into two glasses.

So not a maid but like a male maid, I guessed. Butler? I could see that. Perhaps more comfortable for a bachelor than a woman would be.

"Where is he now?"

"He lives in quarters out back." Stoppering the decanter, Jackson handed me one of the heavy glasses.

Separate "quarters" for the manservant and real crystal glasses in the two-story library. I felt like I'd stepped into an episode of *Lifestyles of the Rich and Famous*. Maybe Robin Leach was hiding behind the curtains.

"Cheers." Jackson tapped his glass against mine, then took a sip. I mimicked him, taking a deep gulp.

Fire. Fire and burning acid down my throat. I coughed, choking. My eyes watered and my insides felt as though I'd swallowed molten lava.

"Whoa there," Jackson said, hurriedly taking my glass and setting it and his aside. "Bet you're not used to that, right?"

I wanted to say, *Ya think?* but couldn't, because I was still trying to remember how to breathe.

It seemed like all I ever did around Jackson was embarrass myself. It was a wonder he still thought me competent enough for employment.

"I'm okay," I finally managed to say, though my voice sounded half-strangled. "Sorry about that."

"No, it was my fault. I should've offered you wine or something."

Oh *now* he figures that out. "It's okay. I'll just sip it. Just took too large a drink, I think." Yes, when one drinks battery acid, one doesn't suck it down like a Coke from McDonald's.

"Okay then, why don't you sit down, take a breath, get your bearings back." He handed me my drink again and took a seat on the cherry leather sofa. After a brief hesitation, I sat by him, again carefully putting what I thought was an appropriate amount of space between us, eighteen inches, per the cultural norm.

I took a deep breath and caught a whiff of his cologne that I'd gotten to smell up close and personal this morning. It was a deep musky scent that perfectly accented the room, having taken on more of the flavor of his skin during the day. Yum. I always thought Jackson looked most at home behind a computer monitor, but he looked so at ease here, maybe I'd been wrong. He looked very . . . male . . . in the best possible way.

"I don't understand what's going on," I said. "First last night, then this. If they're trying to scare me to death, they're doing a very good job."

Jackson was silent, appearing deep in thought as he stared into the distance. I took a careful sip of my whisky. It didn't burn quite as bad this time, now that I knew what to expect.

"You've been on the project a few days now," he said at last. "Anything jump out at you as worthy of this kind of attention?"

I hesitated. This was where it could get dicey, especially if I were wrong. And it would be even worse if I were right. "Maybe."

Jackson focused on me, his dark eyes intent, and nerves fluttered in my stomach. This could be a shot in the dark and I could be completely wrong. If I were, I'd look like a complete idiot. Something I tried to avoid if at all possible.

"The pieces of the software, the different teams," I began, "none of them know what the others are doing. But when you put it all together, it creates a picture that has me worried."

"Explain."

"It's tracking a user's online movements through everything—social media, e-mail, their physical location, websites they visit, what they buy—in one piece. Yes, there's already software out there that tracks websites and shopping. But this analyzes user-generated content and where they go in meatspace."

"And that concerns you?"

"What concerns me is the part that's *not* there."

"Which is?"

I swallowed. This was the going-out-on-a-limb part. "If someone were to code the right kind of search algorithm, they could predict behavior, rather than just analyzing it."

"I don't see anything wrong with that," Jackson said, finishing his whisky.

"But it's Big Brother taken to the extreme," I persisted. "We don't even know if it's the DoD, Homeland Security, the NSA, or the FBI who ordered this kind of software. It's the surveillance that Edward Snowden revealed . . . times ten."

"So you're an anarchist now?" he said with a wry smile. "People can't expect privacy. Not anymore, and certainly not online."

"I'm not saying it's violating their privacy and I sort of agree with you, but this takes it one step further. Because right now the big picture is missing that piece. The purpose of the software. There's been no marketing hook or anything like that for commercial development. It's just tracking everything."

"Then there's nothing to worry about, is there," he said. Getting up from the couch, he refilled his glass and mine. I hadn't even realized I'd drunk it all.

"I think there is. I think someone is writing that code and they're going to add that missing piece once everything else is done and it'll be too late to uninvent the wheel."

"Your job isn't to worry about all the possible applications," he said, handing me my glass. "Deliver the software. Fulfill the contract. Let me worry about who wants it and what they're doing with it."

He sat down again and this time I noticed he sat closer to me. Not touching close, but inches apart rather than a foot. That made it difficult to concentrate on what he'd just said, especially when I took a breath and the aroma of his cologne was stronger.

My glasses were slipping and I pushed them up my nose, arranging my chaotic thoughts into order. Important things first. Extraneous thoughts of *he's so sexy* and *he smells so good* would have to wait.

"I'm worried. Not just about which government agency ordered this software, but for myself and my niece, too. Mia's just a kid."

"I don't like this. Two incidents in as many days is too much, even for the damn government. I'll send security to keep watch at your apartment. Will that make you feel better?"

That was a relief. My only recourse other than Jackson was the police, and we'd already had that discussion last night. They could do nothing and it was likely I'd be in even *more* danger if I tried to get them to help me, or that would put Mia in the crosshairs. I was sure Jackson's security people were top-notch and expensive.

"Thank you," I said. "That's a load off my mind."

"Another week and this will be done," he said. "Wyndemere won't be on the books anymore."

"So you think we should still deliver?" I asked. "Despite what I just said?"

"We were hired to finish the software. It's a little late at this point to pull out."

He had a point there, but still . . . it was my neck on the line, not his.

"That's why you just focus on the job," he continued. "I'll fill in Freyda on what happened and that they need to increase security in and around the building. I should've called her earlier."

"Why didn't you?"

"Wyndemere likes their secrecy," he said. "Pushing buttons about which government agency is paying the bills for their contracts makes them itchy."

I nodded, glad that he was going to have that awkward conversation. Sometimes it paid to *not* be the boss. Tipping my glass back, I emptied it. Whisky was yummy once you got used to it. My belly was warm like a banked fire burned inside, but in a good way.

"Thanks for listening," I said. "I'm not trying to be a nervous Nelly and I know sometimes software ends up being used for things that aren't exactly altruistic, but this just has a bad smell to it."

"It's what I'm here for." He rested a hand on my knee and squeezed lightly, then patted it.

I stared at his hand, still resting on my leg. Jackson didn't seem to notice the intent attention I was paying to his appendage. He was sitting back in the couch, his posture one of easy relaxation as he took another swig of whisky.

The warmth of his palm seeped through the denim I wore until it felt like a brand. My mind was racing with possibilities, all of which I discarded as ridiculous romantic fantasies. I wasn't so hard up for a boyfriend that I'd attack my boss in a fit of lust just because he touched my leg. Maybe. But it would be really nice to have someone. Not just for intimacy, but to be viewed as an attractive, sexual woman. Clark had made me realize even more acutely how much I was missing.

All my life, I'd been the smart one, the geek, the know-it-all. The only thing anyone had ever admired about me had been my intellect. And that was okay. I was proud of what I'd accomplished and thankful I'd been blessed with extensive brainpower.

But deep inside, I wanted to have a man look in my eyes and tell me I was beautiful and that he wanted me. It was an embarrassing admission, that I wanted this, but I couldn't help it. I wanted what I wanted.

It would be a fantasy come to life, but a fantasy that was also never going to happen, especially with Jackson. Billionaire, genius, beat-off-women-with-a-stick entrepreneur. He was so far out of my nonexistent league, he'd laugh himself silly if he knew the fantasies I'd entertained over the past few years.

But his hand was still on my knee and he showed no inclination to move it. So I didn't move either. Might as well enjoy the touch while it lasted. And my bruised ego from last night with Clark could use the TLC.

I was getting sleepy, what with the adrenaline letdown and the two glasses of whisky. My eyes were heavy, and more than anything I wanted to lean over those four inches and rest my head against Jackson's shoulder. But I knew better than to do that. After last night's mortifying rejection, I didn't need another.

*Though he had stuck his hand down my bra this morning . . .*

No, he'd been helping me not get burned. That was all. Social cues were hard enough without letting my hopes make something out of nothing.

My head was heavy on my neck so I leaned back, resting against the couch. I sighed, my eyes slipping closed. That was better.

"How's the new boyfriend?"

The words penetrated the fog in my brain, but I didn't open my eyes. The lids were too heavy to bother.

"Bad," I mumbled. "And he's not my boyfriend."

"Why not? Did something happen?"

I nodded. "It was awful."

"Why?"

I pried my eyes open. Everything came into focus really slowly. Rolling my head back, I saw Jackson's face above mine, looking at me. I blinked once. Twice.

"Told him something I shouldn't have. We're done now."

His brows rose. "What did you tell him?"

I could tell right away by the tone of his voice that he was replaying our conversation in his head about me not talking to anyone about work. I rolled my eyes, which was a mistake because it made me a little dizzy.

"Not work," I snorted. "Told him I was a virgin. He was grossed out. I left. Done."

Silence. My eyes drifted closed again. So tired. I needed to get home. It was past my bedtime.

"You're a virgin?"

The question echoed in my head. I nodded. "I know. Pathetic, right?"

"And he was . . . grossed out?"

I grimaced. "Don't really want to talk about it, 'kay?"

His hand tightened on my leg, squeezing again. "Yeah. Sure."

Mmmm. I liked him touching me and I was loath to move. But I needed to get home. Sitting on Jackson's couch, drinking his whisky and letting him touch my leg, was doing nothing to dissuade my romantic fantasies about him. With a sigh, I opened my eyes and sat forward. The room tilted and I waited a second for it to right itself.

"Where are you going?" Jackson asked, his hand tightening on me.

"It's late. I need to get home. Bedtime was . . ." I glanced at my watch. ". . . an hour ago." I couldn't remember the last time I'd missed bedtime.

"Bedtime?"

"Ten thirty." I slipped off my glasses and rubbed my tired eyes. Today had been long.

"You've been drinking. You're not driving home."

Oh yeah. He was right. That would be bad. "I'll get an Uber."

"Don't be ridiculous. Then you'll have to come back for your car. You'll stay here tonight."

I couldn't have heard him correctly, but he looked perfectly serious.

"That's . . . that'd be . . ." I searched for the right word. "Wouldn't that be weird?" I ended up blurting.

Jackson raised an eyebrow. "That wasn't a badly phrased come-on, if that's what you're wondering."

I flinched. "No, of course not. I didn't think—"

"The idea of you sharing my bed has crossed my mind," he interrupted. "But I don't usually proposition women when they've been drinking."

I stared, my mouth agape. He hadn't just said that he'd thought about sleeping with me, had he? I replayed the words inside my head. Yes, he had. I blinked. Should I say something? What could I possibly say? *Yes, please* sprang immediately to mind.

"The house is plenty big and then I'm not liable if you leave and get in an accident." Jackson stood and took my hand, pulling me easily to my feet. He stood so close, we almost touched, but I could see his face clearly, even without my glasses.

"Um, okay. Thanks," I said, deciding not to address what he'd said about being in his bed. I was transfixed by the way he was looking at me, his dark eyes fringed in thick lashes that I'd never seen this close. The line of his nose was straight and led to lips that looked very soft.

"Come with me."

"Okeydokey."

I trailed after Jackson, his hand still curled around mine. It was easy to pretend we were holding hands rather than him merely leading me to a guest room.

We walked down the hallway to a staircase that arched from one side of the grand foyer to the other, both sides reaching up to the second-story balcony, overlooking the space below. A huge chandelier hung from the ceiling and I craned my neck to look at it.

"That's beautiful," I breathed, watching the light from the hundreds of crystals dance across the marble floor.

"Thank you. Lance tells me it's a bitch to clean."

His wry humor surprised a laugh out of me. He glanced at me, his lips curved in a sardonic half smile. We'd reached the foot of the stairs and Jackson slid his arm around my back as we started up.

"Don't want you to fall backward," he said softly.

If I did fall, it'd be because I was swooning, not because I was drunk. The house was amazing and Jackson was even better. If someone had told me last week that I'd be spending the night at his house, I would have had them checked in to the psycho ward. Getting in a car chase seemed a small price to pay for this unexpected treat.

Just as I was thinking how awful it would be if I actually *did* fall down the stairs in front of Jackson, I tripped. There was a split second of *Oh shit!* then Jackson's arm was around my stomach, catching me. And it would've been oh-so-romantic if it had ended there, but I hadn't expected to be caught and my feet got all tangled with his, and before I could grab the railing to stop myself, we both went down.

I squeaked, my arms flailing, and my elbow slammed into Jackson's nose. Horrified, I scrambled in vain to reverse direction, put on the brakes, anything. Luckily, we were near the top and just hit the last couple of steps, but that did little to assuage my ego, especially when I heard the breath whoosh out of Jackson's lungs when I landed on top of him with all the grace of a dancing hippo.

"Oh my God, I'm so sorry! Are you okay?" I tried to right myself, but at some point his arms had locked around me. Probably trying to make sure I didn't topple backward. I was afraid to look up at Jackson, flat on his back against the steps. Had I given him a bloody nose as well as knocking the wind out of him?

"Holy shit, China," he wheezed. "Why didn't you just knee me in the groin while you were at it?"

I was absolutely mortified. "I'm so sorry," I repeated plaintively. I tried to scramble up again, but his hold on me tightened.

"Keep it up and you *will* knee me in the groin."

I froze, belatedly realizing I was straddling his leg and indeed, my knee was dangerously close to family-jewel territory. Considering the number of women who'd probably been to Jackson's house, I doubted this particular embarrassment had ever before happened to him. No, it took *me* to do that.

"Can you get up?" I asked. "Do you need me to call someone?" Where was his butler guy?

He snorted. "It takes more than a little thing like you to put me out of commission." Rolling over, our positions were suddenly reversed with my butt on the stair and his knee between my legs. He held himself above me and our eyes locked.

"If I didn't know you better, I'd say that was a cute little trick," he said.

My eyes went wide. "I would never—"

"I know."

"That would be unforgivably dangerous, not to mention reckless." His lips twitched. "I know."

I couldn't read the look in his eyes, but it shut me up. My gaze dropped to his mouth. His lips looked soft and were Right There. A kiss from Jackson Cooper would be right near the top of my bucket list (not the very top, though—that was reserved for visiting the Doctor Who Experience in Cardiff someday).

Then he was on his feet and hauling me up as well.

"This way," he said, and this time he didn't take my hand.

I swallowed my disappointment, suddenly *really* glad I hadn't given in to that insane urge to kiss him. He probably thought of me as a particularly amusing employee or kid sister . . . who'd actually told him I was a virgin. Why in the world had I done that? Apparently, the real life reaction to that information was akin to a bucket of ice water as opposed to what Harlequin said.

Too distracted and distraught to pay much attention to the room he led me to, I self-consciously tightened my ponytail and looked at the floor, half listening to his commentary.

". . . and the bathroom is private and through there," he was saying. "There should be plenty of linens, towels, toiletries, anything you might need. If you do find you need something, I'm just two doors down."

I nodded, staring at the toes of my tennis shoes. "'kay. Thanks."

"I'll have a report in the morning on that car and if they found anything. And the security I sent to your place already texted that everything is quiet there."

"Okay." I needed to text Mia and tell her I was staying with Bonnie tonight. I didn't like lying, but it probably didn't set a good example for me to be staying the night at a man's house, even if it was purely platonic.

"Are you okay?" Jackson asked.

"Sure. Just tired." *And was never, ever going to find a man interested in me.*

"Hey." He stepped closer and lifted my chin with his fingers. Our eyes met and my breath caught. "For what it's worth, I think your non-boyfriend neighbor is a fucking moron."

My eyes widened, not just at his words but at the vehemence with which he'd spoken them.

"Really?" My voice was that breathy female thing that without fail made me roll my eyes when I saw it done in a movie. Now I thought maybe I knew why they sounded that way.

He didn't answer. Instead, his gaze dropped to my mouth, and I had the nearly overwhelming urge to lick my lips. Just when I thought the waiting was going to kill me, Jackson leaned down and pressed his lips to mine.

It was gentle and sweet . . . and made butterflies take flight in my stomach. His hand cupped my jaw, sliding along my skin in a way that sent shivers through me. I'd been right. His lips were softer than satin.

Time stretched longer than it was in actuality. When he lifted his head, I was breathless. I knew I had stars in my eyes—or maybe hearts—but didn't really care. Jackson Cooper had just kissed me. *Me*. China Mack.

"Really," he said, his voice roughened in a Dean-from-*Supernatural* kind of way that made me want to rip off his clothes.

Before I could decide to pursue clothes ripping or figure out what to say, he was gone, melting into the darkness down the hallway. I heard his door open, then close.

I closed my door, too, part of me elated at this unexpected turn of events. But the part of me that was too cynical to believe things like this just happened to me—that part wondered at the timing, especially considering how Jackson had not said much about the software that was nagging at my brain, except that I shouldn't worry about it. In my experience, when someone tells you *not* to worry about something— that's exactly when to start worrying.

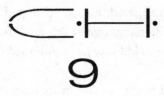

9

I slept like a rock despite the weirdness of my interaction with Jackson. I figured the whisky probably had something to do with it. When I woke up the next morning to the sound of my phone's alarm, it took me a minute to pry myself from the bed, which was the best mattress I'd ever slept on. And the sheets were to die for. I rummaged around for the tag, memorizing the manufacturer once I found it. I had to get some sheets like this.

After my shower, I emerged from the bathroom to find a tray waiting by the bed. A silver coffeepot and a fancy cup sat on it, along with the usual accompaniments. A covered plate emitted a mouthwatering aroma of bacon and when I lifted the lid, I wasn't disappointed. It was like being in a ritzy hotel, only without the hefty price tag. Fresh eggs, bacon, and coffee delivered to my bedroom almost made up for having to wear the same clothes two days in a row (minus the underwear because no way was I doing that). The thought made me squirm a little as I chomped a piece of bacon. Jeans weren't the most comfortable attire when going commando.

I texted Mia, who texted back that she was going to go shopping at the mall today. Oslo had put money in her account and she was going to take a cab. Since the mall was only a few miles away, I said it was okay.

*But make sure you text me when you get home*, I wrote. I felt a little guilty that I'd been working so much this week and we hadn't spent much time together. I'd have to take her to the movies or something this weekend. Luckily, she'd made friends with that other teenage girl who lived a few houses away, though for the life of me I couldn't remember her name. And she'd make more friends at school, I was sure.

When I went exploring downstairs, I followed the residual smell of bacon and found a stranger in the kitchen, putting away dishes.

"You must be Lance," I guessed.

"I am. Good morning." He smiled and seemed friendly. I judged him to be in his early- to mid-twenties and he wore plain black pants with a black T-shirt. With dark hair and almond skin, he reminded me of Tiger Woods, his heritage a mix that was indeterminate but had combined to produce a uniquely attractive man.

"I must have you to thank for breakfast," I said. "I'm China, by the way."

"Nice to meet you, China. And you're welcome."

I glanced around the immaculate gourmet kitchen. I wouldn't know what to do with half the appliances and gadgets I saw. "Has Jackson come down yet?"

"He went for a run," Lance said.

Oh. Wow. Okay, now I felt like a total loser. He was exercising while I'd been sleeping in and eating breakfast.

"I'd better get going then," I said. "Thanks."

"Have a good day," he called after me as I left the kitchen.

Okay, now to find my keys. I pushed my glasses up my nose as I looked around. The house was a huge maze. Where was the library we'd been in last night? I was sure I'd left my keys in there.

I ventured down the hallway, cautiously peering into rooms as I passed. A parlor or formal living room, a room with a piano . . . no library.

A door at the end of the hallway looked promising, but when I opened it, I realized I'd stumbled onto Jackson's home office. I knew immediately that I should leave but . . . it was Jackson Cooper's home office. Maybe I could take just a quick peek . . .

The library had been amazing and his office wasn't far behind. Beautiful windows stretched high up the walls to form a massive bay window. The floors were hardwood like most of the rest of the house. And in the middle of the room was something so out of place, it looked space-age.

A black chair, complete with a headrest and leg rests, sat in the center of a silver metal circular platform. A metal arm curved over the top of the chair, suspending two enormous flat screen monitors at about eye level.

I'd seen this before. It was supposed to be the most advanced, ergonomic workspace there was . . . and it could be yours for a mere twenty-five thousand dollars.

"Wow . . ." I breathed, stepping closer. The door swung closed behind me, a soft snick as it shut. I barely noticed. I had to try it. I couldn't *not* try it. Just sit in it for a second . . .

The seat was configured for Jackson, who was quite a bit taller than me, but I managed. I eased the desk portion into place and sat back. It really was perfect, keeping my neck and arms aligned without any strain.

"This is amazing."

At the sound of my voice, the screens flickered to life. I froze like a deer in headlights. Oh crap. What if Jackson had a camera in here or something? He could fire me for doing this. Yeah, I'd better get my ass out of this chair and go home.

The screens caught my eye as I moved the keyboard tray out of the way. Code filled the window open on the right while several other windows on the left screen showed runtime views and a DOS window scrolling text.

Hmmm . . .

Even as I knew I shouldn't read the code, I glanced through the lines, automatically running it through my head. I paused on a line that was calling a remote procedure, recognizing it as part of the Wyndemere project.

Frowning, I looked for the app name at the top of the window. Jackson had warned me big-time to leave confidential files at work, and yet here he was at home, working on this application, which was called . . . Vigilance. I had no clue what that was. It wasn't in any of the project files.

That bad feeling I'd had last night was back full force, only now it was a sick curdling in my stomach. Jackson had told me not to worry all right. Was this why? Was *he* the one writing the missing piece? And what was I going to do if he was? And why hadn't he told me?

Voices echoed down the hall, one of them I recognized immediately as Jackson's. Panic struck.

*Oh shit.*

I didn't want to imagine what would happen if he caught me and I suddenly realized that no one knew where I was, not even Mia. She thought I was at Bonnie's. If something happened to me . . .

Scrambling out of the chair, I ran to the door, then skidded to a halt. The voices were right outside the door.

". . . where she went? Her car's still here," Jackson was saying.

"I haven't seen her, but I'll check upstairs. Maybe she forgot something in her room."

"Yes, do that."

Looking around frantically for a place to hide, I saw a tiny space behind the leather couch by the bay windows. I dove behind it just as the knob began to turn.

It was a really good thing I was a small person because it was a tight squeeze.

Jackson came in and I could see his shoes as he stopped. My breathing seemed loud so I covered my mouth with my hand, waiting. If he decided to work from home for a while, it was going to be a *really* long day.

He continued over to his chair and paused again. I knew the monitors were still on, there was nothing I could do about that. I waited, heart in my throat as I watched.

After a moment, I saw him move back toward the door. I let out a careful breath. He'd probably just logged off. It was surprising anyway that he'd been logged on when I'd come in, but then again, I doubted he thought someone would be in his personal office besides himself.

The door opened and he left. He'd just been running, so surely he went upstairs to shower. I hoped. I waited longer, counting to thirty before coming out from behind the couch. Cautiously opening the door, I peered out, but the hallway was deserted.

Obviously, the library was in the opposite direction and that's where I headed, moving double time. I ran into no one and found my keys on one of the tables in the massive library. I was nearly to the front door when I heard, "There you are."

I swallowed down a curse. I'd nearly been out the door into freedom. Turning, I pasted on my best fake smile and pushed my glasses up my nose. I held my keys so tightly, I could feel the metal biting into my palm.

"Good morning," I said to Jackson. "Lance said you were out running." Now that I could see him above the ankles, I could appreciate all that his business attire hid. And boy, was it ever worth taking a moment.

He wore loose navy-blue shorts and a white tank. The muscles in his arms looked cut from marble, they were so perfect. His skin even glistened slightly with sweat.

It was enough to almost make me forget that I could be in danger. Almost.

"Just got back. We couldn't find you."

The question was there, unasked, and he waited for the answer. I jingled my keys.

"Had to go find these," I said. He looked unconvinced, so I kept going. "And I had all that strong coffee. Caffeine is a diarrheic, you know."

He glanced away, his lips thinning, and his ears turned pink. Had I just embarrassed him?

"I mean, it can really tear up your stomach if you're not careful," I said. "You might want to apologize to Lance for me. I tried to find some matches—"

"That's fine, that's fine," he interrupted me, holding up a hand. His ears were bright red now, and I would've laughed if I didn't already have one foot out the door.

"See you later!" I called out, almost but not quite running for my car. I didn't breathe easily until Jackson's house was in my rearview mirror.

Since it was Saturday, Wyndemere was practically deserted and I got a lot of work done. Some members of the team were working the weekend, too, so I had three meetings, following up with coding problems I'd found and working through resolution ideas. By the time I left, it was dark and my stomach was cramping. I was really looking forward to my usual Saturday splurge of Thai food.

My phone buzzed as I was getting in the car. It was Mia.

"Hey, Aunt Chi. Jen asked me to go to the movies and spend the night tonight. Can I?"

A little of my guilt lifted. Jen was the teenage daughter of one of my neighbors and she'd invited Mia to a sleepover. That was a good thing, even if it did leave me a little jealous of how quickly she could make a friend.

"What movie?"

"*Age of Ultron.*"

"You haven't seen it yet?"

"I've seen it six times, but Jen hasn't seen it."

Of course she'd seen it six times. I'd only seen it four times. "Yeah, that's fine. I'll see you tomorrow." Then I remembered something. "I have a pedicure appointment tomorrow afternoon. Want to come along and get one, too?" That was a girly thing to do, which was totally unlike me, but Bonnie had made me go a year ago and I'd gotten addicted. Mia should love it.

"Yeah, absolutely!"

I smiled. Score one for Aunt Chi. "Okay then. Have fun. Do you need money?"

"Nope. I'm good. Thanks."

My regular order of chicken satay and quinoa salad was waiting for me when I arrived at Thai Palace. A little hole-in-the-wall place, it had the best Thai food I'd ever tried. Once I'd found it, I refused to eat Thai from anywhere else.

It felt good to be home and by myself for a change. This week had exhausted me. The date that had gone well with Clark, then the evening that hadn't gone so well. My chest ached and I could feel embarrassment creeping in when I thought about it, so I tried not to.

Dealing with a whole team of new people and new personalities for the job at Wyndemere was difficult, too. While John was still being a pain in the ass, the others had behaved professionally, and lunch with

Lana had been nice. John hadn't come in today, which was fine by me. I needed the weekend to think the situation through, then I could deal with him on Monday.

The security men Jackson had told me about sat in a car across the street. I'd noticed them immediately upon entering the subdivision. I was suddenly glad Mia was somewhere else tonight, I thought as I closed all the curtains and blinds. Munching on my salad, I peered through a crack in the curtains, watching the car.

It felt weird to be under surveillance, even if it was just for security.

I flipped on the television, half watching *Doctor Who* as I ran the code I'd read this morning at Jackson's through my head again. I didn't have a photographic or eidetic memory per se . . . but I did have a really good memory for things I'd read.

The code had called the outside procedure and was returning data on GPS location. But what was it looking for? It was plenty fine to track whether someone was shopping for new cars and then pop up an ad on their smart phone, telling them the Toyota dealership nearby was having a cashback bonus sale. But the marketing data wasn't there. Instead, all the pieces of the software pointed to it looking for something. A pattern. But what pattern? And who was doing the looking?

I was finishing up my chicken satay when there was a knock on the door. I froze midchew. There was literally no one I wanted to speak to this evening. Except maybe Mia, but she had a key and wouldn't knock. Maybe if I pretended I wasn't home, they'd go away.

I muted the television and waited. The knock came again, this time with more persistence. What if it was the security guys? What if something had happened to Mia?

Shit.

Setting aside my chicken, I climbed off the couch and hurried toward the door. I didn't have a peephole, just window panels on the side, and what I saw when I looked through them made me wish I'd stayed on the couch.

"I know you're home, China," Clark called through the door. "I just want to talk to you for a few minutes."

"Go away."

"China, please. Let me in. Give me a chance to explain."

Give him a chance to explain why he'd acted as though I had the plague when I told him I was a virgin?

"Why should I bother?"

"Because otherwise I'm just going to stand here shouting through your door all night. Do you want that kind of attention?"

Dammit. He had a point. I didn't want attention period, much less the kind of attention that would result in the neighbors calling the cops. I pulled open the door, part of me wishing I looked like I had on our date night, instead of wearing jeans and my *It's LeviOsa, not LeviosA* T-shirt with my hair in my usual ponytail.

"What?" I asked, not bothering with friendly preliminaries. I pushed my glasses up my nose.

"Can I come in?"

At this point, I didn't think it mattered, so I shrugged and headed back to the couch. My chicken satay was getting cold. I didn't bother looking at him, just returned my gaze to the television. It was fake, though. All my attention was on him.

Even my disillusionment wasn't enough to make him look less gorgeous, I thought sourly as he sat next to me on the couch. Hair perfectly in place, a long-sleeved charcoal Henley fit like a second skin, and jeans that hugged the muscles in his thighs.

*Asshat*, I thought sourly, resurrecting Mia's new endearment for him.

"I don't blame you for being upset," he began. I took another bite of satay, chewing savagely as I gave him the side eye. "Really upset," he amended. "It just took me by surprise. My reaction wasn't a reflection on you."

"Oh, really?" I snorted. "I asked if it was a problem and you said, let me quote, 'Yeah.' How am I not supposed to think that's about me?" I shook my head, tearing off another bite of chicken.

"Your first time . . . it should be with somebody . . ." He trailed off.

"Special? Someone I love?" I finished for him. I was angry at him and embarrassed for myself. Like I wanted to talk about this at all, much less with him. "Whatever. I'm twenty-three years old, soon to be twenty-four. I'm not waiting around for Mr. Right, who may never appear. I'd just like a Mr. Knows-What-He's-Doing."

Which was the blunt truth. I didn't sugarcoat—I'd had to do that all week—and after he'd hurt me the other night, I had to bite my tongue from following my comment up with an insult. The urge to hurt him back was a hard one to overcome, but I should want to be the bigger person. I didn't really *want* to, but I could pretend.

Clark sighed and scrubbed a hand over his face. "I can understand that," he said. "Let's try again."

My eyebrows flew upward. "Excuse me? I'm supposed to *want* to have sex with you now?" He was crazy.

"No, no, that's not what I meant. I mean, let's start this over, go to dinner, hang out, get to know each other more." He paused. "I really want to get to know you better, China."

Hmmm. I chewed, forking another bite and showing it to him. "I've already eaten." Message sent: *I don't think so*. He'd had his shot, embarrassing and hurting me terribly. I didn't see why I should give him a second chance.

"We can just hang out then, and talk," he said, smiling carefully. One adorable dimple showed. Dammit. And his eyes were just so damn blue . . .

I shrugged. "I'm watching *Doctor Who*. You can stay for a while, if you want."

"Where's Mia?"

"She's staying the night with a friend."

"I love *Doctor Who*."

I studied his oh-so-innocent expression, then snorted. "Liar. You've never even heard of it."

"Okay . . . so maybe I haven't watched it. But I *have* heard of it." He smiled wider and now I couldn't help the tiny answering smile curving my lips. Clark was just too damn good-looking and too charming for mere mortals.

"This is what you want to do?" I asked, still disbelieving his sincerity. "You want to spend your Saturday night here, with me, watching *Doctor Who*?"

"If you'll let me. I have a bottle of wine at my place I can get, and we'll just hang out, watch TV, talk, whatever you want."

My mind flashed through all the possibilities and repercussions. Was it worth it?

"Okay," I said at last. "But I don't give third chances."

Clark's eyes were sincere as he looked into mine. "Understood."

I gave a short nod. "I hope it's white and not red. I'm not a huge fan of red wine. Though scientifically proven to be a healthier choice when choosing an alcoholic beverage, it gives me heartburn." As I'd learned the other night when I'd had red wine with my pizza when Jackson had shown up. Which had been confirmed after the three glasses of merlot with Clark. I'd gone through six Tums that night.

"I'll keep that in mind," he said with a grin. "Be right back."

True to his word, he reappeared with a bottle of chilled white wine and two glasses.

"I don't know the correct pairing of wine to Thai food," he said, settling again beside me. "So I took a guess. Chardonnay?" He handed one of the glasses to me.

"A Riesling or chenin blanc is generally considered to be the best pairing, but I'm not a stickler for propriety." I took a sip. It was pretty good.

We watched for a few minutes. I waited, knowing it would come. I didn't have to wait long.

"So . . . what's the premise of this show?" he asked.

With a sigh, I paused the show and launched into an abbreviated version of the Newbie Guide to Doctor Who. It turned out to be a longer explanation than I thought because he kept asking questions and getting me sidetracked, especially when arguing the validity of traveling through time and whether or not it was feasible *or* advisable.

"I've read that whole Grandfather Paradox thing," Clark said, refilling my glass. "It's the plot of the Terminator movies, basically. If you murder your father or your grandfather before you were born, then you'll never have been born. But if you were never born, how could you travel back in time to murder your father?"

"But the Terminator movies prove the Novikov Self-Consistency Principle," I said, warming up to one of my favorite subjects. "That principle states that even if you did go back with the express purpose of killing your parent, the laws of physics remain intact so that your parent must have already survived the attempt on their life because you've already gone back in time and are part of history."

"So you're saying that Arnold never had a chance because he'd already been there and tried that and failed."

"Yep." I grinned.

He shook his head. "You've obviously put a lot of thought into this."

I shrugged. "I've seen the movies several times. Two was the best." That was how I'd spent my last birthday. I'd broken from routine long enough to watch a Terminator marathon.

Clark was looking at me in That Way—his eyes soft, his lips curved. He was sitting really close, his thigh pressing against mine. I felt warm and I didn't know if it was the wine or just his proximity.

A knock on the door startled me. I glanced at my watch. It was nearing midnight.

"Who the heck could that be?" I muttered, climbing off the couch. Clark stopped me, his hand closing on my arm in a vise grip.

"Let me check," he said, also on his feet. "You stay back."

I couldn't argue, because he was already on his way to the door, not that I was sure I would've. If he wanted to be cannon fodder for a possible serial killer, he could be my guest. Though I doubted serial killers knocked first.

Clark opened the door. I hung back a little, but peered around him anyway.

"Who the hell are you?"

I barreled forward because I knew that voice.

"I could ask you the same thing," Clark said, easily blocking me from forcing my way in front of him. "It's late."

"Where's China?" Jackson asked.

"I'm here," I said, pushing my head underneath Clark's arm where it was braced on the doorjamb. My shoulders couldn't fit, but I could twist my head up to sort of see Jackson standing there.

"You know this guy?" Clark asked. "An ex?"

A giggle escaped before I could clamp my lips shut. Too much wine. I cleared my throat.

"I'm her boss," Jackson said, his voice as sharp and cold as a blade.

"Jackson, this is my neighbor, Clark. Clark, meet my boss, Jackson." I squirmed more until I finally escaped the prison of Clark's body.

"*The* neighbor?" Jackson asked, his gaze sharp on Clark.

"What does he mean, '*the* neighbor'?" Clark asked me.

"Yeah," I said to Jackson.

"You're right," Jackson said with a sneer. "He looks like a dick."

My jaw fell open. "I didn't—"

"Watch your mouth, asshole," Clark shot back. "I'm not the one knocking on her door in the middle of the night."

"I'm not the one getting her drunk," Jackson snarled.

This time I got a word in edgewise. "Wait—stop, both of you. Jackson, why are you here?"

Jackson was staring daggers at Clark, who returned the look three-fold, which gave me a slight pause. Clark, who usually appeared so Boy-Next-Door, looked downright dangerous. They were both of a comparable height though perhaps Jackson edged out Clark by a mere inch, but that still left them towering over me.

"Jackson," I repeated. He finally dragged his gaze to mine.

"We need to talk. In private." He looked pointedly at Clark.

I turned to Clark. "I'm sorry, but I'll have to chat with you tomorrow."

He studied me, probably trying to see if I meant it. It took a moment, but finally he said, "Yeah, sure. I'll come by tomorrow."

Before I could say anything, Clark pressed a quick kiss to my lips. He gave Jackson a hard glare as he passed, which Jackson completely ignored, as though he didn't even exist or wasn't worthy of his notice.

"May I come in?" he asked.

I retreated into my foyer and he followed me, closing the door behind himself. I stood awkwardly in the middle of the room as Jackson surveyed everything, his gaze pausing briefly on the nearly empty bottle of wine and two glasses before moving on.

"One of your team was found dead tonight," he said. "You didn't answer your cell and given what's happened the past few days, I got concerned. I would've sent the security team up, but I was afraid they'd scare you."

It took me a moment to process that. My hands became cold and clammy and my knees felt weak. *Physical signs of shock and fear*, I thought. "What happened?" I finally asked.

"Terry was killed in a car wreck tonight."

Terry. The older guy who'd been absolutely professional about everything. Who'd responded to my requests and inquiries with alacrity.

We'd hit it off immediately and I'd known we would work well together. And we had.

"How?"

"Lost control. Hit a tree. Died before emergency personnel got to the scene."

I turned away, closing my eyes and rubbing a hand over my forehead. That just really, really sucked.

"Did he have a family?" I don't know why I was torturing myself. There wasn't anything I could do about it now.

"A wife. Thirty-some years. Two kids, grown and moved away. Three grandkids."

Tears stung my eyes. Grabbing my half-full glass of wine, I downed it.

"You don't think it was an accident, do you." It wasn't a question and Jackson didn't pretend.

"No, I don't."

We were both quiet for a moment.

"So what now?" I asked.

"Any idea why he was killed?"

I shook my head. "He was great. Very professional. Actually had his team's work checked in for final review Friday evening. A week early. I commended him in an e-mail I sent out to the team leads this morning." I'd hoped John would take a hint from his older and more experienced colleague.

"At least his work is done."

I looked at Jackson, shocked into silence at his cold statement. "Really?" I finally managed. "That's what you have to say? The man is dead, likely murdered though it looks like an accident. And you're talking about the project?"

Jackson was suddenly right up in my space. "I want this project over because every day that passes, I regret putting you in charge of it," he gritted out. "People are being killed. For all we know, you could be next. And I don't want that on my conscience."

His sentiment was both frightening and self-serving. He loomed over me, his eyes glittering in the low light from the television. He looked alarming, the muscles in his body tense, as though poised to strike.

"I can take care of myself, Jackson. And I'll try not to get killed so you can still sleep at night."

He broke away and shoved a hand through his hair. "Jesus Christ, China. You're what, twenty-two? Twenty-three years old? You have no idea what you're dealing with. You're too smart for your own damn good and if I had any sense at all, I'd kick you off this project."

That ticked me off. I'd had enough of making people believe my competence rather than focus on my age. "Then why don't you?" I snapped.

Jackson froze, his eyes on me. The air was thick with the tension emanating from him.

"Because I need you."

I'd been all ready to blast him with the reasons he couldn't get rid of me, but his words shut me right up.

"Need me how?" I finally asked, afraid to hope for what I wanted to hear.

"What do you mean? I need you to finish this. No one has the expertise you do and I can't get someone up to speed quickly enough."

My heart sank and I turned away so he wouldn't see the disappointment in my eyes. "You seemed like you were doing just fine with the code I saw on your computer this morning," I said, then immediately regretted my words.

Jackson's hand flashed out and wrapped around my arm, dragging me back to face him.

"What did you see on my computer?"

The low menace in his voice made my mouth go dry. How stupid of me to blurt that out, especially when I'd taken such pains that he not see me in his office.

"N-nothing," I stammered. "I-I was just angry and wanted to antagonize you."

"Tell *no one* anything about what you might've seen. Promise me."

His grip tightened to the point of pain and I winced. "You're hurting me."

He let go immediately and I stepped back, wanting to be beyond his reach. To my dismay, he followed me. My back hit the wall and I had nowhere else to go.

"Promise me."

I didn't see any way out of his demand, and I was scared of what he'd do if I refused. "I promise."

His body was so close to mine, we were nearly touching. I didn't understand what was going on, why he was so adamant. Terry's death seemed to really alarm him—and it alarmed me, too. But that didn't explain his bizarre outburst. And it didn't explain why he was looking at me like he had last night, and showed no intention of moving away.

Lifting a hand, he caught my long ponytail between his fingers. The strands of hair slipped slowly through his touch like a caress. A shiver crept down my spine, but not in a bad way—in a this-is-getting-good kind of way, which was just weird. *I* was weird. Jackson had practically threatened me in my own home and I was quivering like a dog waiting to be petted.

His eyes had me mesmerized, their dark depths gazing into mine as if he could see into my soul. Leaning down, his lips barely brushed my ear.

"You like when I'm close to you, when I touch you," he murmured. The warmth of his breath against my skin made my eyes drift shut. He'd moved closer and I could feel the tips of my breasts brush against his chest.

"I-I never said that," I managed. It was taking all I had not to tip my head just a fraction so that his lips would touch me again.

"You think I can't tell? That I haven't noticed the way you look at me?"

His hand rested on my hip, his palm large and warm. His other hand gently tugged my ponytail so my head tilted to the side. His lips pressed against my neck, right underneath my jaw, and my pulse rocketed skyward.

"Your heart's beating so fast," he murmured, pressing light kisses down my throat. He paused at my carotid artery and I felt the warm wet touch of his tongue. His leg had moved between mine, the hard length of his thigh pressing against the softest part of me.

It felt amazing, but the shock of it startled me to my senses. My boss—who was doing something that he wouldn't tell me about but could be part of why someone was killing people—was seducing me. I'd officially entered the Twilight Zone.

Maneuvering my hands between our bodies, I gave him a hard shove. It took him by surprise enough that it pushed him back a couple of feet, enough for me to scramble away from the wall.

"What the hell are you doing?" I was pissed off. This was the second night in a row he'd done this—come on to me with apparently no other intent than to embarrass and humiliate me. "You can't do this, you know. I *work* for you. This is sexual harassment."

"Is that how you view it? Am I harassing you?"

I hesitated. Lying wasn't in my nature and no, I didn't view it as harassment. "I just don't understand what you're doing, or what you want from me." Plain speaking. Always preferable, in my opinion.

Jackson turned away, shoving his fingers again through his hair, which was sexy as hell. It made his normally perfect hair all mussed, making his edges turn harder and the professional businessman disappear.

He didn't answer right away, instead he picked up the wine bottle and poured the rest into my empty glass, then took a long drink. I waited, arms crossed over my chest. He was going to answer me if I had to stand here and stare at him all night.

"You and I," he began, "we're similar in ways I've never found with anyone else. It's . . . disconcerting. Don't get me wrong, I know you've been interested in me for a while. But I don't date employees." He finished the wine in his glass in one long swallow.

My face was burning hot. He'd known I was utterly infatuated with him? How . . . mortifying. It was pointless to try to deny it, so I didn't.

"So your solution is . . . to threaten me?"

He turned sharply. "I wasn't threatening you. I need you to do what I say, for your own good."

"Why? What's going on? What are you working on?"

"I can't tell you. And even if I could, I wouldn't."

All cylinders were firing in my brain as I puzzled through his words. "Does it have anything to do with what I was talking about last night?"

After a pause, he said, "Remember what happened to Terry, and be careful. Are you on track to deliver on Friday?"

I nodded. "It'll be tight, but I can make it happen."

"Okay. We'll meet Monday morning for a status report." He headed for the door.

"Wait—" I put a hand on his arm, stopping him. "That's it? You kiss me, twice, and now you're just going to leave?"

"If we're counting, I kissed you once," he corrected, his lips twitching into a smirk. "But if you'd like, I could kiss you again."

I let go of him as if I'd been burned. "No. No more kissing. You're my boss and besides, I'm . . . seeing . . . Clark." Had to search for the right word there.

Jackson frowned. "The dickhead neighbor?"

"He's not a dickhead. I just . . . took him by surprise with my unexpected revelation." I didn't want to use the V-word again.

"So all's forgiven?" The derision in his voice was hard to miss.

"What do you care?" His sudden interest in my personal life was throwing me off balance.

"Because he's outside your normal routine."

"What are you talking about?"

"You are someone for whom 'spontaneous' is a dirty word. Your schedule is mapped out weeks in advance, with no deviation. Now, suddenly, you're letting a man you barely know into your apartment, telling him personal things about yourself?"

I ignored that last part. "What do you know about my schedule?"

"Tonight's Thai and gaming. Tomorrow is a pedicure, groceries, laundry, and grandma. Am I right?"

A chill went down my spine and it wasn't even a tiny bit good.

"How do you know all of that?"

"It doesn't matter."

"The hell it doesn't! Have you been stalking me or something? Did you hack into my system here at home?" I scrambled to think of where and when my webcam had been over the past few weeks. "Have you been watching me?"

"I haven't been stalking you, don't be ridiculous," he scoffed. "Did I have to know all about you before I assigned you to Wyndemere? Yes."

I was furious. "Has *anything* you said been true?" I asked. "Or have you just been trying to manipulate me?"

Jackson sighed. "Don't turn this into a thing, China—"

Final straw. "Get out."

"China—"

"I said get out." I was furious and hurt. Jackson was a shit and I was no closer to understanding why he'd done the things he had or what was true and what was false. All I knew was that I was done . . . at least for tonight. "I may work for you, but this is my home and I want you gone."

Jackson's jaw clenched. He looked intimidating, towering over me, but I stood my ground.

"This isn't over," he growled. "Monday. My office." He yanked open the door and strode outside.

"Fine!" I called after him in a fit of temper. Not my best comeback, or even in the top ten, really. I slammed the door shut.

I didn't consider myself an emotional person, but I was ready to cry. I was embarrassed that Jackson knew so much about me, yet I knew so little about him and his motivations. I couldn't help how attracted I was to him or how he fascinated me. He was right—we were similar people. I'd never found someone who could understand me. *Really* understand me. I had a sneaking suspicion that Jackson did. And none of that had changed, no matter how angry I was. If anything, I found him *more* intriguing now.

I was *so* weird.

Then there was Clark. I should like him instead. He was a nice, normal guy who was drop-dead gorgeous and for some bizarre reason, he liked me. And I liked him. He certainly gave me butterflies, which was a good thing. And he *wasn't* my boss. Also a good thing. We were miles apart in personality and interests, but opposites attract, right?

I thought hard as I got ready for bed, pulling on my *Star Wars* pajamas. Yes, logic dictated I put aside my adolescent infatuation with Jackson and pursue a grown-up bona fide relationship with Clark.

But as I settled into bed, pulling the covers up precisely in a fold underneath my arms and staring at the darkened ceiling, I realized that was a lot easier said than done.

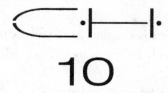

# 10

A banging on my door woke me the next morning and I stumbled out of bed, rubbing the sleep out of my eyes. I hadn't slept well and I tried to comb my hair with my fingers as I crossed through the living room to the front door.

The knock came again as I pulled open the door. "Stop," I pleaded.

Clark stood there, one hand still poised to knock, holding a drink tray with two Starbucks cups in the other. His brows flew up when he saw me.

"I woke you?" he asked.

"Ya think?" I snorted, then turned away, letting him follow me inside. I headed for the couch as he shut the door. Grabbing a blanket from the basket on the floor, I tucked it around me as I burrowed into the corner of the sofa. "What are you doing up so early on a Sunday?"

"I was worried about you," Clark said, sitting next to me and handing me one of the cups of coffee. I sniffed appreciatively. I always *wanted*

Starbucks on Sunday morning, but was just too lazy to actually get in my car and go get it.

"Why? I'm perfectly fine." I took a careful sip. Pumpkin spice. Yum. I'd say it was a lucky guess, but I was a middle-class white girl, so it wasn't like it had been a total shot in the dark that I'd like that particular latte flavor.

"Your boss was here last night, on a Saturday night, being all dick-like and controlling." He looked at me. "You're telling me none of that is worrying?"

Clark was freshly showered and shaved, the dampness of his hair making it an even darker shade so it was nearly black. He wore a blue long-sleeved shirt that had three buttons, the top two undone. The fabric stretched tight across his broad shoulders and showcased the depth of his chest from front to back. He wasn't a supertall guy, but he was a *big* guy.

Suddenly self-conscious, I combed my fingers again through my hair, which lay in long heavy waves over my shoulders. My pajamas were as far from sexy as it was possible to be, though they were really comfy.

"Sometimes my job can be a little demanding," I said with a shrug.

"A little demanding?" The sarcasm was hard to miss. "What the hell do you do? I thought you were a computer programmer."

"I am . . . sort of." I took another sip.

"What do you mean, 'sort of'?"

"Well, it's just that I'm a bit more than your usual programmer," I tried to explain. "The stuff we do, it's really advanced and cutting-edge. We create software and tech that sometimes have their origins in science fiction. We make it real." It was one of the coolest things about my job, and I could feel excitement curling in my belly. "Things you could only imagine being able to do in the future, we are actively creating every day."

"Like what?"

Okay, not a whole lot I could say here since so much was secret, but there were a few things. "Things like . . . a computer chip inside your head that can do things, trick your body. Like control your appetite if you're wanting to lose weight and make you think you're not hungry. Or to curb the urge to smoke or drink. Even control pain receptors in your brain.

"Say you're in the military and you're a solider. You get hurt on a mission but need to keep going. Your pain could be controlled without something performance-reducing like morphine. Same for people with chronic pain. Imagine those suffering from debilitating illnesses being able to control their pain without drugs."

Clark didn't seem to share my enthusiasm. "A chip in your brain to control your body?"

I nodded. "And that's just one thing. Biotech. We do other things, too."

"And you think that's a good idea? You don't think that could be abused?"

"Everything can be abused. You can't stop that. But I don't think we shouldn't invent the future just because someone might use it in a way I find personally distasteful."

"Sounds like you're rationalizing," he said.

"I'm not. It's just the way it is." I took another sip of coffee. The blue of Clark's shirt perfectly matched his eyes. Not that that was relevant.

"I can see why your job could be dangerous. I'd imagine there's a lot on the line with what you guys do."

"Especially this current project," I said. "Though I haven't quite figured out why." That was something else that had kept me up last night.

"What do you mean, you don't know why?"

I hesitated. "It's complicated. And a couple of people have died under suspicious circumstances. I was followed the other day."

His eyes narrowed. "You were followed?" he asked, his voice sharp.

"Yeah but my car kicks ass, so it was okay."

His hand on my arm stilled my attempt to take another sip of my latte. I glanced at him.

"It's *not* okay."

The stark worry in his eyes took me by surprise. "Why do you care?" I asked.

"I care because I've gotten to know you, and I like you," he said. "I care because . . . you're alone and young and you've done incredible things—*are doing* incredible things. You've taken yourself from being a Nebraska farmer's daughter to working for one of the most advanced tech companies in the world. That may be not a big deal to you . . . but I think you're fucking amazing."

Clark blurred in my vision and I had to set down my coffee to hurriedly wipe my eyes. No one had said anything like that to me before and it shocked me how much I was affected by his earnest words.

It felt so good to have someone say those things to me. My family had always known me for being ubersmart. It wasn't a big deal. To have a man like Clark look at me as though I was admirable rather than just an aberration . . . it rocked me.

Clark rested a hand on my head, stroking down through my hair, then repeating the gesture. I didn't look at him, afraid if I did that, he'd stop.

"And I'm not about to let anyone hurt you because you're too cerebral to realize you're in danger."

His murmured words struck me as slightly odd—how could Clark, an HR rep, possibly be able to do anything to keep me safe? But I didn't say anything. If he wanted to play Superman to my Lois Lane, that was fine with me. Everybody needed their fantasy delusions.

He urged me closer and it didn't take much for me to give in and lean against him. He wrapped his arms around me, which made me feel all warm and cuddly. Clark smelled really good and I took a deeper breath, trying not to be too obvious. He still stroked my hair and I would've purred like a cat if I could, but I totally couldn't roll my Rs.

The air grew thick in my lungs and maybe it was just my imagination, but it seemed as though Clark's touch changed from comforting to a slower, more sensual caress. If I tipped my head back just a few inches . . .

The rattle of a key in the lock had me jerking guiltily away from Clark as Mia bopped into the house.

"Hey, Aunt Chi! I—" She stopped abruptly when she saw us, her eyes going round as proverbial saucers. "Oh, gosh, I'm sorry. I didn't mean to interrupt the morning after—"

Oh. My. God. "You're not interrupting," I hurried to say, my cheeks aflame. "Clark was nice enough to bring me coffee this morning. I was up late last night. Working."

The grin on her face said she didn't believe a word of it, but what could I do?

"Um, yeah, thanks for stopping by, Clark," I said, scrambling off the couch. "Mia and I have pedicures scheduled today so I'll catch you later."

"Sure, okay." He got up and I walked him to the foyer.

"Thank you for the coffee."

"It was my pleasure. I'll see you soon."

It was cold out and I wrapped my arms around myself, sliding my fogged glasses down my nose a bit so I could watch him walk back to his place. A little sigh escaped. He was sooo pretty . . . and the view from behind was pretty darn good, too.

Clark glanced back just as he got to his door and totally caught me staring at his ass. Crap. I shut the door fast, but not quick enough to miss his grin.

"Look at you, Aunt Chi! Way to go!"

"It is *not* what you think," I insisted, ignoring her attempt to high-five me. "He really did just bring me coffee."

"Oh." She looked crestfallen, then brightened. "So I guess he groveled and you guys made up for whatever he did the other night?"

I wasn't sure how much groveling had been involved but . . . "Yeah."

"Good. I'm glad. Because he is *really* hot," she said with the kind of enthusiastic appreciation only a teen girl could produce.

Shaking my head at her, I headed for my bedroom. "I'm going to shower. Our appointment is in an hour, then we need to hit the grocery store."

"Okay, but we're going to have to make a stop at the pet store, too."

"Why?" I turned back around to find her peering into the fish tank. Oh no . . .

"Because The Doctor bit the dust." She poked the little gold lump floating on top of the water.

Shit.

"But I always have Helen," I said to the manager of the nail salon. "Every Sunday."

"Helen called in sick today," he said for the third time. "But Hugh is available." He gestured to the man standing by us, waiting.

"It's okay," Mia said to me. "I'm sure he'll do a good job." She smiled at Hugh.

"But . . . Helen does my toes . . ."

"It'll be fine." Mia pulled me toward the back, following Hugh.

"I've never had a man do my pedicure," I whispered.

"It's the same," she reassured me.

But it totally wasn't and after I stopped him endlessly "massaging" my legs—twice—and he tried repeatedly to ask me in broken English if I wasn't liking my pedicure, I decided I'd had enough.

"Um, I need to get going," I said, grabbing my shoes. Mia glanced at me. Her toes were already drying, the dainty pink nails flawless. "Sorry."

He was still trying to ask me if there was something he could do to make my pedicure better as we were heading out the door. Now I had naked toes and would have to deal with naked toes all week long.

Not only did we have to stop by the pet store and buy a new Doctor, but we had to go by the office supply store in order to get Mia everything she needed for school Monday morning. Grocery shopping was an experience as well because she took exception to my food—or lack thereof. I stared in wonderment at my now-overflowing refrigerator.

Mia didn't eat school food so she wanted to take her lunch. But apparently she was a princess because she didn't eat the stuff I'd taken for lunch when I was her age. No peanut butter and jelly sandwiches for her with a side of potato chips.

No, she liked to make salads with freshly chopped lettuce and veggies, sandwiches on ciabatta bread, and fruit with cream cheese dip as a snack. Plus assorted cheeses and crackers, various kinds of energy and vitamin drinks, and cranberry bagels with strawberry cream cheese for her breakfast.

"I'm glad she at least eats healthy," I muttered to myself.

We'd spent the rest of the afternoon and evening rearranging my office to be her bedroom. Mia had insisted she have her own space. "Especially if you and the hottie next door decide to get a little more cozy," she'd said with a wink.

I'd chosen to ignore her comment, grunting as I lugged my Iron Man out of the room and into the hallway. Inch by inch, I managed, but no way could I get it downstairs to my bedroom, so I left it in the corner at the top of the stairs. It didn't look too bad there, I decided, and the sharp ache in my lower back agreed with me.

The bus schedule for school had been downloaded, the coffeepot readied, and clothes laid out for her first day. As I hugged Mia goodnight and went to my room, I felt all the jitters of a new mom sending her baby off to kindergarten for the first time. Would they be nice to her? Would she find friends? Would she like her classes and her teachers? What if the bus crashed on the way to school? They didn't have seat belts on those things.

It was something new to worry about, as if I didn't have enough on my mind, all of which combined to keep me staring at the ceiling a long time before I got to sleep.

◆　◆　◆

"And you've got your lunch?"

"Yes."

"And you're sure you want to ride the bus? Because I could take you."

"I'm sure."

I chewed my lip as I watched Mia shrug on her jacket. She looked perfect, in black leggings with a long, baggy gray sweater and a patterned scarf around her neck. I would have looked like a burnt marshmallow in that outfit. She was skinny and tall enough to pull it off while looking like a teen supermodel. Her shoes were heeled ankle boots that she said were called "booties."

"If you need anything, just call or text," I said. "And make sure to text when you get home, okay?"

Mia sighed as she slung her backpack over one shoulder, then smiled at me. "I'll be okay, Aunt Chi. I promise."

I hugged her one more time, marveling at her calm demeanor. The first day of school had always made me a panic-stricken mess. Learning a new schedule, new faces, new teachers—I'd hated it all. Until my routine was established, I barely slept.

"I gotta go," she said, squirming away. "Jen's waiting for me."

"Okay, okay. Have a good day."

"You, too," she called back as she hurried outside. I watched until she met up with Jen, then closed the door.

Jackson had said he wanted to meet first thing this morning, but that wasn't going to happen. Another member of my team was dead and the rest of them had to be freaking out. I'd sent an e-mail last night calling for a meeting at 9:00 a.m.

Now, I sent Jackson an e-mail politely requesting he reschedule until after I'd met with the Wyndemere people. Well, not really a request, per se. More of an I'm-not-going-to-be-there-so-you-might-as-well-save-face-and-reschedule e-mail.

I was right about the team. For once, even John was on time when I walked into the conference room. Lana and George were there, too, and all three of them wore grim expressions. Lana's eyes were red rimmed.

"I know you've all heard about Terry," I said once I'd taken a seat. "I wanted to address that today as well as talk about where we go from here."

"Where we go from here?" John interrupted. "*Where we go* is to dump this damn project. Both Tom and Terry dead within a week of each other? It's crazy."

"Why does the project have anything to do with it?" Lana asked him.

"You can't be that naive," he shot back. "He'd completed his part, she even said so in that e-mail." He pointed at me. "Then he winds up dead in a car wreck?" He turned to me. "Seems to me that none of this started happening until Cysnet got involved."

I stiffened at his accusation. "What are you implying?"

"Tom was the only one who knew the big picture, and he's dead. Now you and Cooper know, and Terry's dead. So why don't you tell us the big secret. At least then we might be able to protect ourselves."

He did have a point, much as I disliked the man personally. All three of them were now looking expectantly at me. George had maintained his silence, observing the interaction between John and me. I made a decision.

"Tom was the one who decided to keep all of you in the dark as to the other components," I began. "Not the client. And I think I know why." I explained what I'd been thinking about the potential of the software, and they immediately saw what I had.

"Who's writing the integration algorithm?" George asked.

I thought of what I'd seen on Jackson's computer. "To my knowledge, no one."

"But that doesn't make sense," Lana said. "There's no point to any of our pieces without that."

"I know."

"If this is a government project," George said, "then there's no way they won't be using this. Antiterrorism and keeping America safe will be used as an excuse to be even more invasive with citizen surveillance."

"Fuck." John's muttered curse was echoed on George's face. Lana just looked confused.

"Why is that a bad thing?" she asked. "We want to be safe, want to find terrorists before they strike."

"Exchanging privacy for security," George said. "Privacy can never be regained and security is never guaranteed."

"If word gets out that Wyndemere is the author of the software that enables this, it'll be a public relations nightmare," Lana said.

"Yes, but the stock price will go through the roof because every other government is going to want that same software," George added. "It'll make the company millions."

No one replied. It didn't take a rocket scientist to see the dilemma and none of them were idiots. It was like building the software equivalent of the atomic bomb. You couldn't *un*invent it.

"What we're going to do is finish the project," I said. "I know Jackson is having a conversation with Freyda today about security concerns."

"What we should be doing is shutting down this project and going public," John argued. "It's too dangerous to continue. Not to mention if we go public, then they'll be forced to destroy the software. We don't know whose hands it's going to end up in and we can't take the chance it'll be someone like the NSA or worse, a foreign power."

"No way can we do that," Lana shot back. "We'll be fired immediately and hit with lawsuits."

"The whistle-blower program will protect us," John retorted.

"I'd rather not take my chances," she said. "I don't want to end up dead."

"No one said anything about being dead," I said firmly. "The police didn't find any sign of foul play with Tom and so far, Terry's death is still being considered a car accident. Let's not get carried away." Not that I was under any delusions that their deaths were mere accidents, but I had to keep the team calm and on task the best I could.

"We need to figure out who is writing the integration piece," George said. "Someone is, and I'm guessing they're getting paid pretty well to do it." He glanced at the others, then to me.

"It's no one here," I reiterated. "And we're accelerating work as of this moment. Have your teams finish their modules, work around the clock if you have to. Check in any code that's out and sign off on your area. I'll inform you should plans change."

"But we can't do that—" John began.

"End of discussion," I cut him off. He looked like he was ready to explode, but he kept his silence. Lana just looked worried, and George's expression was indiscernible.

One by one, they got up and filed out. John was last and the look he shot me before he went out the door made me glad he wasn't a permanent employee of mine. I would've fired him by now.

My thoughts were spinning as I headed back to my office. I needed to get in touch with Jackson and tell him where things stood. I'd been told by the man in the car to finish the software and I hadn't. Now Terry was dead. So was his death on my hands? And why were they killing the very people who were trying to finish the software?

I stood at my desk, staring at the blank computer screen, thinking. Terry and his team had finished their part of the project early. I'd sent an e-mail to him, copying the team leads, commending him for his work. Were we being eliminated? So no one would know what we'd done? Exterminate potential whistle-blowers.

The code on Jackson's computer nagged at me. I needed to see more of it, but was at a loss as to how. I wasn't arrogant enough to think I'd be able to hack through his home network's firewalls. Was he writing the software? And if he was, why would he keep it a secret?

Mia had texted me when she got home from school and had seemed cheerful. I was anxious to get home to her and hear how her day had gone. Although I'd checked my e-mail religiously, I hadn't received any messages from the team saying the software was in. The silence worried me. I was as worried about finishing the software as I was about *not* finishing it. It seemed as though we were damned if we did, and damned if we didn't.

"Have a good night," the security guard manning the front desk said to me as I passed by.

"You, too," I replied, glancing around the forlornly empty lobby. My steps echoed on the tile as I walked toward the entrance, which was quite a feat since I had rubber soles on.

I felt the guard's eyes on me as I left and it gave me a creepy sensation, though I knew he was just doing his job. When I stepped outside, the chill wind took my breath away. It had dropped twenty degrees since I'd gone inside this morning.

Pulling my long-sleeved shirt closer around me, I hurried for my car across the lot. Only a few vehicles remained, scattered randomly like pieces on a checkerboard. The wind whipped my ponytail around into my face and I impatiently shoved the strands away. My *Star Wars* pajamas were sounding pretty darn good.

I had just reached my car when I heard someone call my name. Startled, I turned and saw Freyda hurrying toward me.

"I've been waiting for you to come out," she said when she neared. She glanced around into the dark woods at the edge of the lot, her body language screaming nerves and fear.

"What's the matter?" I asked. Her demeanor was light-years from how she'd been the one time we'd spoken. Then she'd been very calm and collected—typifying "professional."

"I don't want to stand out here, exposed like this. Can we get in your car and talk?"

"Yeah, sure." I unlocked the doors and we got inside. It wasn't warm, but at least we were out of the chill wind. "What's going on? Are you all right?"

Freyda shook her head. "I haven't been all right since this damn project started."

I could relate.

"Freyda, who is it for? I know it's government, right? Which department?" In other words, who wanted the software badly enough to hold a gun to my head?

She hesitated, her eyes darting out the windows again. "You have to swear to me that you'll keep secret what I'm about to tell you."

Now it was my turn to hesitate. Sweeping vows of silence before I knew what I was promising to keep secret weren't really my thing.

She clutched my arm. "Swear to me." Her eyes were wide and fearful and she was deathly serious.

"I swear."

She took a deep breath. "The software is called Vigilance and yes, it was commissioned by the government."

My heart sank. The software on Jackson's computer had been saved under the same name. It was highly improbable that it was a coincidence.

"Which department?" I asked.

"The NSA. But they started the project three years ago."

"Three years ago? It's taken three years to write?"

"No, of course not. It was the Snowden thing. That hit the press and the NSA got their funding cut. They pulled the plug on the project. Until six months ago."

"What happened six months ago?"

"They started the project again, but it was under the radar. Black budget."

Shit. Black budget was for classified and secret operations. That didn't sound good.

"Haven't you had black budget contracts before?" I asked.

"Of course," she said. "But this was different. I thought the NSA was behind reviving the contract, but it wasn't."

"Who was it?"

Freyda's eyes grew bright. "It's all been on my shoulders all these months," she said, her voice little more than a strained whisper. "I'm not supposed to tell anyone, but Tom is dead and now Terry." She swallowed. "I'm so scared. I don't know who to trust or why they're killing us."

"Who is it?" I asked. "Who commissioned Vigilance?"

Two things happened in immediate succession. The first was that the windshield in front of Freyda broke, shattering into a spiderweb of cracked glass. The second was that a hole appeared in the center of her forehead.

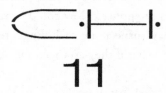

# 11

Freyda still had tears in her eyes, her expression tight with fear. I was frozen in shock, watching in horror as her body slumped against the door.

Adrenaline kicked in at the same time that my brain started working again. I punched the button to start the engine, threw the car into gear, and stomped on the gas. Rubber squealed on the pavement as I tore out of the lot.

My rear window exploded and I screamed, instinctively ducking down while still trying to see to drive. I swerved, narrowly missing a light post. Stomping on the gas again, I yanked the wheel, squealing my way out of the lot.

Freyda's body fell my way, landing against my arm. I shoved her away, disgust warring with terror. I'd never touched a dead body before, and now there was one in my car.

I glanced in the rearview mirror, worried the shooter was following me, but saw no one. That didn't mean I slowed down, though. Instead, I sped up until I hit the highway, then better sense prevailed and I adjusted my speed to the limit. Being pulled over by a cop wasn't what I wanted right now, not with a dead body in my front seat.

My head was jumbled. I didn't know what to do. All I could think about was trying to get away as quickly as possible.

It took ten minutes of mindless driving before I was able to think clearly. Should I go to the police? How could I even explain what had happened? Would they suspect me of killing Freyda? And powerful people were involved. What if they arranged for *my* silence as they had Freyda's?

My cell phone buzzed in my pocket and I dug it out, hitting the button to answer without looking at the caller ID.

"Yeah?"

"China?"

I didn't recognize the voice. "Who is this?"

"It's Clark. Mia gave me your number. Are you all right? You sound weird."

"No, I'm not all right. I'm very much not all right." My voice was strained and I could see the hole in the back of Freyda's head. My stomach turned over.

"What's the matter? Where are you?"

"I'm driving. But Freyda—" My throat closed up.

"Who's Freyda? What happened?" Clark's anxious voice in my ear made me swallow and get hold of myself.

"Someone shot her. She's dead, in the front seat of my car."

Silence. Then, "Holy Christ," he muttered. "Okay. Drive home. Right now."

"I can't bring her body to my house!"

"I'll help you take care of it. Trust me, China. But you need to get home. How far away are you?"

I glanced around. "About five miles."

"Okay. I'll be waiting for you." He ended the call.

I didn't know what to think, except I was grateful not to be alone. Clark would help me. I had no idea *how* he'd help me, but I wasn't going to question it at the moment.

Taking a precaution I hoped I wouldn't need, I reached for Freyda's limp hand, lifting it to press her index finger and thumb to my rearview mirror. Once done, I quickly dropped it, a shiver running through me. Now I'd deliberately touched a dead body, too. Another shudder.

When I pulled into my driveway, Clark was waiting, as he'd promised. He was yanking open my door before I'd even gotten the car to a full stop.

"Are you all right?" he asked, catching me as I nearly fell in my haste to get out.

"She's dead," I blubbered, only now realizing I was crying. "They shot her right in my car, right in front of me . . ."

Clark took me in his arms. "Shh, it's okay. You're okay."

I clung to him, my whole body shaking now in the aftermath of the adrenaline rush. We stayed like that for a few moments until I calmed down. I never thought I'd be that girl cliché who just needed a strong man to feel safe, but I couldn't deny he made me feel protected.

Looking past his shoulder to where Jackson's security guys were supposed to be, I saw they were gone, which sent a chill down my spine. Why weren't they there? Unless they'd thought I wouldn't be coming home tonight . . . but I'd think about that later. Right now, I still had to figure out what to do with Freyda.

"I guess we should call someone," I said, reluctantly stepping back. I sniffled and wiped my nose on my sleeve. I was sure I looked a wreck, but didn't particularly care.

"No," Clark said, surprising me.

I stared. "Why not? What are we going to do with her body?"

"I'll take care of it. You go inside my house and lock the door. Don't answer it for anyone, understand?" He brushed his fingers across my forehead and they came away bloody. "You're cut."

"I am?" I touched my head and winced. Ow.

"It's stopped bleeding, but you need to go lie down."

"I don't understand. How are you going to 'take care of it'?"

"Do you trust me?"

I hesitated, then nodded. What choice did I have?

"Good. Now go inside. Lock the doors. I'll be back soon."

He watched me until I was inside, then I spied through the window as he got into the driver's seat of my car and backed out. Only when the taillights disappeared around the corner did I step back.

Mia.

Grabbing my cell phone, I called her, anxious fear curdling my stomach until she finally picked up.

"Aunt Chi, where have you been?" she asked. "Reggie brought by a pizza even though he said you hadn't called yet. I saved some for you, but he seemed worried. Said you always call Monday nights—"

"Are you okay? Is everything all right there?" I interrupted her chatter.

"Yeah, sure. I'm doing homework. Today was awesome. I love my classes, though my calc teacher is kind of a jerk. Where are you anyway?"

"I'm . . . at work," I said. "I needed to work late tonight and forgot to call. But I should be home soon."

"Okay, well don't work too hard! See you soon!"

"Okay. Bye." I ended the call. Relief that she was okay made my knees weak and I dropped onto the sofa, my head in my hands.

This wasn't how things were supposed to be. My life was a boring one of computer coding, varying ethnic takeout, and the never-ending quest for the perfect bra. Not secrets and murder and people threatening me.

Time passed with agonizing slowness and my eyes grew heavy. My body was feeling the aftereffects of shock and I just wanted to sleep.

Unable to stay upright, I curled up on the sofa, resolving to rest for only a few minutes.

The next thing I knew, I was being jostled and lifted. I struggled to open my eyes, realizing too late that I was no longer on the couch and that Clark was carrying me.

"Wait, what—" I mumbled, but he cut me off.

"Shh. Almost there."

Taking me through the foyer and kitchen, I found myself being laid onto a bed that smelled faintly of Clark's cologne.

"Stay here," he commanded. He left before I could say anything.

I sat up and hugged my knees to my chest. I was freezing, my whole body shaking. Shock and trauma were catching up to me, the logical part of my mind was analyzing my physical and mental health. I was also trying to figure out how and why Clark had been able and willing to help so fortuitously tonight, and none of the answers I came up with were good.

Freyda was dead. Terry was dead. Tom was dead. Who would be next? Me?

Clark was back, carrying a small medical kit and a glass with some amber fluid in it. He handed it to me and I could smell it was alcohol of some sort. I didn't have to be told what to do. Tipping back the glass, I emptied half of it in one swallow. The liquid burned going down, but I was prepared this time.

Grabbing a blanket, Clark wrapped it around me. "You're in shock," he said, as if I didn't already know. Sitting on the bed next to me, he tore open several antiseptic wipes from the med kit. "This is going to sting a little."

He began cleaning the cut at my temple and I winced. He was quick and thorough, cleaning the blood off my face as well, then applying a bandage to the wound.

"It's not deep enough for stitches," he said. "Head wounds just bleed like crazy." He set aside the kit and tugged the blanket closer around me. "Feeling any better?"

I rubbed my eyes. "What did you do with Freyda?"

"I have friends," he said simply. "They'll find Freyda's body, just not in your car."

"How can you possibly have friends like that?" I blurted. "Are you in the mob or something?" He said nothing, which only made the dread inside me grow. "Who are you?" I asked. I might be naive, but I was far from an idiot, and if Clark was really in HR, then I was Kim Kardashian.

"What are you talking about?" he asked. He even had the nerve to look confused. "You know who I am."

"Sure I do." I looked at him and waited. It took a moment, then the fake innocence vanished from his face.

"Fine," he said, his voice flat. "It'll be easier like this anyway."

My eyebrows flew up. "Excuse me?"

"I know about the software Wyndemere is writing. Vigilance."

He couldn't have shocked me more if he'd recited the periodic table of elements. In order. I'd placed bets inside my head on the mob theory. "H-how do you know that name?" I asked.

"I make it my business to know about everything Jackson Cooper touches. And that includes contracts he takes with shady companies like Wyndemere."

"Wyndemere isn't shady," I protested.

"You're going to tell me that three people dead on the same project isn't the least bit suspicious?"

He had a point there. "So why are you telling me this?"

"The timeline is moving too fast to go with Plan A," he said. "So I'm improvising Plan B."

"And Plan A was . . . what? Me?" I wasn't imagining the sick feeling in my stomach. "Gain my trust, sleep with me, then pry secrets from me via pillow talk? Only I'm a virgin, so . . . eww?"

He didn't even flinch, his blue gaze steady as he replied. "I'm sorry, China. You're a nice girl, but I don't think you really comprehend the danger you're in."

In a way, I wasn't surprised. It explained a lot. The sudden, unswerving interest in me from an incredibly gorgeous Superman lookalike for one thing. Tonight's events, for another.

I cleared the unexpected—and unwanted—lump in my throat. "I see." I'd had many years to perfect my poker face to show that names, insults, and stares didn't bother me, and I donned it now. "And I'm just supposed to take your word for it that you're the 'good guy'?" I made quotey fingers with one hand while the other kept tight hold of my blanket.

"I just arranged to dispose of a dead body for you," he said. "And I didn't *have* to tell any of this to you. I *chose* to."

Okay. I guess on a sliding scale of niceties, with buying me flowers on one side, getting rid of a dead body was pretty much as far as you could go on the other. But something still bothered me and I decided to face it head-on.

"But . . . it was all an act?" I asked. "The dates, the wanting to start over, pretending to find me oh-so-interesting and irresistible?" *Bitter, party of one.*

Something flickered in his eyes and he glanced away. Standing, he took the empty glass from me. "Sorry, China. Business and pleasure don't really mix." He walked out of the room.

My devastation plunged a knife into my gut, so painful it robbed me of breath for a moment. The pain echoed through me in waves. I closed my eyes and sucked in a deep breath. This was why I was so careful and didn't let people close. The hurt and rejection wasn't worth it. Computers didn't talk back and they didn't reject me.

Staying another moment in Clark's bed—if that was even his real name—was out of the question. I got to my feet and redid my ponytail, using my fingers to comb through my hair until it was smooth. It soothed me, made me feel closer to the normal China. When I finished, I was heading out of the room just as Clark was coming back, refilled glass in hand.

"Going with Plan C? Get me drunk and drug me to make me talk?" Flirting might be hard for me but I could do bitchy just fine.

"I thought you might still be in shock," he retorted, then tossed back the drink himself. He swallowed and our gazes locked. His jaw was tight and his expression unreadable. I looked away first.

"I just want to go home." I pushed past him, intent on getting out as quickly as possible. My dignity was barely intact, but I held my head up.

His hand locked around my arm, bringing me up short. "Not so fast. We need to talk."

I yanked my arm away from him, then feared I'd left some skin behind. "You treat me like that and expect me to meekly sit down and listen to you? I don't think so." Turning on my heel, I walked as fast as I could toward the front door without actually running. I'd just yanked open the door when Clark's hand slammed it shut.

"I don't want to make you stay," he said in my ear. "But if you don't cooperate, I will."

Well, that left me little choice, now, didn't it.

"Fine." My body was stiff with tension and more fear than I cared to admit.

Clark eased away from me, his hand still firmly on the door panel. I didn't look at him as I sat in one of the chairs. "Now what? Threatening me seems contrary to getting me to cooperate."

He lowered himself into the chair opposite me. "You'd be surprised. Now we discuss Vigilance and Jackson Cooper."

"I signed a nondisclosure," I said. "I can't just start rambling on about customers' business or my boss."

"You'd rather be the next target?"

"I probably already am, so what does it matter? I write software, that's all." I swallowed as my palms grew sweaty. "And you haven't told me who you're working for or why you're obsessed with Jackson."

"Obsessed is a strong word," he said. "He's a leader in the tech industry and has ties to people that would give you nightmares. And you don't need to know who I'm working for."

"I do if you want me to tell you anything. I don't have anything to lose at this point, so give me one good reason to cooperate with you. You've already proven yourself to be an adept liar and manipulator." I crossed my arms over my chest and waited.

We were locked in a battle of wills and for once, he caved first.

"Fine," he said. "I'm a former military intelligence officer. I got out a few years ago, but in case you haven't noticed, the CIA hasn't exactly been on the ball with their intel over the last decade. Budget cuts and opinion-poll-sensitive politicians have reduced the CIA's recruitment of human intel."

"Human intel?"

"Yeah. You know, spies."

Oh.

"So they've been . . . outsourcing," he said.

"Outsourcing spies? How?"

"They pay for information, help with data collection and analysis. And in turn I'm autonomous in my sources, methods, and missions."

"Autonomous? But . . . doesn't that also mean you have no cover? No backup? No government agency to protect you?" It sounded incredibly dangerous.

Clark shrugged. "It's the price you pay for the kind of money I make."

I thought of his used Honda. Either he didn't make much . . . or that had been part of his cover as an HR guy.

"And being *autonomous* in your methods . . . means you're not subject to rules of engagement or mission parameters or guidelines other than not breaking the law," China said.

"Or if I do break the law, don't get caught."

I narrowed my eyes. "You're not being very reassuring."

"I'm not here to hold your hand. I'm here to stop bad people from doing bad things, however I need to do it."

The look in his eye told me he was dead serious. His comment about not getting caught echoed inside my head. I didn't trust him, but my options were limited . . . or non-existent.

"So now you know who I am and what I do, let's discuss Vigilance," he continued. "This software goes further than anything before in evaluating online behavior. People are dying—being killed—for it. Everyone who's tried to cooperate has ended up dead. You were my shot at staying under the radar."

"What do you mean *everyone who's tried to cooperate?*"

"Tom was the one who originally contacted me," he said. "We have a mutual . . . friend. He told me about the software, but he didn't know who'd commissioned it. He was worried about Vigilance falling into the wrong hands."

"And Tom committed suicide . . . supposedly."

"Exactly. I contacted Terry next, and you know what happened there. Whoever has the Wyndemere team under surveillance is very, very good."

"So you decided to go for a less direct approach with me," I guessed. "Why?"

He checked off on his fingers. "You work for Cysnet, not Wyndemere. You're a woman, you're very young, and you don't look like you could pose a threat to anyone."

Well, at least I didn't have to worry about him beating around the bush in an attempt to spare my feelings.

"I'm sorry to burst your bubble, but they already know who I am," I said. "A man threatened me the other day, got in the back of my car and told me not to make the same mistake Tom did. He said Tom was having second thoughts about delivering the software."

He frowned. "You told me it was an attempted carjacking."

"I lied."

His lips thinned. "And you didn't think it would be a good idea to tell someone that you were threatened? I thought you were supposed to be a supersmart genius?"

I took offense to being called stupid, even obliquely. "I *did* tell someone," I retorted. "I told Jackson. And for all I knew, you were in HR, remember? What would the point have been in telling you?"

That had been the night he'd begun seducing me, and would have, if I hadn't told him I was a virgin. So apparently my virgin status had been so off-putting, even Clark—who thought that getting me to talk was a matter of life and death—still had decided to change tactics.

The realization was even more demoralizing than the actual events had been.

"So tell me everything you know about Vigilance," he demanded.

I eyed him. "You still haven't given me any reason to trust you, but you have given me a lot of reasons to walk out that door."

Clark's expression grew hard. "Fine. One word: Mia."

My stomach dropped. "You asshole," I hissed. "She's sixteen."

"Then don't make me do something you'll regret."

That sick feeling in my stomach morphed into helpless anger. Helpless because he had me and he knew it. I refused to put Mia at risk, no matter what I had to do or who I had to cooperate with. And at the moment the most direct threat to her was staring at me, waiting for me to talk.

"Just so we're clear," I said. "I tell you what I know, you swear to leave Mia alone."

"I swear," he said, and I was tempted to believe him. But he was also an accomplished actor. And I was shit at reading people.

"She's my responsibility," I said stiffly.

"You have my word."

I doubted I could actually trust his word, but it was better than nothing.

Starting at the beginning, I went through the different parts of Vigilance that had been delegated to teams—social media monitoring, e-mail text searching, Internet queries and browsing history, GPS location and tracking, deciphering of third-party encrypted communications, all of it.

". . . so the software is making a profile of who that person is—what they do, who their friends are, the places they frequent, the things they buy, everything they put in writing whether it be a comment on a Facebook status or an e-mail sent to their boss."

"Don't Google and Facebook already do that?" Clark asked. "I shop online for airfare to Hawaii, I see Google ads for surfing lessons in Waikiki."

"True, but that's different. Google's only looking at one part of your life via what you put into its search engine. This software goes even further. It's the most complete kind of tracking and monitoring system in existence."

"But it's not finished," he said.

"Yes, it is. The final code from Wyndemere has been checked in and is waiting to be compiled. But there's a missing piece that has me worried."

"What's that?"

"The algorithm that searches through those profiles and sets flags," I said. "That's what hasn't been written." I thought of Jackson and the code on his home computer, but wasn't about to tell Clark about that. "It's not necessary for the software to run—but without it, what's the purpose of the software?"

"We need to find out for sure," Clark said. Reaching into his pocket, he pulled out a tiny USB drive. "Can you get this in Jackson's computer?" He handed it to me.

"Why Jackson's? What's on it?" I asked.

"Jackson because I have reason to believe he knows a lot more than he's telling. And this is a program that will install a back door into his system."

I felt sick to my stomach. "You want me to enable you to spy on my boss. Jackson Cooper. Billionaire, genius entrepreneur and owner of Cysnet. A man like him has lawyers who have lawyers. If he finds out or catches me, he could have me arrested, prosecuted, sue me, basically destroy my life, with a couple of phone calls." I could imagine the hell my life would become if Jackson found out. He'd be livid.

"I need to know."

"Why *don't* you know?" I retorted. "This is supposed to be a government contract. You work for the government . . . sorta."

"No government agency commissioned the software," he said flatly.

"Th-that's not true," I stammered. "Freyda confirmed it tonight, before . . ." I couldn't finish the sentence.

Clark leaned forward, his elbows on his knees and his gaze intensifying. "Yes, tell me what she said. Why was she in your car?"

I hated this. I hated that I had no way out of doing exactly what he told me to do. He'd lied to me, threatened me and Mia, tried to gain my trust only to betray me later. I didn't trust Clark. Obviously, he'd do whatever he had to in order to get the information he was selling to the CIA. And if I got hurt or killed in the process, tough crapola. The only person I could depend on was myself, which meant I'd better hold what little I knew close.

"She wanted to discuss the status of the project," I said. "She was anxious for it to be finished and delivered." Some of that was true.

"You said she confirmed it was a government hire."

"She didn't have time to tell me much of anything," I hedged.

Clark's eyes narrowed, but I just stared back. I'd read that you can tell when someone is lying because the first thing they do is break eye contact. The second is they blink a lot. I kept my gaze steady on him.

A buzzing sound interrupted our silence and Clark answered the phone he pulled from his pocket.

"Yeah?" He listened for a moment, then his gaze returned to me, suspicion etched on his face. "Are you sure?" More listening. "Check out her home and vehicle as well as the parking lot. She might've left it somewhere or dropped it." He ended the call.

"Freyda's missing one of her cell phones," he said to me.

I frowned. "She had two?"

"Yes. One for work and one for personal. She's missing the one from Wyndemere."

"Weird because I bet she always had it with her," I said.

"Did you take it?"

I raised my eyebrows. "Seriously? In between being shot at and dealing with the fact that someone was murdered in the *front seat of my car*, you think I had time to search and rob the body?"

He considered that, then nodded. "You're right. It's doubtful. Now when can you plant that in Cooper's system?"

"I don't know. It's not like we're buddies and I go over there for dinner."

"He kissed you the other night."

My face went hot and my hands clenched into fists. "You've been spying on me?"

"Nothing is private. You should know that." He looked unrepentant. "My point is that he likes you. Use that."

"So you want me to . . . what? Sleep with him and hope he likes pillow talk?"

Clark stiffened, his expression hard. "I didn't say you had to sleep with him. But you can get close enough to plant that."

I got to my feet. "I'll do what I can." I headed for the door and pulled it open, pausing to turn and say, "And thanks so much for all your *help* tonight." It wasn't hard to miss my sarcasm. I slammed the door behind me even knowing how teenager-temper-tantrum that was.

It wasn't until I got home and locked myself in my bathroom that I dared to pull the phone I'd taken off Freyda from its hiding place inside my bra. Thank God for Victoria's Secret elastic.

I turned it off before anyone might try and track it. I'd have to hack into it to find out what information it contained, including which secret government brainchild had resurrected Vigilance.

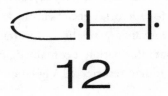

# 12

"What happened to your head?" was the first thing Mia wanted to know. She'd been in her room when I'd come home but had emerged fairly quickly when she heard me.

I rummaged in my closet, trying to find a T-shirt to lay out for work tomorrow. As often as I could, I picked out my clothes the night before because it saved time and was more sensible than waiting until morning. Of course, "as often as I could" really meant "every night without fail."

"What did you do with my *X-Files* fandom T-shirts?" I asked, digging for the one that said *Sure. Fine. Whatever.* It fit my mood.

"What color is it?"

"Black. Gray. I don't know." I rarely paid attention to color, just what the shirts said.

She pointed. "Darks are on the right."

"'Darks are on the right.' Whatever," I grumbled, wondering when I'd find time to reorganize my closet. Though the *Trust No One* shirt was probably a better choice, I didn't want to be too obvious about my state of mind.

"So what happened to your head?" she asked again.

"My windshield had a piece of rock go through it," I lied. "Some glass cut me."

"Oh my God! While you were driving?"

"Yeah, but I'm okay, obviously. It was just a scratch. Tell me about school."

Mia gave me the rundown on her classes and her teachers, going on at some length about the advanced calculus teacher. ". . . and I tried to show him another way to reach the same value, but he said I still had to do it the other way or I wouldn't get credit."

"You know as well as I do that you have to do it their way, even if you're ten times smarter than they are," I said, finally finding my T-shirt. I pulled out a flannel shirt with a tiny black-and-white checked pattern. "Get the grade, then you can do what you want."

"I know, but it's ridiculous. He should've been glad to see another solution. My way was much easier and more intuitive than his."

I could sympathize. Most of the high school teachers I'd had were uncomfortable with me being smarter than them, especially since I'd barely been into double digits while taking advanced geometry. I'd also made the mistake once of correcting a teacher in front of the class and I'd paid the price. I still remembered him ridiculing me while everyone snickered.

*"Why thank you for that," he said. "Shall I let them know you get an extra cookie with your milk this afternoon?"*

"Did you make any new friends?" I asked, shoving aside the embarrassing memory.

"Yeah. There's a group of girls Jen introduced me to," she said. "They want to go to the movies tomorrow night. Can I go, too?"

"So long as you're back home by ten. Tuesday is a school night. Speaking of which," I glanced at my watch. "Two minutes until *Supernatural.*"

Mia was off the bed like a shot. "That's long enough to make popcorn. I'm on it."

I grinned as I followed her out of the bedroom. It was nice having her there, even if it now took me three times as long to pick out clothes for work.

I didn't try to get into Freyda's phone until I'd left the next day. I didn't know if I was being watched at home or someone was listening in somehow. So I was up at the crack of dawn, leaving a note for Mia that I'd gone into work early. I also didn't want Mia to see the damage to my car and have to explain how it happened.

Except when I went outside, I saw that my car was completely whole again. Both the front and back windshields had been replaced. It would appear the CIA also specialized in twenty-four-hour car repair, not that I was complaining. Likewise, the interior was spotless as well.

"My tax dollars at work," I muttered to myself.

By 7:00 a.m., I was buzzing the doorbell on an apartment building on the west side of downtown. When there was no answer, I buzzed again and the intercom crackled.

"No one I know would be visiting at this hour," said a familiar voice.

"It's China," I said back. "Let me in."

"I'm still in my pajamas," he argued.

"I've got something special for you," I said, hoping that would do the trick. Sure enough, a few seconds later, the door clicked open and I grinned.

My friend Yash lived on the top floor of the three-story building and I took the stairs, unwilling to wait for the elevator. He was one of the small group of people I gamed with twice a month. I knocked on his door, then let myself in.

"I've only drank half my coffee," he complained as I entered. He was wearing a matching pants and shirt set of striped pajamas, complete with bedroom slippers. All he needed was a robe and nightcap to complete the look.

"Good because I could use a cup while you look at this." I thought of tossing the phone but decided against it after considering his lack of any kind of sport-related skill. I set it on the counter instead.

"A cell phone? You do know I am already familiar with these devices." His dry humor made me grin.

"Yes, I'm aware. But *A*, this isn't mine, and *B*, I need you to hack into it." I poured myself a cup of coffee from his way-too-complicated machine. I could fix myself an espresso or latte if I could figure the damn thing out. Internal combustion engines? No problem. But a five-hundred-dollar espresso machine stumped me.

"Intriguing," Yash said, looking over the phone. "I assume it can be tracked?"

I nodded. I'd turned it off last night to prevent that very thing. "Yep. You'll need to have a jammer running before you fire it up."

Yash examined it. "Looks like a two-step verification system. ID and PIN."

"I thought that might be the case."

"You have a fingerprint?"

"It's in my car. Just need your good camera." A fake fingerprint could be made relatively easily, provided you had a really good print available. Take a high-res photo, clean it up in Photoshop, print it on transparency with a laser printer, and you had a template. Brush on a thin layer of glue, let it dry, peel, and stick. Voila: a fake fingerprint. Good enough to fool most phone sensors anyway.

"It's in my office," Yash said, waving vaguely toward the hallway.

I knew where his office was and headed down the hallway. As usual, his apartment was spotless. Fastidious to a fault, Yash had a cleaning woman come three times a week. He worked as a consultant because, frankly, no one could afford to keep him on staff permanently. Not that he needed to work, having made his fortune writing games for smartphones, but he'd go nuts sitting around with nothing to do. Which was why I'd brought the phone to him. No one knew cell phones and their operating systems better than Yash.

Yash's office was as organized as the rest of the house, and the camera I needed was in its place inside its case on a shelf. Taking it outside, I took several close-up shots of the fingerprints on my rearview mirror before returning to the apartment.

"One of those should work," I said, setting the camera on the kitchen table. "Any idea when you'll get a chance to crack it?" It was a polite request so I didn't sound anxious, but I knew Yash would start immediately. He loved puzzles and challenges.

"Don't rush me, you know I hate that," he groused. I just hid a grin at his crankiness. Yash was all prickly on the outside, but he'd do anything for his friends, of which I was lucky enough to be counted among those select few.

"You'd know I'd never rush you, Yash. It's just important. Shoot me a text when you crack it."

He glanced up at me, his eyes peering over the top of his glasses. "How important?"

"Galactic." Our code word for urgent, end-of-life-as-we-know-it important.

His perpetual frown deepened. "What did you get yourself into, China?"

"Trust me, you don't want to know. I just need whatever info you can find on that phone. Especially anything about something called Vigilance." It was a shot in the dark, but I had no other leads at the moment to try to figure out who'd hired Wyndemere or who was killing people.

Yash sighed dramatically. "All right. I'll get it done."

"Thank you." I gave him a quick peck on the cheek before he could shoo me away.

"None of that," he complained. "You'll give me your germs."

"You can't fool me—I know you love my germs," I tossed over my shoulder as I headed out the door.

I had an unpleasant surprise when I got to Wyndemere: my security badge wouldn't work.

"I was just here last night," I explained to the security guard as he typed my ID code into his computer terminal. "It should work."

"It says here that your clearance has been revoked," he replied, looking at his screen.

I stared open-mouthed at him. "But . . . that can't be. I'm still working on a project—"

"China!"

We both turned to see Lana hurrying toward us from the elevators. She came past security and took my arm, propelling me toward a corner of the lobby.

"We have to talk," she said.

"I can't get past security. What's going on?"

"It's Freyda. She was found shot to death late last night." Lana looked scared, her face pale and her eyes wide with panic. "John didn't come in today at all and George isn't answering his cell."

My stomach turned over.

"That's not all," she continued. "The software. It's gone. All of it. The entire project file wiped out."

Oh no. "There are backups, I'm sure—"

"The whole system was hit by a virus. It's corrupted everything. The backups they're trying to restore have been useless. Everyone is having meltdowns."

I was stunned, momentarily at a loss as to what to say. My gaze was caught by a news van pulling up outside. "Oh no. Look." I pointed and Lana turned. We watched as three people got out of the van, one obviously the camera-ready reporter.

"You have to leave," Lana said. "I haven't told you the worst part."

I turned back to her. "What could possibly be worse?"

"They think *you* did it."

That phrase, *feel the blood drain from my face*, came to mind. I never knew that was an actual Thing. Until now.

"How . . . why . . . how?" I stammered.

"You were the last one to check in the files. They have security footage of you and Freyda in the parking lot, her getting into your car. Then she was dead this morning."

"I didn't kill her!" But the proof—my bullet-shattered wind-shields—was long gone.

"Someone used her credentials to remotely access the project and copy the files. They have a log, but whoever did it rerouted through so many servers, they couldn't pinpoint the origination. They're assuming corporate espionage."

"And they suspect me?" I was incredulous, stunned, and kind of pissed off, too. The idea that someone would think I did that—

"You need to go. Now," she said. "I know it wasn't you, but everything looks really bad right now. If you want to clear your name, you're going to need to find the stolen software *and* the person who stole it."

"But . . . but . . . where do I go?" I didn't have anywhere. I went two places: work and home.

"Go to my place," she said, then rattled off an address. Thank God I had a good memory. "The garage code is zero eight one five. I'll meet you there tonight. Now go, before the police arrive."

I hurried to my car, giving the news people a wide berth. As I left the lot, I passed another news truck going in. Wyndemere attacked by a virus was big news, along the lines of Microsoft going down.

Going straight to Lana's sounded like a bad idea. Sitting around all day waiting wasn't in my disposition. I thought of going to Clark's, but if the police were looking for me, they'd be watching for me at home.

As I was driving aimlessly, my phone rang. It was Jackson.

"What the hell is going on? Where are you?"

So much for a *Good morning, how are you?* I thought sourly.

"I'm driving. I just left Wyndemere."

"I'm watching the news and they're saying a Cysnet employee hacked Wyndemere and stole proprietary software. What the fuck is going on, China?"

I winced at the fury in his voice even as nausea threatened to overwhelm me. Oh my God, this was really happening.

"I didn't do it, I swear," I choked out, horrified to realize I was close to tears. "I was working late last night and then Freyda cornered me in the parking lot and wanted to talk, but then they shot her, right through my windshield—"

"Wait, what? What did you say?" he interrupted. "Someone shot at you?"

"Yes. I'm okay, but Freyda's dead," I blubbered. I quickly swiped the back of my hand across my wet cheeks.

"I'm at the house. Come here."

I was only a few minutes away from Jackson's place. "O-okay," I croaked out, trying not to outright sob. My life was falling apart in the span of a week. It was insane. This shouldn't be happening to me.

When I pulled into Jackson's driveway, Lance had one of the five garage doors open and motioned me to park inside. Duh. Of course. If anyone was looking for me, my boss was sure to be questioned and having my car in his driveway was pretty much a dead giveaway.

"I'll take care of it," Lance said with a smile as he took my keys.

I handed them over and headed inside, where Jackson was waiting for me.

I'd had time on my way over to get control of myself so I wasn't crying anymore. But my eyes were swollen and I was still sniffling.

He was standing there, wearing black on black again, his cuffs turned back and a Rolex gleaming on his wrist. His shoes were polished to a gleaming shine and his hair was perfect, the wave in front beckoning a woman's fingers to run through it.

All of which made me feel like a complete frump. My *X-Files* T-shirt, long-sleeved flannel on top of that, jeans, ponytail, and glasses were woefully out of place next to him. I felt too young, too dumb, and too awkward.

*Suck it up, China,* I told myself. *You're no model and never will be. But you're smarter than ten of them put together.* No, not a nice thought toward other women, but sometimes you had to tell yourself what you had to in order to keep your chin up.

"Start at the beginning," he said.

I took a deep breath, then told him about how Freyda was waiting for me in the lot last night and what she had said.

"She was so scared," I said, remembering the fear lining her face. "And then . . . she was dead." As hard as I tried, I couldn't stop my eyes from filling again. Embarrassed, I rubbed my eyes underneath my glasses, which was why I jumped when I felt arms around me. I hadn't seen him coming.

"Jesus, China," Jackson said, pulling me into his arms. "Thank God you're okay."

I had no idea why he wanted to hug me, but I wasn't about to complain. It was the safest I'd felt in two days. Clark's words and suspicions whispered inside my head, but I'd worked for Jackson for four years—had been infatuated with him for six. I couldn't just toss away the trust and loyalty I had for him. The USB drive seemed to burn a hole through my pocket and I had no idea if I was actually going to do what Clark wanted me to.

Jackson held me tight, his arms wrapping around me, and I could smell his cologne and the scent of his skin. It was heaven. For the hell I'd been through in the past twenty-four hours, this was almost worth it all.

But I was fooling myself. And it would only be a huge disappointment later when I came crashing down to reality. Jackson didn't want me. He was being supportive, that was all. I needed to remember that. Guys like him didn't fall for geeky, awkward girls like me. Jackson Cooper may be a geek, too, but he was a *cool, rich* geek. Even if he *had* said he'd thought about sleeping with me, which was just confusing.

Clearing my throat, I pushed away from him. Maybe it was my imagination, but it seemed like Jackson resisted for a split second before letting me go.

"Um, anyway," I said, stepping back, "Lana told me this morning that the software was remotely uploaded last night using Freyda's account, which is impossible, because she was dead. All the files have been deleted and the virus unleashed into their network is wreaking havoc. And apparently, Wyndemere suspects . . . me." I swallowed. Hard.

"Lana told me that to clear my name, I needed to find the software *and* the person who stole it."

I'd been looking steadily at about the middle of Jackson's chest, but now I took a deep breath and raised my eyes to meet his.

"Please tell me the truth," I said. "Was it you?"

Jackson's gaze was steady on mine. "Why would you ask that?"

"Because I saw," I said. "On your computer. You were writing code that you had no business writing."

"You told me you *didn't* see anything."

"Yeah, well. I lied."

Jackson let out a sigh. "Of course you did."

"Tell me," I repeated. "I deserve to know the truth."

"The truth is that I never should have brought you on this project," he said, turning on his heel and leaving the room.

I followed in hot pursuit. "What's that supposed to mean?" I asked, having to walk double time to keep up with his long strides. "It's not my fault that Wyndemere is involved in something shady and dangerous."

"I didn't say it was," he replied, stopping so suddenly I nearly ran into him. He'd led us to a room I hadn't been to before and held the door open for me to enter.

I walked inside and found a media room with a huge flat-screen television and leather furniture that looked very heavy, very plush, and very expensive. The carpet felt as though it swallowed my feet. But my attention was on the television screen. It was the reporter I'd seen at Wyndemere, and she was live on the air.

". . . haven't confirmed whether this was a terrorist cyber-attack or an act of corporate espionage," she was saying. "The company spokesman declined to answer any questions at this time. Anonymous sources, however, are telling us that employees of Cysnet—the company owned by entrepreneur Jackson Cooper—are thought to be behind it. There has been no word on whether the death of Freyda Jain, found this morning in her car, is somehow related."

Jackson muted the television. "See what I mean? The lawyers have already been calling."

"You didn't answer me," I said, ignoring his comment. "Did you steal the software?"

"If I did, why do you think I'd tell you?"

Ouch. Burn.

I pushed aside my injured pride and got right up in his space. I had to tip my head back pretty far, but still. "Because my ass is on the line," I gritted out, poking my finger hard into his chest. "That's why."

Jackson snatched my hand in his and jerked me closer. "Don't you think I know that?" he hissed. "It's precisely why I can't tell you anything."

I shook my head. "I don't understand."

"You're too young, China. Naive. Like that neighbor of yours that you're so willing to invite into your home and into your bed. His identity is a complete sham. Granted, they put some work into it, but track him back a few years and he disappears."

Oh no. He knew about Clark. "What are you saying?"

"He's not who he says he is," Jackson repeated. "His trail disappears. He's either law enforcement, or a spy."

"But he said he's in HR," I bluffed, frantically thinking of what to do.

"He lied." Jackson's eyes narrowed. "You don't seem very surprised."

I didn't know what to say. I was an awful liar and I'd already lied twice today. It wasn't something I usually did. Jackson's dark eyes stared into mine, as if he could read my mind. What would he do if he found out Clark was threatening me into enabling a hack into Jackson's network?

"You already know, don't you," he said, and it wasn't a question.

"I . . . guessed." Which was true.

"Please tell me you didn't confront him," he said.

"Um . . . well . . ."

He dropped my arm, turning away and cursing under his breath. Shoving his fingers roughly through his hair, he rounded on me again. "Do you have any idea what he could have done to you? How easily he could make you just disappear?"

Yes, Clark could, actually, and no . . . I hadn't considered that. I winced at the thought.

"What did he say?" he asked.

I panicked. There was no other word for it. And I did the first thing that came to mind.

I kissed him.

Not just any kiss. Nope. Not me. I *threw* myself at him, locking my lips to his and wrapping my arms around his neck. This had the unfortunate effect of causing him to stumble backward, unbalanced by my sudden attack. For once, luck was actually on my side because his leg hit the couch and he abruptly sat. Since I was attached to him like a barnacle to a sinking ship, I went down, too.

*Recover recover recover.* The mantra went through my head as I scrambled, straddling his lap. I tossed my glasses aside and smooshed my mouth to his again. I had no plan for what I'd say when I was done trying to distract him. I'd just wing it.

His lips were warm and soft, so it wasn't as though kissing him was a hardship. Add in the fact that he smelled better than a fresh server right out of the box, and I wasn't faking my enthusiasm.

Jackson's hands wrapped around my upper arms, forcibly pushing me away until I had no choice but to break our kiss. I sat back and our eyes locked.

Oh shit. He was so pissed, I just knew it. What was a graceful face-saving way out of this?

Um, yeah, that ship had sailed.

I couldn't bear to look at him anymore. I'd made an utter fool of myself.

Just as I was trying to figure out how to climb off his lap without falling on the floor, Jackson lifted his hands from my arms to cup either side of my head. Surprised, I lifted my eyes. His gaze was intense, his brow furrowed. Then he was kissing me.

It wasn't like when I kissed him. It was much, much better.

His lips moved over mine, insistent and firm. For a moment, I did nothing, then it was as if my brain finally connected with my body. *Jackson was kissing me. REALLY kissing me.*

Opening my mouth, I pressed closer to him, wanting him to deepen the kiss, which he did. His tongue brushed mine, sending a wave of desire through me.

Reaching back, I tugged out my ponytail. I had good hair. Mia had said so. Maybe Jackson would like it.

That had been a good move because no sooner had my hair settled around my shoulders and down my back than Jackson was pushing his fingers through it. His hand cradled the nape of my neck, pulling me closer. The other hand went to my hip.

*I'd been in this position with Clark not two nights ago and it had ended in disaster.* I couldn't help the thought running through my head. If Jackson did that to me, I didn't know if I'd ever find the courage to kiss another man.

But even those dark thoughts faded away as the moments ticked by and Jackson continued to kiss me, his mouth becoming more demanding. Not that I needed encouraging. I was plastered to him, my breasts smashed against his chest, my fingers in his hair, and my hips pushing down into his. Not that it seemed he minded.

Both his hands moved to clutch my hips, his fingers digging into my flesh through the denim. He pushed up, pulling me down so that the hard length of him pressed between my thighs.

Blood pounded in my ears, heading south. I tore my mouth from his, dragging in a breath. His fingers trailed through my hair, then closed into a fist, pulling my head back and exposing my throat to his lips and tongue.

I felt on fire. Both his hands had my hair and tugged gently, keeping my back arched toward him.

He tugged at my shirt, pulling the sleeves down my arms. I unwound my arms from around his neck long enough to shove the fabric off, letting it fall to the floor.

The world spun and suddenly I was on my back on the couch, Jackson braced on his elbows above me. I was breathless, my eyes wide as they stared into his. The look on his face was one I knew I'd never forget.

He wanted me.

I knew it in an instant, in the instinctual way women have known for centuries when they're wanted. Built into my DNA was something deeply feminine that recognized the hunger in his gaze, in the set of his jaw, the line of his lips.

The knowledge sent a curl of pleasure through me. I smiled. It was amazing, how having the man I wanted look at me like that could make me feel . . . sexy. I'd never felt sexy in my life. Ever. Never ever. But man, did it feel good.

I threaded my fingers through his hair and up his scalp and his eyes slid shut. I pressed him toward me, delighted when he readily complied. His kiss devoured me, sending my lucid thoughts shattering into a heady fog of want and heat and desire.

Jackson tugged on the hem of my T-shirt and I lifted up long enough for him to pull it over my head. He froze with the fabric still tangled in my fingers.

I looked at him, but he was looking at my chest. Suddenly, I was superglad I'd worn my Dream Angels champagne lace push-up with matching boyshort lace panties.

"You're beautiful," he said, his voice a rasp of sound that went right through me.

He sat back on his knees, which is when I noticed my legs were wrapped around his hips. Hmm. When had that happened?

I was distracted by his hands at the fastening of my jeans. The brush of his fingers against my bare stomach sent tremors through me. I was mesmerized by his face as he unzipped my jeans and dragged them down my legs. I really hoped he took my socks with the jeans because they *so* did not go with my bra and panty set.

I was in luck because he did take the socks. But that wasn't the luckiest part. That was when he looked at me as if I were birthday cake and ice cream . . . and it wasn't even his birthday.

All of my grandma's Harlequins didn't prepare me for how it felt when he slid his fingers underneath the lace of my panties and between my legs.

I sucked in a sharp breath when he touched me. He was looking at me, watching my face, as his hand moved. My thighs were spread and I felt like that word they used in the novels . . . wanton. The lights were on and Jackson was watching my reaction to his touch.

"Are you still a virgin, China?" he asked, his fingers sliding between my folds.

Words were beyond me. My heart was racing and my mouth was utterly dry. I could only nod.

"But you've done this, haven't you? Touched yourself? Made yourself come?" His fingers moved deeper, stroking me, barely brushing the little bit that ached the most.

A whimper escaped me, something between a sound of pleasure and a request for more.

"Did you know that if a man takes off a woman's clothes and finds her with matching lingerie, the saying goes that *he* wasn't the one to decide they'd be having sex?"

That startled a huff of laughter from me, which quickly melted into please-may-I-have-some-more sounds when he slid a finger inside me. My eyes slammed shut.

"Is this what you wanted?" he asked.

I pried my eyelids open. Jackson's eyes were darker than I'd ever seen them, a look of intense concentration on his face, as though he were memorizing everything. His gaze lowered from my face down my chest and stomach to where his hand was moving under silk and lace. The Adam's apple in his throat bobbed as he swallowed.

"What is this, Twenty Questions?" I managed to ask in between my moans.

He didn't answer. Instead, his finger moved faster, sliding in and out of me. Each time, brushing that spot that was making me fast lose any semblance of control or dignity. I wanted to touch him, but he was beyond my reach. Raising my hands over my head, I clutched at the couch, digging my fingers into the leather.

I bit my lip to try to quiet my moans, which seemed a little loud, and squeezed my eyes shut.

"God, you are so beautiful, so passionate," he murmured. "I knew you'd be like this."

Reaching for whatever part of him I could find, I tugged on a fistful of his shirt, bringing him close enough to kiss me. He got the hint, his tongue plunging inside my mouth with the same desperation I felt.

Adding a second finger to the first, he spread my legs wider. I gripped the back of his head, holding him tight as we kissed. His mouth swallowed my moans when his fingers moved faster and harder. I could feel my orgasm hovering close, and apparently so could he because he was making sounds, too, his lips pressing hard against mine.

Jackson getting more turned on in direct reaction to my arousal was an intoxicating thing. Nothing spoke to that sexual part of me more than being seen as sexy and desirable in my most vulnerable state. It was a fire that fed on itself. The more passion overcame me, the more Jackson desired me, which made it even easier to give myself over to the heat between us and rushing through my veins.

Stars exploded behind my eyes and I made a noise somewhere between a scream and moan. My fingers dug into Jackson's shoulder, wanting more, even though my body was too sensitive to handle it. I could feel the spasms inside clutching his fingers, an altogether new sensation, and an amazing one. His thrusts slowed to a slow stroking that prolonged the spasms until tears leaked from my eyes and I had to tear my mouth from his just so I could suck in air.

Jackson's mouth moved to my neck, kissing the spot underneath my jaw where my pulse beat wildly. My skin was so sensitive, it sent a shiver through me.

"You are incredible," he murmured in my ear, causing my lips to curve in a tired smile.

"I could say the same to you," I replied. I'd never felt this way before, so sated, yet I wanted more. I wanted *him*.

I reached for his belt, tugging on it. My hand brushed his erection and he moaned. The sound was intoxicating. *I'd* made him do that. I paused working on his belt to stroke him through the fabric of his slacks and he moaned again, his lips seeking mine with an urgency that was deeply satisfying. He wanted me. Just as much as I wanted him.

A sharp, loud rap on the door to the room made me yelp. In a second, I'd pulled my knees to my chest and was scrambling to find my clothes. Jackson was already hissing curses under his breath, which I heartily agreed with.

"Here," he said, tossing a blanket over me as I struggled to turn my T-shirt right side out. I hurriedly pulled the blanket up to my neck, making sure all my extremities were covered as he went to the door. Though he only opened it a few inches, I could see Lance standing beyond.

"I'm very sorry to interrupt, sir," he said. "But two FBI agents are at the door, asking for you."

*Oh crap.*

"Did they say what they wanted?" Jackson asked.

"I believe they're looking for your guest."

Upgrade that *Oh crap* to *Oh shit.*

"All right. Tell them I'll be with them momentarily." He shut the door and turned back to me.

I threw off the blanket and scrambled into my clothes. "The FBI?" I asked, yanking the T-shirt over my head and stuffing my legs into my jeans. "They're going to arrest me, aren't they?"

"We don't know that," Jackson said. "But it doesn't matter anyway. I'm not going to tell them you're here."

I stopped in the middle of dragging on my long-sleeved shirt. "You can't lie, Jackson. Not to the FBI. You could go to jail for that."

"I don't plan on going to jail," he replied, stepping over to me. Reaching under my collar, he lifted my hair free. "And neither are you."

"The software is missing and I'm the prime suspect," I said. "If I don't find out who has it, they'll pin it on me. I'll go to prison for the rest of my life."

"*You* won't find out who has it," he said. "*We* will. I can help you. And the first person I'm going to ask is your mysterious neighbor."

Alarm shot through me. "No, Jackson. Stay away from him. Promise me." Clark was a dangerous guy and I didn't want Jackson within a hundred yards of him. Clark already suspected Jackson of doing something illegal. Jackson showing up on Clark's doorstep, demanding answers, was a recipe for disaster.

He frowned. "When I come back, we're going to discuss your neighbor and what exactly he told you. Until then, stay here."

I opened my mouth to argue, but then he was kissing me. One of those deep, mind-wiping kisses that melted my bones.

"I'm glad he knocked when he did," Jackson murmured against my lips. "I don't want our first time—your first time—to be rushed on a couch. I want you in my bed."

Another shiver went down my spine, his whispered words conjuring images in my head of our naked bodies entwined, sweat-slicked skin, gasps and moans of pleasure . . .

He stepped away, the clicking of the door abruptly ending my fantasy, and my eyes flew open. Damn it anyway. He was going to go out there and lie for me, putting himself and his business at risk. I couldn't prevent him from doing that . . . but I could leave. Jackson had too much to lose to risk it all for me. Besides, I had my own idea as to who had stolen that software.

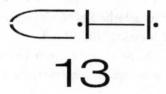

# CH

# 13

Slipping on my glasses, I exited the room, turning right toward the back of the house rather than left. As I'd hoped, there was a door leading out onto an expansive deck. To my right, catty-corner, was a small bungalow, which is where I headed.

The front door was unlocked—Lance should know better—and I went inside. Walking through the almost too-tidy house, I found what I hoped was the door to the garage. Keys were sitting on a small entry table and I snatched them up.

"Sorry, Lance," I murmured. "I'm just borrowing."

Lance owned a silver Lexus. Huh. Jackson must pay well. I slid inside, admiring the black leather. Very nice.

Ten minutes later, I was on the highway, heading home. I had a stop to make along the way, though, because the last thing I wanted was someone finding Mia and using her as leverage against me, just as Clark had threatened.

The part of my brain not trying to figure out my next step was busy reliving the last hour with Jackson. I couldn't believe we'd actually made out on his couch, that he'd *wanted* to make out with me. God, he was an incredible kisser . . .

I was lost in memories for a moment, a blissful state that lasted until I began wondering *why* he'd been kissing me. I'd wanted to distract him at first, but it ended with him distracting me. Because now that I thought about it, he never had answered my question about what he was doing writing software for Vigilance. He'd only said he had no intention of going to jail.

An ick feeling spread through my stomach. I hoped Jackson hadn't been using me, too, the way Clark had. I didn't think I could handle that.

I pulled into Mia's school half an hour after I left Jackson's. It took another ten minutes to find the right office and get Mia. She began peppering me with questions the minute she saw me.

"Why are you taking me out of school early? Aren't you supposed to be at work? Is it my dad? Did he fly down here to take me home or something?"

I didn't reply as we walked through the parking lot, half my attention listening to her, the other half scanning the parking lot for anything unusual.

"Where's your car?" We'd stopped at Lance's car.

"I had to borrow this one," I said. "Get in."

Mia seemed to sense my anxiety and tension, because she took a good long look at me and stopped asking questions.

We were halfway to my destination before I figured out what to tell her . . . and what not to tell her. I took a breath.

"Mia, I'm in some trouble," I said, "and I need you to just listen, okay?"

"Okay." She was serious, her blue eyes solemn as she looked at me. I glanced back at the road.

"It's my job. They . . . suspect that I've done something wrong. Something against the law."

"You would never—" she burst out.

"I know," I interrupted. "But I have to find out who did. Unfortunately, the people who think I did it . . . they're looking for me. And I don't want them to find you while I'm working to clear my name. So . . . I need you to stay with a friend of mine. Just for a while."

"A friend?" she asked. "Who is she?"

"Um . . . it's not really a she."

"Please, Yash," I hissed. "It's just for a few days."

He didn't stop pacing. "You want to leave a teenager . . . a *girl* . . . in my apartment? Overnight? Are you out of your mind?"

"I'll owe you one," I cajoled. I wished Bonnie had been home, but she was in class and hadn't answered my call, which wasn't unusual when she was in the middle of one of her four-hour culinary classes.

He stopped in his tracks, staring in horror through the closed French doors to where Mia was checking out the kitchen. "Oh my God! She's touching my things!"

"She's looking in the refrigerator, Yash," I said, impatient. "It's lunchtime. She's probably hungry."

"What am I going to do with her?"

"Nothing," I said. "Just . . . feed her, park her in front of the TV—it doesn't matter. She's not a toddler. It isn't as though you need to entertain her. I'll be back as soon as I can."

"But . . . people don't stay here," he fretted. "*I* stay here, but not people." Yash was literally wringing his hands.

"Buck up, Yash. It'll be fine."

"I have a teleconference in half an hour. Do you think she'll be quiet for that?"

"She's not a dog either," I harrumphed. "If you ask her to be quiet, she will. Did you get into the phone I left with you?"

"Of course I did," he said, waving a hand impatiently at me while he watched Mia take a container from the fridge and open it. "I left you a voice mail, didn't you get it? It's over on my desk. The security has been removed and I modified the GPS to transmit at a random spot about ten miles away, so it's safe to turn on."

I left Yash anxiously watching Mia's every move and retrieved the phone. I read through the latest text messages that had come in before Freyda's murder. George, John, and Lana had all texted via a group chat regarding the software and who had checked their files in, per the decision I'd made earlier that day.

Then there was some discussion about the project and their safety. Freyda had told them she'd talk things over with me and get back to them. There were a few messages after that, but nothing more from Freyda.

I scrolled through her messages and contacts, especially those from the last few days, pausing on one with just the initials PCOS. The texts from PCOS were much more cryptic and there were only a few.

*Status?*

Freyda had replied, *Nearly finished. I'm seeing to it.*

*Remember the nondisclosure.*

And that was it. Not exactly a red flag, but enough to warrant more information. I hesitated, then typed, *What's in the nondisclosure?* and waited. It didn't take long for a response.

*You're brave, using a dead woman's phone.*

Shit. They knew. Of course they knew. But that still didn't stop the chill that went down my spine. *Why would you kill her?*

*Who said I did?*

I stared at the screen. They texted again.

*I want the software. And I know who you are . . . China.*

My whole body broke out in a cold sweat. *I don't have the software,* I texted, deciding to ignore confirming or denying who they thought I was.

*It's dangerous to lie.*

*Is that a threat?*

*It's a fact. Deliver the software. We're prepared to go to extreme lengths to obtain it.*

*Who's 'we'?* I texted.

Silence.

*I'll be in touch* . . . I hit Send. Okay, so the people who'd resurrected Vigilance—the mysterious government agency Freyda had been on the verge of telling me about—didn't have it. Whoever had stolen it didn't work for them. Which meant whoever had stolen the software was another party entirely and I had no idea who that might be.

The only clue I had was that the person had used Freyda's log in. Very few people would have access to that information. And at the top of my list was John—who hadn't gone into work today.

"Any way you could find out who this is?" I asked, showing Yash the entry for PCOS. He paid me no attention. "Hey. Yash." I waved the phone in front of his face to finally get his attention. "Can you find out who this is?"

"Hm? What? Oh. Oh, yes. I suppose." He took it from me. "She's eating my leftover spaghetti Bolognese."

"That means she likes your cooking," I said. "I've gotta go. I'll call you." Opening the doors, I saw Mia slurping up some noodles.

"Hope it's okay," she said around a mouthful. "There was lots and I'm starving."

"Yash said it's fine," I lied. "Listen, I'll be back, okay? Just stay here—don't go home and don't go back to school—until I come for you."

"You're really worrying me," she said. "Is there anything I can do to help?"

"Don't worry about me," I said, giving her a quick hug. "Just stay here. That's what you can do to help."

The concern in her eyes echoed inside my gut, but I had to leave. Hiding my head under a rock was only going to get it chopped off sooner.

It took me longer than it should've to find where John lived. It was midafternoon by the time I pulled up to the ranch house in a nice suburb of Raleigh. It wasn't exactly the bachelor pad I'd envisioned.

A two-story colonial, its front yard was well tended with a huge oak tree taking up most of the space. The houses here were relatively close together with the plots extending behind them into lush backyards.

I drove by at first, to see if I noticed anything out of the ordinary, but from the outside it appeared as though no one was home. Still leery, I parked on the street rather than in the driveway. Images of Tom's widow, crying in their home, and Freyda, dead in the front seat of my car, crowded inside my head. And then there was Terry, victim of a supposed car accident. If John was involved, he wasn't going to just confess to me and come quietly to the police. But if he *wasn't* involved, chances were good he was a target and needed to be warned.

I took a deep breath and got out of the car. My name needed to be cleared. I was betting that one of the members of the team had stolen Vigilance. John had argued hard to shut down the project and go public. I wouldn't put it past him to steal the software and destroy the backups himself to make sure that happened. And if he had, then odds were he was already gone from here.

Maybe I could hack into his system and find out more. If he was innocent—which I highly doubted—then I had nothing to worry about and maybe he could help me figure out who *had* used Freyda's credentials to steal the program.

Making my way to the front door, I rang the bell and waited. A minute went by. Nothing happened. I tried again, waiting another minute or two, but still no one came. I peered through the window next to the door, focusing my gaze past the gauzy translucent curtain.

The foyer was hardwood and held only a small table on which sat a stack of mail. Beyond the foyer, I saw a set of stairs leading up, and what was perhaps the kitchen past that. Then my gaze went no farther because there, lying on the floor, I could see a pair of legs. They weren't moving.

Jerking backward, I reached for my cell phone, only to realize it wasn't there. A cold rush of adrenaline poured through me. Was it John? Was he dead? What if he needed help?

I hurried from the front to the back of the house, knowing it would be far easier to break inside farther away from prying eyes. I knew CPR and rudimentary first aid—courtesy of living forty-five minutes away from the nearest hospital growing up. I might be able to help John.

A decorative stone wall provided a big enough rock to sail through the glass sliding doors. I winced at the cacophony of noise, then wrapped my hand inside my shirt so I could reach in and unlock the door.

The fact that the body on the floor hadn't moved when I'd broken the glass wasn't a good sign and I was right. I skidded to a halt in the middle of the kitchen linoleum, bile rising in my throat. Whoever was killing the team no longer felt it necessary to make the deaths look like an accident.

John lay in a pool of blood, eyes open, with half the back of his head splattered against the wall. I closed my eyes and took a breath, but it was no use. I ran for the sink and threw up.

Tears stung my eyes as I heaved. I wanted to lash out, rail at the world, at *someone*, for the deaths of these people. Horror stalked me and I had no idea who was doing this. But I was done trying to do this alone. It was time to call the police and let the chips fall where they would. Maybe they could at least protect me, Lana, and George. We were all that was left.

*And Jackson.*

The scuff of a shoe behind me made me scream as I whirled around, for a split second terrified I'd find John had risen as a zombie about to attack me. But John was still dead on the floor . . . and Clark stood over him, his eyes on me.

I stood frozen in shock, unable to believe what I was seeing. Clark? Here?

It took longer than it should've for me to put two and two together—yes, I'm supposedly supersmart—and when it did click in my head, the instinct for survival kicked in hard. He was the one killing people and he'd played me.

Snatching a steak knife from the butcher block at my elbow, I held it out in front of me.

"Stay back, Clark," I warned.

"What are you doing, China?" he asked, remarkably calm for someone who'd just killed a man in cold blood. "Put that down before you hurt yourself."

I flipped the knife so I was holding the blade rather than the hilt, then I flung it. As I'd intended, it landed in the wall behind Clark, approximately two inches to the side of his head. I snatched another knife from the block. They weren't weighted properly, but I could make do.

"Holy shit, China!" he exploded. "You could've killed me. What the hell?"

"Don't try to tell me you're not behind this," I retorted. "You know too much. Too conveniently calling me when Freyda was shot. Now you're here."

"I didn't kill John," he said, "and I didn't kill Freyda."

"I have absolutely no reason to believe you."

His eyes narrowed. "Then answer me this: why are you still alive? I could've killed you several times over by now."

Sirens screamed in the distance and I realized I was in a bad position. What if Clark pointed the finger at me for John's murder? I was holding him at knifepoint. And who was going to warn Lana and George?

I edged toward the entryway, careful to keep him in my sight. "Don't follow me," I warned. "Or next time, I won't miss."

The door was at my back and I reached behind me, closing my hand on the knob. Clark was watching me.

"Don't leave, China," he said. "Please. I can help you. Protect you. I don't want your body to be the next one I find."

That was a sobering thought, but I shook my head. "I'll take my chances."

I twisted the knob and jerked open the door, having to turn my back on Clark.

"Wait!" he called. I glanced back. He was pointing a gun at me. "You can't leave, China."

I swallowed. The gun looked very serious and that old saying went through my head, the one about bringing a knife to a gunfight.

"I'm not staying," I said. "If you don't want me to leave, you'll have to shoot me." A gamble, yes. But he had a point—he hadn't killed me yet and he'd had ample opportunity. So for whatever reason that he hadn't, I was hoping it was enough to keep me alive a while longer.

Our eyes were locked and I took a deep breath, my heart racing and my palms sweaty. I hoped that if he did shoot, he wouldn't miss. Gunshot wounds didn't exactly feel like butterfly kisses.

But he didn't shoot, and after a tense moment of our Mexican standoff, I sprinted out the door and across the street to Lance's car. Turning my back on a loaded gun was the hardest thing I'd ever done. Every instinct in me resisted it, but the fight or flight response was full force and I ran like a horde of demons was after me.

I saw Clark in the rearview mirror watching me before I disappeared down the road. Clark knew a lot more about this than he was telling me. I didn't want to think that he'd killed John. Or that he might kill me . . . eventually.

Lana lived twenty minutes away from John but it was thirty with traffic. I was shocked I didn't get in a car wreck, as jittery as I was. Plus, I hadn't eaten since breakfast and what little had been in my stomach was now in John's sink. My blood sugar was low and the adrenaline had sapped me.

I distracted myself by admiring my knife-throwing skills. My father had insisted I do some kind of outdoor sport when I was young and since I had twisted an ankle playing basketball, got a concussion playing soccer, and had nearly suffocated from an asthma attack playing baseball, I'd asked for self-defense lessons. Learning how to throw knives had made me feel badass, even as the shortest kid in my grade. I never thought it was a skill I'd actually use, though.

Lana had given me her address and garage code, and I clutched the knife I'd taken from John's as I entered her house. I was terrified I'd find someone waiting to kill me—kill her—and I could barely hear as I crept through her kitchen from the garage, the blood was pounding in my ears so loudly.

My palms grew sweaty and I switched the knife from one hand to the other so I could wipe them on my jeans. I could hear no one and the house felt empty, but I didn't trust it. Why would Lana be spared when John, Terry, and Freyda hadn't been?

It took me an hour to search every cranny of Lana's house, stepping slowly and silently around each corner, but I found no one. I was peeking behind a shower curtain when something touching my legs made me scream. (I was getting so good at screaming, I'd have to apply for a role in a horror movie soon.) But it was just a cat, blinking calmly as it looked up at me before winding around and through my legs.

"It's just a cat," I muttered, hearing how out of breath I was from panic alone. If I didn't calm down, I'd hyperventilate myself into blacking out, which would really suck.

I went upstairs and was drawn to the room Lana must use as an office. A laptop sat on the desk, screensaver scrolling across the monitor. I stood looking at it. Trying to get on would be violating Lana's privacy. Then again, these were extenuating circumstances.

And no one was here to ambush Lana. Hmmm.

That fact alone drew me closer until I sat down in the leather office chair. Toggling the mouse made the screensaver disappear and a log-in dialogue box appear.

I had nothing with me to attempt a hack. None of my usual tools that I could use to bypass the security, or even just pull the hard drive and access it via another device. All I had . . . was Clark's tiny USB drive he'd given me to plug into Jackson's system.

Digging it out of my pocket, I stared at it. I didn't know if plugging it in would be a good thing . . . or if it would lead the bad guys right to me.

The image of Clark, staring after me as I ran from John's house, flashed through my mind. I had no reason to trust him, no logical reason, and yet . . .

I plugged in the USB drive.

Nothing happened for a moment, then the screen flickered. Just slightly, and if I hadn't been watching so close, I wouldn't have noticed. Whatever "they," i.e., Clark et al., wanted to accomplish with Jackson, was now going to be with Lana instead.

The cat was wrapping itself around my ankles again when I heard a footfall on the wooden stairs.

I jumped to my feet, guilty as a teenager sucking vodka from their dad's stash on a Saturday night. Could I be in a worse place than in her office? But it wasn't Lana that came around the corner.

"Jackson!"

Emotion and relief overcame logic. I threw myself at him, clutching him as he caught me up in his arms.

"Thank God," he murmured in my ear, holding me so tight it was hard to breathe, but I didn't mind. "You scared a decade off my life, leaving like that."

I was trying so hard not to cry that I couldn't talk, and it took a massive amount of effort to get control of myself. When I could finally breathe again, I tipped my head back to look at him and opened my mouth to speak.

But he was kissing me, his mouth hard and urgent, his tongue stroking mine with fevered intensity. I was overwhelmed. I could do nothing but hold on to him, standing on my very tiptoes as he kissed me. One hand in my hair, the other wrapped around my back. I felt safe for the first time all day.

When he let me come up for air, I pried my eyes open, finding his dark gaze blazing as he looked at me. My limbs felt boneless, and I wasn't sure I wouldn't have crumpled in a heap if he hadn't been holding me.

"Umm . . . hi," I managed.

His lips twisted. "Hi." Then they flatlined.

We spoke at the same time.

"What the fuck are you doing here?"

"How did you find me?"

I flinched at the barely leashed anger in his voice. "Lana told me to come here, plus I was worried she would be next." I repeated my question. "How'd you find me?"

"Process of elimination," he said. "And I assumed you'd try to do something stupid and altruistic like try to protect the remaining members of the team."

I pouted a bit at *stupid*. "Some would say it was heroic," I argued just under my breath.

He gave me a look. "Lance's car is also LoJacked."

Figured. Here he was trying to make me think he knew me oh so well when it was the damn car that had led him straight to me. Whatever. "Stupid or not, someone is killing everyone who worked on Vigilance."

"You realize that includes you," he shot back.

The lump in my throat grew like the Grinch's heart inside that little measuring device, until speech was impossible. To my dismay, Jackson blurred in my vision. I blinked rapidly, trying to clear things.

I heard him mutter a curse, then he dragged me into his arms again. His lips pressed the top of my head, against my hair. My body gradually relaxed and I was able to regain my composure. I'd cried more in the past week than I had since Rose was trapped forever in that alternate universe apart from the Doctor. Or when they'd cancelled *Firefly*.

"Are you all right?" he asked.

I nodded. "It's been a long week," I managed, reluctantly extricating myself from his embrace.

He was scrutinizing me and I glanced away. I wasn't a weak person—you didn't get to where I was, doing what I did, by being weak—and I didn't want Jackson to view me as incapable of handling whatever was thrown my way. My nervous breakdown could wait until later.

"I have to tell you about Clark," I said. "You're right, he's not who he says he is. When I confronted him, he told me he was ex-military intelligence. That he contracts out to the CIA now for human intel."

"He told you this?"

I nodded. "He's particularly interested in you and what you're doing."

"That's . . . not good, China," Jackson said. His expression was grave, alarming me.

I frowned. "Why not? The CIA, those are the good guys. And if they're watching you, it doesn't matter. You've done nothing wrong, right?" He didn't answer, his eyes on mine. "Right?"

The slamming of a door downstairs made us both turn in reaction. Oh God. Had they come for Lana?

Jackson must have thought the same thing because he gripped my arm and hauled me close, looking frantically around the room. He spied a closet door and dragged us inside, closing the door softly behind us.

It was cramped and we were pressed close together, back to front. His arm was around my midriff, holding me tight. If it were any other kind of circumstance, I might have enjoyed it. As it was, though, I was terrified, especially when I heard two men talking.

"Is she here?" one asked.

"Not yet," was the response.

"Thought she was supposed to be here by now?"

"Well, she isn't. So what do you want to do?"

They were close, right outside the room, and they were here to kill Lana. If they found Jackson and me, I had little doubt they'd kill us, too.

It was hard to breathe, the darkness felt stifling. Moving my hand, I held on to Jackson's in a death grip. His hand felt strong and dry covering mine. I closed my eyes and focused on breathing. Passing out from terror would be a really embarrassing way to go.

"I'll wait here, you go on ahead. That way we don't lose any time."

"You sure?"

"Yes. I'll call you when I'm done."

"All right."

I strained my ears, listening. I could hear footfalls on the stairs, growing more distant, but I couldn't tell if it was one set or two.

"Don't move." Jackson's whisper was barely audible and his lips were right by my ear. I gave the tiniest of nods so he knew I understood.

Honestly, did he think I was going to launch myself out of the closet and yell "Surprise!"?

But it was a good thing I didn't because I heard something from inside the room. Someone was still here, and they were moving around.

Jackson repositioned us, silently moving me to the side. When he withdrew his arm from around me, I panicked, latching on. Was he going to try to confront the man?

"It's okay," he whispered in my ear. I frantically shook my head *no*. He squeezed my hand, then pried it from his arm. "Trust me."

I bit the inside of my lip so hard, I tasted the tang of blood. I felt, more than heard, him take a deep breath, then he opened the door.

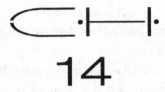

# 14

In the movies, the good guys burst through closed doors in a flash of noise and overwhelm the bad guys. But Jackson didn't do that. He opened the door in a slow, steady way that was nearly silent.

Peeking between his body and the doorway, I saw a man sitting at the desk. As the door opened, he glanced around curiously. But by that time, Jackson was nearly upon him and he had no time to react.

The crunch of bone against bone made me wince when Jackson's fist met the guy's jaw. He'd been reaching for the gun in his side holster, but Jackson grabbed his wrist and bent it backward. The guy yelled as the bone snapped. Another punch from Jackson and the guy slid to the floor. He didn't move.

Holy shit. I'd never seen Jackson do anything like that before, and I wasn't going to lie . . . it was pretty darn hot (as Mia would say).

"I had no clue you could do that," I said.

"Being bullied as a kid means you learn how to fight," Jackson replied. He bent down and took the gun from the man's holster. Searching his pockets, he retrieved a cell phone as well.

"*You* were bullied?"

He glanced at me, frowning. "Of course I was. You told me you were, too."

"Well, yeah, I just . . . hadn't thought of you as being someone who was bullied."

"I was little for my age, smarter than everyone else, and poor. What do you think?"

An image flashed in my head of a scrawny boy in hand-me-down clothes carrying a stack of books, then being knocked down by a crowd of bigger kids. It struck a pang of sympathy in me, and was so unlike what I'd imagined Jackson to be as a kid. Not that I'd spent a lot of time wondering about that, but if I had, it wouldn't have been as a skinny, poor, picked-on kid.

"So you learned to fight?" I asked.

"Absolutely." He glanced up from where he was scrolling through the phone. "Didn't you?"

"I learned how to throw knives."

A sudden grin split his face. "That's badass. Love it. Did it help?"

"Did it for the school's talent contest. No one bothered me much after that." One of my few good memories from school. The auditorium had gone absolutely silent when I'd thrown five knives at a human silhouette target, hitting the center of the head, the chest, each hand, and the last one landing right in the groin.

"What are we going to do with him?" I asked. The guy was still out cold.

"Grab his feet."

Between the two of us we managed to get him into the closet, not being particularly careful about how many of his body parts we knocked against the door frame and wall. Jackson lodged a chair underneath the door handle, locking him in.

"Let's go," he said.

We were nearly to the front door when it swung open and Lana stepped inside.

"Thank God," I breathed. My heart couldn't take much more of this. For a split second, I'd thought it might be that guy coming back to check on his buddy.

Lana looked shocked to see us. "What are you doing here?"

Okay. Weird question. "You told me to come here," I reminded her. "I went to John's first, but they'd already killed him. I was afraid you were next."

"And you would've been," Jackson said. "The man they sent is locked in your office closet."

"Locked in my closet," she repeated, still looking stunned. "Wh-what are we supposed to do with him?"

"You should probably call nine one one," I suggested.

"Yeah." She looked dazed, but obediently dug her cell phone out of her pocket. Dialing, she walked into the living room.

"So what do we do now?" I asked Jackson. "Someone still has that software and the cops think I did it."

"We'll hide you until I can figure out who took it," he said.

"The cops are going to be watching your house."

His lips twisted. "True. But they won't be watching the cabin I have outside the city."

"Cabin?"

He nodded. "Got sick of the paparazzi constantly knowing where I lived and driving by, taking photos whenever I'd leave or bring a . . . companion . . . back to the house."

And by *companion* I knew he meant a woman to spend the night. Part of me was instantly and insanely jealous of all of the nameless, faceless women Jackson had been with. Which in and of itself was *crazy*.

We weren't an "item." He was my boss. Although we had really good chemistry, at least from my point of view, and judging by that little scene at his house earlier. I hadn't imagined the passion between us.

I stamped down on my rabid-girlfriend/stalker feelings and tried to focus. "No one knows where it is?"

"Nope. I bought it under Lance's name. I don't get there as often as I wish. Maybe someday."

Lana walked back in before I could reply. "I've called them. They're on their way. Did you find out who'd stolen the software?"

"I was sure it was John," I said, "until they killed him. Which leaves George." It was so unexpected. He was of an earlier generation where loyalty to your employer was paramount.

"Do you have access to the system?" Jackson asked her. She nodded. "Let me get on. I might be able to trace who touched the files, regardless of log-on ID."

"Okay, follow me."

I watched Jackson and Lana head back upstairs, then noticed he'd left his phone on the table. Just as I picked it up to take to him, it rang. Without thinking, I answered.

"Jackson Cooper's phone."

There was a pause. "China, is that you?'

Wow. *Really* weird. "Um, yeah. Who is this?"

"Don't hang up," the man said, which was never a good sign. "It's Clark."

"Asshat."

"Excuse me?"

"Sorry. My pet name for you. What do you want and why are you calling Jackson's phone?"

"You planted that USB drive, didn't you?" he asked.

"Yeah, but not on Jackson's system," I said. "It's on Lana's. She works for Wyndemere."

"No. No, she doesn't. She's a sleeper agent. She works for ISIS."

I stared straight ahead, unseeing, my mouth agape. "Wh-what?"

"The program uploaded to her system and started sending us information right away," he said. "She's the one who stole the software from Wyndemere. Now she's covering her tracks."

My head tried to catch up with what I was hearing. Lana was an ISIS sleeper agent? But . . . why?

"I don't understand," I said. "How does this software help ISIS?"

"You said it yourself," Clark replied. "It's the perfect targeting software, collecting all that data. All it needs is an algorithm. With the right one, it's the perfect recruiting tool. Their recruiting has increasingly come from social media: Twitter, Facebook, Pinterest, Tumblr, YouTube, you name it. If they were able to pinpoint specific people who would be vulnerable to their message, they could increase their members by astronomical numbers."

I could follow Clark's logic, but still couldn't reconcile Lana as being an ISIS agent, "But . . . she's a woman," I said at last. "ISIS hates women, treats them like chattel."

"Which is why they're the best to use," he said grimly. "No one suspects them."

Suddenly I realized . . . Jackson was upstairs with Lana. Alone. Panic flooded me.

"Oh my God," I breathed into the phone. "You've got to help us. What if she tries to hurt Jackson? Or me?"

Clark said something, but I couldn't hear because just then, the door opened and two men walked in. Both of them average height, dark olive skin, dark hair . . . and each holding a semiautomatic weapon.

I opened my mouth to scream, but one of them was on me in an instant.

"Don't even try it, bitch," he hissed.

"China? What's going on?" I could hear Clark in my ear, but couldn't respond. My eyes were glued to the gunman's. Dark and empty, his gaze sent a chill down my spine. And there was also the cold press of the gun's barrel to my forehead.

I didn't protest when he took the phone from me, dropping it to the floor before stomping his huge booted foot down on it. The glass and plastic shattered into a million pieces.

"She said they were upstairs," he told the other guy, dragging me to a kitchen chair and forcing me to sit. "Go get them."

Jackson. They were going to kill him. And he had no warning. And they were going to kill me anyway . . .

I screamed.

Blinding pain hit me as the butt of the gun hit my temple.

My head was going to fall off. Surely. There could be no other recourse for the massive ache that made me long to be unconscious again. Though perhaps I should be grateful I was waking up at all.

I pried my eyes open, my brain beginning to catalogue my surroundings and situation before my emotions could catch up.

I was somewhere dark and cold, and I could barely feel my fingers, though that wasn't entirely because of the cold. My wrists were tied behind my back, likely with a zip tie if the pain cutting into my skin was any indication. The ground beneath me was concrete, as was the wall at my back.

A noise caused me to jump, and light flooded the room. Someone had opened a door and the sudden brightness blinded me. I barely had time to see the silhouette framed in the open rectangle before another person was shoved into the room. They stumbled and fell, the air whooshing from their lungs as they hit the floor. Their hands were tied, too, and I winced as their arm and ribs caught the brunt of the fall. Then the door slammed shut again.

I was frozen for a moment, unsure who was in here with me, then I heard a slight groan.

"Jackson?" I whispered. "Is that you?"

"Who else?" he rasped, grunting slightly.

I had to get out of the zip tie. Part of me was amazed that they'd actually used something so ridiculous to secure me. Everyone knew how to get out of a zip tie. Maybe they thought I wouldn't know because I was a girl or something. Idiots.

Bending my knees, I swung my arms under my feet, moving them so my hands were in front of me. Using my teeth, I adjusted the zip tie so the little square fastener was right in between my wrists before getting to my feet. I settled my elbows on my hips, took a deep breath, and flung my arms down and apart with all my strength, using my hips for leverage. The plastic bit into my skin, stinging me, but the tie broke and I was free.

Easy peasy.

I hurried to Jackson, my eyes adjusting to the darkness. Ambient light was coming from somewhere, enough for me to see that he wasn't bound with zip ties, but with a thin nylon rope that wound around his wrists at least a half a dozen times. No way was he going to be able to do what I had done with the zip tie.

He sat up with some effort and that's when I saw his shirt was dirty and torn. Grimacing, he worked his jaw for a minute, which was when I noticed the blood on his face.

"Jackson, what happened to you?" Putting a hand on his cheek, I gently turned him so I could see his face better. There was a cut by his eye, and his lip was split and bleeding. It was too dark to see bruises, though, and I didn't know if that was a good or bad thing. My stomach churned at the thought.

"Let's just say I didn't come quietly," he replied. "Especially when I heard you scream."

I swallowed. "What happened?"

"Lana didn't even react," he said, "which was when I knew. Those men hadn't been there to kill her. They were *working* for her, with her, whatever—not trying to kill her. In hindsight, I should've been more suspicious of her."

"You're being too hard on yourself," I said. "She had me fooled, too." My personal animosity toward John had gotten in the way of logically considering *all* members of the team.

"Are you all right?" he asked. "Did they hurt you?"

I shook my head, glancing away. "Not really." Which was an understatement. My head was pounding like someone had set up a jackhammer behind my eyes that was intent on drilling through my forehead.

"You're lying," he said flatly.

Damn. I really needed to play poker more. "Did you see outside?" I asked, changing the subject. "Where are we?" It was too big of a space to be Lana's basement, and it had an industrial feel to it.

"I don't know. They blindfolded me for the ride here."

"What do they want? Why didn't they kill us?" Not that I wasn't grateful to still be alive. "They have the software, but the algorithm hasn't been written yet," I said. "Do you think they'll want us to write it for them?"

He said nothing.

"Jackson?"

"It's written, China," he said, finally looking at me. "I wrote it."

My heart sank. "But . . . why? And why didn't you tell me?"

"I was compelled to do the coding . . . by someone very powerful. I couldn't say no."

"Who compelled you?"

"The president."

I stared, waiting for the punch line that never came. "You're serious."

"Yeah," he said with a sigh. "I wish I wasn't."

"How?"

"The NSA pulled the plug on Vigilance but the president reinstated the program under a presidential directive, which is a bit like an executive order, but not made public. In the name of national security, he can authorize expenditures, order actions, and more. Tom was supposed to write it, but couldn't. He came to me. Once he told me what they wanted, I refused because I saw what you saw. In the wrong hands, this software would be a powerful weapon. Even in the supposed 'right' hands, it's a vast overreach of domestic spying."

"What happened when you told him?" I asked.

"Tom hadn't realized, but he agreed with me. He refused to provide them with the algorithm, so they killed him. That's when I knew I had no choice but to write it."

My thoughts were spinning. "But . . . they killed people. That's . . . that's incomprehensible. Our own government wouldn't murder its own citizens."

"They would if it means no one will find out about the software," Jackson said, his tone one of dry bitterness. "That's why Tom and Terry died. Tom was a warning and Terry had delivered his part. But they took pains to make both look like an accident. Someone else killed Freyda and John."

"It's Lana and those men," I said. "Clark told me she's an ISIS sleeper agent. I helped him hack her computer and he called and told me what they'd found. She stole the software from Wyndemere for ISIS."

Jackson ground out a curse. "It's exactly what I warned them about. In the wrong hands, it's a powerful weapon."

"We have to get out of here," I said, feeling panic curling in my belly.

"I know."

"They're going to make you give them the algorithm, then they'll kill us."

"China! I know."

His outburst shut me up. He was right. I wasn't telling him anything he didn't already know.

Frowning at me, he asked, "Didn't they tie you up?"

"Yeah, but they used zip ties so, you know." I shrugged, holding up my wrists. "Didn't take long to get out of them."

It looked like he was thinking about smiling for a moment. "You do realize that ninety percent of the population wouldn't know the first thing about how to get out of a zip tie."

I frowned, turning this over inside my head. "Really?"

"Really."

Huh.

"Let me see if I can untie you," I said, moving to get behind him, but he stopped me.

"No."

"No?"

"No. Don't waste time on that. You need to get out of here."

"I'm not leaving without you," I protested. "Don't be ridiculous. Besides, even if I wanted to, I couldn't. We're locked in here."

His eyes slid closed and he winced, as though the desperate nature of our situation was just now hitting him. I crouched down next to him.

"Let me work on the ropes," I said. "Please. It can't hurt."

His eyes shot open. "China, listen to me. You have to understand who these people are. You're a woman, they're extremists. To them, you're less than nothing. The fact that you're still alive isn't a good thing, not if you don't escape."

His words were so intense, his dark eyes burning into mine, that my hands faltered at the ropes.

"Wh-what do you mean?" I asked.

"China, they will rape you," he said. "Probably to death. Or at least until you're begging to die. It's what they do."

My blood turned cold. I stared at him, not wanting to believe it.

"That's why you've got to run," he said. "When they come back—and they will—I'll distract them to give you some time. But you have to run. And don't look back."

I still couldn't speak. It seemed unreal, the horror of all this. How could I just leave Jackson behind?

As though he could read my mind, he said, "Promise me."

My eyes filled and I slowly shook my head. "I can't. I can't just leave you—"

"You'd rather die at their hands? They'll make me watch, you know. Watch as they make you bleed. Is that what you want?"

Tears spilled over. "No," I whispered. "I don't want that. But I don't want you to die."

"I'll think of something," he said. "But you're the first priority. You've got to get away. Then you can send help."

I knew he was placating me, that if I did get away, by the time I found someone to come help him, he'd probably be dead. But I nodded as though I believed him. "Okay."

His body relaxed and his eyes closed again. Leaning forward, he rested his forehead against mine. "That's my girl," he said softly, then pressed a kiss to my skin. His hands combed through my hair.

Wait a second. His hands . . .

My eyes flew open. The ropes were on the ground. "How did you do that?" I asked.

He smiled, tucking my hair behind my ear. "You're not the only one with a few tricks up their sleeve."

For a precious moment, we just touched and looked into each other's eyes. I had so many things I wanted to say . . . but no words formed on my tongue. I was just glad—really glad—that we'd had this time together.

"Don't look at me like that," he said.

I had to swallow before I could speak. "Like what?"

"Like we won't see each other again."

I didn't reply. Things didn't look good and I didn't see any point in lying to each other. Or myself.

"Let's get in position," he said, getting to his feet. Giving me his hand, he helped me up as well. "You stay behind me, and when I distract them, you run."

I nodded, though I felt on the edge of hysterical tears. He squeezed my hand as we took up a spot next to the door.

"Cheer up," he said. "It's Tuesday. Chinese food and DVR catch-up night. If Mia hasn't deleted all your *Castle* episodes to make room for her *Grey's Anatomy* recordings."

Oh God, I was going to bawl, and not just because Mia probably *had* deleted all my *Castle*s.

The door opened and suddenly watching TV was the furthest thing from my mind.

Jackson launched himself at the man who'd opened the door, knocking him aside. There was another guy right behind him and he began pulling at Jackson. In seconds, it was a full-fledged brawl.

"Go!" Jackson yelled.

I backed out the door, flinching when one of the men hit Jackson. His grunt of pain was nearly my undoing. But I couldn't let him do this for nothing. That thought more than anything sent me scurrying backward. Forcing myself to turn, I broke into a run.

I found out fast that I was in the basement of some kind of multistory building. By sheer luck I ran down the corridor and turned the corner right into a staircase. I didn't look behind me as I sprinted up.

A door blocked my path but when I slammed into the crossbar, it opened, thank God, or that would've been a real short trip.

I was in a lobby of sorts, with a long expanse of open space between me and the exit. Crap. I'd seen enough movies to know what happens when you ran into open space. *Blam!* Shot in the back. But it wasn't as though I had any choice either.

Every step felt like a mile and I was sure I had at least a dozen guns trained on the back of my head, but nothing happened. Any moment, I expected to feel the pain of a shot. The exit was just feet away and beyond was the inky darkness of outside. I could just see the faint remnants of twilight clinging to the horizon above the treetops.

"Stop!"

I faltered, my immediate reaction was to do exactly what I was commanded, but I kept going. My hand reached for the door . . .

A shot rang out, shattering the glass right in front of me. I screamed, instinctively covering my face with my arms as I shoved my way through the door.

More shots followed but hitting a moving target was hard, and in another few yards, I was out of range.

I kept running, trying to figure out where I was. The neighborhood didn't look familiar and frankly, I was just glad it was a neighborhood and not out in the middle of the woods somewhere.

It was dark and I had no idea what time it was, but I saw golden arches at the end of the block and everyone knew a Big Mac Attack could be satisfied twenty-four hours a day.

I burst into the McDonald's, not caring that everyone turned to look at me.

Sizing up the nearest customer—a teenage boy with a Panthers hat on—I gasped, "Phone. I need to borrow your phone."

He was holding his cell and just stared at me. Maybe he was inebriated? His thought processes weren't working very fast?

"I don't have time for you to think," I said, snatching the phone from him.

"Hey—!"

"Stop." I held my hand up in front of his face. "Be quiet." I hit the button on the phone and dialed.

*"This is nine one one. What's your emergency?"*

"There's a man being held captive," I said. "In a building close to my location."

*"Where are you?"*

I turned to the kid still staring at me, who looked like he was pouting now. "Where are we?" I asked him.

"Fuckin' McDonald's." He rolled his eyes.

"The *street*," I said. "I know we're in McDonald's. What street is it? And watch your language. Would you kiss your mother with that mouth?"

It was something I loved about the South. Mothers drilled manners into their kids and they did not let them forget it. The boy's cheeks turned pink and I knew he was no exception.

"Rudolph and Fifteenth," he said a bit sullenly. "Ma'am."

"That's better." I repeated the address to the operator, along with directions from the restaurant to the actual building at the end of the block. "Please hurry. There are at least three people there that are armed. I believe they intend to harm him." I hung up before she could ask my name and handed the phone back to the kid.

"Thanks."

I stood by the windows to wait, checking the time every few minutes. It felt like forever by the time the cops drove by, lights flashing and sirens wailing. I hightailed it down the street after them, watching anxiously as they went inside, guns drawn once they saw the bullet-shattered windows.

Expecting them to pull out Lana, Jackson, and the gunmen, dismay filled me as they exited, twenty minutes later, empty-handed.

I hurried over to one of the cops. "Excuse me, but I heard gunshots earlier. What's going on?"

"We had an emergency call, but no one's inside," he said. "They must've taken off before we got here." He headed for one of the patrol cars.

I felt sick. I hadn't gotten help in time. What would they do to Jackson to get him to give them the algorithm?

I didn't know what to do, how else to help him. But then I realized . . . I knew somebody who might.

I rapped sharply on Clark's door, wondering if he was asleep. It was nearing midnight and I prayed he was home.

It hadn't been as hard to get home as it could've been. I'd gone back to that McDonald's and used that same kid's phone to call a cab. The driver had not been happy that I had to go inside my house to get money to pay him, but he hadn't had a choice. Then I'd gone right next door.

I knocked again, not letting up until the door suddenly flew open. Clark stood there, holding a gun. He was wearing jeans . . . and that was all.

"Don't you ever wear a shirt?" I blurted, shoving past him into his apartment. I was so tired, I felt like I could hardly keep on my feet.

One eyebrow rose as he followed me to where I collapsed on his couch. "By all means, come in. And I was in bed. You're lucky I stopped to put on pants or you'd be getting even more of an eyeful."

*Clark slept naked.* I ignored the fact my unhelpful logic provided, instead focusing on what troubled me more than his lack of proper nighttime attire. "So Jackson and I get captured by ISIS agents . . . and you're *sleeping*?"

"I warned you, or tried to. I had no idea what happened after that. Neither your nor Jackson's phones were traceable. Until I heard something from you or saw either of you dead on the news, there was nothing *to* do. So I slept." He shrugged and sat on the chair opposite me. "What would you have had me do?"

I didn't know. What he'd done was . . . logical. But still . . . "I'm glad to know my being in mortal peril didn't keep you from getting your beauty rest."

His lips twisted. "In my line of work, you sleep when you can because you never know when you'll get another chance. Like now. I'm guessing you're not here just to provide me with a recap."

I swallowed and shook my head. "I need your help. They still have Jackson."

"Lana?"

"Yes. I escaped and went for help, but they were gone when we got back. I don't know where they've taken him, but they're going to torture him until he gives them the algorithm he wrote. Then . . . then I think they might kill him."

Clark's eyes narrowed. "He wrote the algorithm?"

I nodded.

He cursed, then scrubbed a hand over his face. "Okay, so we have to stop ISIS from getting the software, which will have the ancillary effect of saving your boss from dying."

I nodded again.

He sighed. "Then I'm glad I got a nap in."

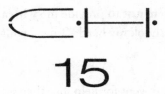

# 15

I raided Clark's fridge while he finished dressing and doing whatever else he was doing. I heard the sound of metal against metal and winced. Looked like he was going armed. I should be, too, but the gun Jackson had given me was still in the glove box of my car, which was sitting in his garage.

And at some point, I should probably give Lance back his car keys.

"So what's our first move?" I asked around a mouthful of the ham sandwich I'd thrown together, extra Miracle Whip. At least he'd had that instead of real mayonnaise. It was so much better on a sandwich.

"I called a friend who works for the CIA," he said, eyeing me as I took another huge bite. "There's been a spike in cell traffic in the area that they're pinpointing, since I told them what to listen for. They nail down the cell phones they're using, track them, we'll get a location. It shouldn't be much longer."

I nodded. "Sounds like a good plan," I mumbled, shoving the rest in my mouth. That sandwich had tasted like Thanksgiving dinner, I'd been so hungry.

"Were you starving?" he asked with a frown. "Because I gotta tell ya, I've never seen a woman scarf down a sandwich that fast."

"I haven't eaten all day!" I protested, looking around for something to drink. A Pepsi sounded really good. Or better yet, a Red Bull. "Can we stop at the gas station for a Red Bull?"

"*We* aren't going anywhere," he said. "I am. You can stay here."

I rolled my eyes. "That's dumb."

"Excuse me?" He actually looked taken aback.

"Which part is surprising?" I asked. "That someone disagrees with you or that I think you're dumb?" I wasn't being a smart-ass, I honestly wanted to know. Clark worked solo and seemed to be fairly competent at a dangerous job, so really it could go either way.

He was silent for a moment. Then, "You're serious."

"Of course."

Clark just shook his head, tucking the very large gun he was holding into a holster underneath his arm, shrugging into a black leather jacket.

"You realize you look like an utter cliché," I said. "The gun, the jacket . . ."

"All your hot-guy fantasies come to life?"

I snorted. "I don't have hot-guy fantasies." Which was *so* not true, but what Clark didn't know wouldn't hurt him. "And I am coming with you, because if Jackson sees you without me, he may not cooperate."

His cell phone buzzed and he glanced at the screen. "Got it. You wanna play hero and put yourself in harm's way, that's your choice. But don't think I'm going to rescue you rather than going after the bad guys."

What a charmer. "It wouldn't be logical for you to behave otherwise," I said with a shrug.

Clark's blue eyes narrowed. "Do I sense sarcasm?"

"I don't do sarcasm."

"Riiiight . . ." he drawled, his expression skeptical. "Whatever. Let's go."

I didn't know where the Honda had gone, but the car we took was a pearl-black Mercedes I instantly fell in love with. I would've inspected it more, but the worry for Jackson I'd shoved in the back of my mind would no longer be ignored, especially now that we were on our way to get him.

What if we were too late?

"You've gotta calm down," Clark said, pulling me from my thoughts. I glanced from the road to him, surprised.

"What?"

"You're about to rub the skin off your hands, doing that," he said, motioning to where I was twisting my hands in my lap. "And your breathing is fast enough to border on hyperventilating. I'm not opposed to leaving you passed out in the car, but I doubt you'd be pleased."

He was right. I was working myself into a state, which was crazy. Worry and anxiety wouldn't help Jackson. I'd done everything I could as fast as humanly possible—fate would determine what happened next. All of which sounded great, but didn't make me feel even a tiny bit better.

"I . . . just don't want him to be hurt," I said, turning to look out my window. I was dangerously close to tears and really didn't want Clark to see me cry.

"Job security? Or is it personal?"

The last thing I felt like doing was talking about my feelings with Clark. "What does it matter?"

"It doesn't. Just curious."

I pushed my glasses back up my nose and cleared my throat. "So where are we going?"

"Looks like they headed for the hills."

Which was actually the woods. We'd gone deep into Carolina back-country when the car finally rolled to a stop nearly an hour later. But there was nothing around us but trees.

"Where are we?" I asked.

"About a quarter mile away," Clark said. "It wasn't like I could just pull up to the front door. There's a reason they're out here."

I chewed a nail, staring into the impenetrable darkness outside my window. "And it's just us against them?"

Clark snorted. "I'm good, but I don't have a death wish. A contract security team should be meeting us." He reached into the backseat and pulled a black backpack into his lap. Digging through it, he unearthed a small radio. Thumbing a button on the side, he said, "Team alpha, in position, over."

After a moment, the radio crackled. "Copy that. Team bravo. ETA is ten mikes."

I frowned. "I know what a klick is. What's a mike?"

"Stands for minutes," he said. "You sure you want to do this?"

My throat was suddenly dry and my palms were wet, but I nodded. "Yeah."

"Okay then."

We got out of the car and he locked it, plunging us into darkness. It was colder than I'd expected and I shivered. My skin crawled at the unrelenting night and my heart rate doubled.

"Take it easy," Clark said. "Put these on." He handed me something heavy and I fumbled with it before he took it from me and settled it on my head. A moment later, goggles slid over my eyes but I still couldn't see.

"Was this supposed to help?" I asked. "It's still dark."

I felt his hand at my temple and a nearly silent click, then I could see.

"Infrared goggles," he said. "Night vision with their own invisible light source."

"That's cool." The panic in my stomach receded. The trees still looked intimidating, but at least now I could see them. "I can see where I'm going."

"That is the point. Follow me, and try not to make noise."

I was glad I had on jeans and tennis shoes because the pine trees grew thick and close together, which kept undergrowth to a minimum, but branches still scraped my arms and legs as I followed Clark. The forest floor was a bed of pine needles, which kept our steps silent.

Cicadas were loud as well as other nighttime creatures that I tried not to listen to. I preferred the darkness of an open field in Nebraska to this claustrophobic canopy of trees.

"Where are we—"

A hand clapped over my mouth, silencing me. Clark's goggle-obscured eyes were inches from my own.

"Quiet." His voice was barely above a whisper. I nodded so he knew I'd understood.

"We're almost there," he said. "The rest of the team will be waiting."

I wondered how many people made up the "rest of the team," but didn't dare ask. He obviously didn't want me to speak.

We kept going, stopping once we saw a clearing in the trees and a building. It wasn't fancy—just a square with windows—but was pretty big. A drive was around the side and three SUVs were parked there. We'd come around from the opposite direction.

Lights gleamed from the windows, bathing the surrounding ground in a slight glow. Clark had crouched down behind a copse of trees and bushes several feet away and I headed toward him.

"Don't move."

A voice in my ear and something cold and sharp at my throat. I froze, fear flooding me.

Clark glanced around and I wanted to warn him, but in the next moment he'd made a hand gesture to the man behind me and I was suddenly released.

"Sorry about that. Didn't know you were a friendly," he said.

I sucked in air, realizing I'd been holding my breath. He came around and I saw he was dressed all in black and outfitted in more heavy artillery than Clark. The same IR goggles we wore adorned his head as well.

Clark beckoned impatiently to me and I bit back the angry retort on my tongue. It would've been nice if they'd known I was coming, too.

"Give me your goggles," he said, sliding his off.

I did as he asked. "Is there anyone else who's going to try to kill me tonight?" I asked, not quite able to let it go.

"Just everyone inside that building."

Well. Okay, then.

I glanced around, my eyes adjusting to the new lighting conditions, and saw that three more silent figures dressed like my attacker had arrived. They didn't say anything as he and Clark conversed quietly. It was military speak about where they were going in, who'd go where and do what, etc.

"The drone overhead is reporting seven heat signatures," one of them said, showing Clark something on a device, maybe a phone or tablet. "We think your guy is in this room, here." He pointed.

"Two guards on the outside, another inside—probably your interrogator. The others are here, here, and here." More pointing.

I tuned them out, the word "interrogator" making panic curl like a fist in my gut again. Jackson was in there. Worry ate at me and I was anxious to go get him.

"You sure you want to come?" Clark asked me.

Startled, I jumped. I hadn't even noticed that he was done planning. "Absolutely."

"Then take this," he said, handing me a pistol. "And try not to shoot any friendlies."

I swallowed, nodding. "Got it."

"Remember—my job is to stop ISIS. This isn't a rescue mission . . . for anyone. If we can get him out, we will, but he's not the primary here."

I looked at him. His expression was serious, his eyes hard. He wasn't the friendly Superman-neighbor and now I wondered how

I'd ever been fooled. Just looking into his eyes sent a chill down my spine.

"You've already said that, and I have an excellent memory." My voice was quiet, and if there was a hint of accusation as well, then I couldn't help it. I'd gotten the message loud and clear. If I didn't get Jackson out, he might not make it out at all.

"Jackson is in the far west corner room," he said. I looked blankly at him. He rolled his eyes. "Over there." He pointed to the other side of the building, toward the back.

"Got it."

"Stay in the back. Stay out of the line of fire. Wait until you hear us call out *Clear*."

"Nice to know you care."

"I don't. I just don't want to have to file the paperwork."

Any quick-witted retort (that I'd think of in about thirty minutes) was lost on him because he'd already turned away and was talking with the other men. They all took a good look at me, sizing me up, I thought. No one looked impressed.

I lifted my chin. I may have been a foot shorter and about a hundred pounds lighter, massively less armed, without any proper training or body armor, no experience in combat . . . where was I going with this? After that depressing litany, I'd forgotten.

The men split into two teams and I followed Clark and the two men with him. The other two headed around back while we went toward the front.

Adrenaline filled my veins in a cold rush and my hand holding the gun was shaking uncontrollably. I held it with both hands now, recognizing the same design as the one Jackson had given me, which was good. And I really hoped I wouldn't have to use it.

The men moved silently, one opening the door, which was unlocked, then filed in. I waited and nearly jumped out of my skin when the bullets started flying.

The noise was unimaginable, worse than in a movie, because this was real and it was right behind me. I prayed the wood at my back was thick enough to stop a bullet. I heard yelling and the crashing of glass, then more gunfire erupted in the back of the house.

My knees were jelly and wouldn't hold me. I sank down, my arms instinctively covering my head with my arms. I would have gladly stayed there if I hadn't heard a muffled "*Clear!*" Sporadic gunfire was still going on in the back, but hopefully would be over soon.

I crawled to the door, peeking inside to find total chaos and destruction. Two bodies were on the floor, not moving, and I was relieved to see that neither was Clark or his men.

Shakily getting to my feet, my gun hung loose in my grip as I headed through the foyer to a hallway leading left. I heard more shouts, then another "*Clear!*" which I took to be a good sign.

At the end of the corridor were doors on my left and right. The two guards who'd supposedly been there were nowhere to be found. I assumed they'd gone to join the fight once the attack had begun.

I wasn't as lucky as Clark had been. This door was locked. I was stymied for a moment, then remembered the handy-dandy lock-picker I was carrying. Also known as a semiautomatic.

Yes, I totally closed my eyes like a girl when I pulled the trigger, but it worked. The doorjamb had disintegrated and I pushed the door open.

Jackson was lying face down on the ground. He wasn't moving.

"Jackson!" I ran forward, dropping to my knees next to him. I carefully set down my gun so I could turn him over onto his back. I put my ear against his chest, a sigh of relief escaping when I heard his heart beating strong inside his chest. "Thank God," I murmured. There was additional bruising on him and his shirt was torn and dirty, but I couldn't tell if anything was broken.

Blinding pain hit the side of my head and I was knocked over, sliding a couple of feet with the force of the blow. Stars danced in my vision and my limbs felt weak as I tried to right myself. Lana stood there—well, two of her actually—holding a metal pipe. As I watched, she leaned down and picked up my weapon.

"Get up," she ordered.

"What did you do to Jackson?" I asked, my tongue feeling thick. Tears of pain leaked from my eyes, but I managed to regain my footing. The room listed and I braced a hand against the wall to steady myself.

"He'll be fine. If he'd cooperated, then we wouldn't have had to try to persuade him. As it is, I think you'll do. Put that on." She motioned and I looked where she'd pointed. The room was pretty basic with a couple of windows and a bare floor—aside from the computer and screens sitting on a metal table. But she hadn't pointed there. She'd pointed to a vest resting on a chair.

I walked over, almost knowing what I'd find, and I was right.

"I'm not putting this on," I said.

"Put it on or I'm going to aerate your boss," she snapped. "Where should the first hole go? His knee? His neck? Someplace nonlethal, so he can just bleed to death."

The sweet, slightly homely middle-aged woman I'd had lunch with was nowhere to be seen. Lana's expression was hard, her eyes ice-cold. It was as though she was an utter stranger. The resolve in her gaze told me there would be no reasoning with her, no argument that might alter the course she'd chosen. The hand that held the gun pointed at Jackson was rock steady.

Gritting my teeth, I gingerly put on the suicide vest, the weight heavier than I'd anticipated. It had to be at least twenty-five pounds.

"What exactly are you going to do with me wearing this?" I asked. "I blow up, so do you."

"I control the trigger, not you." She brandished what looked like a key fob. "So don't worry about me, though I appreciate your concern."

Jackson stirred, wincing as he sat up.

"Perfect timing," Lana said. "You weren't amenable before. Let's hope you will be now. China's joined us."

He turned and spotted me. I could tell in an instant that he'd recognized the vest and what it was by the tightening of his jaw. Getting to his feet, he said, "I'm not going to give you the algorithm. Not even two lives are worth that software."

Footsteps in the corridor and Lana moved quickly, shoving me forward so when Clark appeared in the doorway, I was inches from him.

"One wrong move and we all get blown sky high," she warned.

I stared at Clark, who had absolutely zero reaction that I could see. His gaze took in the situation, then he spoke into a mic by his mouth. "Fall back. Target is not secure."

"That's right. Fall back," Lana said from behind me. "I have unfinished business."

Clark's eyes met mine and I could see in his how this would play out. It was in his best interest for the vest to explode, taking out Lana and the better part of the installation with it, including the software. Two birds, one stone, and a couple of collateral-damage casualties.

Sweat trickled down the back of my neck and my vision blurred as my eyes filled. The weight of the vest felt as though I was carrying my own tombstone.

"Sorry, China," Clark said. Then he was gone.

"So much for 'no man left behind,'" Lana snorted. "Turn around so Jackson can see you properly. Jackson, upload that algorithm or she dies."

He hesitated and in that moment, I didn't care about the software or who it would hurt or any of it. I just wanted to live. I hadn't asked for any of this. I could've gone home today when I'd escaped, not found a way to try to rescue Jackson.

"Jackson . . ." I couldn't stop from whispering his name in a plea. I was only twenty-three years old. I hadn't even had sex yet, or fallen in love, or done any of a thousand things I wanted to do.

He headed for the computer. In seconds, I could hear the clicking as his fingers flew over the keyboard. A few minutes later, he said, "It's done."

Lana's gunshot made me scream and I watched in horror as Jackson crumpled to the floor.

Glass shattered and I screamed again, tears streaking my face. Lana jerked, her eyes widening. Red blossomed on her chest and she looked down, her mouth agape. I stared, hands covering my mouth, as she collapsed.

I was frozen, my eyes first drawn to the shattered window with a hole in the center. Someone had taken a sniper shot to kill Lana . . . but not before she'd shot Jackson.

I ran to him, skidding on blood on the floor. "Oh my God . . . oh my God . . ." There was a wound on his left side, as though she'd been aiming for his heart. But she'd missed.

"Don't move, China."

Immediately disobeying, I spun around to see Clark had come back.

"I said don't fucking move. You're a walking bomb."

Oh yeah. How could I forget?

"Please take care of Jackson first," I begged. "He's bleeding pretty bad."

He didn't look like he was even listening, instead, reaching for my vest.

"No! Jackson first." I batted his hands away.

"Are you fucking kidding me?" he snarled. "True fucking love, right?" He snorted, but sank down on the floor next to Jackson, brandishing a knife. In seconds, he had Jackson's shirt off and was pulling out some kind of med kit from his own supplies.

A movement out of the corner of my eye made me glance toward Lana. She wasn't dead. She was reaching for that key fob thing that had fallen out of her hand and landed on the floor beside her.

"Clark!"

He spun around and saw in an instant what was happening. I expected him to shoot her, but he didn't have a gun in his hand. Instead, he grabbed me, stuck his hands inside both the sleeves of my vest, and yanked.

I expected not to survive the next moment—who yanked at a bomb?—but I took a breath, then another . . . and nothing happened.

Lana had the fob and she was staring at me, looking confused. She'd hit the button but . . . no explosion. As I watched, her gaze went still and her body relaxed. Her eyes didn't close.

"What the hell did you do?" I yelled, rounding on Clark. "You tell me not to move, then you go pulling random shit out of this thing? You could've blown us both up!"

"Oh, I'm sorry, Miss Know-It-All," he sneered, sinking down next to Jackson again. "I've forgotten, exactly how many suicide vests have you seen? Ten? Twenty?"

I didn't answer.

"Exactly. I've seen more than I care to count, and too many up close and personal. I pulled out the detonator. A piece of wire up both sides. Easiest way to disarm the damn things."

Oh. "That's not what they do in the movies," I grumbled.

"Yeah, well, this ain't fucking Hollywood, now, is it."

By now he had ripped open the med kit and was working on affixing it to Jackson. It was some kind of special bandage. He stuck it to the wound, then wrapped it tight around his chest. In the middle of moving him, Jackson woke.

"Motherfucker," he gritted out, his face creased in pain.

"Man up," Clark retorted. "The bullet went through. You'll be fine. Just don't bleed out."

"Fuck you."

"Maybe later, princess. Your girl still is a walking bomb."

Jackson's gaze cut my way. "You've got to delete the software. It uploaded to their server. Hack into it. Delete it."

I spun around, rushing toward the computer. Clark was inches behind and grabbed my ponytail, stopping me in my tracks.

"Ouch!"

"I removed the detonator, but I'd still prefer you not be wearing twenty pounds of C4."

"I've got to stop that software," I said.

"Then hold fucking still." He took the vest off of me gingerly, despite the lack of detonator, then I plopped down into the chair.

It took me approximately thirty seconds to take in what was showing on the screens and the current connectivity and status. The software Jackson had uploaded was already gone, but the IP address he'd connected to was still there.

It took me another sixty seconds to connect to my own home server and log in. From there, I copied over the tools I needed and began running software in different windows, testing the firewall on the other side. It was a good one, but not great. I heard Jackson talking to Clark behind me.

"Call this number. They'll send a helicopter. Get me to the hospital."

"Must be nice to be rich," Clark said, but I still heard the tone of numbers being dialed. I refocused on my work.

"Where are you at, China?" Jackson gasped out. I winced, hearing the pain in his voice.

"Through one. They have a DMZ. Working on the firewall into the LAN."

"Faster," he said.

My fingers flew and I tuned out everything, focusing on the firewall blocking my path. It was tougher than the other one and I had to be careful it didn't lock me out. But it worked and I was scrolling through the internal network in minutes. I began deleting everything, uploading another program to start rewriting sectors of the disk, preventing any kind of recovery once the deletion was finished.

"Done," I said with a thrill of satisfaction. "It'll finish bricking the disk soon, but the software is gone. Deleted."

"Good—"

I spun in my chair in time to see Jackson drop into unconsciousness.

Jumping up from the chair, I hurried back to him, cradling his head in my lap. "Is he going to be okay?" I asked, smoothing his hair back.

"I called his people. Told them the situation. Let's see what his money can do for him."

Clark's tone was bordering on indifferent, a bloodstained hand scrubbing over his face. He looked tired.

The sound of a helicopter stopped me from saying anything more. Clark got to his feet and left the room. I stayed with Jackson until men began pouring into the room with equipment and a stretcher. I was shoved aside, but I didn't mind. I wanted them to take care of Jackson.

When they lifted the stretcher up and rushed it from the room, I followed. They let me on to the helicopter and just before we took off, I glanced around, looking for Clark. But he was gone.

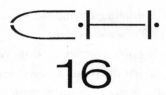

## 16

"But when are you coming home?" Mia asked.

"You're dangerously close to whining," I said.

"It's been two days, and the news said Cysnet and you were cleared of all corporate espionage charges. That it was an inside job. The reporters left this morning."

"I'm just going to make sure Jackson gets home okay, then I'll be home. Go ahead and order Chinese. I'll be home later tonight, I'm sure."

"You've been there almost constantly."

"Job security," I lied. I hadn't wanted to leave Jackson's side since the helicopter had brought us here. He'd been wheeled into surgery immediately and I'd paced the hallways until the doctor had come out and told me he would make a full recovery.

"Okay, but I need to catch you up on my calculus teacher," Mia said. "We got into it again today."

I sighed. "If you'd stop correcting him, this wouldn't be a problem."

"I can't help it."

The nurse wheeled in a very irritated-looking Jackson.

"Gotta go," I said to Mia, ending the call. "So how's the patient?" I asked Jackson.

"Ready to get out of here," he grumbled.

I gave the long-suffering nurse a look of silent apology. The doctor had said he could leave this morning and, by golly, that's what he was going to do. Being Jackson Cooper could get a lot done very quickly, and less than twenty minutes later we were sliding into a black Mercedes. Lance was driving.

"Let's go home," he told Lance, pulling me into his arms.

I nestled close, tucking my head underneath his chin, careful of his wound. We hadn't discussed my constant presence in the hospital. I hadn't offered to leave and he hadn't said I should. So while I'd gone a couple of times to shower and change, I'd come back each time.

"Are you feeling all right?" I asked as the car got underway. It was late evening.

"I'm fine. The surgeon did a wonderful job and I've had excellent company. My ego is still fighting for recovery, but the rest of me is in good shape." His wry tone made me smile.

"The ego battered by not being able to avoid a bullet when you were trying to save the girl?"

"You make it sound all heroic," he teased. "For what it's worth, I'm not accustomed to the role of martyr."

"Then why did you upload the software?" I asked. "You had to know that she'd kill us both anyway."

"I thought there was a chance she could be lying, or that if I gave him more time, Clark could save you." He hesitated, his fingers lifting my chin so our eyes met. "It seems I have . . . feelings for you. Strong feelings I wasn't even fully aware of until you were threatened." His smile was rueful. "And here I've always prided myself on *not* being a cliché."

My stomach had somersaulted when he said he had feelings for me, and I struggled with how to react, what to say. I decided on the truth.

"I have feelings for you, too," I said softly. My gaze drifted from his eyes to his mouth. He was such a good kisser . . .

"Well, that's good," he said, one side of his mouth lifting higher than the other. "I'd hate to think of being rejected by the first woman I've ever legitimately been shot for."

I laughed. I couldn't help it. Despite the trials of the past few days, I was falling in love with the man of my dreams. And it was very possible—maybe likely—that he felt the same.

Lance pulled into the driveway of a house that wasn't the one I'd been to before. I glanced questioningly at Jackson.

"The house in the woods," he reminded me. "I thought we needed some privacy."

Lance held the door open for us and I followed Jackson inside. The downstairs was shrouded in shadows, but I could see the outlines of furniture against a wall of windows. Dim lights shone above the counters in the kitchen, which I glimpsed before he began climbing upstairs. The floors were all hardwood and Lance was nowhere to be seen, thank goodness.

"So . . . I'm just going to stay here?" I asked, my voice a little squeaky as I followed him down the hallway. "With you?"

He stopped suddenly and I found myself pressed against a closed door, his mouth on mine. It took my breath away. When he finally came up for air, I was overwhelmed.

"Yes. With me."

Okay, then.

"Open the door for me, sweetheart," he said, his voice a low rasp that sent a bolt of heat right through me.

Reaching behind me, I turned the knob on the closed door, then gave it a push. Jackson pushed me backward through the opening. Not bothering to look around, I clung to him. I couldn't resist stretching upward, fastening my lips to the skin of his neck where it met his shoulder.

His sharp intake of breath encouraged me and I licked his skin. Mmmm . . . a bit salty, very warm, and softer than I'd imagined.

He kicked the door shut and the room was lit only by the moonbeams shining through windows lining two walls. No blinds were lowered, so we could see the outline of pine trees and the stars glistening above them.

There was a huge white bed in the middle of the room. When I saw it, my heart rate tripled. I wanted to be in that bed. With Jackson. I wouldn't have thought I'd want Jackson as badly as I did so soon after our ordeal, but then again, I'd heard about and read numerous anecdotes over my life about those who had brushes with death wanting to reaffirm life.

Jackson set me down very carefully on the bed, then stood. I was immediately dismayed. Was he going to leave me? I reached out and snagged a fistful of his shirt.

"Don't go," I said, and it sounded more like a plea than a command.

He disengaged the fabric from my fingers, then kissed my knuckles. "I wasn't planning on it."

Jackson began to unbutton his shirt, and I was transfixed. My eyes had adjusted to the moonlight, making it nearly bright enough that it seemed as though a light was shining through the room. He undid one button after another and my mouth grew drier with each expanse of skin as it was revealed. By the time he was tugging his shirt from his slacks and tossing it aside, the flesh between my legs was throbbing.

His shoulders and arms were so big and hard . . . the muscles flexing as he undid his belt. Even with the bandage on his chest, he looked amazing.

Jackson stood unembarrassed in front of me, my eyes devouring him as his body was revealed, inch by glorious inch. I didn't think I'd ever seen anything more arousing than Jackson watching me watch him undress.

"We're not getting interrupted this time," he said, setting one knee on the bed and leaning over me. I fell back against the pillows and he followed me down, resting half his weight on me. He kissed me and it was as though we'd been lovers who kissed for ages. No longer any awkwardness, just mouths and tongues meeting in joint desire. The taste of him was familiar now, as was his scent.

Scent. Wait a minute.

I inserted a hand between us and pushed. He lifted his head, his brows drawn together in a frown of confusion. "What? Are you okay?"

"I want a shower first."

The look of surprise on his face would've been comical if I'd been in a mood for laughing.

"Seriously?"

I nodded. "We've been in the hospital around sick people and germs all day . . . it feels gross." And now that was all in my head, my arousal and desire had completely gone. "Please? A shower?"

With a surge, he got to his feet, then pulled me up, too. "If you want a shower, then that's what you'll have," he said.

Taking my hand, he drew me through a doorway, switching on the light. I took a good look around while he turned on the shower.

It was a gorgeous bathroom, with a deep, claw-foot tub and a standing shower enclosed by glass. The shower had a giant, round head in the ceiling that poured water like a rain cloud, with additional spigots in the walls to spray toward the center. Steam was already rolling when Jackson turned to me and tugged at the belt of my jeans.

"Wait, what are you doing?" I asked, holding the hem of my T-shirt down. He tugged my hands loose anyway.

"You said you wanted a shower. I'm giving you one."

Holy shitballs. "*You're* giving me a shower?" It was like one of my romance novels! I was so excited and yet . . . "It's really bright in here."

Like, could-see-my-pores kind of bright. "I look better in low lighting. And amazing in full dark."

Jackson laughed, a low rumble that made me smile, too, and despite my shyness, I didn't resist when he tugged the shirt over my head and pushed my jeans down my legs. In another moment, he'd added my seafoam lace matching bra and panty set to the pile of clothing.

"I beg to differ with that assertion," he said. "You are beautiful." And since he said it while his gaze roamed over my face, hair, and chest, the look in his eyes soft and warm, I believed him. The massive erection he was sporting didn't hurt either.

It was the first time I'd seen a man fully without clothes—a real live one, that is. I mean, like everyone else I'd paused, rewound, and rewatched Hugh Jackman's naked behind in *X-Men*. (I may have even paused the video. Twice.) But this was different, and my pulse was racing so fast, I was nearly light-headed.

"Come with me."

He didn't have to ask twice.

The water was deliciously hot and his skin was warm. It was like standing in warm rain. Another first: the first time I'd ever been fully naked, held against a man who was likewise naked. Which prompted a thought, and though Jackson was kissing my neck in a delicious way that sent shivers through me, I still spoke.

"What's the difference between *naked* and *nude*?" I asked, tilting my head so he could reach farther underneath my jaw. Mmmm, yes, just like that . . .

"Naked and nude?" He sucked my earlobe into his mouth and his hands moved down to cup my rear.

"Mmmhmm . . ." Okay, maybe I should have rethought the whole talking thing while doing this.

"Well, *naked* implies that being without clothing was something of an accident," he said, his knee nudging my thighs apart. "Whereas *nude* implies intent."

"Intent?"

"Intent to be bad."

His hand slid in between my legs, stroking me, and I lost track of even that little bit of conversation. Water sluiced over our skin as he spread my legs farther apart. His finger pushed into me and I moaned. I clung to him, my breasts pressed against his chest. His erection prodded between my legs and an answering flare of heat echoed deep inside me.

Abruptly, he stepped back, his hands retreating to my hips. "My apologies," he said. "You wanted to wash, correct?"

My mouth was slightly agape in surprise, but then I saw the twinkle of mischief in his eyes. Ah. Revenge then. He wanted to play. I could do that.

"Absolutely," I said, reaching for the bar of soap sitting in a silver dish attached to the wall. I kept my eyes on his as I lathered my hands, then slid the soap down each arm, then back to my neck. I took my time soaping my breasts, watching the Adam's apple in his throat move as he swallowed and his eyes grew darker when they met mine.

There was a seat along the back wall and I lifted my leg to rest one foot on it, slowly dragging the soap down my leg, then back up my thigh. I had my back slightly turned toward Jackson so I could only see him out of the corner of my eye.

Pretending obliviousness, I took my time washing between my legs, letting my slippery fingers slide between my folds. Part of me couldn't believe I was doing this, that I could be so bold in front of Jackson. The other part of me was shouting *YOLO!* and *Carpe Diem!*

I gasped in surprise when he grabbed me by the waist, spinning me around. He sat me on the bench and dropped to his knees. His hands pushed my legs apart and then his head was *there*, and his tongue was on me, inside me, and it was better than I'd ever imagined it would be.

I wanted to keep my eyes open, because the sight of Jackson—his dark head between my pale legs and the water cascading over his back—was something I wanted to memorize for forever. My fingers threaded through his wet hair and he lifted his eyes to mine. It was a shock, the burning desire in his gaze. He watched my face as he licked me and I struggled to keep my eyes open, but then I couldn't any longer.

My eyes closing must have been a signal to him because he intensified his caress, nuzzling me and sucking on a part of my body I hadn't ever considered suckable. I made more noises of approval, which he echoed. His fingers dug into my thighs as he pulled me closer to the edge of the seat. Then he did this thing with his tongue, so fast and sweet . . .

I came in a shattering climax that had my cries echoing against the glass. I had fistfuls of his hair, my body still trembling inside, as he gentled the strokes of his tongue. My breathing was more like panting as I pried open my eyes.

The look on Jackson's face was a mixture of lust and satisfaction. I knew without a doubt that he wanted me, and it was the most intoxicating feeling on the planet.

Raising my arms up, I turned off the water by the taps above me, then stood.

"I think I'm clean enough now," I said, combing my fingers through his hair. "Take me back to bed?"

Jackson pressed a kiss to my abdomen, then stood. I heard his knees pop and I winced.

"Ouch," I said. Now I felt kinda guilty. Here he'd been kneeling on the hard, marble floor of the shower—

"Totally worth it." He winked at me.

Huge bath sheets were on a heated towel rack next to the shower and he grabbed one, wrapping me in it before getting another for himself. I watched with interest as he quickly scrubbed the water from his hair, then did a cursory job of drying his chest before tossing the towel aside.

He scooped me up and I kissed him as he carried me back to the bed. When he lay me down, he unwrapped the towel slowly, as though to prolong the Big Reveal. It made me smile.

"Best Christmas present ever," he murmured, catching my smile.

"But it's not Christmas," I teased, admiring the way the light from the bathroom illuminated the muscles in his arms and shoulders.

"You're right," he said, feigning puzzlement. "That means you'll have to think of something to top this when Christmas rolls around. Good luck with that."

I was bare before him now and ideas for a witty reply flew out the window. My mouth went dry at the sight of him. His body was beautiful with not an ounce of fat anywhere, which made me think I'd definitely have to make sure he never caught a good look at my ass.

His . . . manhood? Member? Staff? I didn't know what to call it that wouldn't make me blush. All my romance novels used words like that, but somehow I thought Jackson would probably laugh out loud if I complimented the size and stiffness of his "rod of pleasure."

Best not to call it anything at all, I thought.

Though I couldn't take my eyes off it. I was lying down but remembered what he'd done in the shower and abruptly sat up.

"My turn," I said, tugging at his arm until he obliged, laying back against the pillows on what I internally had already assigned as "his" side of the bed.

I called to mind every sex scene I'd ever read where the heroine had done this particular act for her hero, wondering how to begin exactly. I hoped my enthusiasm would make up for a decided lack of experience.

Okay, I had to call it something. *Mr. Happy* sprang to mind. It did kind of look like he was smiling . . . Decided then, I scooted in between Jackson's spread legs and tossed my hair over my shoulder (without the neck cramp this time—Mia had taught me well). Mr. Happy looked pleased at this turn of events, judging by the way he jerked a bit when my breath touched him.

I took that as a good sign. Tentatively, I licked the tip, and could've sworn I heard Jackson gasp. I liked that, so I did it again, a longer and slower lick this time. I saw his fist clench the sheet.

A sudden surge of power filled me. I could give him this and he was utterly enraptured by it, just as I had been in the shower. It was a heady feeling, and an aphrodisiac unto itself. The actual act wasn't bad either. His skin was soft as silk, the shaft hard as a rock, and I fitted my lips around the head, letting him slide into the warm cavern of my mouth.

"Holy shit, China," he breathed as I took him deeper. I couldn't get him terribly deep before my throat rebelled, but I just let him slide out, then did it again.

"Jesus . . ."

Okay, invoking the Lord's name meant he *really* liked it. That was good. Sounds were good, kind of like an instant opinion poll of how I was doing. But I didn't want this to be boring, so I put to use one of the racier scenes I'd read in the Harlequin Desire series (and reread, read, and reread again).

I slid one hand underneath Mr. Happy to cup his balls, squeezing gently. The other hand I curled around the shaft as I took him again in my mouth. I sucked lightly, tracing my tongue down the underside, then back up. Instant opinion poll analysis said this was a Good Thing, so I did it again.

Turning him on was having a major impact on my desire as well. The more noises he made and the harder he got, the more into it I was, little moans in the back of my throat sending little vibrations through Mr. Happy.

"Oh God, China," he said. "Holy fuck."

I raised my eyes to see him watching me. The corners of my lips lifted in a seductive smile as I circled the sensitive tip with my tongue, then deep throated as far as I could, which turned out to be all the way down. Yay me—I always was a quick learner. Judging by the mingled curses Jackson gritted out, and gasps, he appreciated my quick aptitude as well.

Closing my eyes, I inhaled deeply, recalling a line I'd once read in a racy Judith Krantz novel. She'd said until you'd smelled a man precisely *there*, a woman couldn't possibly know him. I had to agree.

Suddenly, he pulled away, his hands closing on my upper arms. Without any warning, he was tossing me back against the pillows, settling between my legs and kissing me with a voracious hunger I readily returned.

"Are you sure?" he murmured against my lips. My eyes flew open.

"You're kidding me, right?"

He snorted a laugh. "Just wanted to verify."

"'Jackson, ya big stud, take me to bed or lose me forever,'" I quoted. To my delight, he replied.

"'Show me the way home, honey.'"

I grinned, pulling my knees up and spreading my thighs a bit wider to accommodate him. He sat back on his heels and took Mr. Happy in hand, guiding him into me.

*This was it*, I couldn't help thinking. And I was suddenly *really* glad I'd waited for Mr. Right and not just Mr. Knows-What-He's-Doing. I think I'd gotten both.

The feeling of him slowly filling me was indescribable, but I'll try anyway.

Intimate. Erotic. Vulnerable. Pleasurable. The heat of him inside me, the way he looked in my eyes as we became one, the pause he made before pushing in all the way and the twinge inside that faded almost instantly. I'd never felt more feminine in the best possible way than when he was deeply seated inside me and we both let out sighs of pure pleasure.

"Are you okay?" he asked. His voice was slightly breathless.

"*Okay* is grossly inadequate to describe this," I replied. This time my smile wasn't one of humor, but that of a woman whose man looked utterly enraptured. "Don't you think?" I wrapped my arms around his neck and pulled him closer.

"Thinking isn't on the agenda at the moment," he replied. He pulled out a bit, then entered me again, making my eyes slide shut.

I agreed, but couldn't vocalize it, because then he was moving with more purpose and my hips mirrored his. My legs circled his hips, lifting to meet his thrusts.

His hand cupped underneath my knee, lifting it higher, and I was glad I was flexible enough to accommodate this position because it felt really, really good.

"Kiss me," he breathed against my lips, a rhetorical request since his tongue slipped inside my mouth to dance with mine.

Kissing was so much better when it was during sex, I decided. It gave everything a whole new—and welcome—intimacy.

I had no idea how long to expect things to last—the romance novels always glossed over the specifics—but it wasn't quick and it wasn't so long that I'd get a cramp in my side. It was . . . perfect. When I wanted him to move faster and harder, I told him, and he did, and it was incredible. Judging by the sounds he was making, he liked it that way, too.

I could feel myself hovering on the edge of an orgasm and when it rolled over me, it was the best I'd ever had. Turned out masturbating was to actual sex what watching *Star Wars* on a fourteen-inch screen was to watching it in 3-D on an IMAX.

It was kind of nice that I finished before him because not only could I concentrate on his body and his face, but his cock against my overly sensitive flesh made a friction that kept the aftershocks going. Oh wow . . .

Jackson's body spasmed into mine, groans falling from his lips. I held him closer, arms and legs twined around him. His face was buried in my neck when he stilled, then he was kissing me again.

"You're amazing," he said, pressing his lips to my cheek, my nose, my forehead. "And beautiful."

"Well, don't move more than two feet away or I won't be able to see you," I said.

Jackson laughed, rolling over onto his back and pulling me with him until I lay on top of him. My feet only reached his midcalf as I rested my head against his shoulder.

"Was it worth the wait?" he asked softly. His fingers combed through my hair, arranging it gently down my back.

"Yeah," I said. "Definitely." I looked up at him, resting my chin on my folded arm. "I'm glad I waited. You were worth it."

The next moment, I was reconsidering my candor as something changed slightly in his eyes.

"I'll take that as a compliment," he said lightly, and gave me a smile.

I wondered what this meant for us. If it was a one-time thing, or if this meant we were In A Relationship. But all those romance novels had one thing in common: never ask first, *especially* after the first time you have sex with someone. It was nice, though, that I could now relate to the burning questions those heroines always had.

His eyes were kind, if a bit more shuttered than they'd been "during," and it was a nice moment just looking into them. Turning my head, I rested my cheek against his chest. His breathing was even and I fell asleep to the sound of his steady heartbeat.

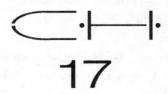

## 17

I woke slowly, my body aching in strange places, and it took me a moment to remember where I was and what I'd done. Had it really happened? Or had I dreamed it? A glance to my right confirmed it. Jackson was lying on his back, asleep, his chest bare above the sheet which was drawn up to his waist. At some point, I must've rolled off him.

Without waking him, I slid out of bed. I was too keyed up to sleep more, even though the sky was just now lightening with dawn. We'd had sex. I was no longer a virgin. Plus, I was starving.

Retrieving my clothes from the floor of the bathroom, I pulled them on before tiptoeing downstairs.

It was a gorgeous home, one of those log cabin places meant to look rustic but in reality a luxury residence that was a far cry from the pioneer days. Something smelled good and I followed it to the kitchen. Black granite countertops and high-end appliances outfitted the place. I was drawn to a note by the oven.

*Thursday is breakfast-for-dinner night.*

I smiled, opening the oven to see that Lance had left a quiche Lorraine for us to eat. I hadn't ever asked how Jackson had known about my schedule, but at the moment it made me feel warm and fuzzy inside that he did. Technically it was closer to breakfast than dinner time, but I wasn't complaining. Jackson and I had been too . . . busy last night to bother checking the oven.

"That looks good."

My scream at the voice behind me was immediately muffled by a hand over my mouth. I was hauled backward against a man's chest and the voice spoke in my ear.

"Don't scream, China. It'll just piss me off. And I'm already pissed off, having to hunt you down out here in the middle of the fucking woods."

Clark.

Little by little, he lifted his hand from my mouth. "What are you doing here?" I hissed. I was acutely aware that his arm was locked around my waist and that my back was pressed tightly against his chest.

"Looking for you, obviously," he retorted, his sarcasm thick.

"Let me go." I squirmed and he released me. Whirling to face him, I hurriedly backed up, putting some space between us. "What do you want?"

He looked me up and down, then raised one dark eyebrow. "Looks like your virgin status is a thing of the past. Am I right?"

My face had to turn six shades of red, judging by the heat in my cheeks. "That's none of your business." I decided not to say anything about how it *could've* been his business, but he'd rejected me. In hindsight, a good thing.

Clark's lips twisted, but he let it go. "I'm guessing Jackson has fully recovered?"

"He's doing all right, yeah."

He leaned against the counter, crossing his arms over his chest. I wondered if he was armed, then thought that was probably a given.

"His company is safe from being sued and the FBI has dropped their investigation. On top of that, he got the girl. I'm guessing he's sleeping well tonight."

I felt vastly underdressed and without my usual armor, whereas Clark was wearing dark jeans, boots, a dark gray T-shirt and a black leather jacket. Somehow I thought this was more his usual attire than what he adopted for his HR persona. And it didn't help that his gaze kept sweeping down to my bare legs and feet.

"What do you want, Clark? A thank-you?"

He gave a careless shrug and crossed his arms over his chest. "I won't hold my breath."

"You told me you didn't do rescue missions," I said. "So who fired the shot that killed Lana?"

Clark shrugged. "She was a real bitch. And you're welcome."

"What the hell are you doing here?"

Jackson's voice came from behind Clark. I hadn't seen or heard him come in the room.

Clark didn't do anything for a moment, then his expression smoothed. "Looks like your boyfriend is coming to the rescue," he said to me in a low, conspiratorial tone. "How's it going, Jackson?" He turned slowly.

Jackson stood a few feet away, gun in hand. "Why are you here? How did you find us?"

"We have some unfinished business," Clark said. He opened a cabinet and took down some plates, seeming completely unconcerned that a gun was pointed at him. "Finding you was easy. You really think putting this place in Lance's name would fool anyone?" He snorted, opening the fridge and taking out a beer. "Some genius you are."

Popping the top, he took a long swallow of the beer, then glanced at us as if he'd forgotten we were there. "My apologies," he said. "Did you want one, too?" He motioned to the fridge.

My mouth was agape in shock and Jackson just looked pissed.

"No? Suit yourself. Food smells good though. Let's eat while we chat. I'm starving."

He took the quiche out of the oven and set it on the counter. My stomach gave a noisy growl as the aroma filled the kitchen. Looking over at Jackson, I shrugged and started going through drawers until I found the utensils.

I took the loaded plate Clark handed me and walked past Jackson into the front room. A fire burned in the huge, brick fireplace and there was an overstuffed, oversized chair right next to it that was calling my name.

Curling up in the chair, I set my plate on my lap and dug in. The boys could figure out their business or fight or whatever. I just wanted to eat.

A few moments later, Clark came in, sitting in an armchair across from me. Then Jackson, who took the sofa. He carried a plate and set the handgun right next to him within easy reach.

"The lovebirds aren't sitting together?" Clark asked. He leaned toward Jackson. "Maybe you weren't as good as you think you were."

Jackson ignored him. "China says you're CIA."

Clark took another bite. "Not quite true, but close enough." He glanced at me. "You wrote the algorithm. You still have that software. I want to know who you're selling it to."

"Who says I'm selling it to anyone?"

Clark rolled his eyes. "You're a businessman, you make money—it's what you do. I could make a phone call right now and have the FBI on your doorstep, arresting you."

"You won't leave here alive if you try," Jackson threatened.

"Relax, lover boy," Clark said. "I said I *could*, not that I *would*. I'd rather know what you're going to do with it." Using his fork, he pointed at Jackson. "You're hiding something. You going to fess up? Or do I have to beat it out of you?"

"I'd like to see you try."

"Don't tempt me."

"Will you two knock it off?" I interrupted. "You sound like teenagers. And not very smart ones at that." I looked to Clark. "He's not going to do anything with it."

"Bullshit," Clark said.

I looked at Jackson. "Tell him."

There was a long pause before Jackson answered.

"It's not up to me," he said.

"What does that mean?" I asked.

His gaze swung to meet mine. "I told you who wanted that software done. Just because Lana tried to steal it doesn't mean it's over. They're still going to want it."

"Who is *they*?" Clark asked, his voice sharp.

"Why should I tell you?" Jackson shot back. "You can't be trusted."

"I also just saved both your lives."

"The *software* is what's going to keep us alive. I'm not giving up the only protection we have."

"You don't think someone's going to kill you for it?"

"It's my bargaining chip."

They were at an impasse, staring daggers at each other. I didn't know which side to take, so I kept quiet. I could understand Jackson wanting to keep secret the fact that the president's own people had ordered the software. But Clark had put himself on the line to save us, so he couldn't be just a mercenary.

The silence was interrupted by the buzzing of Jackson's cell phone in his pocket. He glanced at the screen, then answered it.

"Jackson Cooper." He listened for a long moment, then glanced at me. "Yes, I know." More silence. "Okay. I'll be there in half an hour." He ended the call.

"That was my lawyer," he said. "Now that I'm out of the hospital, the board is demanding a meeting to discuss what happened, and reporters are wanting a statement. I need to go do damage control."

Dismayed, I said, "But I thought I was in the clear. That Cysnet was in the clear."

"You are, but they're still nervous about Cysnet's name being attached to what was initially reported as corporate espionage. The stock has taken a dive over the past few days."

Crap. I chewed my lip, setting aside my plate since I wasn't hungry anymore. Not with this now happening. "Jackson, I'm sorry—"

"None of that," he interrupted, getting to his feet. "You can stay here until I get back, but don't worry. I'll take care of smoothing things over."

"I can't just stay here," I said. "I don't have my things." I did so hate to be without my stuff. It made me vaguely uncomfortable. "And there's Mia. She's been by herself now for nearly two days, which means I'm a terrible aunt and guardian . . ."

"Your car is back at my house and trust me, you don't want to be there right now. Reporters are crawling all over the place."

Oh God. The thought of being on TV, peppered with questions by reporters who had no idea of the difference between software and hardware made my head start to pound. I leaned forward, resting my head in my hands.

"So I'm just supposed to hide here indefinitely?" I asked.

"I'll take her home," Clark said.

I glanced at him in surprise. Since when did he want to be all help-ful? Last I checked, we'd ceased being useful to him.

Jackson looked suspicious. "Why would you do that?"

Clark shrugged. "I've got time to play taxi."

Jackson looked about as skeptical as I felt, but what choice did I have? "It's fine," I said to Jackson, getting up and walking over to him. I tipped my head back to meet his eyes, his hands settling on my hips. "I'll be fine. Go do what you need to do, okay?"

"You're sure?"

Not a bit. "Absolutely." I smiled my awful, fake smile, then remembered how bad I was at that. I still didn't trust Clark, but I'd put Jackson through enough danger and trouble already. He didn't have to escort me home when his business was on the line.

Jackson's grimace said I wasn't fooling him, but I gave him a little push. "Go on. Go. I'll be fine."

"Call me when you get home," he said. Before I could reply, he kissed me. His hands slid to the back of my neck, his fingers tangling in my hair and sending a shiver through me. This was a different kiss than before. A sated, possessive, deep kiss.

When he pulled back, I was a little breathless and I knew my eyes were too wide and bright, but I couldn't help it. It was all so new and so . . . wonderful. I couldn't even stop the stupid grin on my face. I may as well have had a neon sign over my head: *Just Had Awesome Sex with Her Dreamy Boyfriend*.

"You two need a few minutes? Shouldn't take more than seven, right? Nine, tops."

Clark's sarcastic drawl was ice water over my head. I'd almost forgotten he was there.

Jackson ignored him, pressing a kiss to my forehead. "I'm going to change. Call me later." I nodded, watching him as he headed upstairs to the bedroom.

I may have stomped over to Clark. "I liked you a hell of a lot better when you were in HR," I hissed.

A lifted eyebrow. "Boring?"

"Nice."

"Nice *is* boring."

Whatever. "Let's go."

I was temporarily flummoxed when I opened the door. It was pouring down rain and we were in the woods, which meant there was a sea of water and mud between the door and the driveway. The path was paved, but muddy water cascaded over it.

"Will you melt?" Clark asked, his voice at my ear.

I shot him a look of irritation. "I'm not wearing my rain boots. Just my tennis shoes." Rain boots were definitely necessary. Wet feet were very uncomfortable, unsanitary, and led to colds, possibly even pneumonia. If I stepped out that door, I could wind up in a hospital.

"It's just water."

"It's *muddy* water." And cold. And wet. And did I mention dirty?

"For fuck's sake," he muttered. Before I could retort, he scooped me up in his arms. I squealed, then clung to him as he stepped out into the rain.

I was drenched before he'd gone five feet and I kept my head down, my face in his leather jacket, until he opened the car door and stuffed me inside. He hustled around to the driver's side as I was getting my breath back. I began shivering almost immediately.

"Are your feet dry?" he asked.

"Mostly," I stammered through chattering teeth.

He glanced at me, then shrugged out of his jacket and tossed it in my lap. "Here. Put that on."

"I d-don't need your j-jacket," I protested.

"Yeah, you do."

"I don't—" I began, but he cut me off with a sharp glance.

"That T-shirt is see-through now."

I glanced down. Shit. He was right. Of all the days to wear white. My seafoam lace bra was clearly visible through the sodden fabric. I hurriedly shifted his jacket. Luckily, he was a lot bigger than I was so it covered me entirely.

"Sorry," I muttered.

"Don't be sorry. I appreciated the view." His smirk was unrepentant.

He started the car, giving me a welcome distraction from the embarrassment that comment brought about. "This is more what I pictured you driving than the Honda," I said. It was a Porsche Cayman. Two hundred seventy-five horsepower, one hundred sixty-five miles per hour top speed. First a Mercedes, now a Porsche. I couldn't fault his taste, but exactly how many cars did he own? "Is this the Black Edition?"

Clark shot me a glance. "You know cars."

I shrugged. "A little."

"Why do I get the feeling there's nothing that you know only *a little* about?"

I responded with a question of my own. "Who's the real you?" I asked. "The really nice guy who bonded with me over *Doctor Who* and Chinese food? Or the smart-ass secret agent guy who buys and sells information to the CIA?"

He glanced at me, his blue eyes unfathomable. "Why do you care?"

I didn't know the answer to that. "Is Clark your real name?"

He looked back at the road. "Does it matter?"

My lips thinned. "Fine. Don't answer any of my questions. I don't care."

There was silence for a few minutes. I watched the road. The leather jacket smelled really nice and I huddled underneath it. It was only about an hour after sunrise, but the sky was so overcast, it looked dark still. I stared out the window, trying to recapture my earlier joy. It wasn't until we were parking in my driveway that he spoke.

"You wouldn't ask if you didn't care," Clark said. "And I can appreciate that. But I'll be out of your life soon. So it's really . . . unnecessary."

I studied him. For some reason, his words struck me as sad. "Unnecessary for someone to care about you? Don't you have . . . a family? A girlfriend? Friends? People who care about you? What do they think of the life you lead? Don't they worry?"

The half smile he'd had faded entirely and his expression grew shuttered.

"It's best for people in my line of work not to . . . cultivate . . . relationships." Then he smiled and it was like one of my fake smiles, only done much better than I could do. It didn't touch his eyes, which looked . . . empty.

I'd been right. It was sad. And I didn't want to ask any more questions.

"Can I wear your jacket inside?" I asked. It had stopped raining, but my T-shirt was still soaked.

"By all means."

I slung the jacket over my shoulders and hurried inside, not checking to see if he followed, though I was sure he did. The leather jacket was a nice one and I was sure he'd want it back.

Mia was still asleep, as early as it was, and after a steaming ten-minute shower, I felt more normal. I pulled on jeans, my favorite *Firefly* T-shirt—*Curse your sudden but inevitable betrayal*—a long-sleeved button-up over that, and socks. My glasses were sadly water-stained so I had to take a few minutes to clean those up. I couldn't stand any kind of smudge on my glasses.

My hair was half wet and half dry, so I just brushed it out and left it down since trying to wrangle it up into a ponytail in that state was a recipe for a tangled disaster. Twenty minutes after I got home, I was back in the living room, except Clark was nowhere to be found.

"Clark?" I called, wondering if he had left after all.

"Up here."

I looked back up the stairs, my jaw hanging open. Surely he wouldn't . . . I took the steps two at a time.

"This is impressive. I've gotta say."

He was surveying my "storage room" with a look bordering between amazement and disbelief.

"You shouldn't be up here," I said stiffly. "I didn't invite you to look through my things."

"You were taking a while," he said, picking up my handmade wand (willow, twelve and three-quarter inches). "I didn't think you'd mind."

"Well, I do."

Setting down the wand, he reached for something else. I felt like Yash, wanting to wring my hands at how he was touching my stuff.

But instead of a collectible, he picked up a framed photo, half-hidden behind a display of Funkos.

"Who's this?" he asked.

I knew what photo he had. It was the only photograph in the room. I didn't have to answer, but I did anyway. "My mother, with me, when I was five." I remembered the photo and the day we'd taken it. The circus had come to town so Mom had decided she and I should go. There had been a fake lion kids could sit on for a photo, and she'd stood beside me, an arm around my shoulders, as we posed. Both of us looked so happy.

Reaching for it, I took the photo from Clark and replaced it on the shelf. "Please don't touch my things." I turned and left the room without another word. I didn't like to dwell on my mom's death, even now.

I made a pot of coffee, carefully *not* thinking about my mother. Clark must've gotten the hint about prying through my home because he appeared a few moments later, taking a seat on one of the stools at the bar in my kitchen.

"Lana's computer sent a lot of helpful information," he said. "I forwarded most of it on to the CIA for analysis. With luck, we'll be able to find more agents like her here in the US, just waiting for their orders to activate them."

All of that was good and made me feel better about how things had gone down—at least I'd proven useful—but something he said struck me as odd and I turned toward him, carton of half-and-half in hand.

"Why just most of it?" I asked.

"Excuse me?"

"Why did you only forward on most of it? Why not all of it?"

His lips twitched. "Not much gets by you, does it," he said. I thought that sounded like one of those rhetorical questions that didn't need an answer, so I didn't supply one. "No," he continued. "I kept the file she had on you."

My hands went cold. "What file? Why would she have a file on me?"

"She had the file because she was interested in everyone the government is interested in. You're one of those people."

"Don't be ridiculous," I said. "Why me? I'm from Nebraska and the only thing even slightly interesting about me is that I'm smart. Big deal. Lots of people are smart."

"That's what I thought, too," he said. "Why would the government have a file on you? What's so special about you?"

The coffee was done and I poured two cups. "I don't think I'm special," I said. "All my life, I just wanted to be normal. Like all the other kids. I didn't want to freak out when my peas touched my carrots, or be obsessed with the rhythm of the rain hitting the window. When someone told a joke, I wanted to be able to laugh like everyone else, not five seconds later once I realized it was a joke.

"I don't know what the file says and right now, I don't care." I faced Clark, placing his coffee on the counter in front of him. "I'd rather just forget it, go about my life as it was before all this happened. I was happy."

"Were you?" His question seemed serious enough, and it made me pause. Had I been happy?

"I was . . . content," I replied. "Happiness is an illusion, isn't it? Fleeting, leaving you more *un*happy in its wake for having experienced it. Isn't it better to just be content? No high-highs, no low-lows. Just . . . an evenness to each day with nothing unexpected."

"I don't know. You looked pretty happy this morning."

My gaze dropped to my coffee and my face got warm. Yes, I'd been ecstatic this morning. It was intoxicating, that kind of happiness. And dangerous, too. How long could it last?

"You know, I could use someone like you," he said. "It's always handy to have a computer and tech expert around."

I took a careful sip of my coffee. "You're offering me a job?"

"Maybe. Are you interested?"

"I work for Cysnet. Why would I want to change jobs?"

"Well, first of all," he said, "it's usually a bad idea to sleep with the boss." He waggled his eyebrows at me. "Secondly . . . do I really need another?"

I wasn't amused. "You've lied to me and used me from the beginning," I said stiffly. "Used me in a very personal way, I might add. You tried to gain my trust and make me think you were interested in me in . . . *that* way." I couldn't say the word *sexually*. "Then you drop this bomb on me about who you supposedly really are and who you work for, and threaten my niece to make me do what you want. And now you think I'd want to work for you?" I snorted in derision, then leaned across the counter toward him. "This might come as a shock to you, *Clark*, but if I quit Cysnet, I'd have a dozen companies and government agencies banging down my door to get me to come work for them. I don't need you and your pity job offer, even if I am sleeping with the boss."

The amusement had faded from Clark's expression and his face was blank now, his eyes unreadable. "Fine," he said, getting to his feet.

I expected more, but he said nothing else, just shrugged on his jacket and headed for the door. Tentatively, I followed. He pulled open the front door and for a moment, I thought he wasn't going to say anything else. But he turned at the last second, nearly causing me to run into him.

"For the record," he said, gazing down at me. "The reason I didn't sleep with you wasn't because I didn't want to." His gaze traveled over my face before coming to rest on my eyes. "Believe it or not, there's still a part of me that's not a complete dick."

My eyes were wide at his admission, and it did kind of make me feel better. His eyes dropped to my mouth and I was abruptly reminded of the chemistry between us that had burned so hot for such a short time. I swallowed, scrambling for what to say, but before I could think of anything, he'd pressed a kiss to my cheek.

"And yes, my name is really Clark," he murmured, his warm breath a caress against my skin.

Then he was gone, beeping the Porsche unlocked and pulling open the door. Before he slid inside though, he looked at me again. "By the way, your fish is belly-up."

Well, crap.

He peeled out of my driveway and down the street in a flash of black metal and sleek lines. Yes, that suited Clark much more than the Honda.

I was about to go back inside when a familiar sight greeted my eyes and I paused. My Mustang was coming down the street, Lance behind the wheel. A grin spread over my face at seeing my baby. I'd missed her.

"Here you go," Lance said, handing me the keys. "The boss thought you'd need your wheels back ASAP."

"Thanks," I said. "Do you need a ride back?"

"Nah, I'm good. An Uber's on the way."

"Okay then. Thanks again!"

I went back inside to finish my coffee and get to the paper first before Mia woke up.

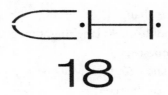

## 18

". . . and I saw Polly sneaking out of Walter's room at five in the morning," Grandma said. "Can you believe that? Last Wednesday, she was sneaking out of Franklin's room. I swear, that woman gets around."

"I thought Franklin died?" I asked.

"No, that was Frankie, not Franklin."

"Ah." Grandma was giving me the gossip from Viagra Wednesday in the retirement community, which turned into Walk of Shame Thursday.

"Betsy and I were having lunch Friday and she said she couldn't sleep Wednesday night from all the noise going on in the room next door."

"I thought Betsy had her own place?"

"She had to move into the main house when she broke her hip."

Something occurred to me. "Grandma, what in the world were you doing up at five a.m.? You hate early mornings."

Silence.

"Grandma, you weren't sneaking out of someone's house, were you?" The thought of my granny doing the Walk of Shame made me nearly laugh out loud.

"Don't be silly," she said with a snort. "I much prefer them sneaking out of *mine*. At least I know when the last time my bathroom's been cleaned and my sheets changed."

"Grandma!" I couldn't help laughing, though. I'd come by at least some of my OCD honestly.

"You hush," she said. "And put Mia on the phone. I want to talk to her. And be sure to feed that cold."

"Fine, fine, but I thought it was starve a cold."

"Feed a cold, starve a fever," she corrected.

"Right." Hauling myself up off the couch, I took the phone upstairs to what had become Mia's room and handed it to her as she lay curled underneath a mountain of blankets. "Grandma wants to talk to you."

But as I was shuffling back downstairs, the blanket I had wrapped around me trailing behind me like the train of a gown, I rethought the wisdom of letting Mia and Grandma speak to each other when I heard Mia say, "Guess what? China has a *boyfriend*."

Great. Not only had I undergone the third degree over why I hadn't called last Sunday and why I was calling tonight, which was a Tuesday, but I'd no doubt undergo another interrogation about Jackson the next time I called her.

And I'd have to talk to Mia about calling Jackson my boyfriend. We hadn't discussed specifics like titles. I didn't want him running for the hills the way the hero always does in the romance novels. He always comes back, of course, when he realizes he can't live without the heroine, but why chance it?

Jackson was in the kitchen when I got back downstairs. "They didn't have chicken noodle soup, but they had tomato," he said, unloading a paper bag on the kitchen counter. I stood next to him, wrapped in a blanket and holding a box of tissues.

"I don't know if Mia likes tomato," I said, my voice all nasally. Then I coughed. "Ugh. I hate being sick."

"If Mia doesn't like tomato, then I'll go get something else for her," he said patiently.

"Okay. Thank you." I shuffled back to the couch and let him take a bowl up to Mia, who was in bed watching TV to nurse her cold. The damn rain had made us both sick so now we'd missed two days of school and work with sore throats, coughs, and runny noses.

Jackson had been great. Once the publicity had blown over with the company and he'd explained to the board about Lana, things had quieted down. You could almost say life was back to normal, except *normal* had never been this good to me.

"It's been a while since you caught up on your DVR," he said, dropping some fish food in the tank for the newest iteration of The Doctor. "Want to watch *Castle*?"

"I don't want you to get sick, too," I said.

"I'll be fine." He settled on the couch next to me and pulled me over so I was half lying on his lap, then tucked the blanket around me.

We watched *Castle* for a while as the evening grew late and his fingers combed through my hair. I nestled closer to him, then noticed Mr. Happy was wide awake underneath my cheek. Smiling, I turned on my back to look up at him.

"Feeling amorous?" I teased.

"Well, your head is down there so it's not like I could exactly help it." His smile was soft and his eyes gentle as he looked at me. "But you're sick and I'm sure making love is the last thing on your mind."

"No, no, I feel a lot better," I insisted. I pressed his palm against my cheek. "See? No fever. And I haven't coughed in a while. I think the soup did the trick."

He frowned slightly, feeling my forehead, too. "Are you sure? I don't want you to have a relapse—"

"I think The Doctor would prescribe some TLC," I said, shooting a look at my fish tank. Sure enough, this one was still alive. So far. "And multiple orgasms have been known to cure very serious illnesses. So really, you'd be doing me a favor."

I got an outright belly laugh on that one. "All right then. Let no one say Jackson Cooper refused a woman in need."

To my surprise, he scooped me up in his arms.

"What are you doing?" I squeaked.

"It's called carrying," he said, heading for the stairs. "It's generally considered to be a grand romantic gesture."

I grinned, looping an arm around his neck. "If you can carry me, blanket and all, up the stairs then I'll certainly consider it a grand romantic gesture. Though your back may not appreciate it."

He snorted, easily climbing the staircase. "Yeah, that blanket really sends it over the edge. I don't think I can handle it."

"Smart-ass."

It turned out sex *was* good for colds, or at least for clearing the sinuses. And as we lay naked in bed together, those questions that had plagued me a week ago fluttered to the front again. This hadn't been the second time we'd slept together—Jackson had come by the night Clark had left. We hadn't talked much because we'd been tearing each other's clothes off once he was two steps inside the door.

"So . . ." I said, drawing little circles on his chest with my finger. My head was against his shoulder as I nestled inside the crook of his arm.

"Yes?" he asked when I didn't say anything else. His voice rumbled in his chest.

"Um . . ." I hesitated, trying to figure out how to put into situationally acceptable words what I wanted to know. "I was wondering . . ." And as usual, social etiquette failed me. "Are we just friends with benefits or is this a boyfriend/girlfriend thing?"

Jackson's chest bounced a little as he chuckled. "Was that the tactful or blunt version?"

I sighed. "It's the China version."

He moved and I twisted so I could see him. "I don't mind the China version," he said with a soft smile. "And for the record, it's whatever you want it to be."

Frowning in confusion, I said, "But that's not how it works. It's supposed to be mutually agreed upon. Not dictated by one partner."

"What I meant was that I'm very . . . taken . . . with you," he said.

I stared, processing this, then a smile split my face. "I'm . . . taken with you, too," I said. "But I've never had a boyfriend before."

"Does that mean you do or don't want one now?"

Stretching up, I brushed a kiss to his lips. "It means I do."

His hands cupped my rear, readjusting me so I lay on top of him, my thighs cradling Mr. Happy. "Good. But I'm not giving you my letter jacket."

"Fine with me. Just so long as I get to drive your car sometimes."

"Deal."

"Deal."

It was Friday night and I had a new schedule—dinner with my real bona fide boyfriend. Jackson was going to pick me up at eight, which was still two hours away, but I was ready to go. Since Mia had made plans with a group of friends, I'd asked her to do my hair and makeup before she left. So now I sat gingerly on the edge of my sofa, trying not to wrinkle the shirt she'd ironed for me.

It was a fancy shirt with buttons and not even a T-shirt underneath. A deep scarlet color and soft to the touch, she'd said it looked fantastic on me with my dark hair and "ivory" complexion, which I took to be a pleasant euphemism for pale as death. The sleeves were long but she'd rolled them back and put a silver bracelet on my wrist. She'd even made me tuck my shirt in to my jeans, which were also new and much tighter than what I usually wore. I squirmed, trying to break them in more. Maybe I should do some squats?

My doorbell rang and I got up, wondering who that could be. It wasn't pizza night, so it wouldn't be Reggie. Not the neighbor either, since no one had moved in since Clark had moved out. Was it Girl Scout Cookie time of year yet? I loved Thin Mints . . .

But it wasn't anyone I recognized. Two men stood on my porch, waiting for me to open the door. And they didn't look friendly. I stepped back from the window, thinking fast as to what I should do. Should I call someone? Jackson? The police? But they hadn't *done* anything to me, just rang my doorbell. Maybe I was overreacting?

As I was thinking all this, one of them knocked. "We know you're in there, miss. We're with the Secret Service. Please open the door."

A word I never, ever uttered fell out of my mouth. I knew I had to open the door, but I would rather have opened every *Star Trek: The Original Series* action figure I had that was New In Box.

"What do you want?" I said once I'd pulled open the door.

"We'd like you to come with us," one of them said.

"Not without ID."

They both obliged, showing me badges and cards proclaiming them to indeed be members of the Secret Service. They looked authentic, though if that wasn't convincing enough, the guns in holsters underneath their suit jackets looked very real indeed.

"Where are you taking me?" I asked, still standing in my doorway.

"Someone needs to speak with you," the one who'd spoken before said. "We'll bring you back shortly."

They waited for me to decide, which was polite since I didn't think saying no was really an option. I grabbed my keys and my phone, but the talker stopped me.

"I'm sorry, but your phone will need to stay here."

Alrighty then.

They escorted me to a waiting sedan, engine running, and all three of us got in the back. I thought for a moment they'd blindfold me, but they didn't. Which was a good thing because I totally would've gotten carsick and thrown up on them.

We drove down to Research Triangle, parking underneath a small, four-story building. The garage was deserted and the men flanked me as we followed the driver to an elevator in the corner.

My nerves were raw by the time we exited the silent elevator. I hadn't asked any more questions. I knew they wouldn't answer anyway, so I saved my breath.

The corridor was functional and not especially welcoming. It ended overlooking a large room that spanned ten feet below the fenced walkway. A sort of high-tech NASA design lay below, with screens on the wall in front and three rows of workstations facing it. They weren't ascending though, instead all rows were on the same level.

"What's this?" I asked the men in confusion. But they'd already turned and headed back to the elevator.

As far as I could tell, I was alone, so I walked down the metal steps to the floor for a closer look. All the workstations were on and displayed the same logo on their log-in screen. Stopping in front of the nearest one, I read aloud.

"The Price of Freedom Is Eternal *Vigilance*."

"Exactly."

I squeaked and spun around, startled. A man was walking toward me who looked vaguely familiar, but I couldn't place him.

"Who are you?" I asked when he'd stopped in front of me.

"I'm Stewart Gammin," he replied, holding out a hand for me to shake. I did so automatically. "You may have heard of me."

My memory supplied the connection. "You're the president's chief of staff." Which made something else click. Freyda's phone contact—PCOS.

He smiled, though it wasn't the practiced, friendly smile of a politician. More that of a bureaucrat who'd been told that it was required to occasionally be nice. With dirty blond hair and brown eyes, he was a good-looking man. Maybe six feet tall and somewhere between the forty- to forty-five-year-old range. His suit was well-tailored and his shoes polished to a gleaming shine.

"Yes, that's correct. And you're China Mack."

"How do you know me? Why am I here?"

"We've been keeping tabs on you for some time," he replied. "You're one of the most intelligent people in the world. An incredible asset to our country. And now your country has need of you."

"What are you talking about?"

"I'm talking about this." He gestured to encompass the room. "I'm sure Jackson has told you that the president ordered Vigilance to be finished, despite the NSA's public difficulties. The president has the ability and authority to make such things happen *and* keep it out of the papers."

Something clicked in my head. "Wait a minute . . . PCOS. You're the one Freyda was talking to. You're the one who killed her. Or had her killed." Which was really bad news . . . for me. Especially since I'd just blurted it out like that. Subterfuge wasn't my thing.

"I did not kill her nor any other member of the team," he said. "We believe that was NSA operatives, trying to get this project shut down."

"Why would the NSA want it shut down? Aren't they all about spying?"

"The president is afraid there are moles inside some of our most secret agencies, including the NSA, working against our national security. We don't know who they are or who they're working for. That's why we need you."

"Me? Why?"

"Jackson delivered the software to us. No one else. We're the only ones with a copy of Vigilance up and running." He nodded toward the wall with the screens. "But now we need someone to head the program."

He looked at me and I looked at him. It took me a minute.

"No . . . really? Please say you don't want me to do this. I hate that software, think it's a huge overreach and dangerous—"

"Which is precisely why you're the best person to run the program," he said. "The president requested you, specifically."

I snorted, pushing my glasses back up my nose. "Nice try. Like I'm going to buy that."

Stewart smiled blandly again and clasped his hands behind his back. "Regardless of whether you believe it, it's true. But the most pressing concern is getting the right person to head this project. You talk about how dangerous Vigilance is . . . would you not want to make sure it wasn't abused? You'd be in the best position to do so. And we could find those responsible for the deaths of your friends."

That was tempting, but . . . "Vigilance should be destroyed."

"A genie cannot be put back inside the bottle."

We stared at each other. The sick feeling in the pit of my stomach told me what I was going to do. I couldn't turn my back on something like this, not when I'd been one of the people who'd helped build it. And he was right. So many people would be awed at its capability and wouldn't be able to resist abusing it . . . in the name of keeping the American people safe.

"Does Jackson know?" I asked.

Stewart shook his head. "He does not. We arranged for his delivery of the software and our relationship with him is at an end. He'll be compensated for his time and the . . . issues he had to deal with."

"Yeah, being shot was one hell of an 'issue,'" I said dryly.

"That was unfortunate. We weren't aware of Ms. Miller's . . . ties," he said, frowning slightly. "Which is another reason why we should use this software. If we'd been using it before, we would've found Ms. Miller before she killed John and Freyda. Vigilance will save lives . . . *if* it's in the right hands."

Dammit. I could feel myself caving. I didn't see what other choice I had. Knowing this was out there, being used by a secret department of the US government, would keep me up nights.

Finally, I nodded. "Okay. I'll do it." And it felt like I'd just signed the rest of my life away.

Stewart smiled for real this time. "Excellent. You won't regret it, I promise you. There is no greater honor than being of service to your country, I can assure you."

*Until they stabbed you in the back*, I thought.

"Your position will be Division Head and you'll be given an extensive list of possible recruits to vet. You'll know better than we what technical skills are needed. As for the intelligence side, we thought it would work best if you had someone with extensive field ops experience and widespread contacts in the community." Stewart glanced over my shoulder. "Ah, and here he is now."

I turned and my stomach dropped somewhere near my toes.

Clark was striding toward me.

"Let me introduce you to—"

"We've met," Clark interrupted, halting in front of me. "Good to see you again."

The smirk on his lips made me realize my jaw was hanging open. I closed it with a snap.

"You knew about this," I accused. My hands were clenched into fists.

"First thing you should learn about spycraft is that just because you know something, doesn't mean you're allowed to tell anyone." He glanced toward Stewart.

"When are we set to go live?"

"As soon as your staff is hired."

Clark's gaze returned to me. "Then we'd best get to work, right, China?"

"I'll leave you to it then," Stewart said. "China, paperwork will arrive via secure courier in the next few days. Please review it carefully."

He shook my hand and I got a good look into his eyes. They were calculating—as cold and impersonal as his handshake. I had little doubt I meant next to nothing in his version of The Grand Scheme of Things and that if I ceased being useful, I might be next to die under suspicious circumstances.

"I'll be sure to do that," I said.

He nodded, then headed toward the stairs. In another moment, he disappeared down the corridor.

"Shall we?" Clark asked. "You have a lot to get caught up on."

I raised my chin. "Not tonight, I don't. I haven't signed anything yet. Besides, I have a date." I spun on my heel and followed the path Stewart had taken. I'd just hit the top step when Clark called after me.

"You're going to have to quit your job at Cysnet," he said. I glanced back at him. "And Jackson can't know why."

My gut twisted. He was right. But just because I quit working for him didn't mean we had to break up. It actually solved a problem—sleeping with the boss. There was that silver lining I was looking for. I actually smiled.

"You're right," I said, resuming my path. "I'll see you on Monday." I waited until I was about to disappear behind the wall, then poked my head out. "And since I'm now technically your boss, be sure to arrive on time. Have a good weekend."

The look on his face made me smile wider and was the rainbow over my silver lining.

Maybe this wouldn't be so bad after all.

# ACKNOWLEDGMENTS

Starting a new series is always fraught with doubt and uncertainty, so I'd like to thank the following people who believed in this new character and story:

Kevan Lyon, my agent. I don't think anyone was more excited about China than you.

Maria Gomez, my editor. Working on each new series and each new book is always a true pleasure. I'm so very blessed to have you!

Melody Guy, my developmental editor. I love to hate getting an e-mail from you! Your hard work makes my stories so much better and when I get the nod of approval from you, I know it's For Reals.

My amazing beta readers: Shannon Patel, Tiffany Kimble, and Nicole Duke. Your input as avid and critical readers is invaluable to me.

My family, for being supportive and long-suffering as I made my way through another book.

And you, the readers, for picking up yet another book of mine. Thank you for following my work and loving each new heroine—from Kathleen, to Clarissa, to Ivy, to Sage, and now . . . China. I hope you love her.

# ABOUT THE AUTHOR

Tiffany Snow has been reading romance novels since she was too young to be reading romance novels. Born and raised in St. Louis, she attended the University of Missouri in Columbia, earning degrees in history and social studies. Later she worked as an information technology instructor and consultant. At last, she now has her dream job: writing novels full-time. Married with two wonderful daughters, Tiffany makes her home in Kansas City, Missouri. Visit her website, www.tiffany-snow.com, to keep up with her latest projects.